FOOL'S

FOOL'S GOLD

FOOL'S GOLD

Books by

KATHERINE NORBERG

You Can't Wallpaper My Igloo
Memoir
Mrs. Jones Steps Out of Bounds
Women's Literature

Annie Cooke Mysteries
Assisted Murder
Murder Goes A-Hunting
Murder Goes to Auction
Murder On Little Cat Feet
Cozy Mysteries

Birthplace of the Winds
Historical Novel

A Cry from the Reeds
Short Stories

FOOL'S GOLD

HISTORICAL NOVEL
ALASKA

KATHERINE NORBERG

FOOL'S GOLD

CONTENTS

KATHERINE NORBERG

THE LAW of the YUKON

This is the law of the Yukon
and ever she makes it plain:
"Send not your foolish and feeble;
Send me your strong and your sane.

This is the law of the Yukon,
That only the strong shall thrive.
That surely the weak shall perish,
And only the fit survive.

--- Robert Service ---

PROLOGUE

YUKON, CANADA
August 1896

He went by several nicknames: Stick George (for his association with the Stikine Indians) and Siwash George (he proudly considered himself a real Siwash native).

While these titles did not have much of an impact, there was one moniker—"Lying George"—that did do him harm. He came by it honestly enough through his talent for embellishing the truth, often stretching it beyond all reasonable boundaries. However, if additional truth be told, much of the time he was more precisely dealing in outright lies.

So, it really shouldn't have surprised him that his earnest accounts of finding gold in a tributary of the Klondike River called Rabbit Creek fell on skeptical ears all around.

Throughout the summer, people just smirked and rolled their eyes at George Washington Carmack, fortune seeker, erstwhile adventurer, and inveterate liar.

It came to pass however, that despite the universal skepticism that surrounded him, facts seeped into the narrative that caused his audience to revise the prevailing judgment.

At some point his shotgun-shell full of gold dust and his fabulous tales of discovery of potential riches must've certainly gained traction, because after but a few days, every creek around his claim was filled with boats, and every hillside became a potential claim.

It wasn't long before the Klondike crawled with humanity

from all parts of the world. People had been electrified by tales of rivers and hills filled to the crests with gold for the taking.

Dawson, formerly consisting of a few tents scattered among the bushes along the banks of the Klondike River, became one of the biggest towns west of the Mississippi. The population number made a quantum leap from the recent past into the present. Rabbit Creek became Bonanza, and the entire area became fittingly known as Eldorado.   In the space of time (a little over a chaotic year) some fortunes were made against extraordinary odds, most were not realized, and some were made only to result in eventual crushing losses. For every success, there were countless failures with many lives lost.

But still humanity poured in.

Most of those who farsightedly decided to make their fortunes in goods instead of gold did manage to thrive. By assessing the needs of the growing population, and catering to those needs through creative enterprise, they fulfilled their dreams to the tune of great profit.

Meanwhile, those who just kept dreaming of gold and settling for nothing less mostly ended up living a nightmare.

PART ONE

THE GOLDEN STEPS

-1-
SOUTHEAST ALASKA
1897

THE MEETING

The voyage had been long, troubling, and exhausting. They were late in arriving. And the lamentable thing, Harold knew, was that things were going to get worse, not better.

There was no time to relax, no time to lick wounds, and certainly no time to catch up on sleep.

Because he planned on buying a horse to pack his outfit up the pass, he made his decision to get to the Klondike by going up White Pass instead of the better-known Chilkoot Trail. By making this decision, Harold knew the dye was cast to seal his fate for the next few months, and maybe forever.

As he looked down from the deck of the dingy, coal-dust-coated tug on which he had sailed from Seattle, he could see slimy mud flats that extended five miles up the inlet to the tent town of Dyea and the beginning of the Chilkoot Trail. He was eminently thankful that, instead, he only had to get his belongings to nearby Skagway to get to White Pass via the Skagway Trail—in his estimation, a much easier proposition.

And his estimation was tenuously built on hearsay from the mouths of people stepping off ships in Seattle harbor—people who were dizzy with euphoria brought on by sudden wealth, or by crushing disappointment brought on by woeful misfortune.

They all rambled on with half-truths and exaggeration—not to say outright lies—about the conditions surrounding the whole gold rush venture. The words "gamble" and "risk" never got great billing. Neither did "danger" or "death." Insanity reigned, spurred on by mass singleness of purpose.

"It's a fool's paradise," one of the wiser tongues maintained, as they stood by and watched most of the fools that were still in the making.

"Yeah, but all you have to do is have Lady Luck smile upon you just once…"

There was no logic or reason involved. You just couldn't argue with the dreams of crazed men.

The hodge-podge accumulation of humanity that had sailed with Harold on the two weeks' voyage from the lower forty-eight had now crowded around him in the shambles that was the deck, craning their necks to get the first view of what lay in wait for them.

Included among the group that had begun the voyage with him, was a sad, and even more bedraggled motley group of individuals. They were the "lucky" souls who'd been rescued, a few days out of Seattle, from their rapidly sinking sternwheeler—a ship that had been transformed from what it had been originally designed for: river travel—into a barely seagoing vessel.

"They had no idea how to load the vessel," informed one of the lucky survivors, his disgust quite apparent. "There were piles of stuff all over the damned deck. No order or system whatsoever. It was asking for disaster. Fools all."

The ship had indeed been very inexpertly loaded; the food being added haphazardly to huge piles of belongings. All of this had acted as unintended ballast, so that as the passengers had eaten their way through the food supplies, the vessel slowly keeled over, trapping and drowning many of the passengers, including women and children.

The wailing and panicked cries were impossible to forget.

The only thing that loomed in the future of the ones who had been saved—if they still had or could somehow obtain the funds—was a trip back to where they had started. Otherwise, they had to take their chances at making their fortunes in the most lawless city in North America.

Skaguay.

Later, the spelling would change.

From what Harold had heard, it was worth your life to roam its muddy streets. In all probability, if you didn't lose your life, you were certainly running the risk of losing your property, your security, and even your health, especially mental.

Yet all the misgivings that might figure in the hearts of the single-minded prospectors paled in comparison to the madness that permeated their brains; madness for the "color" waiting for them at the end of the trail... color in quartz veins, color in rushing waters and mud, color in the deepest gravel, and, the greatest undoubtedly most satisfying of all: color in the gold-pan or sluice-box.

Like most of the vessels disgorging masses of fortune seekers, Harold's boat needed to draw deep water, so it couldn't go all the way up the shallow mudflats to Skaguay itself. Passengers had to find a way to move their belongings from the ship to the beach, preferably above the tide line.

In the uncontrolled madness that followed the arrival of the boat, Harold was able to flag down a man rowing a small skiff that he might get help to ferry his outfit halfway to the mean high tide mark. Although the ship's company had promised to deliver everything to Skaguay, the captain was refusing to include the lightering of the baggage to shore. So, passengers were on their own to see things through.

"Hey! Hey! Over here!"

Harold waved some dollar bills in a risky attempt to ensure the rower's loyalty, wishing he could afford the luxury of getting his possessions all the way to the uppermost beach, instead of just part of the way.

Competition for the smaller vessels was fierce, and a few overly eager passengers fell into the water in their panic to hire someone. No one helped get them back on the boat, and they had to swim to shore or grab on to the smaller boats. Terrified horses, oxen, and even goats were pushed over the side and left to swim to shore. Some suffered broken limbs, and some remained mired in the mud, their owner's loss.

Harold knew through the grapevine that the thirty-foot tide would come in swiftly, holding all the people, animals, and piles of property at its mercy. Having had good luck hiring a rower, he had his boxes deposited just above the rising tide. Knowing there was no time to waste, he immediately began the grueling task of securing his belongings on land.

Slogging to and fro through the boggy mud of the beach, to get everything out of jeopardy above the high-water mark, it took him ten trips, the last just as the saltwater was lapping at his one remaining load.

Once he was high enough on shore, he dropped down next to his pile in an exhausted state the likes of which he had never experienced. Blearily he watched as others railed in vain at the sea because they hadn't been able to rescue everything. The flour, sugar, yeast cakes, baking soda, cereals and dried products that had been so carefully counted and packed were now fish food. Family heirlooms and prized mementos had floated away or suffered irreparable damage.

Grown men sat on the beach crying openly in frustration as they faced the undeniable fact that their dreams were over. One man beat his son until he his arm was so sore, he couldn't raise it. Apparently, the young man had not pulled his weight by packing a heavy enough load on his back.

Others stared with empty eyes, overwhelmed with thoughts of the tasks that lay ahead. Still others refused to pay the locals they had employed who had fallen short of fulfilling their agreement to ensure the safe delivery of the property.

Bloody fights ensued. Shots rang out but it wasn't enough to dislodge some people from their mental torpor so weary were they from their recent battle against the elements.

When he had rested a bit, Harold looked around, not certain of what his next step should be. Then he figured he should check on and maybe consolidate some of his baggage. The more he could organize things, the easier they would be to transport.

He was about to get up to repack a few things when he looked up in time to see a tall, serious-faced, gun-toting young man approaching him with long decisive strides.

-2-

SHOOT FIRST

Extremely wary of strangers in this lawless environment, Harold immediately stood up in a defensive position. He'd seen the fights that had been brought on by people attempting to appropriate the belongings of others. He'd also seen the crooked dealings of some men who professed to "guard your outfit" while you tried to find lodging or food in town. When you came back, you found that parts of your outfit had been sold behind your back.

It seemed to Harold that he was beginning to recognize a gang of men who conducted this "business" as a coordinated group. He decided never to leave his stuff but didn't know how to go about moving it as one lot.

"I've been watching you, Sir," the stranger said to Harold as he approached, a grim smile on his face. "You seem to be on your own and in a difficult position."

Harold looked at him, his suspicion obvious. He wondered if there was something he had overlooked. He eyed the pistol on the other man's hip.

Seeing his puzzlement, the pleasant looking stranger went on.

"What I mean is, it's very difficult to keep things secure when you don't have another soul to keep a lookout for you."

Harold was beginning to suspect a sneaky ploy to separate him from his belongings just like the ones he had observed all around.

"I think I have managed well enough so far..." he began in a huff, ready to refuse help, but then his voice died off as he realized the truth. He was, indeed, in a fix.

The stranger smiled at the realization dawning on Harold's face.

"Don't worry," he said shaking his head and smiling benignly. "I don't belong to the Smith gang. I have a real and honest proposition for you."

"Smith gang?"

Harold was ignorant of any such thing but remembered the plotting and dealing of some overbearing characters he had witnessed in the past hours.

"Yes, you know...Soapy Smith's men—they're all around. They just about run this town, and believe me, you don't want to be on their wrong side."

He pressed his lips together and raised his eyebrows meaningfully to emphasize his point.

"Or their right side, come to think of it, as it would be a totally false association. The only reason for them to befriend you is to take advantage at some point. Best stay away and out of their business completely."

"Well, how do you do that?" wondered Harold aloud, sitting down again, overwhelmed.

Fatigue mixed with desperation were gaining ground.

The stranger put a booted foot up on one of Harold's boxes, bent his knee, and rested his forearm on his thigh. His other hand idly encircled the butt of his pistol.

"Well, that's what I'm trying to propose to you."

He thought for a moment, as if trying to figure out the best explanation. "You see, I'm sort of in the same position you are, except that I have the added complexity of having a woman with me. My...uh...wife."

Harold just sat, somewhat taken aback by this piece of news. There weren't many women around. Most people didn't think women had the fortitude required to be successful in ventures of this type. And even if they did, they certainly wouldn't have the actual desire to undergo hardships of such great magnitude.

"Yes, we've recently...uh...married. She wasn't ready to say good-bye at such an early stage in our marriage. The only alternative was to...well...stick with me. So, we boarded the same poor excuse for a ship that you did. All the time we were aboard, we both observed you and decided that, if you'd agree, we'd place our lot in with yours to divide the labor."

He shrugged.

"Almost all the people with experience say having a team of three greatly improves the odds. That is, if you can stand each other for the duration."

He smiled grimly, letting his words sink in.

There was silence for a few moments while each man processed the situation.

Just then a loud argument broke out a few stockpiles away.

The two men looked at each other and stood up quickly. The stranger immediately pulled out his Colt .45, holding it ready to fire. They both saw a group of men pushing and shoving. Then one broke out at a dead run toward town.

"Stop! Thief!"

"Someone, stop him!"

There was general pandemonium as a group took off in the same direction, many slipping in the ooze that had formed because of the thousands of feet, hooves, wheels and sled-runners that had churned the muddy ground like so much butter.

The stranger re-holstered his Colt and shrugged at Harold.

"Well, nothing new there," he said. "I hear it happens every day, several times a day."

Then he stuck out his hand, his smile radiating friendliness.

"By the way, my name is Gunther Jorgenson, from Minneapolis."

"I'm Harold Beasley, most recently from Seattle." He grasped Gunther's hand. "I'm originally from Chicago, but that was a while ago."

Gunther nodded.

"If you talk to anyone in this place, you'll find out that there are people from everywhere wandering about. And, by everywhere, I mean all over the world. Americans aren't the only gold-crazy people."

He smiled knowingly.

"And the foreigners don't even know the language. I don't understand how they get along and know what to do."

Shaking his head in wonder he continued.

"And the rest...well...they may speak English, but they're just as inexperienced."

"Well, that would describe me as well," stated Harold ruefully, almost ashamed. "I've never been on an expedition of any sort..."

"Well, you look hale and hearty enough," laughed Gunther. "I saw how you handled your outfit."

He shook his head and pursed his lips in disgust.

"By contrast, some of these gentlemen have done nothing more physical than sit behind a desk all day; accountants, writers, teachers, and worthless lawyers. They've never lifted anything heavier than a pencil."

He chuckled derisively.

"I'm grateful for my hard life as a rancher," he added. "It'll pay dividends, sooner or later."

Harold shivered suddenly.

It was late September—some would call it early fall, but a very cold wind was picking up, and it reminded him that getting a good parka was on his agenda. It seemed rather like early winter. Working hard to move his boxes had bathed him in sweat—sweat that had now turned cold. He knew that a good parka, possibly native-made, would serve much better than the Mackinaw coats that were in general use. He raised his collar and buttoned up his coat.

Seeing his new associate looking uncomfortable, Gunther made a suggestion.

"How about if we put our stuff together? We can hire someone to watch it while we do errands and warm up in town."

He was all business.

Not having a better plan, Harold decided that he should trust this man.

There was really no choice. He had the fleeting thought that Gunther's Minnesotan roots would stand him in good stead in Alaska's harsh environment. It was a good sign.

So, he slowly nodded his assent.

As Gunther's outfit was closer to town than Harold's, they decided to consolidate Harold's belongings to add to Gunther's. At that location it would be more convenient to keep tabs on it.

Taking turns packing Harold's belongings, they had moved everything by late evening.

Then Harold met Gunther's wife.

-3-

GROCERY LIST

The honky-tonk piano was agonizingly and incessantly loud, not to mention off key.

The three of them were seated at a rickety wooden table among dozens of raucous patrons who were either sitting next to them at other small tables, or lining the "bar," their muddy boots dropping great clods of dried mud forming little piles.

All seemed to have so much to say in very loud voices, talking over each other as they drank expensive liquor—expensive, but not necessarily high in quality. Their talk in this tent-saloon revolved around tales bandied about whose truth couldn't easily be ascertained. To hear them, you'd have thought that gold nuggets were as plentiful as cherries on a tree, ready to be plucked from the Klondike with great ease. Others insisted that, on the contrary, there was nothing to be gained by facing the impossible hardships of the trail, and only fools were likely to attempt the journey.

"Don't know which is worse," shouted Gunther so that his wife and Harold could hear over the bedlam. "The bragging, the whopping lies, or the wrong notes."

Harold took a swig of his watery beer and nodded distractedly. Although he tried to tear his eyes away from her, they always slid back to her face as if drawn by a magnet.

Gunther's wife.

Earlier, a college student, who had come to Skagway, as it was later spelled, to try his luck as a packer, accepted Gunther's promise of pay—half now, half later—for guarding their outfits.

Gunther felt that he was too young looking and inexperienced to be one of the marauding gang members. Not certain on his own the best course to follow, Harold deferred to Gunther's superior experience in the matter. Not knowing any better, he was now glad to have some direction.

So, they took a chance and left everything under his guard while they ate at one of the fly-by-night restaurants that had popped up along the muddy thoroughfare un-aptly named "Broadway."

The menu, which sometimes differed drastically from one day to the next, was a reflection of whatever the owners could get their hands on. If you were lucky, there was some kind of meat; if you weren't, you'd have to make do with rice mixed with some soggy vegetables. On some days, a watery soup was the lonely main fare.

Harold and company were lucky to dine on some decent fish and reconstituted dried potatoes. After the meal, they thought they'd stop in at the *Nugget* to get a feel for the town.

They made their way into the large tent that claimed to be a "saloon." The enterprise that operated under that vastly inflated term boasted a few tables, a six-foot plank that served as a bar, and two or three unsteady-looking stools.

They put some chairs around a table, sat down across from each other, and apprehensively ordered beer. As they waited, Harold took stock of his newest partner.

Despite her slightly bedraggled state, she was the most attractive woman he had ever seen.

Dark ringlets framed her fresh face, as dark brows and lashes set off her startlingly green eyes. Her full lips parted as she conversed in animated fashion to present very straight white teeth. And although she sensibly wore bulky men's clothes instead of the impractical women's fashions of the day, Harold could tell that a slim lithe body resided within.

Her name was Sarah.

Harold half-heartedly blamed the length of time he'd been away from civilization for his being so smitten with her. He didn't know what else it could be, and, at the same time, he was very uncomfortable about it.

This was someone else's wife, after all.

But still. The attraction was extremely difficult—not to say impossible—to suppress.

"...so it probably would be a good idea to buy one, don't you think, Harold?"

Harold stared blankly at Gunther. He had no idea what the subject of the conversation had been.

"Uh...sorry. I was thinking of something else...What were you saying?"

Gunther frowned for a moment, pursed his lips, and then continued.

"What we were saying is that we should probably buy a packhorse to get our stuff up the pass. They're expensive but can be a big help. With a packhorse we could make better time to Lake Bennett and start our boatbuilding sooner. I don't know how much lumber is available up there to construct boats. They might run out."

"Actually," answered Harold, nodding in agreement. "That's why I chose the Skagway Trail. They say it's easier to go up White Pass with horses than the Chilkoot. I was planning on buying some kind of pack animal, myself."

"Well, you know what they say: great minds think alike," approved Gunther, emptying his glass and leaving a line of foam above his upper lip.

"After we get out of here, let's pay the damned fees and rent a campsite. It won't be comfortable, but at least we'll have a temporary base of operations."

As they discussed the plan, Harold noticed an older man, probably a miner, morosely nursing a few ounces of drink, barely balancing himself on one of the stools. Every once in a while, he'd look at them and shake his head, talking to himself all the while. Then he'd look off into the distance and shake his head again.

Suddenly he stood up and lurched over to their table, bracing himself on it with both hands. Sarah quickly pulled her head back her face twisted in instinctive and barely concealed distaste.

His sleeves were shredded at the elbow and cuffs, his vest pockets were torn, and it was impossible to tell the original color of his pants. The three instinctively held their breaths to avoid taking in the terrible smell that hung all about him.

"You folks are headed for disaster," he croaked, shaking his head slowly, his greasy hair spiking out beneath his knit cap. He pointed a grimy finger at them and smiled mirthlessly revealing brown teeth and black spaces where others might once have been.

"You have no idea..." He cackled and shook his head again, gesturing to the outside. "Horses you say? Have you taken a gander at those nags? Any idea what they've been through?"

He waved his finger in warning. "Take it from me. You're better off on your own...using your own backs."

He stumbled and grabbed Gunther's arm to steady himself. Gunther looked even more disgusted than his wife had. He pushed the man away and then wiped his hand on his thigh. The man ricocheted against a guy at the bar who promptly pushed him away too. He ended up on the floor.

Harold couldn't help feeling sorry for him as the burly bouncer grabbed him and dragged him across the rough floorboards to the tent opening, ejecting him at the last moment.

In the great scheme of things, he hadn't been any more of a disturbance than most of the other loudmouths in the saloon. His forced exit probably had much more to do with his negative financial status; he was just taking up room that a paying customer might occupy.

When the three of them had left the saloon, they looked around for a camp in which to put their outfits and spend the night.

The young college student who'd been guarding their stuff accepted more pay to help them get everything to the campsite. They all agreed that he was worth every penny.

They put up Gunther's tent.

There wasn't much room for worrying about modesty in their canvass shelter, but Sarah managed to hang a sheet somehow to make a privacy barrier between Harold's bedroll and theirs. She took it down during the day to make moving around in the tent easier. Then, every night, it went back up.

The next morning, while she stayed in camp to watch over their boxes, the men went back to the main street to see what they could find to complete the inventory of items required by the North-West Mounted Police to cross the border into Canada. If you didn't have what they said you needed, they wouldn't let you into British Columbia. You could forget about the Klondike.

Each person needed a certain amount of food and equipment. Gunther figured that travelling together, they could split the equipment. They would still be required to have three sets of the food on the Canadian government's list:

400 lbs. flour
35 lbs. rice
100 lbs. beans
50 lbs. cornmeal
50lbs. oatmeal
100 lbs. granulated sugar
8 lbs. baking powder
2 lbs. soda
36 yeast cakes
15 lbs. salt
1 lb. pepper
½ lb. mustard
¼ lb. ginger
25 lbs. each evaporated apples, peaches, apricots
25 lbs. fish
200 lbs. bacon
25 cans butter
10 lbs. pitted plums
15 lbs. soup vegetables
50 lbs. each evaporated onions, potatoes
24 lbs. coffee
5 lbs. tea
48 tins condensed milk

5 bars laundry soap

40 lbs. candles

60 boxes matches

They could share responsibility for the equipment, which had to include a steel stove, a gold pan, granite buckets, a cup, plate, knife, fork, two spoons, two frying pans, coffeepot, pick, hand saw, whipsaw, whetstone, hatchet, two shovels, three files, draw-knife, axe, three chisels, twenty pounds of nails, butcher knife, hammer, compass, jack-plane, square, Yukon sled, two hundred feet of rope, fifteen pounds of oakum, and, most importantly, a canvas tent.

The Mounties also regulated the clothes that were needed per person. Harold had most of the items required: three suits of underwear, a mackinaw coat, two pairs of mackinaw trousers, twelve pairs of wool socks, six pairs of mittens, two over-shirts, two pairs of shoes, two pairs overalls, and a suit of oilskin clothing. He still needed to buy two pairs of snag-proof rubber boots–his present ones had suffered greatly in the mudflats—four blankets, four towels, a rubber-lined coat, and five yards of mosquito netting.

"These boots aren't new," complained Harold, as he inspected what he was planning on buying in one of the roadside shacks that passed for a retail shop. "Look. There's mud all over and a split in one of the soles."

"Well," replied the woman merchant who was pedaling the boots. "You wear twelves, right?"

Harold nodded.

"Twelve and a half, actually."

"Well then," she answered, her scorn very apparent. "You don't have much choice. Not too many guys have feet that big and our supply of large sizes is small."

Harold looked confused.

"All right, but why are they used? What does that have to do with the size? His eyes narrowed as he looked more closely at one of them. "And ...is this blood?"

She put her hands on her hips and gave him a patronizing look.

"These have some mileage on them...yes..." she assented crossly. "People on the trail leave 'em because once you're past the mud and into the snow they're too bulky and cold. Not too many men have gone up there in elevens or twelves. Like I said...You don't have much choice."

"But this pair doesn't even match." Harold said pointing out a difference. "And this one," he said, picking up a different pair, "isn't even a real pair. Both boots are for left feet."

He eyed the merchant who looked back at him balefully, hands still on her hips, apparently not the least bit concerned. In fact, Harold felt she was actually challenging him.

At that moment, Gunther appeared, having made his way back from another merchant to where Harold was trying to make a purchase.

"You know," he said in a low voice, having caught the tail end of the exchange. "Those boots have probably made the trip up and back several times. This enterprising merchant sends someone up after them or goes up herself. They're dug out of the mud, or the snowbank, or the ice, and brought back down here. If you buy them, you'll probably be at least the third person to use them. Maybe more."

Not sure if he was being cautioned or encouraged, Harold closed his eyes as much in disbelief as distaste. As the merchant had said, he had no choice.

Wishing he'd had the foresight to make this purchase in Seattle, he forked over the money to pay an incredibly inflated price for used and damaged boots—the mismatched pair.

He left the two left feet pair in the shop.

The merchant's parting smirk was firmly planted in his brain and left a bad taste in his mouth.

Later, on the trail, every time he put them on, he couldn't help wondering who had worn them before him.

He was positive there were a few dried bloodstains inside one of the boots, and there was a split in one of the soles that would undoubtedly provide an opening for loose pebbles, guaranteed to irritate you no end.

Not to mention the probability of soaking his feet.

He also wondered what had happened to the two right feet of the other pair.

-4-

TALES OF WOE

Many of the people at the campsite got together around their evening meal to gain information from whatever source they could.

After having made several purchases around town, all the while avoiding whatever their instincts told them could be a scam, Gunther and Harold returned to their tent, planning on consolidating their boxes and canvas bags. According to the scuttlebutt circulating, Harold guessed that he had made a mistake in bringing up a shipping trunk.

"They're left all over the place up high," related a man who, having lost his outfit, had come back down to Skagway. His overloaded horse had stumbled and fallen backwards down a precipice to land far below, way beyond reach.

"They're much too bulky and heavy," he continued, referring to the trunk. "Everyone puts everything in canvas packs, makes a wood frame with straps to get over the icy pass. Horses can't go past a certain point."

He looked at Harold, who was hungrily spooning some stew into his mouth.

"If I was you," he said nodding his head for emphasis and pointing to the steamer trunk. "I'd ditch that thing."

But one of the most useful conversations they had was with a woman who had ventured up White Pass with her brother at the end of July. She told them all about her misadventure.

She and her brother had planned on using their past experience in running a restaurant to open one up on the

American side of the border with the Yukon Territory, such as Fort Yukon. They had heard that the town of Circle could support several restaurants as well.

Among their heavy boxes were a few of their prized kitchen utensils that would serve when they started their business. They also planned on maybe opening a temporary one on the trail, using their own supplies, to feed the stampeders. The woman actually carried packages of dough among her clothing so that it would rise with the help of her body heat. When they stopped along the way to prepare a nightly meal, she would make bread using the dough, and bake it in the sheet metal stove. It was amazing what the men would pay for a small portion of bread in their daily struggle to get enough food.

Then, halfway up, her brother fell ill with what they were pretty certain was meningitis. There was no medical help to be had as she stayed by his side while his fever raged, and the nape of his neck caused him such pain that he spent the last day of his life screaming.

Her brother's death put an end to her dream at least temporarily. She used an abandoned sled with missing planks to drag his body back to town where he could be buried in a halfway decent manner. She would under no circumstances leave him on the trail over the winter like had been done to some of the other men who had died of various causes, their bodies frozen until the spring thaw. Many had died suddenly of food poisoning by eating rotten horseflesh served by some of the so-called roadside cafés, and the others fell prey to any microbes that their run-down conditions couldn't fight: influenza, pneumonia, and a variety of infections. She seemed surprised that her constitution had allowed her to survive.

Harold, who was still considering buying a couple of horses or mules to pack the outfits up the pass, wanted to know more details about this approach.

"Do you see that sorry fellow over there?" the woman asked Harold, pointing to a shapeless form half lying on the muddy ground and half leaning against a broken tree trunk.

"If you really want to find out about the trails, and what you need to be prepared for, you should probably engage him in conversation. He went up with the first bunch of people hoping to make it to Lake Bennett before everything freezes."

She pursed her lips in a wry expression, as she went on.

"Now, he doesn't have enough money to go forward or backward, and he's barely existing in between."

She nodded encouragingly, gesturing toward the man.

"Take him a bowl of food and he'll be your best friend."

Then, with a grim smile, she gathered her voluminous skirts and went off to her tent.

After a consternated three-way silence, Sarah spoke up.

"Why don't we invite him over here for a bit of food and see what he can tell us. It might be well worth a few ladles of our stew."

The men agreed.

He accepted the invitation with pathetic eagerness, smiling to expose great gaps where teeth should've been. Although it was difficult to read his expression because of the incredible layer of grime on his face, Harold thought he looked relieved.

He told them he went by Jed.

Sarah made sure he was comfortable on a box used as a chair and gave him a bowl containing a generous portion of what was left of their supper.

He scooped the food out of the bowl until there wasn't a morsel left. Then he cupped the bowl tightly to his chest as if just holding it there gave him sustenance. After a minute, he relinquished it, his eyes not straying from it. Sarah took pity and scraped the last spoonful out of the pot for him. When she handed the bowl back to him, he looked so grateful it was almost as though he had fallen in love with her.

Harold could quite understand it.

The more he was close to Sarah, the more he had to suppress his feelings for her. It was beginning to monopolize his thinking process, a fact that did not bode well for a situation that promised close quarters living for weeks...maybe months. While he knew all about the dangers of close-living alienating partners—he had no idea about the opposite predicament.

He noticed tightness in his chest as he pictured it. He was unable to figure out a way to deal with this strange new emotion.

After Jed had scraped his bowl clean for the second time, he sighed and wiped his mouth on an incredibly grubby sleeve, leaving a small swath of cleaner skin. The others could now see that he had a scar across both lips.

Gunther sat down on the ground next to him and began to ask some questions.

"Maybe I should just go back to the beginning, and you can take from it what you will," Jed suggested, looking around as if searching for something. "You wouldn't happen to have a little whiskey on you, would you...?"

After receiving some negative headshakes, he pressed his lips together and looked disappointed. "Talking goes so much better if you can wet your whistle a little..."

"Tell you what," said Gunther, surreptitiously raising his eyebrows at the other two. "After you relate what you know, we'll stop at the *Nugget* for a small libation. That'll make it worth your while, all right?"

Jed nodded his head with a pleased expression. Then he started his narrative.

The first part of the trail was deceptively easy. The stampeders became quite smug as they were able to lead their horses, oxen, dogs, and even one or two domesticated elk over a wagon trail through flat swampy flats and timberland. But as soon as they seemed safely ensconced in their comfort zone and their guard was down, they were suddenly faced with getting up and over a series of hills separated by a soggy and extremely muddy riverbed crisscrossed by an ill-defined path that was difficult to follow. Devil's Hill was a tortured twisting path no more than two feet wide where many loaded horses fell to their deaths five hundred feet below.

The term "Dead Horse Trail" was soon coined.

Harold, Gunther and Sarah were reminded of the derelict drinker they had met at the *Nugget*. He had warned about this very thing. So had the man on their first night in camp.

If, by great luck, the horses and men avoided the pitfalls threatening their progress on their first true challenge at Devil's Hill, they then had to forge their way through the ten-foot boulders on Porcupine Hill, picking their way around them carefully so as not to get stuck and break legs. Many horses perished there—most were just left behind with broken legs until they were mercifully shot or stepped over and compressed into the earth by foot traffic all the while still alive.

"This," said Jed, pointing to his lips, "is what you get when you venture to close to a panicked fallen horse... too close to a hoof, I mean..."

Rivers of mud delivered the next challenge. It was Summit Hill, a thousand-foot climb dotted with sharp rocks that tore at the horses' flanks and hooves, mud holes that swallowed them and their packs whole, and streams of slimy mud that wove through great barriers made of huge granite slabs.

Overshadowing the trail from the mudflats of Skagway to Summit Hill was a constantly gloomy drizzle of rain that turned every trail into a river of dark viscous glue that mired men, animals, equipment and supplies. The trails were always so narrow that if a problem developed in one area, it held everyone up as they couldn't get past the trouble spot. Sometimes the horses had to stand hour after hour in horrible conditions, without respite, their fully loaded packs crushing their backs. The men didn't want to go to the trouble of unloading them in case there was sudden acceleration, and they wouldn't be ready to move forward.

At this point, Harold wasn't so sure about his horse idea.

"So, you're saying that using horses might not be the best way to go?"

"All I can tell you is that by the time the men reached the summit, there wasn't but a handful of horses in sight," Jed said shaking his grizzled head. "And they suffered greatly. If someone did manage to get to the border, they had to disguise the horrendous cuts and sores on their animals by taking off their packs and replacing them with blankets that they carefully smoothed over the wounds to disguise them."

He raised a forefinger to emphasize his point.

"If not for this trickery, the Mounties would shoot the poor animals to put them out of their misery."

"Sounds more like they should've shot the men," scorned Sarah. "That's awful cruelty you're describing."

She looked at Harold and her husband and raised a finger in warning.

"I don't want to have anything to do with that," she said flatly. "I'll carry twenty loads before I'll inflict such suffering on another being."

His original plan notwithstanding, Harold was now inclined to agree.

Gunther returned late after dropping Jed off at the saloon.

While he was gone, Harold and Sarah rearranged some boxes, cleaned out the tent, and made conversation.

Harold learned that Sarah was a schoolteacher and that her parents had owned a mercantile store bought with the proceeds of her father's medical practice. She had a host of younger brothers and sisters for whom she had been responsible as they grew up, notably because her mother had had a serious illness for several years that kept her bedridden.

In spite of all her responsibilities, Sarah had managed to finish her schooling to get her degree. After teaching all day in a two-room schoolhouse, she would get home and help her father take inventory and stock the shelves. She couldn't remember ever having a day off or spending any time on anything but work.

While Harold heard everything she told him, he couldn't concentrate on her words so befuddled was he by the attraction he felt. He found himself using any pretext he could to brush up against her as they worked. Whether or not she noticed, he couldn't tell. What he could tell was that a degree of guilt was mounting in his gut.

Then Gunther returned and Sarah put up the divider sheet.

-5-

BEST LAID PLANS

After taking into consideration all the information they had gathered, Harold, Gunther and Sarah began to rethink their agenda.

There were rumors going around that White Pass would not be open for much longer. The conditions had reached a point that any kind of stampeding was practically impossible. More people were returning to Skagway than leaving it. And the former had tales of unbelievable suffering, frustration and failure. They spoke of more deaths by disease, accident, and even murder. But the worst were the incidents of cruelty to animals, mainly horses.

Of the three thousand horses that were used in the cruelest ways to climb White Pass, only a handful lived through it. Many of them were not in the best shape to begin with and very few men knew how to load packs on them properly. It wasn't uncommon for two miners to spend an entire day trying to load just one.

If the horse couldn't make it up a slimy path or squeeze between boulders, he was often killed or bludgeoned by his owner and left on the trail for the line of stampeders and their horses to trample over.

Cracked on the head with an axe because he had suffered a broken leg, one such horse had his pack removed by his owner who then left him on the trail still alive. By nightfall, only the animal's head and his tail were left on either side of the path.

He had been ground into the trail, at the same time as his dying body slowly grew cold.

So, all along the trail, horses lay in great rotting piles on what was later called Dead Horse Trail. Their legs snapped in crevices between rocks, their backs broke when they fell backwards, the weight of their packs pulling them over. Most of them were half-starved and weak. They drowned in sloughs and choked in the slime of the deep holes along the way.

On the corduroy roads made to cross bogs and streams, they were disemboweled when logs were pushed up on their ends by the hordes. It was said that some of the beleaguered animals even walked off cliffs in suicide to avoid the suffering. And the men rarely bothered to put them out of their misery. Instead, they returned to town and bought another animal. Often these were bloody and internally damaged from already having been up the trail, their erstwhile owners having given up on their quest.

When Harold heard all this, he made sure to shield Sarah from the knowledge.

The cruelty, he knew, would make her sick.

The town was filling to the bursting point. Idleness became unrest, which, in turn, became crime. Lawlessness reached new heights.

"Well," began Gunther a few days later, after sleepless nights due to shots fired and cries of "Murder!" throughout the night. "What do you think about a big change in plans?"

"Such as...?" asked his wife, clearing the few dishes they had used for a midday meal. "Are you hinting to us that you have a brilliant idea?"

"Possibly," he answered with mysterious overtones. "I do have a proposition to present to both of you."

"Well, don't hold us in suspense," said Sarah, skepticism in her expression. "Let us in on the big idea." She winked at Harold.

"Yes," chimed in Harold. "I'm getting pretty tired of this sitting around listening to a bunch of old bums with bad teeth and noxious body odor. Half the time, you don't know what's the truth and what's made up. I'm all ears."

Gunther put his foot up on a box, leaned his forearm on his thigh, and cleared his throat.

"All right," he said, looking at both of them very earnestly.

"What do you think about going up the Chilkoot instead? We've sort of given up on the horse idea anyway..."

Sarah and Harold were silent.

"It's supposed to be shorter and more direct," he continued, padding his argument. "From what I hear, the success rate of getting to the summit seems to be higher via that route."

Harold wasn't sure how he had arrived at that calculation. He wasn't aware that there had been much research done so far.

"But..." hesitated Sarah. "That means we have to lug everything to Dyea. You think the mud flats are bad here..."

She shook her head in dismay.

"Well," said Gunther. "It's either that or we can the whole thing."

He looked at Sarah.

"Is that what you want?"

She was quiet, her mouth twisted in thought.

"You know I don't like quitting," she said slowly. "I can't imagine what it would be like to go home and have to admit defeat."

She shook her head.

"And after all we've been through so far…" She abruptly turned to Harold.

"Harold. What do you think?"

He was taken by surprise. He hadn't figured that they'd much value his opinion. Most of the time he felt like a third wheel on a bicycle.

"Well...I...uh," he stalled, and then recovered. "I didn't come all the way up here to turn around now." He finished with a firm headshake to emphasize his statement.

"That's what I thought," nodded Gunther. "If we want to go to the next step, I don't really think we have any choice but to go the other way."

Far into the night they were still discussing the situation, trying to figure out how they were going to get everything about five miles north across the redoubtable mud flats of Dyea Inlet. That would be an expedition in itself, and it would only take them to the starting point of the real challenge that lay ahead.

*   *   *

It didn't take long to find others who wanted to make the same switch as Gunther's little group. By pooling their money, they were able to get together with two Swedes who had also come from Minnesota, and who were hell-bent on getting to the Klondike as soon as possible. Thanks to a Swedish grandmother, Gunther had learned a bit of the language, so he was able to communicate with them quite adequately.

In the case of the Swedes, the stop at Skagway had been unscheduled as far as they were concerned. Like many of the people who had actually bought tickets to Dyea, they ended up on the shores of Skagway because the captains of the boats—waterlogged coffins as they came to be known—refused to venture all the way up Dyea Inlet. Thor and Sven had tried to make the best of their situation by immediately seeking a way to get to their original destination. They told Gunther that they had a line on a large dory that would ferry them and their outfits to the Dyea beach for a decent price.

Not bothering to check things out too seriously, and eager to grab the opportunity, Gunther and company paid rent for a shaky wagon in which to load everything from the campsite to the beach and onto the boat. They were able to painstakingly load everything on the vessel—an odd combination of dory and scow— with not an inch to spare.

The owner of the small and wobbly vessel was not very happy with the load, but because the trip would be so short, he seemed to keep his objections to himself. To sweeten the deal, and to increase the chances that everything ended up where it was supposed to, the two Swedes offered to help row.

The top-heavy craft, rolling precariously from port to starboard with stomach-churning regularity, made its way slowly up the inlet, while the men helped with the rowing, being careful to avoid sudden moves as they changed position,

Sarah's knuckles showed white as she grasped the gunwale. All wore grim expressions, their eyes focused on the beach in the distance that was coming closer...but only agonizingly slowly.

Just as Harold was beginning to relax, the boat's owner stopped rowing and announced loudly that he needed extra funding to complete the deal.

The passengers looked at each other, Gunther translating for the Swedes. Not sure who had the upper hand, no one made a move.

Then the pistol came out.

The balance of power shifted to the boat owner.

Having no choice—the passengers dug out the extra money, their eyes glittering with anger. Harold would not have laid bets on whether the object of their anger might've just shortened his own life span. He had no idea what might happen when they had unloaded their boxes, and he wasn't making any guesses. He didn't know where Gunther had stashed the Colt; his coat covered his hip.

After what seemed like an interminable span of time, the craft ground to a halt in shallow water.

The owner, his gun still at the ready, just played the barrel back and forth as the others unloaded boxes, splashing their way to the dry shore. His expression betrayed no emotion; it was as though this was a daily occurrence of little import.

Harold was surprised at how much Sarah packed, then he remembered her telling him how she had spent her youth stocking shelves. Still, she took no extra license for being a woman, and pulled her weight in most efficient manner.

*　　*　　*

"I think we just had the unwanted attention of a Soapy Smith enterprise," mused Gunther as they sourly watched the dory pull away back into the inlet.

"They'd better not have as much sway on this side."

The Swedes didn't seem to realize the significance of their brush with crime. Harold figured that they probably thought that these things just happened in this strange area and were to be expected.

They weren't far wrong.

But Dyea was not the hornet's nest of crime and rough living that its sister city was.

Although much the same characters roamed the muddy streets, conducted business, and tried to make a buck or two at the expense of the strung-out Klondikers, most of Dyea's boom business community members seemed a bit more law-abiding than their Skagway counterparts.

Because the Chilkoot was continually open, people joining the stampede did not have to bide their time in idle talk and drink. The transient population was all about moving in the right direction and getting down to business: the hills.

So, the three adventurers followed suit and made good their plans.

They bought three Yukon sleds that they planned to use above the snow line, until the trail was such that they could no longer be managed. At that point, they would transfer the loads to large canvas backpacks.

Sarah busied herself by packing the sleds so that food and cooking utensils could easily be reached while on the trail.

To travel the first snowless miles, Gunther knew they had a couple of choices. One of these was to hire an ox or horse and wagon to carry the sleds and equipment to the snow line, and the other was to hire a packer.

Without consulting the others, and letting his finances be his guide, Gunther decided on the second choice.

In a way, he felt sorry not to do business with the woman who owned an ox and wagon. She had arrived in Dyea with less than fifty dollars. By baking pies, taking in laundry, and charging men for a lukewarm bath in a tin tub she'd had the foresight to take with her from Seattle, she made enough money to buy the ox and wagon.

Admittedly, the wagon rolled unevenly, and, although the ox was on its last legs, it was still able to move quite a load without giving out.

Apparently, this enterprising woman was making a good living. She was counting on the ox to last until the stampede was over. Fortune made, she was going back to her family in the lower forty-eight.

Her gold would be silver.

-6-

THE TRAIL

As winter weather was imminent, every day that passed made arriving in good shape at Lake Bennett and the Yukon River a riskier proposition.

Gunther behaved as though his coattails were on fire. He raced around town to find items he needed, slogging through the mire that was every street of Dyea. Having heeded the advice of a miner who had been up to the summit and back at the end of summer, he ordered three duck parkas to be made by the town tailor. In order to keep up with the demand, this enterprising merchant had many natives in his employ working day and night.

Later, Gunther took Harold with him to buy a handcart that would serve them until they reached the snow and could transfer everything to sleds. He figured that they'd either take it apart and find other uses for the boards, or they'd put the parts on the sleds for use on the other side of the summit. The cart was the type that could be pulled from the front and pushed on either side with a special rail. It was the perfect contraption for three people. They would have to load all their belongings on it, including the sleds.

"What happens if not everything fits," asked Sarah, very much afraid that she already knew the answer. She had brought along her pride and joy: a treadle sewing machine dismantled for the trip. Something had told her that it could be very useful when they reached their destination. But, it was a bit bulky and weighed a considerable amount.

"What doesn't fit, doesn't go," growled her husband, showing that he was not open to discussion on the matter. "We'll have to decide on what is expendable and get rid of it. Maybe we can find a buyer..."

Sarah just shook her head and continued to consolidate the outfits. Harold did the best he could to help both of them. Assisting Gunther was a trial in patience, while helping Sarah was a gratifying pleasure. He felt a bit like a third wheel, adding his own items where he could. He hoped that Gunther wouldn't get carried away and impatiently throw Harold's things— especially his tools—by the wayside without consulting him. After expressing this fear secretly to Sarah, she assured him that she'd supervise the discards.

He got rid of his useless trunk on his own.

In the end, Gunther had to concede that they could not get everything into one wagonload, even when they considered the three backpacks they'd be carrying. As they easily had over four tons of goods and equipment—thirty-five hundred pounds just in the food that was required by the Mounties for three people— the volume was daunting.

With the last of the money they had budgeted for this part of the journey, they hired a native packer: a Stikine Indian, who had a line on another wagon for rent. He made them a deal for packing and pulling for two cents per pound to the snowline.

The second wagon was hardly what you'd expect; a few boards laid side to side, put together in a steel frame, and fastened to an axle with buggy wheels. Still, it was enough to accommodate the leftover items.

"It only has to last the first five miles," said Sarah, doleful and worried. "But it doesn't look like it can go five yards without falling apart."

Beggars can't be choosers, Harold's grandmother had always said. He thought that saying fit this situation quite aptly.

The wagons finally loaded, the backpacks full, they judged they were as ready as they would ever be. They had observed many teams of men and some families leaving town every hour of the day and night. Photographers took many shots of the stampeders to send back to their newspapers, in this way fueling the fires of gold rush "brain disease" thousands of miles to the south.

Without a backward glance, Harold and his partners set out midmorning of the next day.

"What we don't have, we don't need," grunted Gunther as they rumbled out of town heading for the trail. "There's no room for regrets..."

Harold wasn't so sure about that, but he wasn't about to argue so early in the game. Sarah, her sparkling eyes observing everything, just kept her expression serene.

The beginning of the trail was an easy introduction. They were not wearing their parkas yet. It would've made them sweat, something to be studiously avoided in freezing weather.

There was an actual dirt road that crossed and re-crossed a river through copses of many types of trees. It was relatively easy for the men, in their rubber boots, to trade off pushing and pulling while Sarah remained at her designated pushing station.

Having had experience on this trail, the native packer went ahead. Gunther and company didn't have to worry about where to find the best path—it was just a question of following the packer who was now also their guide.

This worked well the first few miles of the trail, but the packs were heavy, and they took several rest stops. Eventually, they tied Sarah's pack on top of everything in the wagon. Soon the men's packs followed. Along the trail, they began to see signs of things unraveling.

First came the trunks left behind by those who found them too burdensome. They were open and had obviously been ransacked. Framed pictures, fancy clothes, mementos of every type, parts of boats, machinery, even revolvers, and anything that was not absolutely necessary, was abandoned in favor of lightening loads.

Happy that his trunk was no longer part of the equation, Harold saw why there had been a glut of used rubber boots in town. After the trunks, boot after boot lined the trail. He was beginning to understand why. They had served their purpose every time they'd had to ford the streams that crisscrossed the road. But now, as the trail began to climb, the boots were heavy and clumsy and gave little support, almost more of a hindrance than help through the rougher terrain. The sharp rocks sliced the rubber, and he knew they wouldn't be much protection from the cold once they hit snow.

Nonetheless, Harold was not about to leave his boots behind; too much of a waste. Besides just dwelling on principle, he knew there'd probably be a point at which they'd be useful again.

Waste not, want not. Another of his grandmother's oft-repeated sayings.

During one of their rest stops for a trailside meal, he rummaged through his pack to find his leather lace-up boots. The other two followed suit.

As they leaned against the wagon eating the bread and cheese Sarah had packed for their midday meals, they watched contraption after contraption rumble by, some so precariously overloaded that the slightest bump in the road caused worrisome jostling of contents.

Going the other way, their step much less lively, a mostly disheveled and obviously dejected line of people were returning to Dyea, having given up on their dreams of getting to the gold fields. Harold didn't even let his mind imagine the frustration and suffering that must be dogging them.

A constant drizzle and intermittent fog served as a kind of pall over the procession that made its way like a giant silent serpent inexorably heading up the mountains.

All along the way, they saw many men shrug off items they considered expendable, and rearrange the contents of their canvas packs, now a bit lighter. Those men, without the luxury of a wagon, would be making this trip several times to shuttle their total outfits—so-called "back-tripping." Harold felt some pity for them, eminently glad that, with a wagon and partners, he was demonstrably better off.

Somehow, that thought was enough to give him renewed energy as they continued their trek.

"We stop here," intoned the packer, a few hours later, pulling the smaller cart off the trail.

They had reached a place where several camps had been set up to the side of the trail in the mud.

"This Finnegan's Point. You put up tent and stove to cook. Then sleep."

With that he dropped the pack and went off up the trail.

"Wonder if that's the last we'll see of him," ruminated Harold.

"Oh, he'll be back to get the other half of his payment," said Gunther, nodding his head knowingly. "Don't worry. We'll see the whites of his eyes tomorrow morning."

Bone tired, Harold couldn't even afford to give a thought to the next day. Helping put up the tent and rig up the cook stove was about all he could manage. Even a neighbor's invitation to visit the local saloon tent couldn't entice him to leave their camp.

His back propped up against a rock, he just watched as Sarah prepared some of the evaporated food to make a stew. He pretended to be interested in her methods, but in reality, he just couldn't take his eyes off her as she busied herself with pots and tin plates. It really didn't matter to him what she was doing.

He was vaguely aware that Gunther had disappeared, but he didn't waste much energy trying to find out where.

Housekeeping was way more fun without him.

Sometime during the night, he woke up in the dark to find Gunther crawling around him to get to his bedroll on the other side of the tent. He thought he smelled liquor and smoke, but immediately fell back asleep.

The next morning, it was a vague memory. He was nevertheless angry at Gunther for leaving most of the setting-up to Sarah.

"So, where did you go last night?" he asked Gunther, who was busy wolfing down some oatmeal mush just outside the tent.

Gunther slurped some more, simultaneously looking to see where Sarah was. When he saw that she was inside the tent packing the bedrolls, he leaned over to Harold.

"I got into a game," he said in low tones. "Made myself a pretty penny."

He jingled some coins in his pocket. Then he put his finger to his lips and rolled his eyes toward the tent. Harold got the gist of it, nodded in resentful but tacit agreement, and drank the last of his coffee.

So, our man Gunther has a gambling habit.

Harold wondered how much that fact would affect the overall enterprise. He was pretty sure that Sarah would not regard this with her customary equanimity. Her husband's secretive expression made it obvious that he didn't think so either.

After breakfast, the packer showed up, just as Gunther had predicted. Wordlessly, he checked what they had packed and saw they were ready to go. He picked up his pack and grabbed the handle to the wagon.

"We go now," he said unceremoniously. "It snow today."

They rolled across a corduroy road made to go over a boggy area by the person whose name had been given to the spot. Finnegan and his sons had built the log road with the intention of charging everyone who used it. Eventually, as people just barreled roughly by them, they gave up trying to collect the toll. It had worked for a time, but they were a long way from rich.

Far different from yesterday's easy travel across the lowlands, today's trail would greatly test their resolve and stamina.

The Dyea River snaked around as if to attack from several different angles. It had formed a canyon that was near to impassable. Choked with huge boulders, roots that twisted and writhed around rocks and downed tree trunks, the path narrowed until it formed a slit between slick rock faces and muddy dirt banks. When forward progress halted because of some accident—usually a fallen horse—they had to stand for hours before things got moving again.

Sometimes they had to use crude ladders made of logs—at a price—to span deep ravines or gullies and climb from one side to the other. It was almost impossible to pull the wagons across without unloading them. After a few times of unpacking and repacking, they figured it would've been easier just to abandon the wagons and make some extra trips using just their backs, sore as they were.

Many horses perished in this canyon, in the ugliest of ways. And the river was always there to torture everyone as it appeared and reappeared, daring them to cross for what seemed to Harold like the hundredth time.

It took them the entire day to go the eight miles from Finnegan's point to Sheep Camp. By the fifth, snow had started to fall, making the trail slushy and even more treacherous.

The men who had successfully driven their horses all the way through the canyon learned with dismay that their animals had paid dearly for it. Some had lost shoes, suffered terrible cuts and bruises, and had severely strained backs from standing for hours with badly cinched packs and incorrectly packed loads. Reason and pity would dictate that they should be rested for a few days—insanity and greed dictated that they be hustled on.

The three partners eschewed the large tent marked "HOTEL" in yard-high letters, for the privacy of their own tent. Experience now guiding them, they set up camp in record time. Gunther paid the packer, who immediately headed back toward Dyea after more business, wagon in tow.

Sarah suggested that the three of them use their time in Sheep Camp—named for an old sheep hunters' camp—to dry their clothes, especially their footwear.

"Hand them over," she ordered the men. "Get some dry socks on while I rinse these and air them out."

She had seen what days on end of constantly wet feet left in soggy boots could do to a person. In the last camp, she'd been exposed to the negative effects that she wouldn't soon forget. When some of the men close by her camping spot unfastened their laced boots, she was privy to a show she could have well done without. Besides the absolutely putrid smell that drifted to her nostrils, there was often rotting flesh to be observed, albeit unwillingly. She reasoned that to avoid that particular horror, removing footwear and drying it, plus airing their feet out, would go a long way.

It was well worth the trouble.

"Harold," said Gunther in his usual boisterous manner, interrupting his partner's thoughts. "We'd better go and grab as much firewood as we can pack. This is the last place on the whole trail that has any."

They put on clean socks and their rubber boots and went out in the steady snowfall, sled in tow.

As he followed, Harold couldn't get rid of the vision he had of Sarah, bent over, rinsing his grubby socks in a bucket full of melting snow.

There were well over a thousand people in Sheep Camp. They seemed to flow in and out, up and down, busily in perpetual motion.

Trying to get to the shack where they could buy firewood, the two men could hardly squeeze between the tents and shelters that covered every foot of ground. There were piles and piles of goods both for sale and already bought. There were shacks and tents set up to sell every item one might need on the trail and then some.

Harold especially noticed the rubber boots for sale, subconsciously wondering if there was a pair with only right feet among them.

In the business tents, you could get your laundry done or your correspondence mailed. You could buy medicine or tobacco. Some places even sold the "best beds you can buy" and some the most inventive of shelters.

And then, there were the huts and shacks passed off as "hotels."

Food, women, and a spot on the floor to sleep were all available for a price. In one such hotel, as many as five hundred people were fed daily, seated in shifts, and forty were housed at night. They slept side by side and end to end so that it was impossible to get from one side of the room to another without trampling some unfortunate soul.

Socks and shoes hung on the rafters to dry. Before freeze-up, this "hotel" even boasted "running water:" a stream that flowed under a corner of the building.

What was especially noteworthy was that this camp had been completely swamped by a sudden flood a few weeks ago. It had ripped the place to shreds driving most things downriver. That all the businesses were back up and running in such short order was a testament to the energy and enterprising spirit of the merchants.

Of course, some might just attribute it to all-encompassing greed. All felt the pressure of getting back in business as soon as possible. After all, fortunes needed to be made, and as soon as possible.

Harold and Gunther were finally able to get to the places that sold firewood. It was expensive, but absolutely necessary, so they loaded up the sled. There was no telling where the next source would be.

Then it snowed some more.

-7-

TENSE TIMES

The poor animal tottered on unsteady legs. If the wind had been blowing, as it was wont to do, he most certainly would have ended up on the ground, a bundle of bones in a bag of shriveled skin. As it was, he tripped over tent ropes and ran into caches. It was almost as if he was blind, but his unsteady gait was really due to lack of strength; starving, he couldn't control his movements. There was no feed or grazing for him. No comfort, care, nor friend.

"Where is his owner?" asked Sarah, beside herself with anger and frustration as she watched the pitiable brute bump into sleds and wagons, ropes and guy-wires, all partially obscured by the falling snow. She had never seen a horse so thin, so bloody with cuts and abrasions, so disoriented. He finally thrust himself partly inside the tent, seeming to want to get next to the warmth of the stove.

"What can we give him?" she appealed, her hands outstretched to the men camped all around, in a panic to help the animal. "Please, someone, where is his owner?"

Most of the men sitting by their campfires nearby just ignored her pleas or looked away. This poor animal was only one of dozens wandering around the campsite. All had been abandoned by their masters who had realized that the animals had outlived their usefulness, yet they didn't have the fortitude to put them out of their misery. Or they simply didn't want to spend the bullet it would take to do so.

Finally, Gunther had had enough of his wife's loud supplications. Slamming down his supper, he grabbed the animal by the mane and walked him some distance from their tent. It was less than a minute later that Sarah and Harold heard the sharp report of the Colt.

Harold saw Sarah close her eyes and support herself by leaning on a pile of boxes. He got up and put his arm around her.

"It's really for the better," he said, as she nodded, tears welling in her eyes. "The poor wretch is out of his misery, now."

For a second, she leaned against him, shutting out the world. Then, in keeping with her habit, she moved off to tend to her work.

Gunther returned, sat down, and picked up his plate.

He didn't say a word as he finished his supper. Harold did the same, his concerned glance darting to Sarah every once in a while. She seemed unfazed, but he knew she was deeply affected by the cruelty of the experience.

They heard that snow had fallen even more thickly at the summit overnight.

"Oh my God," exclaimed Sarah the next morning, holding the tent flap open, as the sun made a brief appearance between heavily laden clouds. With this short-lived clearer weather, they had a graphic view of what lay ahead.

Above the chaos of erratically placed tents, lean-tos and miscellaneous shelters littering the camp as far as the eye could see, men struggled forward. Up the rocky slopes, the tiniest of motions could be observed as the never-ending line of men bent under their packs, inched its way up the mountainous inclines that reached high to the summit.

"They look like ants from here!"

"Yep, and we're going to be looking like that too," said her husband, lacing his boots. "Many times over."

Sarah let go of the flap and sat down suddenly. Harold was certain that, like him, she hadn't realized just how daunting the rest of the trail was going to be.

"Do you think we'd better leave some stuff behind?"

Sarah must've hated to say it, but the monumental task that lay ahead was obviously making her reconsider what they absolutely needed to take. "I'm sure we could do without..."

"What? The cooking stuff, our winter clothes and equipment, or the food and firewood we need to survive? Maybe you think we can do without the bulky sleds?"

He raised his hands in question and shook his head.

"Tell us, Sarah. What is it you so brilliantly think we should we get rid of all of a sudden?"

Harold thought that Gunther's retort was needlessly cynical and mean. He obviously thought that Sarah was suggesting that he was responsible for packing too much.

"Look, Gunther," Harold said, trying to placate him. "It's a natural reaction she's having. She's not blaming you or anything..."

"Well," continued Gunther on a tear. "Seems to me she was the one trying to keep me from leaving some things back in Dyea. Now, because she finally understands what we're faced with, she's changing her tune."

He flipped open the tent flap and stalked off.

Harold immediately felt guilty. Some of the items Sarah had prevented Gunther from leaving behind had probably been some of Harold's stuff, notably his rather heavy woodworking tools. Sarah bit her lips together in an attempt to keep from crying. She bent over the bedrolls and began to wrap them up for the trip. Harold could see her shoulders shaking.

He went over to her and pulled her upright. Then he put his arms around her in silence, and they stood there for a few moments as she collected herself. Harold tilted his head down until his lips were against her forehead. Instinctively, he kissed her softly, aware of the smoothness and warm smell of her skin.

Suddenly blood invaded his brain in a heated rush, and he panicked.

What was he doing?

He straightened up and gently pulled away from her, daring to hope that she hadn't taken offense at his weak moment.

She looked up at him and smiled that everything was all right. Her lashes were wet, her eyes bright with tears—she used the hem of her blouse to dry them.

"I...uh...I..." Harold was at his wits' end.

"Thank you for trying to comfort me," Sarah said, patting his arm, justifying his action. "Sometimes Gunther's in his own world. He doesn't realize what...what effect his moods have on others." She looked deeply into his eyes. "I'm sorry you had to be a part of it..." With a final pat, she turned and went back to her packing.

Harold stumbled out of the tent, his heart beating hard, his breath coming in short gasps. He inhaled deeply, hoping that the raw cold air would either calm him or knock him to his senses.

Peering into the depths of the gloom surrounding him, he felt no relief. The unending grayness was an apt metaphor for his dread.

-8-

NIGHT GAMES

They didn't see Gunther for the rest of the day and on into the evening. Harold figured that he had found himself another poker game or such.

Would that Lady Luck keep smiling upon him, because if she didn't, everything and everyone would bear the brunt.

Harold was fearful that they had already spent more money than they had originally budgeted for. Everything on the trail seemed to cost three times as much as they had estimated. If Gunther was to have a bad night...well...Harold didn't even want to think about the effect it would have on their situation.

Sarah had spent most of the day packing the sleds according to her own system. One sled had everything they needed to set up daily camps including food, while the others held the equipment and items they would need once they reached the Klondike. Harold packed up the wood and started to take apart the wagon and stack the boards.

When it got late, and Sarah put beans on to cook for supper and fried some bacon, several men came by and offered a few dollars for a bowl of food. They had lost their goods, or they were so poorly equipped that they were obliged to buy what they could all along the trail. Sarah kept putting more food on to cook, adding biscuits, until Harold cautioned that they couldn't spare any more. She looked so sad at not being able to help anyone else that Harold thought his heart would melt.

Finally, exhausted, Sarah put away the dishes, took off her boots and burrowed under the blankets of her bedroll.

"Good night, Harold," she said sleepily. "If you see Gunther before you retire for the night, tell him not to wake me."

Harold put a small precious piece of wood in the stove to give her a bit of extra heat. He battled an overwhelming urge to lie down with her and hold her until she fell asleep. It was all he could do to go out into the evening and check straps and packs to occupy his mind.

In the darkness of the tent, he was in the deepest part of sleep when he was jarred to wakefulness.

"Don't move and be quiet!"

Harold felt a hand over his mouth. He tried to shake it off but was too wrapped up in the bedding to get a hand loose to defend himself.

"Quiet! It's me: Gunther. Don't make any noise and I'll take my hand off. Nod if you understand."

Harold nodded quickly. Gunther removed his hand but stayed put on top of Harold's bedroll, squashing him.

"I can't breathe," whispered Harold. "Get off!"

"All right...Shhhh. Just a second."

There was some moving around and Harold felt the weight lifted off his body.

He was disoriented. What was going on?

Against the muted brightness of the snow, Harold saw the bottom corner of the tent flap go up and he sensed that Gunther was looking outside while trying to hide. He released the flap quickly, and Harold felt the pressure of Gunther's hand on his leg. He took it as a signal not to move.

Outside there was some murmuring of voices and some crunching of footsteps in the snow. They went back and forth in front of the tent. Finally, whoever it was must've moved off because the murmuring and the footsteps faded.

"Okay, Gunther. What the hell's going on? Who was that?"

Harold kept his voice low, but there was no mistaking his concern and displeasure. "What'd you have to wake me up for?"

Gunther had moved over and was sitting on a box by the stove.

He started to talk but Harold interrupted.

"Keep it down. Sarah's asleep. She doesn't want to be awakened." He paused. "Now, what happened?"

Gunther didn't answer right away.

"Look...don't worry. It's nothing serious."

"Yeah? Then why were you telling me to be quiet, and why are you hiding?"

Frustrated, Harold almost forgot to whisper. "Where were you all day, anyway? We could've used a hand..."

Gunther cleared his throat.

"I just went to see if I could make good on a loan. They were having a game, and I ...uh... I had to pay someone back for what I lost in the last game."

"I thought you said you had some winnings," said Harold. "Didn't you just tell me last..."

"Yeah, yeah," was the impatient reply. "I did win some...but at one point I had to borrow to stay in the game. I...uh...kind of sneaked out without repaying... the guy was practically asleep..."

Harold sighed and whispered fiercely.

"Do you realize how you're jeopardizing everything we have? Now you've got a target on your back. Not paying what you owe is tantamount to cheating as far as they're concerned. They'll be after you as soon as it gets light. Jesus Christ!"

Harold couldn't remember the last time he'd been so angry.

"Oh, don't get so riled," placated Gunther, trying to calm things. "I have it figured out. Just listen a second."

Harold was so livid he found it hard to calm down to hear more excuses. He had visions of people with pistols chasing them down the mountain.

"Well, I'm listening...but it'd better be good. Otherwise, I'm going to...to..." He faded for lack of a suitable threat.

"All right, Harold. For Crissakes. Just try to follow...

Gunther was all business as he whispered his plan for evading a possible search party bent on its brand of justice. Harold was not convinced it would work and he couldn't help but be afraid for all of them, especially Sarah. He knew that there was no real law on the trail. If you got on the wrong side of the wrong person, there could be absolute hell to pay. In the end, who was right and who wasn't probably didn't make much difference.

There was no more sleep that night. Gunther woke Sarah up telling her they were starting up the trail right now. Wide-eyed with puzzlement, she didn't object.

Harold was already tearing down the tent and making room in one of the sleds for the stove. There was just enough light from the moon and reflection from the snow that they were able to see to gather all their goods and strap them securely.

A few people were up and about, but the drunkards were sleeping off their debauchery of the previous evening—exactly what Gunther had been counting on. He was planning on getting a half-day's lead on anyone who might remember him. For added protection, he wore his cap down low and wound a scarf around the lower part of his face. It was impossible to recognize him.

"Are you that cold, Gunther?" asked Sarah, puzzled by his gear. "We've just started and I'm sweating already."

Gunther grunted.

"Don't worry about me. Just pay attention to your sled. Don't slide off the middle of the trail or you'll get stuck. And for God's sake keep up."

Harold was happy that he had made sure Sarah's sled had the lightest load. Somehow, he had known that short-tempered Gunther would be impatient with her if she slowed progress, so he had rearranged how the sleds were packed.

The trail started to rise as soon as they left camp. They could only go a few hundred yards without slowing to rest. Gunther was constantly prodding them to keep going. As the climb became more precipitous, they had to bend over so that their upper bodies were parallel to the trail. Harold was beginning to think that the sleds were not the best idea.

"I think I'd rather make three trips with a pack on my back than drag this thing," he breathed as they made a stop.

"Maybe we should just leave them in a cache by the side of the trail and shuttle things on our backs from now on."

Gunther shook his head. He had finally taken off the scarf, but still had his cap on.

"No, no. Not yet. We can't be doubling back just yet. When we get to The Scales, we'll do that."

Harold knew why he didn't want to double back until they absolutely had to. He had to bite his lip to keep from expressing his irritation that Gunther had put them in this position, but he didn't want to upset Sarah.

What in God's name would it take for Gunther to learn his lesson?

So, until dusk fell, they continued across the most inhospitable and treacherous ground.

Because of the snow, they could not distinguish glacier from snow-covered cliff side, or boulder from gravel, or even small snow-filled depression from large holes. Some overhanging clumps of snow looked like they could break loose at any moment and crush anyone in the way.

But still they labored on, bent over double, their feet and back screaming for relief. People were in front of them, people were behind them, and there was nary a space in between. If you stepped out of line, it could be hours before you could find a spot to be able to squeeze back in.

They squinted in the glare of the ice and snow and couldn't slake their thirst until they got to a wider spot on the trail where they had at least a chance to work themselves back into the line.

And the line moved inexorably upwards...ever upwards, like a disjointed human serpent.

They got to a point where they could see that the mode of travel was about to change. Huge piles of baggage were spread around every foot of the trailside. Everything was going to have to be packed on backs from here on, in shifts. Besides the required food, clothes and tools, this included dogs and sleds, pieces of boats, lumber, and all kinds of tools and machinery that men were hoping would save labor later on.

They had arrived at The Scales, at the bottom of the Chilkoot.

It was a terrible and inhospitable spot buffeted by unremitting wind, used to reweigh the outfits before going to the summit in order to readjust the packing fee. And the fee had always risen as precipitously as the pass. Gunther had rewrapped his head with his scarf, but now, in consideration of the weather, it made sense. Harold had dug out a better cap, and Sarah tied a scarf around her hood to keep it firmly anchored.

They would have to spend at least a couple of nights in this place, fighting the bitter wind, the moisture, and the deepening cold. And there was nothing to look forward to besides even more debilitating effort and suffering in the immediate future.

As Herold stared ahead, his breath forming clouds, the Chilkoot loomed in all its ferociousness. The part he could see—the part below the obscuring fog and rain--seemed to be a formidable ninety-degree rise of hard slate covered by snow and ice.

At the sight, his heart sank like a weighty stone.

But more than being daunted himself, he greatly feared for Sarah. He could quite understand that, despite her demonstrated courage and strength so far, she might, at this point, give up the mission.

And, also at this point, he realized that he couldn't continue without her. Not the trail…not the quest…not his life.

In spite of the overwhelming circumstances, this realization and his self-admission of it gave him sudden and unexpected peace in one corner of his mind.

He wasn't going to waste energy fighting it anymore.

-9-

NEXT TO GODLINESS

The night seemed to last forever.

The wind roared incessantly as it fought to crush everything in its path. It inserted its cold dampness into every space, viciously raked every protrusion, and tugged mightily at anything that wasn't bolted or tied down firmly.

At one point, it won its battle with Gunther's tent; the stovepipe split. It was all they could do for Harold and Gunther to re-stake the tent and fit the pipe back together.

By the time they had refastened tent poles and guy-lines, and pieced things back into shape, their clothes were wringing wet.

Naked under blankets, they tried to dry their clothes on a makeshift clothesline over the stove. By dawn that could barely be distinguished from night, they had mixed results. Dog tired, they got up and realized that everything was still pretty damp. Sarah had arisen several times through the night to turn the wet clothes inside out to make the most of the scant heat.

There was no choice. As uncomfortable as it was, they put damp clothing back on, hoping that whatever body heat they could generate would finish the drying job. It would've been too long and involved the dig out a change of clothing that was buried among the packing.

As he helped ferry the goods to the campsite from their previous one, Harold was extremely grateful that they had had the foresight to buy parkas. The attached hood was a lifesaver compared to the coat and hat combination that most men wore. Sarah had been wearing hers since Sheep Camp, Both men decided that now was the time to join her.

Bathing and cleanliness were not uppermost in the minds of the general population at this time, and certainly even less so in the minds of the stampeders. Nevertheless, Harold noticed that every night, no matter what the temperature or the circumstances, behind the modesty barrier that she always managed to fasten to the tent roof somehow, Sarah used a bucket of melted snow to conduct some kind of washing ritual.

He knew it wasn't just vanity; it was a health concern.

All along the trail, the three of them had crossed people who were either very ill, or who were escorting the body of a person that had succumbed to illness. They also knew that even more bodies had been left to freeze alongside dead horses and dogs by the side of the trail.

They heard of the terrible spinal disease that had claimed many lives and had mystified the few medical authorities that had set up back in Dyea. They knew about the infections and the nutritional deficiencies that turned many people around in their tracks.

Sarah had an instinctive impulse to keep things clean, thinking that personal washing would keep unhealthful things at bay.

And, religiously, she continued to wash and dry their socks.

So far, all of it was working. Coupled with making sure their diet included dried fruit and onions, the care of their socks—and therefore their feet—kept them free of illness or infection.

But, merely staying healthy was not a guarantee of skating by without encountering danger. Harold was very aware that there were many other aspects to this expedition that could be just as hazardous to your existence as poor health.

He had noticed that at some of the established rest stops along the way, some men would pull out what looked like a large book. After manipulating it, the men would turn the book into a small counter upon which they placed a shell game.

Unbelievably, the stampeders would willingly lose their places in line and squander their money on a spur of the moment game that was sure to separate them from their tenuous wealth. They always lost, and they never learned.

At the end of the day, the men running the games would pocket hundreds of dollars, pack up their sleds full of false stampede goods, and return to town to sleep in comfort. The next day they would head back up to entice and fleece their next victims.

Gunther slowed down noticeably as they passed the shell games, and, each time, Harold's heart was in his mouth as he was afraid his partner would succumb to the temptation of the game.

"I know I can thwart those cheating thugs," he whispered to Harold at one point, out of Sarah's hearing. "I have a quick eye. I know I could win a game or two."

He nodded with conviction and continued.

"I'll bet they're part of Soapy's gang. Look at how they've stuffed those sleds with straw to make them look like they're packing stuff like they're one of us."

He pointed to one of the gamers.

"Look there. That fellow even has a miner's shovel sticking out of his sled," he smirked. "Great touch of authenticity, wouldn't you say?"

Harold was relieved when Gunther moved on, but he was perpetually irritated that he even had to add this to his list of worries. He had seen murderous intent in the red eyes of the losers. He knew it wouldn't be long before someone found himself at the business end of a knife or a pistol.

But Harold was wrong if he thought it would be a game that would soon cause havoc and death. It turned out to be an argument over something much more mundane.

"What was that?" asked Sarah, startled by a sudden sound, as she began to set up the main meal of the day.

The men stopped repacking their baggage to listen. They heard some shouting and noisy activity.

"My God! It's murder," they heard someone yell. "He's dead! Stabbed!"

"Who is it? Did you see it?"

"Was there a fight?"

"Yeah," added someone, disgust in his tone. "And all over a handful of beans..."

Leaving Sarah to guard their belongings, Harold and Gunther hurriedly threaded their way to the disturbance through the tall snow-covered mounds of baggage strewn haphazardly among tents and shacks.

They approached a group of agitated people trying to get past each other to peer into a tent.

Being taller than most, Harold could look over their heads.

What he saw in the murky depths of the tent was a body bent backwards over a box that had obviously been used as a table. There was an overturned glass and a plate on one corner of it.

The body was motionless.

Harold saw something on it that he couldn't quite make out because of a dark patch in the center of his chest.

At the same time there was a tussle just outside of the tent. Two men were holding a third who was struggling to escape their grasp.

The hue and cry went up.

"Hang him!" someone shouted. "He's nothing but a low-down killer!"

"Yeah, but whip him first! Teach him a damned lesson!"

This was followed by bloodthirsty shouts of agreement and raised fists.

Harold turned around to see what Gunther's reaction was.

He looked up the trail and down, but his partner was nowhere to be seen. Figuring he was somewhere in the gathering crowd, Harold focused his attention back on the noisy scene.

"All right! Everyone, stand back!"

A large man sporting an impressive handlebar mustache waved a pistol in the air.

"There will be no outlaw justice here. Let the man make his case."

There were some angry murmurs, but the crowd stepped back to make room in the middle.

Harold moved back too, wondering how this was going to end, dreading the worst. He had a definite feeling that things were close to being out of control.

There was no formal law on the pass, and he was sure that no one was going to hoof it back to Dyea just to find someone to administer justice properly. Looking around, he didn't see anyone who looked like he was particularly filled with scruples.

In fact, it looked like just the opposite.

Most faces were dark and menacing masks of pitiless wrath. This was true even for the few women in the crowd.

Renewed shouts of "Hang him! Hang him high!" reinforced Harold's fears.

The captive shook as much with fright as cold, Harold was sure. He looked close to tears, his paleness pathological as his dark, red-rimmed eyes shifted from face to threatening face. He seemed to be searching, in vain, for sympathy in a crowd that was voraciously feeding on his panic, eager for a spectacle.

For a split second, his gaze met Harold's, and Harold felt his stomach clench.

Tonight, the bloodthirsty atmosphere in the camp was palpable. It was as thick as the fog that slowly crept down the mountain from crevice to cranny, saturating everything in its path with pervading dampness and cold.

Deciding quickly against becoming involved with the hasty hanging party, Harold pulled his coat tight around himself and strode quickly back to the tent where he knew he'd find comfort and relief.

When he caught sight of Sarah, and his heart missed a beat; it was all he could do to restrain himself from rushing into her arms to release his emotions.

Then, out of the corner of his eye he saw Gunther and was immensely glad he hadn't given in to his impulse.

Seated at their makeshift table, Gunther was eagerly spooning dinner into his mouth. Harold couldn't help but notice a smug expression on his partner's face.

"Have a seat," Gunther said with his mouth full, gesturing magnanimously toward a box they were using as a chair.

"Things are looking up..." He gave Harold a wink and a smirk.

"Odd how things sometimes take care of themselves."

He quickly glanced over at Sarah and back at Harold, giving a slight shake of his head.

Harold took it as a signal that he couldn't say anything else for the moment.

So, he sat down resentfully without a word, as Sarah brought him a bowl of stew made from dried vegetables and a bit of salted meat. She topped it with a biscuit. Harold smiled his thanks as he picked up his spoon.

He so appreciated a woman's touch, however small it might be. Without it, this expedition would be incredibly dreary indeed.

-10-

JUSTICE ON THE TRAIL

As soon as he had finished eating, Gunther made it his business to learn of the fate of the murderer.

He had gloated to Harold that the two men involved were the ones he owed money to. The latest developments had relieved him of the issue entirely. One man was dead, and the other was very severely engaged.

Harold didn't join Gunther in his smug jubilation; he felt it was completely undeserved and unjustified. In his mind, Gunther should've had to make some restitution instead of getting off scot-free.

The murderer had been whipped at a post and sent reeling back down the mountain, warnings ringing in his ears about never showing his face on the trail again. A few of the men who had been heading back to Dyea were to make certain he would get no farther than the town's makeshift jail. After that, it would be up to the authorities to deal with him.

A separate group accompanied the victim's body.

Across the camp, customary activity continued uninterrupted. The incident was soon forgotten. Everyone went back to the business of packing and climbing and dreaming of goldfields.

Harold, however, couldn't just blithely dismiss the event. His spirit had been dampened by the mob mentality that surfaced as soon as an extreme situation occurred. People seemed to tap into their lowest instincts—their basest character.

Harold hoped that the obvious examples of this were not the majority. But he also knew that all it took for bad things to happen was the silence of others. He wondered if he should have made a move in an attempt to quell the situation.

To assuage his guilt, he had a driving need to talk it over with Sarah. Knowing that he would have utmost respect for her judgment, he wanted to gauge her reaction. But Gunther was always in the periphery, so he didn't get the chance.

By this time, over fifty feet of snow had accumulated at the summit of Chilkoot. According to the prevailing information, many men had to make twenty or thirty trips to haul their outfits over the pass. The snow buried everything at either end and made it very difficult for people to find their caches even though they planted long poles to mark their spot by the trail.

Although there was a kind of unwritten law of the trail against stealing, Harold and company decided that one person should always remain with their goods, while the other two did the ferrying. For the umpteenth time, Harold gratefully acknowledged that having three people was a definite advantage.

They left their tent up, figuring that they would be spending some time in it as they returned repeatedly to The Scales for their goods.

The two men loaded backpacks with about seventy pounds each.

A backpack was about the only feasible method for transporting goods. Pack animals could not climb the icy thirty-to-forty-five-degree slope. This was especially true for the stairs that had been carved out of the ice at the head of the pass by enterprising men who charged for their use; the so-called "Golden Stairs."

Even dogs had to be carried over.

The first day of packing up the pass was a lesson. They paid the toll for using the "stairs." and it gave them license to use them from that time on. The men had had no idea how exhausting the trip shaped up to be. While Harold stayed with the cache of goods at the summit, Gunther slid back down the snow-packed incline on his heels and backside taking advantage of the groove that had been worn into the snow-covered mountainside by hundreds of boots and backsides before him. Traveling in that fashion, it only took a few minutes to get back down to the tent. It had taken over six hours to climb in the other direction.

Having realized that seventy pounds was too much, Gunther packed much lighter loads for himself and for Sarah to take up to Harold who was guarding their cache at the summit. They decided they could both go up and then Sarah would stay with the cache as the men went back down for more.

In this manner they managed their outfits, the pile at the camp receding while the pile at the summit grew.

On his way up the path to the "Golden Stairs" for what seemed to be the hundredth time, Harold was bent over double under the weight of his sixty-pound pack. Between loud groans, he sucked in oxygen, often having to use his hands against the uneven, slippery ground to keep his balance, all the while trying to control his frustration at the effort he was having to exert. His groans joined the eerie chorus of others echoing all along the long line of men in the same straights, as they pushed and pulled themselves up by an ice-encrusted rope anchored along the "stairs."

Some of the men were crying as they fell to the side of the line, too exhausted to keep moving. Harold was often tempted to join them in some of the cutout rest areas that had been made for them to lean against the rock face with their packs still on. What spurred him on was the certain knowledge that getting back in line would be almost impossible. Everyone was in lockstep right up against the next striving body; there was not an inch of space between them. If you got out of line, you had to hope that someone would trip, freeing up a small space between two others. If not, you could wait all day to get back in.

How had Sarah been able to keep up the pace?

Harold was continually amazed at her resilience; her physical strength was inspiring—but, above all, her strength of character was what was truly remarkable. He never heard her complain. At the summit, she helped the men assemble their cache and mark it. Back at The Scales, she made dinner and reorganized the campsite. Up the pass, she bent under the weight of her backpack like everyone else and forged her way up the murderous incline in unrelenting fashion. And, every other day, she'd go through the dirty socks routine. Harold tried to do as much as he could to help her. Gunther just seemed to take her work for granted.

"Hey, Harold," he'd say. "Come on...that's women's work. Save your energy for the big stuff." He'd cluck his tongue in scorn and wander off.

Harold could hardly contain his irritation. No wonder many associations dissolved on the trail. It was so easy to rile your partners to the point of distraction. He knew Sarah must've heard the comments, but she never let on. Instead, with a warm smile, she'd thank Harold for his attentions and pat him on the back or arm.

He lived for that touch.

Finally, after an interminable month and a half, came the day that there was only one load left apiece, including the tent. The fact that they knew they were on their last trek to the summit helped give them wings.

Owing to the fact that they had constantly scraped snow off their cache and marked it with a long pole decorated with a bright piece of cloth, they were able to retrieve it without too much problem.

They reassembled the sleds for the downhill slide to Lake Lindeman, on the Canadian side.

But first they had to pass customs and pay duty for their American goods.

The Northwest Mounted Police stood stalwart at their posts despite the blizzards and constant wind. However inclement the weather, they never slackened in their efforts to assess proper duties and inspect equipment. The Americans soon realized that simply obeying without discussion was the best way to get by. If you were lucky, they would let you pass without thoroughly checking your outfit. They were the law, and everyone knew it was a bad idea to complain.

Everyone it seemed, except Gunther.

"First, they arbitrarily set up the border—it's not really where they say—then they expect to be paid for stuff we already paid for. That's some kind of international robbery," he groused. "It's a damned scheme."

"There's no fighting it," counseled Harold, afraid of a diplomatic incident. "The people who bought stuff in Canada on the way up through Victoria have to pay duty on the

American side. There's no way out of paying, one way or the other."

He shrugged. "Best just do it and be quiet."

"Well, I'm not payin' an extra cent," continued Gunther unabated. "They'd better watch it..."

For all his bluster, he stood aside as the intimidating Mounties examined their outfits to make sure they had the required amount of food and equipment. Then they were told what was owed in duty fees. Afraid of an outburst that might get their goods confiscated, Harold held his breath as Gunther reluctantly paid, his ill humor very obvious.

The entire summit was littered with piles of freight covered in a blanket of thick snow. It reminded Harold of a city. The outfits that had been deposited first, were probably not going to see daylight until the late spring thaw, so buried were they by more goods and snow. He felt sorry for the people who couldn't move on because of that predicament. He couldn't help feeling a bit superior at their own success thus far.

Then he heard the voice of his grandmother, loud and clear. "Pride goeth before a fall," she'd say, her mouth a stern line, her finger waving in admonition. To ward off bad luck, he tried to feel humble. The result was questionable.

As there was absolutely nowhere to pitch a tent or have any kind of camp, they paid a lot of money for a stale doughnut and a bitter cup of coffee to fortify themselves for the trail ahead. At least it was downhill...a blissful relief. They would have to do the backtracking as all along, but now the uphill climb would be without energy-sapping loads.

But before they got going toward the next point, Harold couldn't believe his eyes at the sight of those ubiquitous shell game con men who set up shop even up there, just west of the international border. In pursuit of the potential fortune, they were sure would grace them, they plodded on, stalking the exhausted stampeders who made the predictable last-ditch effort at a chance for easy money.

Having dug out little shelves for the men to stop and rest their packs, they built fires out of very expensive wood—it had to be hauled seven miles—to make an attractive rest stop and increase the temptation. With shrieking winds swirling around, the con men plied their trade and pocketed their winnings to the detriment of the hapless men who tried in vain for yet another chance at a blessing from Lady Luck.

If they had only realized that there was no chance involved at all.

It was a forgone conclusion that the only winners were the con men that always had the upper hand. At the end of the games, their victims had to make up their minds whether to go on with even less money than before, or to return to shore and try to get passage home, tails tucked between their legs. Many of them were just sitting, completely dejected, by the side of the trail, gazing ahead, their stares empty and unfocused.

The sun had briefly come out, as the three partners headed down the steep slopes to Lake Lindeman. From the height of the pass, they could see the interminable human line that wended its way down. The challenge was by no means over, but, compared to what they had just been through, it certainly seemed easy to slide down on the Canadian side.

Then the clouds moved back in and everything took on the customary gray and indistinct aura.

After a very wind-blown uncomfortable night, they arrived at the edge of Lake Lindeman and tried to wedge their campsite in among the thousands of tents and half-built boats that littered the shoreline.

It took several more trips back to the summit before they finally had their tons of equipment by the edge of the freezing lake. This time, the trips up were the easy part, as they were empty-handed. Then, on the way back down, they had to use guiding ropes to keep the sleds from sliding too far to the left or right or hurtling down too fast.

They realized that they were too late to build their boat in time for freeze-up. Ice was already forming at a frightening pace. The winter loomed long and cold as they faced months of waiting for spring. At least they had a long time to build a crackerjack boat.

Between Lake Lindeman and Bennett Lake at the headwaters of the Yukon River, there was a rock-strewn canyon—One Mile Rapids—whose tortuous waters had already taken a few lives and many outfits during the past summer.

There was a choice to be made.

"Do we build a boat here and wait for the thaw to float down the One Mile Rapids to Bennett, or do we keep slogging forward over land until we get to Bennett and then build our boat there?"

Grim-faced and indecisive, Gunther looked to Harold and Sarah for their opinions.

"I heard people lose everything going through the rapids between the lakes, and if they don't die in the water, they die at their own hand in despair of having lost their belongings."

Sarah looked dubious. "Maybe we should stick with our sledding system. It might take longer, but we don't risk as much. The Yukon past Bennett is treacherous enough."

Harold was silent, thinking it over.

Winter had everything in its firm grip. Whether they built the boat now and waited for the spring thaw here, or trudged down to Bennett and built the boat there, it would still be months before the Yukon could be navigated. As far as time was concerned, it seemed almost a moot point to him. Avoiding the test of the canyon, on the other hand, seemed wise.

"I'm for going on down to Bennett on foot and building our boat down there," he finally said. "I don't see why we should risk everything, at this point, when we don't have to."

Gunther's mouth twisted in thought and his eyes closed, but he finally nodded in agreement.

"Yeah, you're right. Why subject ourselves to those rapids if we don't have to."

Sarah looked relieved.

So, the pressure to move on under duress was somewhat lessened.

The dangers of the known were definitely better than the unknown. If nothing else, they were quite handy with the sled and the backpacks. Boats were a new dimension to be dealt with as far into the future as possible, after as much planning as possible.

The temperature dipped below freezing.

-11-

THE PITS

He didn't know how she had done it, but when she called them in for dinner, he was flabbergasted to see a feast on the table.

"How in the world did you find a... a bird?" asked Harold, incredulous, as he took off his parka and shook out the crystalline snow from its folds.

He knew what was sitting on the platter wasn't a turkey, but whatever it was, it was definitely in that category.

Sarah just smiled mysteriously as she swept by him and added a few things to the setting.

"And the linen?" asked Gunther, knocking snow off his boots and slapping wood chips from his hat and coat. "Looks to me like you've been messing around digging through the baggage. Isn't that your grandmother's tablecloth?"

Unbelievably, his tone turned what should've been a compliment into something tantamount to a scolding.

They had set up a semi-permanent type of camp, now that they had arrived at Lake Bennett to spend the winter while getting their boat put together in time for break-up on the Yukon.

It had been a relatively easy slide down the mountain from the summit of Chilkoot to Lake Lindeman. Once all their goods were at the lake, they observed how some enterprising miners put together sails and rigged their sleds to take advantage of the ever-blowing wind. The ice on Lindeman was moderately smooth, thereby making progress possible, even easy compared to recent experience.

The three followed suit, loading the sleds to their maximum capacity, making sails out of some of their tarpaulins, rigging a makeshift mast and fastening ropes with which to guide the sled as it was propelled ahead by the wind. Every once in a while, the sleds would get stuck in rough terrain, but for the most part it was smooth sailing—much smoother than a trip along the same route would've been in the water of the treacherous canyon.

Having arrived at Lake Bennett, they were incredibly lucky enough to find a recently abandoned campsite with its own whipsaw pit. The fact that the pit was already built was a huge benefit, saving time and making more money available to buy lumber for the boat.

And now, appropriately, it was Thanksgiving, or somewhere near it, and they were about to sit down to a wondrous meal that Sarah had somehow been able to organize in order to celebrate.

Harold felt incredibly thankful indeed.

She knew they were dying of curiosity as to how she had managed all this, so she let on just a little, just to calm them down a bit.

"Well, while you guys were busy setting up in the sawpit, I was able to do a little research. You'd be amazed at what one can dig up with a little persuasion."

She made a dramatic gesture toward the well-laden table.

"Hope you like the goose. It took a lot of that persuasion I was mentioning..."

Harold would've appreciated anything that was a little different from the usual fare. This was more than he could've even imagined. Not only was there a goose she had somehow roasted, but there were vegetables, bread, and a kind of cinnamon apple compote for dessert. And he really appreciated the lengths Sarah had gone to in preparing a beautiful table.

Suddenly shy about it, he sat down at his accustomed place and took a hold of a napkin.

A napkin!

Civilization epitomized!

There was real cutlery. Real glasses for water. No tin. Harold handled it all in very gingerly fashion, raising the glass to see the light refracted. He had been away from so-called civilization so long he had forgotten the pleasure that could be found in having nice things around.

"What do we need all this fancy stuff for?" asked Gunther gruffly. "I don't need a napkin. I have a sleeve."

Harold looked at him to see if he was joking, but it was impossible to tell. He was busy sticking his fork into the goose to try to pull it apart.

"Wait, Gunther," said Sarah, stilling his hand. "I have something to carve it properly."

Once Gunther settled down, and let his hunger speak for him, they all enjoyed the Thanksgiving meal. Harold tried to make his appreciation obvious, complimenting Sarah on all her efforts—they had been considerable.

Gunther mumbled his way through three helpings of everything. And when he had finished, he belched loudly, stood up to stretch, and went to the bedroll to lie down.

"We'll have to hold up on the sawing," he said, as he pulled a cover over his eyes. "Take some time off, Harold. You're going to need it. It's your turn for the pit."

Harold's heart sank at that reminder.

The "pit" was the lower part of the sawpit, under the platform. It was where one of the partners stood to help pull the whipsaw through logs and the spaces in the platform to make the planks needed to build a boat. The other stood above on the platform, guiding the saw as it was pushed and pulled in as straight a line as possible toward the man below who kept his eye on a chalk line.

For most saws, the downward stroke was the cutting stroke, so every bit of the sawdust, woodchips, dirt, and whatever else happened to collect on the platform cascaded down into the face of the man below. As he had to monitor the formation of the cut above him, he could not close his eyes, nor turn his face away. It was a horrendously aggravating necessity that could certainly not be eliminated or even improved.

And it caused frustration, arguments and outright fights. Harold saw several partnerships dissolve because of it.

As he helped Sarah clean up after the meal, he tried to put it out of his mind for the moment.

"Sarah," he started, as he watched her carefully wash and dry the three glasses they had used. "I just want you to know...that I really appreciate what you did here...with the dinner...I mean."

Sarah wrapped the glasses with some rags and carefully laid them in a wooden box.

"I know, Harold," she said, her voice very low—almost a whisper. "I'm aware that you appreciate what I do...and I'm very grateful. If not for that..." Her voice died as she turned to pack the box away.

They worked in comfortable silence a while longer, until all the traces of the table setting had disappeared into the various packs that were spread around. Harold stuck some logs into the stove and sat down on a box to relax while Gunther's snores punctuated the silence.

Then Sarah came over to him and gently put something down on the table.

Harold was surprised to see a small bottle of what he assumed were spirits, and two cups.

"Gunther's going to be sorry he went to sleep," smiled Sarah, speaking in low tones, as she pulled out the stopper and poured some amber liquid into the two cups. "He's missing the best part of the celebration."

What he doesn't know won't hurt him, thought Harold uncharitably. *He'd only ruin the moment with his loutish ways.*

They sat in silence, smiling all the while, enjoying the warmth of the stove and the fiery flavor of their drinks. Harold let his imagination run. The impending horror of the pit faded, and he was transported to the closest thing to heaven he could've hoped for.

In time, the lighthearted thoughts dissipated as quickly as they had materialized. Reality came back in all its terrible intensity, not to say insanity.

Day after day they toiled in the pit, eking out boards for their boat—a boat that had to withstand the formidable abuse that the Yukon in its various forms was sure exact upon it.

Gunther had a set of plans for the boat that he'd brought along with him all the way from Minnesota, carefully rolled up in one of his many pockets. Every once in a while, he'd consult them, especially when it came to forming the keel and ribs.

"Boat plans from the plains of Minnesota?" cracked Harold. "Lots of those in the cornfields, are there?"

"Did you forget about the thousand lakes?" retorted Gunther. "Fishing is big up there." He shook his head with obvious scorn.

Harold wished he had a partner with a greater sense of humor.

The plans called for a flat-bottomed boat—the easiest to construct and the usual type for navigating rivers. Both men wondered how that design would fare in the turbulent rapids they were bound to face on several occasions.

Both strong men, Gunther and Harold were able to keep the saw cuts straight, the boards even. Harold's woodworking skills were a boon as well. Thanks to in a large part to Sarah's careful menu planning, they were also healthier than many of the men who were mostly on their own—men who ate what was handy and didn't take care of themselves, either because they didn't know how, or because health was way down their list of considerations.

By the time most of them had finished the workday, there wasn't much energy left for thoughtful meal planning. Scurvy was often the result, even though common knowledge provided ways to avoid it. Accidents with tools finished off a few who couldn't heal, or whose injuries incapacitated them beyond hope. They barely had the wherewithal to sell what was left of their outfits and retreat back to Dyea or Skagway.

So, it wasn't surprising then, that after demonstrating their success, Harold and Gunther were called upon to work for others. With money earned for labor, they were able to avail themselves of some useful items for sale around the tent town as well as extra food and equipment.

Sarah opened a kind of two-table restaurant, cooking bacon, flapjacks, and beans in the morning, and stew or soup with biscuits or cornbread at night. Keeping careful track of food supplies, she had to turn away dozens of people at the beginning because the stock was limited. Soon, however, from the money she took in for the meals, she was able to buy food from stampeders who were abandoning their dreams and heading back up the trails for home.

During the afternoons, between meals, she took in laundry that she washed in tin buckets and mended the threadbare clothing that the miners had been wearing non-stop for weeks.

Business in her tent was brisk.

*   *   *

Before long, it was Christmas.

While the occasion was hardly noticed by the miners in their usual hustle of daily enterprise, Sarah and her men were able to celebrate with even more elegance than they had Thanksgiving.

But instead of a bird, they had roasted stuffed rabbit.

Nell had connections—this time someone who knew the art of trapping.

Harold had been able to scrounge some lumber to make a full-fledged table with real legs instead of boxes. He stayed up extra late to finish fashioning a couple of chairs that he presented as a surprise to Sarah on Christmas morning. Her grateful smile made it worth the effort.

"Don't see what was wrong with our other chairs," grumbled Gunther, not above trying a new one out, and tucking his special-occasion napkin under his chin. "You spent valuable time and material that might've been better expended for something really useful."

Harold and Sarah looked at each other and hid their smiles.

By now, they had figured, if Gunther didn't complain about something, he was probably ill. It no longer affected them to any extent, although it did rile Harold that Sarah was continually denied proper gratitude.

He made a point of compensating for it.

And he treasured the warm scarf and socks she had somehow found the time to knit for him.

The temperature hovered near zero.

-12-

NERVES OF STEELE

Their newfound wealth had its negative side.

One day that they hadn't worked the pits, Gunther came into camp and threw a big package in front of their tent.

"Present for you, Harold," he announced with what Harold was pretty sure was a snide expression.

Sarah stopped her cooking and stood up.

"What is it?" asked Harold frowning.

Beware of Greeks bearing gifts.

"What did you...?"

"Open it and find out," said Gunther, his lip curling. "Late Christmas present."

Yes, it was definitely a snide expression. Harold tried to push away rapidly mounting ill feelings.

When he took apart the package his fears were realized.

It was another tent.

A smaller one—basically a one-man tent.

Gunther's face was wreathed in beatific smiles.

"Your own private home," he chuckled. "I hope you like it. Oh...and you'll have to buy your own heater. I have my gift limits."

Sarah had gone back to her cooking. Harold couldn't see her expression, but her body looked a little rigid as she stirred the pot.

"Guy who owned it died," came Gunther's offhanded unsolicited explanation filling the silence. "I helped out his sister by buying it. It was a good deal. And the best part is that now we all have our own place."

He turned to Sarah.

"So... what's for dinner, my Sweet? Soup or stew?"

Then he turned to face Harold.

"Oh, by the way, Harold, you're still welcome to eat with us you know..."

Harold was dumbfounded at this performance. Gunther's monologue, delivered in such casual manner, was the longest speech he had uttered in months.

Not able to suppress the feeling that he was suddenly an outcast, Harold could only nod and carry the tent to one side of the campsite. There was hardly any space on which to pitch it. Guy-lines, baggage, equipment of every description—even animals, littered every inch of space around the tents.

Harold finally found a spot big enough over a lumpy area that no one else had wanted. He dumped the tent and sat down on it, trying to think.

His breath crystallized in front of him as he panted with emotion. He knew he'd have to snap himself out of his sudden lethargy—he couldn't stay immobile like this too long—cold was penetrating his layers of clothing.

He was about to get up when he saw Sarah weaving her way toward him between piles of goods.

"Harold," she said, breathless from the exertion. "Please come back and eat with us. And stay tonight at least. You can set up some boughs for your bedroll tomorrow and get a stove. There's no point in your..."

"But...what about Gunther?" Harold had no desire for a confrontation, nor did he want to insert himself further into a domestic situation. Things were touchy enough in the whipsaw pit.

"Oh...you know...Gunther..." she shrugged dismissively, her jaw set. "He'll go along. He was just trying to...to...exercise some kind of misguided overbearing...I don't know what. Just ignore him."

She tried to make a joke.

"I'm the tent boss anyway..." She tugged at Harold's arm. "Come on back. I got a piece of fresh moose meat for dinner from one of the fellows you helped."

Fresh meat would indeed be a welcome change. Harold found himself salivating at the thought, even though he'd never had moose before.

*   *   *

By now, Harold and Gunther had a sizable pile of boards they were planning to use to build a boat on which their lives were soon to depend. They had often interrupted their own progress in order to help others, especially couples that included a woman. Even though these slender sisters, wives, or girlfriends could stand on the whipsaw platform to pull the saw up and then line it up for their men to pull down for the cutting stroke, the process took almost twice as long as it took the all-male teams. Harold and Gunther hastened the process for them and were paid in some form or another for their trouble.

Because of this they amassed an eclectic collection of goods to add to their outfits. Some proved to be useful like certain tools or furnishings—even food, and some were whimsical like the ostrich-feather hat Harold presented to Sarah that made her eyes sparkle.

Gunther managed to find his usual outlet for spending his liquid earnings. There was plenty of gaming of every sort in which to participate on Bennett. The good part was that the Northwest Police did not let any members of the Smith gang cross the border into Canada to ply their trade. The bad part for people with Gunther's bent was that they kept a tight rein on the Americans that they had let through.

They allowed no guns, inspected belongings, monitored work, and enforced their laws with unshakable resolve. They allowed some entertainment including ladies of the night, but they were strict in administering all businesses, making sure there was no cheating. They also dispensed advice and lent a helping hand in boat and shelter construction.

A more hardworking, morally upright and compassionate group of high-minded men did not exist. Under the able leadership of Mr. Samuel B. Steele, their meticulous record-keeping and deep sense of responsibility saved countless lives. In every situation, they demonstrated undeniable class. At the same time, they received very little appreciation from the thousands of foreigners who descended like a cloud of locusts upon their territory and strained their generous nature with displays of despicable behavior.

Sarah was one person who did appreciate their contribution.

"He has the most perfectly apt name," she prattled over breakfast to her two men, referring to the larger-than-life captain.

"His eyes are steel gray, and he rules this place with an iron fist. I believe him when he says that the Smith gang will never show their faces here. If they did, they'd be sorely disappointed."

Whenever possible, she treated the Mounties to a good meal and dinner conversation. They often came by her tent just for a brief greeting, but she insisted they stay for a meal. If Gunther was at the table, he was uncharacteristically subdued. It was as though just the presence of the law made him nervous.

And he had reason for this. Because the Mounties frowned on anything that might disrupt the peace—like angry losers, Gunther had to be very cagey to indulge his habit. Harold was probably the only one who could tell if he'd had a bad night because, if there was no obnoxious barrage of bragging, it meant Gunther had lost.

While he had felt slighted when Gunther had banished him to live under his own tent, Harold was later glad to be able to use it as a refuge when he needed to avoid his partner. That's what happened when Gunther came to him for a loan after a string of nights devoid of bragging. It infuriated him that Gunther was such a slave to gambling, and he didn't want to enable him further. It was a waste of money that most could ill afford.

After Gunther's calculatingly obsequious request, Harold just shook his head.

"Nope," he said firmly. "I have other plans for my money." With that, he walked into his tent, pulling the door flap closed behind him.

He was relieved not to have to see Sarah's disappointed face as she once again witnessed Gunther's weakness.

*   *   *

"Your boat is number four thousand," a young Mounty announced to them one day, as they were putting the finishing touches on their riverboat, noisily hammering the homemade caulk into every space between boards. He had a notebook and was laboriously writing their names and those of their next of kin in it.

"Four thousand?" Gunther was incredulous. "Is ours the last one?"

"Not by a long shot," laughed the Mounty. "So far, our records show over seven thousand. And there are more all the time."

Under Captain Steele's ironclad supervision, every boat and every single passenger was duly noted and recorded by boat number. It was one of his steadfast principles to be responsible and care for each soul that was planning to make the perilous trip down the Yukon River.

"When the boats arrive in Dawson, we'll know the outcome of every enterprise by checking names off our list. For those who don't appear on the banks of the "City of Gold" after a reasonable delay, there'll be a search. If it's found that they have suffered their demise on the way down, our men will make sure that their next of kin will be notified, and that any money found among lost outfits will be returned to them."

It was a noble exercise in conscientiousness that required great character and energy, and ensured as much safety for the participants as was humanly possible.

And it was a debt that would never be repaid, as the crazed and self-obsessed stampeders never stopped to consider how, despite their pathetic foolhardiness, the Mounties were diligently caring for them at every turn.

*   *   *

By late winter, Lake Bennett had become a place of contrasts. The weather varied with dizzying high and lows. The mountainsides were thawing, while the ice still had the lake in its firm grip. The nights were still freezing but the days grew softly spring-like, flowers beginning to peek through melting patches of snow.

Besides the continual influx of men still coming down from the passes, and a small contingent that had given up and were heading the other way, there were men who waited patiently for breakup of the river ice by sitting around, smoking their pipes. Others couldn't wait, and took off over land, undaunted by the distance they had to cover.

It was a race, after all.

There were others who busily sawed and hammered, filling the valley with constant ear-splitting racket, and there were some who were ambivalent as to the best course to follow. Should they hope for better luck, or should they quit and minimize their losses? Their indecision was their weakness—a characteristic that had no place in this particular world.

Aside from the people who demonstrated singleness of purpose—their goal to get five hundred miles down the treacherous Yukon to the Klondike or be damned, there were the ones who realized that making a fortune did not have to be put off until Spring.

Sarah was definitely one of the latter.

Like the women who plied their nighttime trade from their tiny "cribs" sanctioned and patrolled by the Mounties to fulfill the needs of the largely male population—an expedient way to keep them from committing violations—Sarah could see that many other desires needed to be catered to as well. And the appropriate time was at hand. There was no need to wait to arrive in Dawson to be enterprising.

Despite the great hardships inherent in conquering the Chilkoot and White passes with bare necessities, enterprising individuals looked past these and bent under burdens made up of crates of eggs, perfumed soaps, rare delicacies—even caviar.

No effort was too great. Many were the individuals who bent over double or struggled with packed sleds to freight cases of liquor carefully hidden in creative ways to avoid the scrutiny of the Mounties at the border.

Of course, for some, liquor was more a necessity than a luxury.

Understanding the quirks of the human soul, Sarah realized that people would readily pay incredible amounts for items that they missed from their previous life. To them, rare indulgences were well worth the outlay.

Her two-table restaurant became a five-table, with a small counter for additional seats. She had persuaded her men to build a semi-permanent structure out of the scrap wood from the boatbuilding. They were able to secure an extra stove and built a display case for the luxury items that she had traded for by doing laundry and repairing clothes.

"How do you do it?" asked Harold in wonder, as she closely examined a finger he had hurt that had become infected, throbbing to distraction. "There aren't enough hours in the day to accomplish what you're doing."

"Well, obviously, there are," she answered sweetly. "I've just learned a lot of short cuts for everything."

She held his hand firmly.

"Now, hold still. You have a sliver of something in there imbedded at the edge of your fingernail, and it's going to have to come out."

After boiling some water on the stove, she took out a cup and filled it.

"Well, Sir," she said with a grim smile, holding out the steaming cup. "Let's see what you're really made of. Sit down at the table. You need to stick that finger in this cup as hot as you can stand...no....hotter. We have to purge that pus out of there."

Harold sat down and tried not to wince as he plunged his finger into the water. It was all he could do not to jerk it back out.

"How long do I have to...?"

"Just a few minutes. Then I'll try to squeeze the infection out. I think you'll feel relief right away as it drains."

It worked just as she had explained.

A long sliver of wood slid out with the yellowish discharge that burst from his finger. Sarah gently squeezed as much of the sticky fluid as she could without causing more damage. Then she took a piece of clean cloth from her sewing supplies and wrapped his finger.

Harold's chest was jittery, but it wasn't because of the pain.

The proximity of Sarah's body, especially as she bent over so that her head was almost touching his, was befuddling him. Her hair was loose around her shoulders, and it brushed his cheek. As he had come over very early, she hadn't had time to button everything. He could see the swell of her breast in the opening of her blouse.

"Try to keep it clean, and if possible, keep your hand raised," she ordered, straightening up from her task. "When your finger loses its redness and quits hurting, you can go back to using it. If not, we might have to repeat the treatment."

Harold looked anywhere but at her, hoping she'd attribute the redness of his face to his reaction to the treatment. He felt immediate relief from the throbbing pain of a few minutes ago. Her treatment seemed to be working well already.

"Uh...how did you know to do that?" he asked, rolling his sleeve back down, trying to hide his embarrassment. "I wish I had known to do that the last time this happened. I was about to cut the whole thing off, it was so bothersome."

"Well," said Sarah, rinsing and putting the cup away.

"Before he decided to be a merchant, my father went to medical school. He actually had a practice for a while when I was very little. People couldn't afford to pay him much, so they would give him items in trade for his care. That gave him the idea to open the store."

"So, he was actually both a doctor and a merchant?"

"Yep. It worked out pretty well, and I got training in both."

"And, you were a teacher too..."

As he pulled on his coat, Harold could hardly contain his admiration for her; his soul filled with a very special awe.

Thanking her for her good care, he desperately hoped that he sounded casual doing it.

Stepping out into the spring sunshine to head back to work, he could only think that she was wasted on someone who didn't seem to realize or appreciate what an unbelievable gem she was.

-13-

THE THAW

"Did you hear what happened?"

On a day in April that promised to be much warmer than the last, Sarah was serving breakfast to Gunther and Harold, when one of their neighbors interrupted them, out of breath and sweating profusely,

All three looked at him, obviously in the dark as to what he was talking about.

"What happened?" asked Gunther, pointing to a chair. "Do you want some breakfast?"

"Some coffee if you have it," he said, sitting down with a grateful sigh. "I just came from the head of the lake. A bunch of fellows came down with news of a really bad avalanche back up on the pass." He took a long gulp from a cup Sarah had handed to him. "Lots of bodies..."

Pulling her frying pan off the heat, Sarah sat down with the men to listen.

"You know how the winds have been warmer lately? Well, they say it's because of that—its action on all that snow that fell last week—that the slides started."

"So, no one realized the danger?" asked Harold, sitting back with his cup. "They still kept going up the pass?"

"Oh, yeah," answered their visitor. "You know how they are..."

Harold thought that was pretty rich coming from someone who probably would have done exactly the same thing.

"The only ones to heed the danger were the Sticks—the Indian packers. They refused to work. Everyone else kept going—making the most of the pleasant weather—even after a family was buried in one of the first slides."

"Did they die?" asked Sarah, looking like she was afraid of the answer.

"Well, no. Some of the guys were actually able to dig them out. And while they were doing that, they could hear a lot of rumbling coming from higher up, so they tried to warn everyone to hightail it back to Sheep Camp."

"Let me guess," intoned Gunther. "No one listened."

The visitor nodded.

"Like I said, the only ones to head back to Sheep Camp were the packers."

He shook his head.

"Some of the guys high up, heard the rumbling and, before they knew it, they were suddenly sliding, transported downhill by a kind of solid snow wave. Their arms and legs were sticking out at weird angles, their heads buried, as they were swept along."

The four sat in silence as they imagined the scene.

"I talked to one guy that got out," the visitor continued after a spell. "He was buried under six feet of snow and just about suffocating when he was saved. A lot of others weren't so lucky."

He put his cup out for Sarah to give him more coffee.

"I guess I'll take one of those flapjacks if you have any to spare," he added, eyeing the empty plates with traces of syrup on them. "I missed my breakfast earlier."

Sarah obliged by making a few more pancakes and serving them piping hot.

Between mouthfuls, he continued his tale.

"The worst part was hearing people screaming from beneath layers of ice and snow. Even as others tried to dig them out, their screams got weaker and weaker until...well...I'm sure you get the idea. They found some of them frozen in running position, and some completely upside down." He chewed some more and then raised a finger. "One good thing...There's a lady was dug out twice...and lived to tell about it." He shrugged. "Some people have no luck at all, and then there's those that get an extra helping..."

Days later, more news surfaced about the tragedy.

Much to her gratification, Sarah learned that good old ever vigilant and caring Captain Steele dispatched men to help dig, keep track of the dead, and make sure belongings were sent to family. More bodies surfaced as snow thawed, and some were probably never recovered, but the number of losses was estimated at around seventy. A few more slides occurred in subsequent days, but there were no more deaths reported.

The bright sunlight and longer hours of daylight increased the energy along the banks of Lake Bennett. Streams were flowing down the hillsides surrounding the tent city, flowers were blooming, and the winds had turned gentle and fragrant. Men who had finished their boat building, sat idle by the water's edge, ready to pounce once the ice began to move.

But, in spite of all their willing it to thaw, it held fast.

Lake Bennett had become the busiest boat harbor in America. Boats stationed on the banks extended as far as the eye could see, each laboriously numbered and noted in the records held by the Mounties, led by Superintendent Steele.

It was the lull before the storm.

"You'll be facing danger right away," the Mounties counseled, trying to prepare the thousands of people who were about to take their lives into their own inexperienced hands.

"Miles Canyon will be swollen with water forced through the narrows. It'll be higher in the middle as it absorbs the extra volume. Controlling your boat will take everything you've got and then some..."

Many of the folk listened with only one ear, if they listened at all.

"Nothing can be worse than what we went through up there," they said, jerking their heads in the direction of the Chilkoot and White passes. "What could there possibly be more daunting than that? Going down this river letting the current take us will be as nice as pie."

His cautious nature coming to the fore, Harold didn't ascribe to this philosophy. Some were creating a picture of being securely ensconced in their boats as they casually made their way down a friendly and welcoming Yukon River, stopping along the banks when they felt like it to have a meal over a fire, as though they were on a holiday cruise. Harold thought this was incredibly naïve, if not dangerous. This was no time to let down your guard.

"Have you heard these guys?" he asked Sarah, as they began to take down their shelters and make the packs in such a way that they would fit in the boat most efficiently. "You'd think it was going to be a ride on a lake in a city park," he scoffed. "If you listen to the Mounties... they put a way different complexion on it."

"Yes," said Sarah, nodding in agreement, brushing a shiny dark curl out of her eyes. "And I, for one, take their word for it.

They do not talk through their hats. They've seen what that river can do to people who don't have experience."

She stopped and looked intently at Harold.

"I am frightened, when I think of it. One of the Mounties told me that last fall one fellow was so despondent after losing his outfit twice to the river that he shot himself. And he had a wife and children at home..."

Harold bit his lips and raised his eyebrows.

"You're right. It's not going to be easy. We'll just have to avoid the most dangerous aspects—maybe portage around the worst spots—and be very careful."

"Oh, you two are just nervous Nellies," blustered Gunther who had caught the tail end of the conversation. "We have one of the best boats around, and we'll load it just right. After going over the pass, we know we're strong enough to conquer some river water. At least we won't have any avalanches to deal with."

He threw down a pile of rope.

"Here. I got us this. I figure we can wrap it around all our boxes and packs and have a ready handle in case something does happen, and we need to grab everything."

Well, thought Harold. *At least this shows he doesn't think it's all flowers and rainbows...*

-14-

BREAK-UP

"It's breaking up! Bennett is breaking up!"

Gunfire and shouting assured that everyone lined up for miles along the lakeshore was aware of the news.

It was late May 1998, and the ice was finally easing its grip on the lake. Water could be seen between jagged edges of ice that had been rent apart by the formidable pressure beneath it. Huge, grinding ice chunks forced each other out of the way up the banks. It wouldn't be long before the Yukon broke up too.

Gunther tore up the hill to the tent. Harold and Sarah were tying some of their outfit packs with ropes.

"It's bustin' up! It really is. A whole lot are ready to go. We've got to get a move on."

Without stopping to check very carefully, or to consult the other two, he started to grab some of the goods that hadn't made it to the boat yet.

"Whoa, Gunther. We haven't finished packing those. Just hold up for a moment."

"But we're going to get behind. Let's go. They're getting ahead of us."

"For Crissakes, Gunther. All the ice from lake has to clear first. You want it to crush us before we even get started?"

Harold was getting increasingly impatient with his partner. It seemed that, instead of getting smarter with experience, Gunther was more and more impulsive.

"If some are trying to set off now, they're going to end up crushed to death, or at least lose everything..."

"That's right," added Sarah. "Superintendent Steele says that..."

"You know?" interrupted Gunther, his voice gaining a dangerous edge, his fists clenching. "I've had just about all I can take of 'Superintendent Steele this,' and 'Superintendent Steele that...' You'd think he's God come down to Earth."

He frowned at Sarah and raised a finger in warning.

"I really don't care what *Mister* Steele has to say, and I definitely don't want to hear another word about him."

He paused to take a breath, his forehead still furrowed in anger.

"What I want is to get to the damned gold fields."

Staring intently at the other two, he continued. "And I mean right away."

Then he looked around quickly, found a trussed-up package that looked ready, and grabbed it.

"I'll be down at the boat."

Sarah looked at his receding form as he made his way down to the crowded bank. She gave a barely perceptible shake of the head, and then went back to her task.

It was with great difficulty that Harold had, once again, managed to hold his tongue. One of these days he was not going to be able to, and then there would be irreparable harm, especially if it came to blows. So many partnerships had dissolved in this way. But, in all good sense, he knew that to have any chance of making good on this venture, he had to keep a lid on his ire and his eye on the ultimate goal of reaching the Golden City.

As thousands of men waited impatiently for the ice on Lake Bennett to clear, ready to hop into their boats as soon as it was indicated, others decided to wait for the initial rush to subside before they tackled the canyon and the rapids.

For the latter group, the natural challenges were daunting enough without adding huge numbers of largely inexperienced sailors to the mix. Many were planning on manning a paddle or a sweep with absolutely no experience or practice, and certainly no knowledge of the waters. Some had boats that looked like they might sink in the first hour. In Harold's opinion, they were nothing but accidents waiting to happen, and they would drag others down with them.

Because he did listen to the Mounties and valued their advice, Harold knew that there was very little chance of obtaining new claims in the gold fields anyway, especially ones that would yield that all-important fortune of a lifetime. People already in the Klondike had been working claims for a year, and most good spots were taken. The men who had managed to last the winter without starving or dying of scurvy and the elements, eked out a few dollars per gold pan or sluice box. Most of them blew their earnings when they came to town. The huge success stories—the true ones that had first fueled the feverish national movement—were few and very far between.

So, for Harold, Dawson was not a jumping-off point to other points. It was an end in itself. He planned on using his woodworking skills to set up a lucrative business right in the boomtown. His idea was to take advantage of the gold dust seekers rather than actually be one.

So, hurrying downriver, throwing all caution to the winds, was not his aspiration. In fact, he saw wisdom in doing just the opposite.

Of course, this put him at odds with his partner. He knew it would be next to impossible to convince Gunther that caution was the much better part of valor.

And that was even with Sarah on his side. She too was planning on establishing a business. She would follow Gunther's lead, as it was her place. Nevertheless, it was becoming obvious that she harbored reservations.

She finished securing a canvas bag and came over to Harold.

"I don't know," she said in a small voice, putting a hand on his arm. Her eyes were bright with unshed tears and her lip trembled slightly.

"I'm so afraid Gunther will drag us into needless trouble. He refuses to listen to anything I say anymore."

Harold put his arm around her, trying with great effort to think of something helpful to say that would relieve her worry.

He came up short.

Sarah clung to him, biting her lips to keep from crying. Harold could feel her shaking. Guarding himself against doing something he'd certainly regret, he held her close, letting his warmth envelope her, hoping that would suffice for the time being. She had always presented such a calm front. He hadn't realized the depths of her emotion.

Time stood still.

"Interesting way to get our stuff ready."

It was a most sardonic tone, and it made them both jump. Gunther had come back for more of the outfits. Harold quickly released Sarah, who looked stonily at Gunther.

"Don't you worry about us doing what needs doing," she said, amazingly quick on her feet. "We're not the ones who disappear in the evening, doing God knows what. We don't shirk our load of work."

She walked over to the packages she'd been assembling and went on with her admonitions.

"If I were you, I wouldn't be making any accusations."

Pointing to the pile she'd been working on, she continued.

"Here. These are ready for you." Then she brushed roughly past him on her way out of the tent.

Harold could hardly believe that she had confronted Gunther in this fashion. Maybe she had gained some kind of inner strength from knowing she had Harold's support.

For his part, Gunther looked sheepish, but immediately tried to cover it up.

"What's gotten into her?" he asked without really expecting an answer. "So cranky. She must not be getting enough sleep."

Harold didn't dignify the false conclusion with a response. Ignoring his partner, he bent over and adjusted some straps on a box.

A little worried about the compromising position Gunther had found him in, he was grateful that Sarah had somehow managed to diffuse the situation. He figured that, at the moment, Gunther was probably too guilty and thinking that it would really be bad taste to bluster about other people's faults.

Gunther made good on his intent to leave quickly. Over dinner eaten on boxes on the ground, he announced that he had found someone who volunteered to start the minute the ice funneled out of the lake.

"He invited me to go aboard his boat if I would handle the sweep while he and his partner row in front."

He took a bite of stew and chewed thoughtfully as Harold and Sarah looked at each other in consternation, their forks suspended in the air. Then he continued as though his chosen topic was no more noteworthy than a discussion on the content of the ubiquitous nightly stew.

"So, you two can follow at any point you choose. You can do it right away, or you can take your sweet time. I, for one, will certainly not interfere with your plans."

Self-righteously taking a swallow of coffee, he twisted his mouth into a sneer.

"Who knows? Maybe you can get the illustrious Mr. Steele to nurse you along..."

It took her a minute, but Sarah finally found her voice.

"So...so you're planning on just going off on your own? We're splitting up? What about the outfits? How do you...?"

Gunther put his palm out to silence her.

"I've already taken care of that. I've put some of our stuff on the other boat. Besides, it's only temporary. When you catch up in Dawson, we'll be able to re-combine everything."

Without a word, Harold slowly arose from his seat. He tripped on a piece of rope and accidentally upset the dinner plates and cups as he grabbed the box for balance. So distracted, he didn't even stop to pick things up, but strode out of the tent, blood rushing in his ears.

First, he cursed the day he had met Gunther. Then, on second thought, he took it back because that meant he would've never known Sarah.

It was a frustrating paradox, and he was at a loss for a satisfactory way to deal with it.

Down on the banks of the lake, there was furious activity as thousands of would-be gold seekers turned into instant boat pilots and secured their belongings for the impending challenge. Far into the night, under the twilight skies of late spring, there was incessant shouting, swearing, and knocking of boxes against the sides of boats.

No one slept.

By morning the energy had reached a fevered pitch as the first boats made their way down the remaining miles of the lake to the beginning of the Yukon.

Still smarting from Gunther's decision and total disregard for his partners—which included a wife—Harold watched bitterly from the edge of the lake, as his supposed partner grabbed the sweep on his new associates' boat and began to steer away from the bank without so much as a backward glance.

They took advantage of a stiff breeze at their backs. The black transom with the red stripe receded in the distance, Gunther pulling the sweep slowly from left to right in expert fashion.

Harold could have sworn there was a smug expression on his face.

Standing next to Harold, Sarah watched as well, her mouth a thin bloodless line, her usually pleasant countenance dark with what Harold could only assume was barely suppressed anger, disappointment, and probably hopelessness.

As much as he tried not to, Harold couldn't help wishing his ex-partner ill. At some point, Gunther would have to pay for his selfish attitude. Perversely, Harold hoped he'd be there to witness that moment. It would be a small measure of revenge.

The pressure to make haste now off, Harold and Sarah plodded back to what was left of their campsite. Harold had collapsed his own tent and made a sail out of it that he planned to rig his boat to sail down the rest of the lake. He wasn't sure if, after that, it would be a help or a hindrance in the turbulent waters of the canyon and the rapids. He'd have to seek advice from someone who knew. Once they reached calmer parts of the Yukon, they would simply float with the current.

That evening, Harold was at very loose ends. Alone with Sarah, he was like a horse in an unfenced corral, wondering how far he could indulge his instincts, insecure without the usual boundaries. He chided himself that, with all the worries facing him, he could even be thinking in these terms. It was a very unsettling feeling.

Better follow her lead.

After a subdued dinner of leftovers and biscuits, they had some tea, and sat on their makeshift seats discussing their plans, noting the rapidly emptying campsites around them. The evening was bright, warm, and filled with a continual hum of activity.

The late evening sun illuminated Sarah's face, her eyes jewel-like, defined by her dark brows and lashes, and giving her cheeks a rosy glow. Harold felt a familiar pressure in his chest that he tried to suppress by surreptitiously taking deep breaths.

"I guess we don't stray much from our established intentions," he uttered finally, straining to keep the conversation going to come up with a feasible plan.

"We'll still go to Dawson and open our businesses. I don't doubt our ability to do that. It's just that we're going to have a really tough time with the first few miles after the lake."

Sarah nodded, a morose expression clouding her comely features.

"Well, I don't care what Gunther says. We could use some help...or at least advice. I'm not too proud to ask..."

Harold nodded in agreement.

"Me either," he said. "It's not being weak. On the contrary. It's being smart. I don't mind learning from someone else's experience."

He drained his cup and expressed new resolve.

"Tomorrow, first thing after breakfast, I'll go talk to one of the Mounties. They're always willing to help and they know what they're talking about."

Sarah murmured her assent as she got up to put away the dishes.

As they got ready to spend the night, Harold could not foresee that he would be speaking to the Mounties way before breakfast.

Putting the brakes on his emotions, he set up his bedroll next to Sarah's.

She looked very tired; taking care of the dinner dishes seemed to drain her of any remaining energy. He was afraid that she might become ill from the accumulation of contrary events of the past months.

It had never occurred to him before, but now realized that a real possibility existed that there might be a limit to the strength and resilience she had always demonstrated.

In view of what lay ahead, it seemed like getting a good night's sleep was of paramount importance. Harold tried to force himself to quit thinking of Sarah's proximity even though he lay but inches from her, their bedrolls touching.

It was tantamount to torture, but he steeled himself to fight the temptation to disentangle himself from his bed to slide into hers.

He could hear her soft even breaths.

After a great deal of tossing and turning, he eventually fell into a troubled sleep.

Only a few hours had passed when he was abruptly shaken awake.

"Get a move on, Harold. You need to come down to the lake. Your partner has suffered a setback, and he needs your help."

Harold squinted to see who was reaching into the tent to jiggle his leg. He caught a glimpse of a familiar uniform and realized that the Mounties had come to him before he'd even had a chance to seek them out.

"What do you mean? My partner isn't here anymore." Half asleep, Harold was confused.

"Oh yes, he is. And he's not in good shape. Will you come along with us?"

It wasn't really a request.

Blinking, Harold grimaced as he pulled himself out of his warm bedding, and, after seeing that Sarah's eyes were closed, he groggily followed the Northwest Police down to the bank.

What the hell had Gunther gotten himself into now?

So much for that good night's sleep he'd been counting on.

-15-

THE RAPIDS

He was wrapped head to foot in a blanket, sitting on an overturned boat. When Harold got close enough, he could see his prodigal partner shaking violently.

Harold looked at the Mounty for an explanation. Gunther didn't look like he could say anything.

Sticking a hand out from his blanket, Gunther gestured that the Mounty could tell Harold what had happened.

"No, Sir," said the Mounty shaking his head. "We need to see you to your camp immediately. You need a hot drink and some dry clothes. Let's get up the hill."

Harold wasn't sure if Gunther had insolently rolled his eyes at having to follow orders, but he did get up and follow.

When they got to the tent, Sarah was standing in the opening. If she was surprised to see the small procession heading her way, she gave no indication. Before anyone could say anything, she stoked the fire, poured some water in the kettle, and set it on the middle of the stove to heat.

The Mounty left, but not before he was certain that Gunther was drinking some hot coffee after having changed out of his damp clothes.

It took a while, but Gunther finally stopped shaking and was able to enlighten Sarah and Harold as to how he had spent the time since he had seen them last.

After making it easily to the end of the lake, Gunther and his new partners braced themselves as they glided on to the Yukon River at Miles Canyon.

Two of them were on either side of the riverboat while Gunther handled the sweep that was supposed to steer the boat.

Physically an able man, he learned quickly how to get the best performance out of this oversized tiller. It was clamped to the boat in a special slot in the transom at the stern. He could push left or right against the water from that fulcrum. As long as he kept the sweep in the water, and didn't lose his balance, he could hold the boat true. The other two, each manning an oar, tried to guide the boat and propel it in conjunction with the furiously rushing current.

Gunther's confidence built as they approached the canyon. So far, so good. He felt in command.

But when they reached the beginning of the canyon, it felt like a huge hand reached out and grabbed the boat, dragging it forward with invisible force. Runoff from the melting snows above, added to the water from many small streams, greatly increased the volume of water that gushed into the canyon, causing a huge swell down the center for the entire length of it.

"Stay in the middle!" shouted one of the rowers over his shoulder to Gunther. "We don't want to be pushed up against the damned wall of the canyon. Keep us centered."

Gunther didn't have time to respond. It was all he could do to steady himself and keep the sides of the boat away from the incredibly tall walls of rock brooding down on them, sometimes far enough away, and sometimes frighteningly close. The sweep felt like it had a life of its own. Hanging on to it with all his strength, he could've sworn he had a bull by the horns.

Gone was the confidence of a few moments ago, especially as the canyon seemed to go on forever. Gunther was beginning to doubt he could last all the way.

"I've never been so afraid," he admitted to Harold and Sarah, as he hugged his blanket around him and held his warm cup against his cheek. "I've never been so close to being out of control." He made a face. "It was almost making me sick. I guess my stomach was so tight..."

"So...did you make it to the end of the canyon?" Sarah rubbed his back to get the circulation going. She had to duck around his wet clothes that were hanging above the stove to dry.

"Well, yeah, but that was nothing compared to what came next." He held out his cup for Sarah to refill.

She and Harold waited impatiently for him to swallow some more before continuing.

"I saw the wreckage of lots of boats...I have no idea how many men lost all their stuff...and their lives. The Mounties said there have been several drownings. They record the identification numbers of the boats when they come shooting out of the canyon so they know who hasn't made it through. They actually go back and try to rescue..."

He had a fit of sudden coughing. Sarah patted him hard on the back. He took a quick swallow of coffee to try to suppress the tickle in his throat. It worked, but his voice had become scratchy.

"Anyway...the canyon was almost easy compared to the rapids."

He shook his head in recollection.

"Even before we started down, we saw men in the water, hanging on to rocks as the Mounties threw them ropes. Their boats had smashed against the rocks; they lost everything."

He looked at each of them. "I should've taken that as a warning." Then he looked away as he finished his coffee, raising his cup in emphasis. "But, I wasn't in a position to change the plan. It wasn't even my boat, after all..."

"That's true," muttered Harold. "The time to speak up was long past..."

Whether or not Gunther took offense at that response was hard to determine. He was probably too self-involved to notice any subtleties.

"So, I'll never know if it was really an accident, or whether those two...those two damned schemers did it to me."

His eyes glittered with anger.

"Anyway, we had barely started into the first part of the rapids when the boat suddenly jerked sideways. It took me off balance and I unintentionally lifted the sweep out of its slot. The sudden weight of it as it waved around flipped me right out of the boat."

He shivered violently. "I thought I'd be paralyzed. That water is indescribably cold."

"Like the pass?" Sarah asked, frowning at the memories. "Remember how we were always freezing?"

"It seemed worse than anything we felt on the pass. At least with the snow and the wind, it doesn't get through your parka to the bone right away like being soaked does."

They were all quiet for a moment as Gunther gathered himself to continue. Outside the tent, the activity level was picking up as the morning unfolded. More well-intentioned fortune seekers naïvely made their way down the bank to play into the hands of Fate.

Ignorance is bliss. Harold could hear his grandmother again.

Gunther finished his drink and pulled the blanket closer around him.

"I think I need some food," he said suddenly, as if it was going to materialize in front of him by some kind of magic. "I haven't touched a bite since our last meal together."

He's acting like things are perfectly fine between us. He expects Sarah to jump to it as if nothing ever happened.

Before Harold could say anything, Sarah went over to the pot of leftover stew on the stove.

"There's not much left, Gunther," she said without any kind of rancor. "Give me a minute and I'll warm what there is."

Gunther grunted and kept up his narration.

"I guess I have to reconsider my earlier dismissal of the illustrious Mounties," he said with a bit of ruefulness. "If it hadn't been for them, I'd probably be washing out the other end of the Yukon..."

He shook his head.

"My hands were so cold I couldn't get a grip on the rocks. I was getting swept by everything until they managed to get a rope out to me somehow. I got tangled up in it more by accident than by design. There was a lucky bend in the river that made it possible for me to float up to the bank without too much effort."

Sarah was scraping the bottom of the pot to get every possible morsel for him. Gently placing a half-full bowl on the top of the box they were using as a table, she absentmindedly patted him on the back. He grabbed a spoon and took a sloppy mouthful. Bliss etched itself across his face in the form of closed eyes and a smile.

"Best stew so far," he said with a full mouth, as he raised his spoon in salute. "You're getting better at this stuff..." Then he crammed some more in.

Harold thought that if this was an attempt to compliment his wife, it was a sad one, indeed. And it wasn't about to serve to wipe out any hard feelings.

But, disconcerting as it was to Harold, Sarah looked almost happy.

"So, what happened after they roped you in?" asked Harold, trying for the hundredth time to put a lid on his anger.

"They must've given you a ride for you to have gotten back here so quickly."

"Yep. They just plunked me down on one of their horses—rode double—and brought me all the way back. Sure was easier than that boat ride—except for the lecture part..."

"Lecture?"

"Oh yeah. They couldn't rescue me without giving me a long lecture about safety malarkey and stuff...you know...the same drivel they're always going on about."

"Not exactly drivel, Gunther. Seems like you illustrated their point exactly."

Gunther just shrugged and scraped a last bite together.

"By the way," interjected Sarah, taking the empty bowl. "What about your new best friends? Did they try to save you or anything?

Gunther's face got darker, and he slammed down his coffee cup.

"Those damned-fool idiots did nothing...absolutely nothing to help me. In fact, it was almost as if they had planned it that way from the beginning. They needed someone to handle the sweep through the canyon, but obviously didn't want to share anything further. So, when I fell out of the boat, they just kept right on going."

He shook his head furiously.

"And if anyone ever asks, they'll just plead innocent, saying they couldn't help it. The current was too strong, and they couldn't do a thing about it."

"But couldn't that actually be what took place?" asked the ever-forgiving Sarah. "It's rather difficult to prove intent in this case."

"Well, who died and made you a lawyer?" quipped Gunther, obviously annoyed. "I'm telling you how it was. In case you forgot, I'm the one who was actually there..."

He huffed in irritation, and added, "Why do you always have to doubt me?"

"She's right, Gunther." Harold finally spoke up. "You'd have a very tough time proving anything. I think you'd better cut your losses and forget about it."

Gunther's expression became shifty, his tone superior.

"Oh. So, you're willing to forget about the parts of our outfit that were on their boat? You want to count those losses out?"

Sarah and Harold looked at each other.

"What parts?" Harold's voice had a dangerous edge. "What did you put on their boat?"

"Well, mostly my stuff," he began airily. "And I do believe some woodworking tools went on it...and maybe a sewing machine..."

"What?" Harold and Sarah were of one voice. "You put *our* stuff on that boat?"

"I had to make sure we'd meet up again," said Gunther as if he had done the most reasonable thing in the world.

"It was...well...my special insurance policy that we'd get together in Dawson, you might say. Besides, it was some of the stuff that was packed first and ready to go..."

Harold had finally reached the breaking point.

"God damn you, Gunther! Why didn't you just drown?"

He struck the box with a closed fist, making the cup and spoon on it jump.

"Now we have to catch up with those guys before they decide to sell everything. Son of a bitch! You maybe just ruined all our plans."

Harold was completely beside himself.

"I ought to have you arrested for theft... You're the most inconsiderate, selfish, low-down..."

He couldn't finish.

With a loud groan of frustration, he scrambled out of the tent and staggered away.

-16-

GIVING IN

It did no good for Harold to stay away from the tent.

Thanks to Gunther's selfish moves, Harold and Sarah were now under the gun to get going down the river to recoup their property. As difficult as it was undoubtedly going to be, it was time for Harold to swallow his very justified anger and try to make the best of a bad situation.

But, if Harold was going to have anything to say about anything, the way the little group had been operating was about to change. He was determined not to play second fiddle to Gunther anymore. From now on, decisions would be made without Gunther's input. If it meant they'd have to go on without him—so be it.

Harold was sick to death of having to tiptoe around Gunther's sensibilities and to restrain himself when Gunther's actions were reprehensible.

Having done something he rarely stooped to, Harold had gone to one of the saloons that was left still doing business. He had a few fingers of watered-down bourbon to try to take the edge off his anger. He wasn't really under any illusions that this would work, but the burning in his throat and belly gave him something else to dwell on for a few moments. He really couldn't understand how some men did this for hours on end. He tried some more. It didn't feel that good, especially on his empty stomach.

A couple of hours later, and a few sheets to the wind, Harold headed back up the hill to the tent. He had no idea what he was going to say as he blearily made his way through the area that was now peculiarly bare because of the mostly empty campsites. He was confused and stumbled around.

Suddenly, he felt a hand on his arm.

It was Sarah, and she was trying to get Harold to be quiet.

"Sh," she said quickly, putting a finger across his lips. "Gunther finally went to bed and he's asleep. I guess he finally got warm enough..."

Before she could continue, and without really thinking about it, Harold put his arm around her and drew her to him, planting a hard kiss on her open mouth.

His alcohol-muddled brain having a difficult time dealing with all the implications of his action, he just did what felt right. Kissing Sarah was the rightest thing he could think of.

He loved her. He wanted her. He had denied himself for so long. He was starved.

If he'd been sober, he'd have been surprised that she didn't shy away, and he would've wondered at her response. As it was, he just crushed her body to his and continued kissing her, delighting in the transporting joy it gave him, relishing the gratifying satisfaction.

I could die right now, and be happy about it...

Breathing hard, he finally relaxed his hold on her.

"Oh my God, Sarah," he said, reality descending upon him like a bolt of lightning. "What...what am I doing? Oh my God...can you forgive me?"

Still in his embrace, Sarah put her fingers across his lips again.

"There's nothing to forgive," she said, kissing him quickly to quiet him.

"It takes two to get here, and I'm willing. I love you, Harold. There's no denying it."

She nodded her head slowly. "We both know it was coming to this..."

"But...but..." Harold started, very confused by her assertion. "You...you..."

He wasn't getting anywhere, and Sarah looked amused.

They sat down on the last box destined for the boat. Sarah took both of Harold's hands in hers.

"If you're worried about Gunther...he has no leg to stand on."

Harold just looked more confused, and Sarah continued to explain.

"He has been lying about our relationship. We're not husband and wife."

Harold swallowed, cleared his throat, but was unable to say anything.

"If you think back," she continued, squeezing his hand. "I've never claimed as much. I've never called him my husband..."

She hesitated a moment.

"So, if I've sinned, it's by omission. I have let you believe his story because it was more expedient to do so. A woman without a husband is nothing but a wayward child to some people."

She shook her head gloomily for a second.

"On my own, I would've had absolutely no credibility."

They sat, holding hands, looking into each other's eyes and smiling blissfully.

A soft breeze blew Sarah's curls about her face.

Harold wasn't sure if he was on the same planet of a few moments ago. It just wasn't possible. If he'd had to come up with a positive scenario on his own, it wouldn't have held a candle to this new reality. Finally, he broke his stunned silence.

"Well, you certainly know how to surprise a fellow," he said, his voice shaking with emotion. "You just took a huge weight off my shoulders."

And my heart is lighter than air...

-17-

LOSSES REGAINED

After bailing out near-drowning victims one after the other, the Mounties—again under the direction of Superintendent Steele— decided to institute new rules for getting through the canyon and the rapids.

No more women and children. No more inexperienced sailors. No more overloaded or rickety boats.

Along the banks of the canyon and the rapids there was total devastation of humanity. At the head of the Canyon, men contemplated which action to take: brave the water or pick up and carry their ton of goods around it, through the woods. They had seen the results of a hundred and fifty boats not getting through and ending up as so many large splinters against the rocks. They had seen men drown as their outfits went under. They had seen partnerships break up over devastating losses.

Sam Steele was about to make things easy for them by taking away their choices.

They would have to obey the new rules or pay a fine of a hundred dollars per broken one.

Putting a deputy in charge of enforcement, Steele announced to the nervous mob that women and children would have to walk around the canyon and the rapids. So would the men who didn't have proper loads and boats All boats that were seaworthy would have to be piloted by men judged by the deputy to be competent in getting it through without mishap. And all along the way, the Mounties would be at various checkpoints to keep everyone honest and safe.

With these new rules in effect, Harold and Sarah could plan the last leg of their trip.

"You can come with us if you want," Harold admonished Gunther, when everything was packed in the boat. "But you'll do it our way, and when we get to Dawson, your first order of business will be to find your erstwhile boat partners and repossess our belongings."

Gunther had become a taciturn and glum-faced individual. He didn't take well to orders, but he was smart enough to realize that there was no recourse for an alternative at this point.

Harold had no illusions about Gunther's attitude. He knew that his partner had made up his mind to go along until something more attractive presented itself. It was a game of no confidence.

The plan was to hire a pilot to see the boat through to the other side of the canyon. Once there, for the fee of twenty-five dollars, they would load the boat on a tramway that one of the more enterprising souls had set up with horse-drawn cars to skirt the rapids. After that, they'd put the boat back in the water and float the rest of the five hundred miles to Dawson.

Harold knew that Sarah silently thanked God for the Mounties in general and the superintendent in particular. The latter's sensible approach to safety was very reassuring to both of them. It's not that they weren't prepared to do the hard work—it's that they were much more reasonable than most, more resourceful, and they were willing to recognize their limits.

Once past the most dangerous spots on the waterways, it was easy to float with the Yukon's powerful current under the powerful rays of the summer sun. One side of the river had a cut bank with roots and trees sticking out into the middle that could be the cause for disaster if the boaters were not aware. The other side was usually made of wide beaches with broad sandbars on which the boats might get hung up. So, oars served to keep the boat in the best part of the river.

Harold had made it Gunther's job to keep the boat where they wanted it. Gunther's sour countenance did not deter the other two from enjoying this part of the expedition. Compared to every stage in the past year, this was the easiest and least fraught with danger. Both were determined not to let Gunther dampen their enthusiasm as long as he did what was required of him.

The campsite at night had changed in configuration since Bennett. Quite often Gunther didn't even bother to stay in the tent; he made himself a bed on the boat and spent most of his time there. He'd show up for whatever the other two were making for their meal and then slink off to the river.

Harold was not impressed.

Let him sulk. He's lucky we're letting him be.

Then one evening, as they were finishing their meal, two very grubby looking natives and a mangy dog materialized out of the woods. It was difficult to tell their ages, but Harold figured they were more boys than men.

"You buy?" they asked, pointing to a blanket they were dragging that seemed to have heavy items wrapped up in it.

"Good price."

Willing to humor them, Harold signaled for them to open the blanket so they could see their wares. The boys laid the blanket open to reveal a conglomeration of items. Harold knew that many of them had come from other people's outfits—

probably the miners who had suffered some mishap and needed to trade for money to get home.

Sarah bent over and picked through a few items to take a better look at them. Many were cooking items and tools. Some were native-made mittens and boots. She pushed several items around on the blanket.

Harold was not that interested in buying anything, especially as the boat was already loaded to the maximum allowed. But when he heard her exclaim, and she walked towards him with something in her hand, he perked up.

"Harold. Do you recognize this? Isn't this one of yours? Aren't these your initials carved into it?"

She extended a wooden-handled chisel. Frowning, he took it from her to get a better look. Out of the corner of his eye, he saw Gunther wander off.

After a second or two, he looked up at the boys.

"Where did you get this?"

The boys looked at each other and then down at the ground. Then one of them ventured an answer.

"We trade." He shrugged. "White man from boat."

"Where?" asked Harold.

Another shrug.

"He here." The boy pointed at the ground.

"When?" Harold continued his interrogation.

"One day...before now."

Harold figured they meant the day before. He walked over to the blanket and started to go through the items. By the time he had examined everything on the blanket, he had a pile of tools set aside. Among them were small clamps, axes, more chisels, wrenches, a keyhole saw, a hand drill, a hammer, and even a plumb bob without its string. His initials were on every item.

"How much?" he asked, pulling out a little pouch he kept his coins in.

The boys, disbelieving this possible bonanza, were tongue-tied.

Ignoring the growls of the dog, Harold approached the boys with a handful of coins.

"You take this, and you come with us in the boat. We find the man you trade with."

The boys immediately looked fearful, and they waved their hands emphatically to say no.

"If you want money, you come," insisted Harold, a little surprised that they would refuse the coins.

Before he could go on, they turned around, scooped everything but the tools into their blanket, and disappeared back into the trees, the dog trailing, his tail between his legs.

Consternated, Harold shrugged at Sarah.

"Well, looks like I regained some of my property," he said, still surprised by the fortuitous turn of events.

"Twice stolen. I'm sure these are ill-gotten gains for the second time. Ironic that the original thieves got robbed themselves...and by boys."

He laughed bitterly. "Of course, this is only half of it. I mean to get the rest, including the toolbox, as well as your sewing machine." He looked around. "Where's our faithful companion?"

It was Sarah's turn to shrug.

"I think he's at his usual spot in the boat..."

"Well, that's where we're headed," he said, picking up as many tools as he could. "Let's pack up. I'll bet those previous cohorts of Gunther's are not that much farther ahead if they're stopping along the way to trade the evidence. We'll need Gunther as backup if we encounter them."

Sarah's face showed a little disappointment at the fact that their usual nighttime camping had been interrupted. Instead of sliding into her bedroll next to Harold's, having intimate conversation and falling asleep hearing his breathing, she'd be chasing elusive thieves.

"Don't you want to get your things back?" asked Harold as they made their way to the boat. "This might be our best chance to do that. Chasing after them once they get to Dawson could be a hopeless proposition."

In spite of the late hour, the sun was still high in the sky. The mosquitoes were out in vindictive droves. The only way to escape them was to push off in a hurry.

It was obvious from Gunther's face that he knew what was up. He had been all too aware of the unexpected reappearance of Harold's tools, and it didn't take a great leap of imagination to figure out that they were now hot on the trail of the rest. Harold's brief explanation of his plan was almost superfluous. Gunther's motives might have always been dubious, but he was plenty smart.

The Yukon was littered with men and boats. It was no small task to try to recognize Gunther's former associates. Harold did not hold out much hope, but he was determined to give it a good try. At least they knew what the boat looked like.

There were hundreds of campsites along the banks of the Yukon, as men lay about either relaxing or getting over their harrowing experiences, not the least of which were break-ups of their partnerships.

Partners who could not abide each other after hundreds of miles of hardship, argued insanely about how to equitably divide their belongings. Some stupidly sawed flour sacs in half, split up boats to make two smaller ones, or simply just sawed the boat in half. They argued over every item in their outfits.

Two such miscreants were at a complete loss on how to divide a frying pan, pulling it from each other in a hopeless tug-of-war. The Mounty responsible for this section of the river settled the argument by seizing the pan and throwing into the Yukon. Amazingly, the two men seemed perfectly satisfied with this on-the-spot ruling.

Harold was just about ready to give up for what was left of the night, when they rounded a small bend and saw a narrow beach, obscured by hanging brush. Partially hidden from the main part of the river, a boat was beached, its black transom with a red stripe barely visible. Up the bank, smoke spiraled from a campfire.

They had found their quarry.

As there were other boats milling around Harold's, he knew there would be no alarm if they aimed to pull up at this little beach. Unless they were recognized.

"Get out the mosquito hats," ordered Harold. "We need a little lead time. We can buy that if we wear them. Gunther: get your Colt ready."

Harold was right. The lone figure lying by his campfire hardly stirred as they approached.

"I got nothing to share," he admonished, barely looking up. "Move on if you want to profit."

"Really?" said Harold, sarcasm dripping. "Because that's not what we heard." He looked around. "Where's your partner?"

"Tell me and we'll both know. He took off after some Indians to try to get some stuff. Been gone since supper."

"Stuff?" asked Harold.

The man straightened up and looked more carefully at the three figures in front of him. He was trying to make out their features through the mosquito netting.

"Yeah. Some of our outfit. Some men stole it."

"Really?" repeated Harold. "Don't you mean boys?"

"And don't you mean, someone else's stuff?" joined in Gunther.

He ripped his mosquito hat off. "Remember me?"

Squinting in the late sunlight, the man got up to get a better idea of the people who were confronting him. He walked around the campfire. Then his face changed.

"You? How did you...?"

Gunther had miraculously regained some of his previous aggressiveness. Towering over him, he grabbed the man's shirtfront and shook him, almost suspending him so that only his toes touched the ground.

"No thanks to you, I'm fine. And I'm here to pick up my stuff. Hand it over."

Just about then, they heard someone coming through the brush. Gunther whipped out his Colt and cocked it. He pointed it at the newcomer. Harold gently pulled Sarah behind him to make sure she was out of the line of fire.

The other partner, toting a large, heavy sac, looked fearfully at the group around the campfire, immediately recognizing Gunther. He frowned at his partner.

"What the hell, Jeb? What's going on?" He put down his load and hurriedly started searching his pockets.

"Hold it right there," came Gunther's warning. "You might want to put your hands in the air instead." The muzzle of the Colt put an exclamation mark on his words.

Harold decided it was time to take over the conversation before things deteriorated and Gunther went off half-cocked.

"All you have to do is turn over the stuff Gunther here added to your outfits at Bennett," he stated, his hands facing out in a gesture intended to calm things. "Once that happens, we leave you up to your own devices. No harm done."

The two men looked at each other in obvious embarrassment.

"Well, we...uh...got robbed yesterday. Upriver. By two natives. with a huge really mean dog. They threatened us if we didn't hand over our outfits."

"Threatened you with what?" asked Harold, catching Sarah's eye. "Were they armed?"

"I'm sure they had all kinds of knives on them. You know how the Indians always do. I'm pretty sure they each had a pistol, too."

His partner nodded vigorously.

"Yeah. We had no choice. We had to turn the stuff over."

If the situation hadn't been so tense, Harold would've laughed in their faces.

"Are you sure about all that? Are you sure you weren't sleeping, and woke up to find your stuff gone?"

Their silence spoke for them.

Pistol still pointed at one of the men, Gunther walked over to the sac.

"Well, looky here," he exclaimed, kicking at some of the loot. "I think I see some more of your stuff, Harold. That is, unless these two have HB as their initials. And....there's parts to a sewing machine here too." He looked up at the two men. "Planning on opening a seamstress shop in Dawson, are you? Or do you like to sew your own clothes?"

Not appreciating the humor, the men just stared at the ground. They seemed to know it was useless to object.

After making the two sit down on their hands, Gunther kept them at gunpoint while Sarah and Harold loaded their boat with their repossessed goods.

When everything had been repacked, they left the campfire, Gunther walking backwards with the Colt still pointed. Harold hoped he didn't trip and fire by accident.

As they pushed off to go find a new campsite, one of the men ran to the edge of the water and yelled at them.

"We'll catch up to you in Dawson. We'll see how this ends..."

He was shaking his fist as the boat slid farther downstream.

"He's really brave when the Colt's out of sight," commented Sarah as she found a place to sit at the back of the boat. "I thought he was going to cry when we took our stuff back."

"Somehow, I don't see those two making it in the City of Gold," commented Harold. "The Mounties are going to learn of their reputation. They might as well turn around and go home right now to avoid further pain and heartbreak."

As to Gunther—he stared straight ahead, his mouth set in a grim line.

-18-

CITY OF GOLD

Hugging the right bank of the Yukon so as not to miss the city, Harold, Sarah, and Gunther were beginning to see signs that they were approaching their goal.

More ruined boats lined the banks of the river—some simply cut in half by disenchanted or half-crazed fortune seeker. More reasonable souls tried dividing the goods in efficient ways. Passing "Split-Up City and an island of the same name, the three soon saw the tangled-up channels and islands that marked the confusing area just before the Klondike River's entry into the Yukon.

Gunther decided to appropriate one of the more complete boats that lay abandoned along the way. He had Harold drop him off on a nearby bank so that he could get to it.

Having reached it, he raised an oar to Harold and Sarah to show that he'd be all right.

"I'll catch up with you in Dawson," he shouted. "Be looking out for me." With that, he started to pull the boat out into the current.

Harold had a fleeting thought that he might never see Gunther again.

Then they saw it.

Around the last bend—a rocky bluff—they saw the roaring Klondike River as it emptied itself into the Yukon. Ahead rose a large mountain, and finally, on the far side of the violent meeting of the two rivers, sprawled the new city.

Dawson.

"Oh, Harold," breathed Sarah as she grabbed his arm. "It reminds me of Bennett, only much, much bigger."

As they forced their way across the confluence of the rivers, they could see more detail, and it was mind-boggling.

Hundreds of miles from any established civilization men had created their own brand new one in a very short span of time. Among the hills and trees, and rocky outcroppings, buildings of every description and stage of development showed whitely in the morning mist. They could make out storefronts, cabins, caches for storage, hotels in many stages of construction, markets, saloons, mills, and tents, tents, and more tents.

Harold stood holding an oar in one hand, his other wrapped around Sarah. They were drifting slowly past the thousands of boats already tethered to the beach. He drew her head to him and kissed her temple.

"We'll get it done here," he whispered. "This is our goldmine. If it lasts one year or more, we'll succeed. At the end—because these boom towns always end—we'll go back south with our fortune and set up a small business near Skagway."

He looked into her upturned face. "I want to grow old watching you show our children the finer points of stocking shelves."

Sarah was smiling silently.

"Harold. Do you suppose there's someone here who can marry us? I think I see a church in that little hollow over there."

Harold dropped the oar and gave her a full-fledged kissing embrace. Against the rising sun, Harold, strong and tall, hugged his cherished Sarah, until they formed a single silhouette.

PART TWO

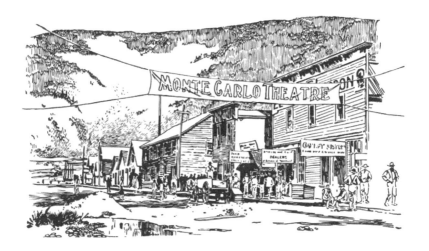

DAWSON CITY, CANADA
1899

FREEZE-UP

DAWSON CITY, CANADA
SUMMER 1899

-1-

COFFEE AND COOKIES

Sarah stood in her small kitchen, hands on her hips in quiet resignation.

The sun's morning rays streamed through the small cabin windows, lighting up columns of floating dust motes irreverently dancing and bouncing off each other in defiance of her best house-cleaning efforts.

It was a lost cause.

Sarah had resigned herself to living in this bustling town of over 40,000 souls. Dawson was by all accounts a full-fledged town with all the good and the bad the definition denoted, despite its dirt roads and paths that, depending on what the skies unleashed, turned from viscous clinging brownish sludge to dried-out grit. It adhered to everything and made keeping a dust-free environment a fantasy.

Every shoe, boot or hem carried with it a little testimonial of where its owner had been. And when it dried, it was just a floating enemy that everyone tried to get used to living with.

Sarah would not have been surprised if her molars had been worn down by unexpected resistance when, in spite of her unflagging guard against it, grit somehow made its way into her best culinary efforts.

"Chew at your own risk" she'd admonish Harold. "I tried dusting today…" Even making sure the cooking-pot lids were securely closed couldn't always guarantee a grit-free stew.

A knock on the cabin door brought her out of her self-pity.

It was so timid she had to convince herself that she'd heard it. The intricate custom-made door-window Harold had fashioned out of the bottoms of wine and whiskey bottles did not reveal a bodily form outside. Either the person who knocked was standing away from the door, or was too short to reach the window.

"Who is it?

"Nettie. It's Nettie V."

Antoinette Beaulieux Vonfurstenberg.

Sarah had to smile.

It was such an imposingly long name for such a diminutive person. No wonder she couldn't see the outline of a head through the glass.

She quickly stepped to the door, undid her husband's elaborate lock, and then the latch.

Out in the blazing sunshine stood a small form, her hair a shining halo, shimmering in the light morning breeze that carried with it the fragrance of summer wildflowers.

"Oh. Please come in Nettie. I'm so delighted you've come to visit."

Sarah touched Nettie's elbow to guide her in. Her guest reached down to remove her shoes. It would've been an exercise in futility to simply wipe them on the mat.

"Let's sit by the window," said Sarah pointing to her kitchen table. "After this winter, it feels so good to soak in all that sunshine. Let me warm up the coffee."

"Oh…" whispered Nettie, her eyes shining in anticipation as she approached the table in her stockings. "*Du café?* Sarah, you have true coffee? *Vraiment?*"

Sarah smiled as she got two cups from a cabinet. "*Mais oui, ma chère. Du vrai café!*"

Sarah was glad that the French she had learned as a child from a neighbor, and further studies in school still stood her in good stead. Nettie's English was improving, but she'd get confused, and slide back into her native French when she became emotional. And all too frequently, many commonly used idiomatic English expressions often served to keep her completely in the linguistic dark.

After pouring hot coffee from the pot that made its permanent home on the cook stove that also served to heat the cabin, Sarah reached for a special tin high up on a shelf. She brought it over, pried off the lid, and revealed a few tea biscuits she had managed to keep out of Harold's clutches.

Nettie's eyes expressed her appreciation as she reached into the tin, selected a biscuit, and took a tiny experimental bite.

"Mmm. *Si bon! C'est si bon!*" She took a sip of coffee to wash the crumbs down, and just looked reverently at the remaining piece of biscuit as if she was reluctant to harm it.

Sarah laughed.

"Oh, Nettie. Don't be so shy. Eat up! I can get more."

Puzzled, Nettie's smooth forehead creased into a frown. She looked up from the biscuit.

"Eat...up? What is that? I don't know you eat up or...or down?"

"Oh...I'm sorry," Sarah chuckled. "It's just an expression. Just...just..." She shook her head in frustration. "*Mange bien.* Dig in.*"

At the last two words, the frown returned.

Sarah sighed and just shook her head again. This translation stuff could bog you down. To avoid more misunderstanding, she made up her mind to be more literal when she talked to her young friend.

There was a comfortable enveloping silence as the two women savored their treats, basking in the sun's soothing rays that streamed through the window. Installing honest-to-God real windowpanes had been a worthwhile investment.

Finally, Sarah gently interrupted the moment.

"You know, Nettie, I remember some of the things you told me about how you made it here...arrived here in Dawson last year, but I never really asked you about your life before. You speak French, so are you from France...or maybe Belgium like many of the...uh... working women in town?"

Sarah was obliquely referring to the section of female society that catered to the preponderance of men in the Dawson population.

Nettie took a sip of coffee and shook her head. She put down what was left of her second biscuit and leveled her blue-eyed gaze at Sarah.

"I was born in *Luxembourg*," she said shrugging, pronouncing it the French way. "Not really any of those, but very close. *Tu sais*...you know...squeezed by Germany and France...and Belgium. But my German cousins and my uncle bring me here." She pointed at the ground to illustrate her point.

"But…what about your parents? Did they think it was all right for you to take off? I mean, to go away from them?"

Nettie took another few sips of her coffee. She shook her head.

"My father… he die from accident of mining," she said. "*Le charbon*…you say…coal. And my mother die because a bad sickness of the throat. The brother of my father took me when I was little. He help me. I always live with him and my cousins. He is priest now."

"Oh," said Sarah a bit surprised. "Does he live here too?"

"*Non, non*," replied Nettie, shaking her head. "He sent me to Dawson. He…my uncle…is a minister of church in St. Michael's at end of the Yukon River…so far away. Only my cousins are with me." She shrugged. "They are looking for gold…like all the men."

Sarah nodded in understanding and got up to get more coffee. She emptied what was left into Nettie's cup and was rewarded with a shy smile.

"So, you came here the long way," murmured Sarah more to herself than making a point, as she put the coffeepot back.

She figured that she and Harold had come the shorter, more brutal way. She turned around to face her guest.

"You sailed from Europe, crossed America, sailed another ocean all the way up to the mouth of the Yukon and then went all the way up the river to get here." She shook her head in awe. "That must've taken months, years…"

Nettie smiled ruefully and nodded.

"I have two birthdays during that *long voyage*," she said. "Now I am grown up, but I start like a child…"

143

Sarah knew that Nettie had probably experienced severe "growing up" lessons on the way to reaching her majority.

She had heard of the harrowing situations that the last long leg of her trip had imposed on those who had undertaken the mission to reach Klondike gold by crossing the huge Territory of Alaska: an endless span of treacherous, dangerous and often deadly geography.

Sometimes the dangers were natural—wildlife or accidents—but more often they were instigated by a diverse hoard of men of varying unnatural goals and values. She didn't want to interrogate Nettie, and risk making her relive any bad experiences. Nevertheless, she was extremely curious, and couldn't resist a small question.

"Where did your trip north on the boat begin? In Seattle?"

Sarah knew that the busy port of Seattle accounted for the lion's share of all manner of sea-worthy and not so sea-worthy vessels boarded by passengers eager to begin their quest for Far North riches. She and Harold had been part of that mob. Seattle made the most sense.

Nettie put down her cup, shaking her head.

"No. We start in San Francisco." She eyed the last biscuit in the tin.

"Help yourself, *Chérie.* I'll get more to keep Harold happy." Sarah pushed the tin toward her guest.

"*Vas-y,*" she encouraged. "Go ahead."

Nettie didn't have to be asked again. It was when she reached slowly into the tin, that Sarah noticed her young friend's hands.

"Oh you poor thing!" she cried out as she gently grasped Nettie's hands to have a closer look. "What in the world have you been doing?"

Nettie colored and shrugged. She bit her lips before answering in a small voice.

"Madame Renée gives me work…sometimes I have much laundry and it must hang outside. I guess…I do not dry my hands very well. Many times, they stay wet when I clean the floors… I cannot always care properly…"

"I should say so!" interrupted Sarah heatedly. She looked closer at the tips of Nettie's fingers. "Look…you have small cuts around your nails and your skin is so terribly chapped."

She bit both lips to form a thin line and shook her head.

"You cannot go on like that. If you don't stop, those cuts will never heal, and may become infected."

She swiftly arose from her chair. "I'm going to get some salve that Harold uses when his hands get chapped from his carpentry work."

She disappeared behind a pile of boxes that served as a temporary division between the living area and the bedroom. Nettie could hear her searching for something. She sat, her shoulders slumped, obviously embarrassed.

"Here it is," said Sarah reappearing, brandishing a container. "Give me those hands."

Nettie submitted without a sound.

"My father was a doctor," said Sarah, as she carefully massaged the salve into Nettie's fingers. "I helped him care for his patients, and I have many of his recipes for various ointments. I use them on Harold all the time."

She rolled her eyes and shook her head. "He's always cutting or bruising himself when he works."

She continued her treatment, concentrating on the tips of her patient's fingers until most of the ointment had been absorbed into the red, chapped skin.

"Do you have gloves? And," she added, as if suddenly realizing something. "Do you have a good coat? That little sweater is not exactly going to keep you warm if the weather turns."

Nettie resorted to her signature shrug.

"I do have some, what do you call them…not gloves…no fingers…"

"Oh, you mean mittens." She nodded. "Well, from now on, you're going to have to wear them all the time until you heal. Even inside."

"But, Sarah. I must work. Madame Renée will…will…"

Nettie seemed genuinely frightened, and at a loss to continue. She sniffed and wiped her nose with her sleeve, as Sarah patted her arm in reassurance.

"I'll talk to Madame Renée," Sarah said gruffly. "She will realize that you will be no use to her if you can't heal those hands. I'll make her understand, don't you worry."

Nettie looked close to tears but kept silent. The treatment over, she hid her hands in her lap.

Sarah put her arm around her friend and patted her shoulder. "I'm going to put some of this ointment in a little tin for you to take with you. Rub it in at least two times every day, just like I did. And," she warned, "keep those mittens on all the time. You must avoid… uh…not do that kind of work for a while."

Opening a squeaky cabinet drawer, she rummaged around for a few seconds.

"There we are," she said, satisfied, holding up a small container and pushing the drawer closed with her hip.

"Perfect for what we need.

It didn't take long for Sarah to scoop some of the ointment into the little tin. She snapped both containers shut, pocketed the small one, and grabbed a shawl from hooks by the door. Then she slipped her feet into one of the many pairs of boots lined up neatly along the wall.

It took a little coaxing, but Nettie finally rose from her chair, and reluctantly put her boots back on to follow Sarah.

Closing and locking the heavy door to the cabin behind them, they set off in the bright sunshine to see Madame Renée.

-2-

CHANDELIERS AND CHUTNEY

The two women picked their way carefully along the rocky hillside path that led to the center of town—a couple of main streets with storefronts, banks, and many saloons of varying stature, importance, and attractiveness. Some were replacements for the buildings that had been destroyed in one of the fires that broke out periodically, and some were glorified tents.

The weather had been dry and hot for a few days—indeed the temperature had been unseasonably high, sometimes soaring to over a hundred degrees. Sarah had misjudged when, out of habit, she had grabbed her shawl.

Accordingly, as they wended their way by different cabins and buildings on their trip downhill, they did not have to deal with the ever-present cascade of mud and slime that the path usually consisted of. Still, they took great care to avoid the hardened ruts, rocks and exposed roots that could cause a turned ankle in a single brief moment of inattention.

Nettie followed at a distance, obviously less than eager to get to their destination.

Upon reaching Front Street, Sarah turned around and waited for her friend to catch up. Then she entwined their arms, and smiled encouragingly as they went forward on the boardwalk, their long skirts swishing in time with their strides.

As they reached the busier sections, the street changed consistency and became the customary mire caused by horses and wagons and heavy foot traffic. In places where there was no boardwalk, they picked their feet up more carefully to avoid the worst of the sludge and were obliged to raise the hems of their skirts.

"Cheer up, *ma chérie*," Sarah reassured her hesitant friend, pulling her close. "This is not going to hurt. In fact, it may mean an easier time for you soon. "

Nettie tried a smile, but it wasn't a success. She pulled back on Sarah.

"But…she will be mad…she hates for her workers to…how do you say it…not do their responsibilities…She will kick me away…"

"Oh, I don't think so." Sarah smiled mischievously. "I have a little ammunition where Madame Renée is concerned. She'll see the wisdom in what I propose."

Nettie didn't even try to ask for an explanation. As Sarah prodded her along, she stumbled a bit in hesitation, looking confused and worried.

They passed dozens of aimless people: great numbers of pale-faced men and a few women, none of whom seemed to have a very busy agenda for the day. There were also many dogs roaming the street, some in packs, snuffling at anything that might resemble a morsel of food. Honky-tonk music emanated from the saloons—the *Dominion*, the *Opera House*, the *Pavilion*, the *Aurora*, the *Mascot*, and even the *Bank Saloon*—as men burst in and out of the doors of the gambling houses and dance halls, a great many tottering on unsteady legs. Sarah could smell ale and stale perfume as they staggered by.

And there were also occasional wafts of sewage and vomit.

In the year she had lived in this town, she had never ventured into these establishments, and, despite her natural curiosity, hoped never to have to. While she only partly believed the diatribes churned out by the local preachers, who insisted that they were pits of debauchery and sinful acts, to her it was more because what happened in their confines was most depressing.

So much money—mostly in gold form—was wasted; so many opportunities were missed, and so many spirits were crushed. Relationships were built and torn apart, commonly on the very same night. At their best, the saloons were places for people to spend some time being entertained—innocently or otherwise—at their worst, they were places of thievery, conflict, and occasional accidental killings. Entering, you were never sure of how your fortune might change, but one thing you could be sure of was that you never left the place in the same shape you had entered it.

Throughout the town, great banners streamed everywhere advertising "Gold! Gold! Gold!" in every form, in every location. The intention was to draw in buyers for outfits, day-to-day items, professional services of doctors, lawyers, dentists and a untold numbers of merchants; some in bona fide structures, some under flapping tents.

If a person had a poke full of the magical dust, one could avail himself of anything from cigars to diamond jewelry, cooking pots, French *pâté* and champagne, all manner of booze and gourmet items, mining equipment, and souvenirs of all descriptions.

The two women stepped down from the boardwalk and farther out into the center of the rut-riddled street to avoid the traffic in and out of saloon doors. In doing so—just in time—they were able to avoid being crushed by the sudden explosion of two wrestling bodies tumbling out of the *Monte Carlo*, one of the most notorious saloons in all of Dawson.

With a little cry from each of them, they shied away, pulling up their voluminous skirts as they went. The wrestling bodies were soon joined by spectators spilling out into the street from the saloon and nearby establishments, eager for more entertainment.

Not being able to bypass the gaggle of rowdy onlookers to continue down the street, Sarah and Nettie were forced to remain in place, and watch the debacle unfolding before them.

After a few moments of writhing in the muck, the two adversaries became unrecognizable—the Dawson mud performed its routine act of obscuring all features and distinguishing aspects of the two men. People stepped back in order to avoid the slogging and splattering, but they kept up their shouting and uproarious encouragement from a safer distance.

Then, amid the jeering and raucous cries of the onlookers, there was a sudden piercing whistle. The crowd immediately quieted as suddenly as it had begun its racket, and, as if by unseen signal, began to part at one end like the Red Sea for Moses.

"It's Captain Steele!" someone whispered loudly, in a reverent tone. "Make way! Make way!"

Sarah felt a wave of relief wash over her. She was immensely gratified to see that the source of the crowd's motion was a purposely striding Superintendent Sam Steele of the Northwest Mounted Police; the man who she felt was singlehandedly responsible for keeping the peace among the American and foreign rabble of this Canadian city.

So much admiration had he and his stouthearted men garnered from the swelling population, that there was no one in town who dared show him the smallest disrespect. He had saved countless lives, and ensured that many men be spared from their own impulsive, stupid, and often deadly acts.

There was no one foolhardy enough to dismiss his authority or ignore his wisdom. If they did, Steele had a place for them: the two-mile-long public woodpile on the outskirts of town.

"Thank God," whispered Sarah to Nettie. "Now we can proceed. Like he always does, Captain Steele will take things well in hand."

Grabbing Nettie's arm and navigating around the milling bodies that still seemed to expect some form of confrontation to liven things up, Sarah forcefully headed down the street. They dodged dogs and men in equal proportion, until they reached the clapboard front of a large establishment.

"*C'est ici*...it is here," said Nettie hesitantly, pointing reverently to a double door that sported curtained windows.

"This is the hotel of Madame Renée."

Then she pointed around the corner to a small alley between buildings.

"I think we must go to the back..."

"No," said Sarah resolutely. "There is no reason that we cannot go in the front door. We are not delivery people." She firmly grasped Nettie's hand and opened the front door.

Coming in from the sunshine, it took a minute for their eyes to grow accustomed to the relative gloom of the main floor of Madame Renée's place of business.

They were in a small entrance lobby with antique chairs and occasional tables. A few renaissance style paintings and sconces adorned the tapestried walls. A sculptured wooden registration desk graced one side of a wide staircase.

A few clients ambled to and fro between the restaurant and the entrance. It was too early for lunch, so the restaurant was mostly empty except for a couple that must've enjoyed a late breakfast, possibly recovering from a night of revelry. The young woman leaning against the shoulder of the mustachioed, vest-wearing, diamond-chain bedecked older gentleman, looked pale and exhausted. Her eyes were closed. Sarah had the distinct feeling that she had caroused a bit too much for her health.

The menu posted by the entrance advertised a list of food items that would've made restaurateurs in the cities of the lower states beam with pride: oysters, lobster, chutney, mushrooms, beef, ham, fruits, cakes, jams and jellies, select cheeses and good coffee. Sarah couldn't help contrasting that with her ubiquitous home menu of mostly beans, hotcakes, bacon, and stew.

The floor of the hotel was covered by imported carpeting, the woodwork was trimmed in gold, the windows boasted fine quality glass, and the furniture and linens were of first quality. The heated rooms were lit with recently installed electric lights.

But the most remarkable furnishing amid the collection, and what stole the show, was the cut-glass chandelier hanging in the dining room, presiding over the entire assemblage.

As Sarah stared at this riveting object, she almost had to pinch herself to make sure she wasn't imagining things.

These were amenities that defied reality. She hadn't seen bone china since having left her parents' house over three years ago. She had no idea that these luxuries could exist in this rough, mud-infested frontier town, and barely a mile from her modest little cabin.

What enterprising person must've seen to the importation of these amazing acquisitions? An enterprising person, she felt sure, who was certainly motivated by driving desire, and who assuaged his or her greed by finding gold in different ways.

Nettie seemed indecisive as to where to go to find Madame Renée. She circled the lobby and stood indecisively by the stairs while Sarah watched attentively, disconcertedly noting her friend's obvious nervousness.

Finally, their waiting was over.

Wearing a radiant white blouse accessorized with a stunning brooch at the high collar, and a dark silk gathered skirt, a tall, distinguished woman descended the staircase, removing her hat as she navigated the stairs. She caught sight of Nettie.

"*Ah, Antoinette. Enfin, te voilà. Oú étais-tu?*"

Frowning, she waved her hatpin like a small sword, smoothing her elaborate hair-do at the same time.

"*Il y a un tas de lessive…*" Then she noticed Sarah moving toward her and started.

"Oh. I am sorry," she exclaimed, embarrassed. "I did not know *Antoinette* had company."

154

She stabbed her hat, inserting the long pin, and hung it on a decorative coat rack by the lobby desk.

"I was just wondering where she had been…"

"Well, I'm sorry too, as it turns out," answered Sarah, taking Nettie by the arm. "She has been with me. I'm afraid that *Antoinette*"—she pronounced it the French way—*"* will not be doing any of your aforementioned pile of washing for a spell."

Madame Renée stood stiffly, consternated. She was not used to being corrected.

"And…you would be…?" she asked, her eyes narrowing, her French accent thick.

"My apologies. I should have introduced myself."

Sarah smiled politely.

"I'm Sarah Beasley, the wife of the carpenter you hired to make your custom bar and stools."

She looked down at Nettie and hugged her briefly.

"And I'm a good friend of Nettie, here."

Madame Renée stood stock still, her eyebrows raised haughtily.

"*Enchantée*, I'm sure," she said, her inflection indicating quite the contrary.

She nodded, continuing.

"Yes, I do, indeed, remember your husband: *un très bel homme, je dois dire…*" she added as a matter of fact, giving her judgment on Harold's good looks. It was a foregone conclusion that she was quite experienced in judging men's looks, after all.

"He promised me good and…*euh*… timely work."

She pursed her lips and looked expectantly at Sarah in anticipation of a response. When Sarah didn't answer, she continued.

"And...he's quite expensive, I must tell you. *Mon Dieu!*"

She rolled her eyes and shrugged.

"So...I have great expectations..."

"Oh, you can be quite sure that the work will be excellent," reassured Sarah, secretly wondering how this order would be filled now that Harold was off somewhere else.

"He's known for it. You will have the most elaborate and finely made bar in the city."

She raised an eyebrow to emphasize her point.

"If all goes as expected, you will be well satisfied." She wondered if the woman got her hint that something was expected of her, too.

Madame Renée had flounced by them with no response and posted herself behind the counter as if using it as a barrier to keep riff-raff away. She pulled some papers out from behind it, and distractedly perused them. The other two looked at each other, not knowing what to expect.

"So," continued the older woman, still eyeing the papers as if they were more important than whatever the business was that Sarah had to discuss.

"You made a statement regarding Antoinette's work. May we know the reason?" She looked up sharply, a quizzical yet challenging look on her face.

Sarah took a deep breath, trying to figure out the best way to explain the situation.

She didn't want to alienate this woman who held Nettie's welfare in her well-manicured hands. Nor did she want the woman to shrug off what she had to say as of no consequence, as soon as her back was turned.

This was indeed a tightrope act that required some diplomatic skill if you expected to remain on top.

-3-

HIGHS AND LOWS

Harold wondered if he had everything he needed.

This was his first foray into the gold mining experience, and he wanted to make sure everything was all it could be. It was difficult to know what you'd need when you had no idea of what was involved.

He carefully took stock of the packs spread out before him that he had piled up in front of his cabin door, in anticipation of his impending trek through the wilderness. He thought back over the chance conversation he'd had that had precipitated a whole new set of events.

*　　*　　*

While buying lumber for his brand-new carpentry business at one of the twelve busy sawmills in town, he'd had a life-changing conversation.

One of the other customers was buying a whole outfit to manage his claim out in the Eldorado area outside of Dawson where many claims had been staked. As Harold struck up a conversation, he found that the young man he was talking to was working alone, with no experience to guide him. It was obvious that he was wholly under that spell of the undeniable, obsessive driving force that made every cautionary consideration recede into the background.

It was no matter if you had no money.

No matter if you had no experience.

No matter either, if you didn't know much about mining.

There were plenty of people to learn from, whether they were willing teachers or not. Everything would be of little importance when the efforts and risks paid off, and you had a fat poke in your pocket.

"Oh, I know it seems foolhardy," he shrugged as he waited for his materials to pile up. "But I'm by no means the only one. It's many a fellow who's trying for the big pay-off by himself. I'll have plenty of company in the same boat."

Harold hardly gave a thought to what he was about to say. His curiosity had the better of him; he was about to make a move without consulting his practically brand new wife.

"What about if I go out there with you and set up your outfit?" He blurted out the words before realizing the impact of what he was saying. "I am an experienced builder. You'll need a cabin."

Astonished, the young man's words failed him. Looking like an oversized fish, he opened and shut his mouth a few times. Then he grinned widely.

"You're just pulling my leg," he smiled. "Making fun of me, are you?"

Harold smiled back and shook his head.

"No. I'm surely not joking. I would be happy for the experience."

Then the enormity of what he was proposing hit him.

"However, I will have to consult my wife," he added hurriedly. "She might have something to say…"

The young man's mouth took on a sarcastic twist. He rolled his eyes as if to say that he had known the offer was bogus all along.

It took a bit more to convince his new friend and potential future associate to put off his trip to the mining area while Harold got his belongings together. They would meet the next day to plan their trip.

Sarah had not been happy.

"But you don't know the first thing about mining," she complained as they gathered the makings of supper.

"How in the world are you going to make any progress? And you say that young fellow you plan to help doesn't know anything either?"

She scowled and shrugged.

"What about your carpentry work? Are you just going to let everything we've been working towards just drop? All our customers will go to someone else…" Her mind went toward Nettie, and how a delay of the bar being built for Madame Renée would affect the young woman's workload and treatment.

Harold walked over to his wife and put his arm around her, ducking the paring knife she had been peeling potatoes with, and was now waving around to emphasize her points.

"It's not going to be that bad," he said, trying to calm her down. "I won't be gone that long and there's always the chance that I might actually make good on the claim, or even just earn some money as a digger. The gravel has already been pulled up to the surface, so all we have to do is the cleanup; the easy part."

He grinned hopefully.

"We might actually scoop up a lot of gold up there…"

Sarah gave him a baleful glare. She shrugged off his arms and flounced off to the other side of the room. Turning around, she put her hands to her hips and raised her voice.

"Have you seen how everything turns out for many of the fellows who have staked everything on the hope that they'll make good? Right now, they are desperate for people to buy what's left of their outfits so they can pay for a trip home. In fact, they have less than nothing, because they usually owe."

She scowled again.

"I, for one, do not want to end up in those straights. I can't believe that you are even contemplating such a foolish venture. We haven't sacrificed, fought the weather, planned a business, invested in all this"—she indicated the boxes and furnishings that populated the cabin—"and suffered—yes, suffered—for you to waste it all on this…this ridiculous and foolhardy venture."

She shook her head and pressed her lips together. Then, pulling some curls away from in front of her face and tucking them behind an ear, she lowered her voice.

"Harold, I just can't agree to this. I just can't."

It was as though someone had let the air out of her sails. She sat down in a heap on a large box, dropped her knife, and put her head in her hands.

At a loss for words, Harold rubbed his jaw. Then he scratched a dark eyebrow. Finally, he pinched his lips with his thumb and forefinger, all in an effort to come up with a convincing argument.

He was accustomed to his wife being most agreeable and even-tempered in every situation. They had always been able to talk about everything and come to equitable decisions satisfying both sides. Facing this recalcitrant and apparently inflexible person scowling at him was extremely unsettling. He didn't recognize his own wife and was suddenly unsure of the best approach. Actually, never before had he had to even ponder a particular approach. They had both always just presented their thoughts and feelings with perfect spontaneity—no subterfuges or ploys had ever been necessary.

Harold was out of his depth.

And he didn't have the luxury of allowing things to play out over time; he had promised to join his new friend in the morning. Under uncommon pressure, he wracked his brain for a most persuasive of arguments.

"All right, my dear," he started, bending down to pick up the knife and stepping toward the potatoes on the table. "Let's look at this from all sides. Rest assured that I'm not going to undertake anything you don't approve of."

He started peeling. He had barely sliced off a potato eye when he felt his wife come up behind him and gently take the knife and the potato out of his hands.

"Give me that before you hurt yourself," she teased gruffly, as she patted his arm in reconciliation. "I guess you deserve a hearing. I suppose I was just angry that you hadn't included me in the decision-making." She nodded. "I realize now that you really hadn't had the chance."

While Sarah continued peeling, and Harold sliced some moose meat, they discussed the new subject in their usual considerate manner. By the time the browned meat, potatoes, carrots, onions, celery and parsnips were simmering in the stewpot with some spices from the small plants Sarah grew on the windowsill, Harold had laid out the plan as he understood it.

"So, we will use all of Henry's outfit—I'll contribute some food and kitchenware seeing as we have plenty—and I'll provide the extra labor and maybe some lumber. He has two horses to load the stuff to the site. He also has the necessary buckets, shovels, rope and firewood."

Harold took a breath.

"But the best thing, really," he added quickly, "Is that he was able to buy someone else's claim at a very good location, at a very good price. The seller was desperate. Over the last year, he had lost his partner to another miner who promised better pay. Plus he got sick—probably from poor diet. He sold to Henry for a song. So, everything basic is already there: the shafts, cribbing, windlass…even the gravel piles ready to be sluiced."

He didn't add the detail that the transaction had been conducted in a saloon, after many rounds of drinks.

"But…how will you do the actual work?" Sarah wanted to know as she got out the flour for biscuits. She had no idea of the meanings of the terms Harold had used. "And exactly what will the work involve?" Her mouth twisted in skepticism. "Do you even know?"

Harold sighed and shrugged.

"I know that one of my jobs will be to make improvements on the existing cabin. That's not a mystery. I think I'm pretty well an expert on that." He extended his hand to encompass their living area to illustrate his point.

Then he continued.

"It's also possible to work for hire for other miners as a digger."

He shrugged.

"After, that…well…live and learn, I guess."

He looked at his wife with a rueful smile.

"It can't be that hard or there wouldn't be thousands of men managing claims."

"Yes, well, I'm not sure how well they're managing," she groused, with obvious cynicism. "I certainly hear about more failures than anything else." She added water to the flour and baking soda and started to knead a sticky ball of dough.

Harold was silent as he watched his wife work. There really was no argument for what she had said—it was all well-known fact.

He leaned over and hugged his wife's waist.

"Where's my champion?" he asked jokingly, his blue eyes twinkling. "Where's my unflagging support? Didn't we promise that to each other when we got married?"

Curling a rebel lock of hair behind her ear, she floured the ball of dough that was now smoother and slapped it onto the table.

Reaching around Harold to grab her rolling pin, she pouted silently. In her mind's eye, she pictured their small wedding ceremony in an unfinished chapel down the hill when they had first arrived in Dawson. She really had felt that she had totally given herself to her new husband. She believed he could undertake anything. On their long and tortuous trip to the Klondike, he had shown himself to be strong, decisive and creative.

And very caring.

His efforts to start a business in this frontier city had been unerring and constant. As a result, they were doing better financially than most of the Dawson population in their situation.

How could she be so skeptical now? His judgment had always proved sound. That wasn't even up for argument.

Then she thought of the many customers she'd had at their little food stand in town. She just couldn't ignore the many stories she'd heard that were mostly about crushed dreams and ruined lives. She couldn't dismiss the hollow stares and gaunt features of the men who had fought for their dreams and lost. With tears of shame streaming down their faces, they would hold creased photographs of wives and children who remained afar, waiting years to hear about good fortune that would surely come their way. For these desperate fathers and husbands, even their trip home was not assured, as it depended on their ability to sell all their belongings, sometimes down to their boots.

Sarah shook her head to clear it of the depressing visions. She had to admit that she was not in the dire straits of the unsuccessful fortune seekers, but she didn't see the need for compromising even a part of the modest wealth that she and Harold had built up so far. It hadn't been easy, and continued success required constant vigilance, effort, and a smart savings plan. The last thing they needed was something to shoot their plan full of holes. Besides, this whole new idea seemed no more than a whim; a whim that was certainly not worthy of making life changes.

Cutting out the biscuits from the thick sheet of dough she had rolled out, and placing each one carefully on a baking tin, she tried to assemble the elements of her case.

As supper took shape, Harold could see that his wife's thoughts were percolating in her quick mind. The stew simmered, and the biscuits baked, sending out comforting and enticing aromas. When dinner was ready, they both sat at the small table facing each other, serving dishes of food steaming fragrantly between them.

* * *

As Harold looked over his packs and parcels, he thanked God for his reasonable and forward-thinking wife. Their dinner conversation had been lively, sometimes becoming heated. In the end, Sarah realized that if Harold did not go on this questionable venture, he would probably regret the missed opportunity for the rest of his life. She was afraid that he would resent her forever if she interfered.

So she relented.

On his end, Harold promised to make the trip back to Dawson at least every two weeks. There were always men going to and fro between the two places; he was certain he could always walk or ride along. He had no true picture of how hard the "walk" through the marshes covered in some real stumbling blocks called large grass tussocks called "niggerheads" could be. Try as you might to step from the top of one to the next, you were more often not able prevent yourself from sliding off into the frigid waters. Rubber hip boots were at a premium in Dawson; totally necessary.

As far as the building contracts he had in town were concerned, Harold had made good blueprints. His partners, Sidney and brother Jake, were very capable of interpreting them and beginning the new projects or continuing what they had already begun. On his trips home, Harold would supervise and make sure everything was properly engineered. He promised that if there were problems, he would delay his trips back to Eldorado until everything was taken care of.

In view of what her husband had laid out, Sarah could not really object on the grounds that everything would fall apart in his absence. To afford Harold's workshop, they had sold their food stand, so she would not have to spend time running that. Her responsibility would be their cabin, her sewing business, and her volunteer hospital job with Father Riley. The only thing she could object to was that she would be on her own and would miss Harold greatly.

"I'll miss you greatly too," Harold had maintained. "You won't be the only one on that score. It's just…it's just that…"

"That some things are worth the sacrifice," Sarah finished the thought for him. "I understand that."

She pursed her lips and closed her eyes.

"I just don't entirely agree with it."

Then she had collected the dirty dishes on her way to the washbasin.

Harold's stomach was in turmoil. Between the excitement he felt about his proposed venture, and the uncertainty that cast a pall on it, he had the added guilt of leaving his wife to all the pressures of keeping things going at home. She'd have to keep money coming in, manage the household, haul heavy buckets of water, keep the woodpile supplied, and fix anything that broke or wore out. It was a tall order for anyone, especially without the protection and help of a husband to count on.

Lying in bed after a busy evening getting everything ready, midnight had come and gone.

Hugging and kissing his wife in the early morning hours as they tried to get to sleep, he was unable to overcome the guilt that was in danger of dampening his enthusiasm.

And, of course, there was that niggling fear of the unknown.

-4-

PARADISE ALLEY

Nettie's lot had improved greatly since her friend Sarah had intervened on her behalf. Against her better judgment Nettie was sure, Madame Renée was allowing her to skip anything related to getting her hands wet and being exposed to the cold. She still had to handle laundry—collecting it around town, stripping hotel beds, hauling sheets and heavy towels to the laundry area, picking up the dried sheets, and then returning them to the beds, but she didn't have to wash anything. No bedding, no dishes, no floors.

Sarah had surmised correctly.

Being a shrewd businesswoman, Madame Renée had certainly weighed the situation, undoubtedly concluding that Nettie's good health was important to the overall business plan.

"Antoinette." she announced one day, as if off the cuff, on her way out the door. *"Nous allons réduir tes responsabilités."*

Pulling on her stylish gloves as she spoke, she went on to explain Nettie's new job description, taking sole credit for the notion, and acting as though it had always been her intention to do so.

The young Belgian girl was almost jubilant as she went about her curtailed chores, pulling her laundry wagon for pick-ups in town, getting accustomed to the mittens that she wore on a nearly constant basis, as her good friend Sarah had advised.

The back street, Paradise Alley, was enjoying a quiet lull before the evening onslaught of customers. Nettie was making the rounds to see if any of the seventy or so "crib dwellers" wanted to have their bedding or laundry washed for a fee exacted by her enterprising boss.

Nettie knew many of the women on a first-name basis, aware that they were false names, posted at the front of their respective "cribs." Identical structures with a window at the front facing the narrowest of boardwalks, these very small quarters had room for just one or two beds on which these women plied their trade.

Nettie felt sorry for most of them, grateful that she'd had family pay her passage, and therefore owed nothing to strangers.

The circumstances under which they had been brought to Dawson were similar to hers, but that's where the similarities ended. The women were forced to conduct business under the watchful eye of their pimps to whom they owed for their passage to the Klondike, laboring under relentless conditions, day after excruciating day. Eventually, they simply wore out from the endless toil, endless exposure to illness, endless enslavement.

Exhausted, and unable to continue any longer, a small number of them brought on final release from daily persecution with poison or a bullet. Oblivion was the goal.

"*Bonjour*, L'il," sang out Nettie as she drew up to one particular crib. "Do you want the services today?"

Hearing nothing, she glanced up at the painted name sign to make sure she had the right crib—they all looked so much alike.

It was the right one: "L'il Bets" was printed in blood-red paint over the window. Leaving a destitute family of nine siblings, she had come to Dawson from North Dakota.

"L'il?" she said again, knocking on the wall. "Bets. Are you in?" She wasn't worried that there was any business being conducted inside, as that business really didn't begin before four in the afternoon. The women of Paradise Alley had the hours of late morning and early afternoon to themselves. Most of them slept to make up for the long hours of the previous night, and some enjoyed just talking to each other, finding support in this particular solidarity. Mostly Belgian, they spoke French or Flemish among themselves in raised voices from their respective quarters.

Nettie knocked again. Not hearing anything, she was about to move on, but the rickety door scraped open, revealing a narrow crack.

"I'm here, Nettie," came a muffled response. "You may come in."

Nettie propped her wagon against the wall, pushed the door open wider, and slipped inside the crib.

There was no room to turn around. L'il sat on the lone bed, hiding her face in her hands.

"Do you have any laundry for me?" asked Nettie. "We will try to be ready by tomorrow…"

With her hands still covering her face, L'il shook her head. Nettie frowned, sensing that there was something wrong. This was odd behavior for someone who usually greeted her with equanimity—sometimes even with good cheer.

"L'il," she said, applying gentle pressure to the young girl's hands, trying to pull them away from her face. "Are you all right? Do you not feel well?"

The response was a loud choking sob. L'il gave in and removed her hands from her face. In doing so, she revealed a shocking sight. Besides the redness caused by tears, L'il's eyes were puffy, her skin around them was black and blue, and her lips were swollen to twice their normal size.

"*Oh, mon Dieu!*" exclaimed Nettie, horrified. "*Qu'est-ce qui c'est passé?* What happened? Who did this?"

She squeezed next to L'il on the bed and put her arm around her, noting with dismay that she felt mostly skin and bones under the girl's thin chemise.

"You must tell me. This must be stopped."

L'il couldn't say anything between sobs. Nettie looked around the minuscule room and saw what she was looking for: a water pitcher.

She quickly rose, pulled her clean handkerchief out from her sleeve, and dipped it in the pitcher. Back at the bed, she held the cool damp cloth to L'il's face, hoping that it would be soothing to her.

"Thank you," whispered the girl. "You are so kind to me…" She took the handkerchief and pressed it to one eye.

"*Mais non,*" replied Nettie, shaking her head. "*Ce n'est rien du tout.* It is nothing at all what I do." She sat back down in the small space next to L'il.

"You must have rest."

Then she had an idea. "Why do you not come and stay in my room for this night? You cannot…um…work like this. *Ce n'est pas possible.*"

L'il looked at Nettie as if she wasn't quite right in the head.

"Not work?" she asked incredulously. She shook her head slowly, and then more vigorously.

"I cannot…cannot do that. I have to give my earnings to Big Sal. She will not let me take time off." She pointed to her face. "This is not enough reason to interrupt money coming in…"

Nettie sat, perplexed for a moment.

"But when she sees your face…? Certainly, she will excuse you, no?"

L'il put the cooling handkerchief on her other eye. She almost snorted at Nettie's questions.

"Never. She never lets anyone off. Even Rosie…when she was expecting in two months…she still made her work. I think that's why Rosie left with that old fellow who only had one arm."

She gave the handkerchief back to Nettie.

"There's no way out." She got up. "I have to get ready…"

It seemed like everyone was locked into the same position. Herself being under Madame Renée's thumb, Nettie understood L'il's situation quite well. Everyone owed everyone. She got up to make room.

"*Eh bien*, at least I hope she puts the man who did this to you far away from here."

L'il shrugged and smiled grimly. "That depends on how many customers we have. You know…money. It's the only thing that counts."

Nodding in complete understanding, Nettie pushed open the little door and stepped outside.

"Just remember what I said about you can stay with me if you would like…"

For a fleeting moment she saw a small hopeless smile of gratitude in the opening, and then the door squeaked shut.

As Nettie continued her rounds of the cribs, she couldn't get L'il's damaged face out of her mind.

Maybe Captain Steele would be able to do something about the abusive treatment of many of the women. She made up her mind to talk to Sarah about it. Nettie had noticed immediately that her friend had great reverence for the superintendent, and she trusted Sarah's judgment. A just man would not put up with the cruelty of the circumstances these women had to endure.

The thing was—and Nettie was certainly not aware of it—the existence of the Paradise Alley cribs was by design of the police, especially supported by Captain Steele himself.

Thanks to the Captain, order was maintained in what could have easily descended into lawlessness, immorality and crime. In a Canadian town that was populated by a great majority of irreverent Americans, it was surprising that order was strictly and successfully maintained, from outlawing guns in town, to keeping the Sabbath. In spite of the drinking and desperation, or the rise and fall of fortunes, Dawson was remarkably free of serious offences.

A mystical aura existed around the stalwart men who represented the North-West Mounted Police. There was talk of some of them working in the coldest weather without gloves, yet not losing fingers. Some suffered what should've been devastating accidents, but miraculously survived without injury. Bearing these facts in mind, even the least law-abiding citizen—the one who would be more likely to flout the law under normal circumstances—never dreamed of doing so in Dawson. It would've been a recipe for disaster for his own comfort and wellbeing. An ill-conceived transgression would be dealt at least with a blue card: a forced ticket out of town, or a sojourn on the public woodpile: the only way he could stay in town.

At any one time, fifty men who had made the wrong choices, labored on the pile, wishing they had been more circumspect in dealing with Captain Steele's men.

"So, why does Captain Steele not stop the Paradise Alley business," asked a distraught Nettie, the next time she visited Sarah. After all, obscenity, cheating, even just working on the Sabbath, were all forbidden and punished. To her, the poor treatment of innocent women seemed more egregious.

"*Mon Dieu.* Those women have a very difficult life. They suffer every day. You should see their bodies. *C'est affreux.*"

"Well," said Sarah, trying to figure out how to explain the captain's motivation. "I agree it seems awful. I know you feel pity for those poor women. But Captain Steele knows what happens when men are left to their own devices when there are only few women around. By regulating Paradise Alley, he controls them, and keeps assault and rape to a minimum."

"In fact," she continued, thinking it over. "I haven't heard of a single case."

Nettie looked at her friend, wide-eyed and puzzled.

Putting a comforting hand on Nettie's arm, Sarah pursed her lips and nodded grimly. "It's not ideal, *ma chérie*, but it's definitely the lesser of two evils…"

One look at her young friend's confused expression made her sigh.

It was translation time again.

-5-

BEANS AND BISCUITS

With his wife's measured good-bye still ringing in his ears, Harold held on to the horse's bridle, not sure who was leading whom through the slippery, marshy path to Eldorado.

He would've thought that with the extraordinary amount of back-and-forth traffic between the mines and Dawson that it would've been much less challenging; more worn away.

Henry had chosen to travel as far from the boggiest part of the marsh in order to avoid the worst of the treacherous tussocks of wild wet grass where traffic was sparse. But it wasn't easy. Nature grew quickly in the midnight sun. Even away from the worst of the marsh, plants and young saplings proliferated with remarkable speed, shooting up where yesterday there had been but a small seedling.

Harold could barely keep up with Henry who was ahead of him with his own heavily laden horse. The slippery protuberances and the unevenness of the path caused him to slip and slide; he was sure that he'd at least twist his ankle—at worst, break one. That he'd get soaked no matter how much care he exercised, was a forgone conclusion.

At first he had been naively dismissive: sixteen miles of muskeg, brush, and some forested areas. After what he had been through getting to Dawson from Dyea, that seemed like a negligible distance and easy going. Add to that no inclement weather to deal with, no huge outfit to drag along, and no stampeders to crowd him out.

175

"It seems as nice as pie," he had said to himself, a bit incredulous.

But now he became aware that this new wilderness itself was a huge challenge. With a comfortable cabin, clean clothes, and more than adequate food—not to mention the attentions of a very efficient and caring wife—he had probably gone soft. Living on the edge was going to take some getting used to again. Harold wasn't sure he was quite up to it.

Then the thought of gold brought him back to his reality: he could take a lot of punishment for the potential reward. What was a little discomfort in the meantime?

An hour later, having crossed several miners headed in the opposite direction on their way back to Dawson, he and Henry sat by a small campfire, out of the way of the main thoroughfare, on a bit of a rise, waiting for beans to heat. Not wanting to spend money, they were planning to forgo a stop at what tried to pass for a hotel in Grand Forks, where the gold-bearing Bonanza and Eldorado Creeks joined together.

Along the way, they had tried to pry news out of the men hurrying back to Dawson as to the state of the mines and any new discoveries, but the answers were disappointingly non-committal. They finally surmised that miners were, in all likelihood, trying to discourage any additional prospecting. There was probably enough of a crowd as it was. Overriding everything on this trek back to civilization was their desire to get to the saloons either to celebrate, or to drown their disappointments.

Harold had a tin plate on his knee with a biscuit on it, a last-minute addition to his pack made by Sarah. He took a second one out of his pack and handed it to Henry.

"Here…this'll help with the beans," said Harold. "It'll give them something to hang on to."

Henry smiled and nodded.

"Yes…I find that I miss my mother's cooking," he said, his smile turning grim. "She could really put up a meal." He patted his stomach and shook his head. "I think I've lost twenty pounds since I left home." He grabbed a stick and stirred the beans warming in their can, propped on the coals. "She'd roll over in her grave if she could see how I eat now."

Harold understood but couldn't really sympathize. His meals had been quite satisfactory lately. But he wasn't going to lord it over his new associate. Besides, things in that respect were probably going to change from now on. Before it was all over, he'd probably have to take his belt in a notch or two.

Too impatient to wait for the beans to heat properly, they filled their small plates and slurped their supper, soaking up the last morsels with their biscuits. The whole process had taken but a few minutes.

The lukewarm beans hadn't gone very far towards easing the hunger pangs. Even including the biscuit. Harold could've eaten three times as much, but he didn't say anything because he had no idea how the food would be parceled out over the next few weeks.

In addition, he could've easily taken a nap, but realized that this was also not in the cards any more than a second helping of food.

Henry tipped over the empty bean can and crushed it with his boot. Then he threw it in the surrounding brush on his way to finding a spot for a call of nature.

Meanwhile, Harold packed up the plates and spoons and kicked dirt over the dying embers of the fire. The horses, tied to a stringy bush some distance off where they could graze, stomped and whinnied, pulling at their tethers. Harold figured they were eager to move.

Hearing twigs snap, Harold assumed his partner was on his way back. He kept adjusting his packs, longingly eyeing the remaining biscuits, but deciding to reserve them for later.

"So, Henry, how much longer…" began Harold, looking up from the pack, suddenly realizing he had company that was not going to answer his question.

Facing him, standing unsteadily, a man with a gray, deeply lined face, waved a knife in what Harold took to be a threatening manner. On some level, Harold felt he should've feared more for his life, but the man looked in such bad shape that Harold was more surprised than anything else.

"What do you want," he barked at the intruder, standing up and hoping that Henry would hear and intervene.

"You got any food? Coffee? I ain't had nothing in…" he faded, stumbling, lowering the knife, and collapsing to a kneeling position right in front of Harold.

That's the tableau that greeted Henry as he reappeared.

He pulled out a pistol that Harold didn't even know he had. They were not allowed in town, and most people didn't even think they were necessary.

"What the hell?' Henry started, opting for a defensive stance. "Where did he come from?" He looked at Harold for an explanation.

Harold raised his eyebrows and shrugged.

"I don't think there's a lot of danger here," he said, pointing to the man who was now swaying side to side, barely managing to stay upright. "He's in pretty dire straights. Wants food."

As if illustrating Harold's point, the man toppled over, his head hitting the ground with a heart-stopping thump.

The potential threat averted, Henry put away the pistol.

At the same time, as they approached to help him up, their nostrils were assailed by the most offensive odor. They held their breath and propped him up against one of the packs, in a seated position.

With but a few thoughts towards their limited food supply, Harold and Henry reopened the food pack and gave their unexpected guest a bit of food and water. At first Harold had thought the man to be well over fifty, but upon closer scrutiny, he realized that caked-on dirt and gauntness had prematurely aged him. He probably wasn't out of his thirties.

When the man seemed to have recovered a bit, he thanked his benefactors, and told them that his name was Jake Morton, ex-miner; ex because he had suffered a terrible leg and foot wound, and had lost his job as a digger on Bonanza.

It was then that Harold noticed that his left pant leg was shredded. Upon seeing the filthy bandage underneath, he realized that the noxious smell that had overwhelmed him was not only unwashed body odor and fetid breath, but most certainly gangrene. A closer inspection revealed that the fellow's wound was suppurating with infection, his flesh dying. He probably had a high fever and was dangerously close to losing his life. Harold had heard enough of his wife's lurid hospital tales to be aware of what dangers this man was facing.

Bearing in mind what he had learned from Sarah, and knowing she had significant medical knowledge thanks to her doctor father, Harold reckoned that Jake needed serious and immediate care. Fortunately, there was enough traffic streaming back to Dawson that they were able to engage a driver of a wagon on his way to town for supplies to take Jake to Father Riley's hospital. It was the poor man's only hope.

Having seen to Jake's temporary comfort in preparation for the trip to the hospital, it didn't take Harold and Henry but a few minutes to load the horses and set off in the opposite direction toward Bonanza and Eldorado.

This venture had taken on a dimension that Harold had never experienced, but he took his cue from Henry who seemed to be taking this last event in stride. The only difference in his demeanor was his hand constantly checking the pistol that was now obvious, strapped to his hip.

Harold had left his illegally owned pistol at home in case Sarah needed it. He seriously doubted that she could ever harm someone with it, even if she was at risk, but he felt better that she had it, non-the-less. It had not occurred to him that he might need it, himself.

By nightfall, which did not necessarily mean darkness, Harold began to see additional quantities of discarded items, trash, and wear and tear on the vegetation, so he knew the end of the road was near. He was bone-tired and sore, nursing a couple of blisters. How could he be so out of shape? He certainly had gone soft since the Chilkoot Trail over the mountains, just a year or so ago.

He didn't have time to wallow in self-disgust. The brush and trees became a huge clearing. But it wasn't a natural one. Brush had been cleared, and trees had been felled in irregular patterns, leaving some standing alone, and some standing in small groups of two or three.

Progressing a little farther, Harold could see where all the downed trees had gone. The hillsides were bare of vegetation, but dotted with hundreds of structures, scattered like a child's toys. Some were easy to understand; cabins and outbuildings, and—a terrible memory: saw pits. Others were strange structures to Harold: long winding wooden connected fences snaking down the hillsides. Between the fences, Harold could see large boxes attached to them. Water flowed through everything by design. There were also tall crisscrossed structures with men hanging on at different heights. Harold knew that all these things were part of the mining enterprise, but what their functions were, he'd have to discover with experience.

By the time they reached the cabin that had come with Henry's claim there was a duskiness to the atmosphere. Part of that was due to the fact that it was well into the early hours of the morning, and part was due to the smoke coming from all the smokestacks, chimneys, and campfires at each claim, smudging the entire hillside.

They tied up the horses, gave them water from a barrel alongside the cabin, loosened their loads, and began to unpack.

"I don't know about you," sighed Henry, putting down a large pack. "I'm about ready to call it a day. We can do all the rest of this tomorrow." He pointed to the squat cabin. "Let's see about our accommodations."

Harold hadn't been holding his breath wondering what those would be. He had told himself to be prepared for things to be very rough.

It took some effort to open the unlocked door; disuse and time had allowed for some swelling of the wood and probably some shifting of the structure itself.

Inside, Harold was glad that he'd had realistic expectations. As he looked around, the builder in him couldn't help envisioning the improvements this new home away from home desperately needed. He couldn't keep visions of his cozy cabin back in Dawson out of his mind.

There was only one furnishing that approximated a bed, and it took quite a creative mind to see it as such. Immediately dismissing it for his own use, Harold claimed a spot on the floor to drop his bedroll.

In a few minutes they had closed the door and flopped down in their respective sleeping areas.

Soon snoring replaced the silence.

-6-

BEDPANS AND BANDAGES

Sarah hurriedly made her way to Father Riley's clinic.

She steeled herself in advance to manage her natural revulsion to rotting flesh, dysentery, and gaping putrid wounds. The good Father needed a great deal of help to tend to the scores of patients lining the hallways of his ramshackle, drafty, and woefully under supplied, understaffed hospital.

In addition to the physically daunting elements, she was determined not to let the rampant misery and hopelessness overwhelm her.

Although she saw the Jesuit priest almost every day, laboring under incredibly difficult conditions, sacrificing himself to help others no matter what illness or malaise had taken over their bodies, she hardly ever saw him eat or sleep. He did not even have his own bed, let alone a room to put one in, and he certainly didn't have a kitchen or dining area. He had given everything up to make room for patients.

His first building, basically a church, had not survived the town fire of almost a year ago. He had built it with very little help, laboring over hand-hewn altar and pews, and homemade vestments. Along with most of the town, his labor of love had gone up in flames and burnt to the ground.

Undeterred by the tragedy, he immediately set about to rebuild. Fortunately, the town contributed to his present building, taking donations, holding bazaars, and raising money any way they could. After all, they knew him to be so self-sacrificing in his efforts, that even non-Catholics enthusiastically supported his cause.

Because he skimped on his own wellbeing, Sarah often took a packet of food that she made him promise he would put aside for himself. Being a realist, however, she suspected that very little of it made its way to his stomach. In all probability, he routinely found what he determined to be a more needy repository for the food. Undaunted, she kept taking her little care packages to him in the hopes that, at some point, he might consume even a small portion himself.

She found him leaning against the wall of the entrance to the hospital, looking pale and haggard. She was not alerted by his facial appearance—she hadn't exactly seen him look healthy on any occasion—but the obvious fatigue and lack of energy did take her aback. He was normally a dynamo that never slowed down.

"Father," she said, putting a hand on his shoulder. "Have you had anything to eat? What about rest?"

She forcefully steered him toward a bench used to seat new patients. He offered no resistance.

"I'll be all right, my dear. Stop fretting. It's nothing but a temporary malaise." He shook his head, and weakly waved her away.

"I'm sure, Father," Sarah went on, placating him. "I'm sure you are quite right."

Then her tone changed.

"But now that I have you in my clutches, you are going to have some of this."

She opened her package and pulled out some bread and cheese plus an ale bottle filled with milk. Brushing aside his weak remonstrance, she tore off a piece of bread and held the cheese so that he could take a bite. He gently removed the food from her hand, and almost delicately took a bite of each item. Under Sarah's watchful eye, he smiled reassuringly, and ate some more. She uncorked the bottle, and he took a long pull, sighing as he wiped his mouth on his thin sleeve.

"Blessings upon you, my child," he said gratefully, suppressing a belch. "I guess I need taking in hand." He shook his head in wonder and smiled at her. "Your husband is a very lucky man…"

At the mention of Harold, Sarah's mouth twisted slightly in mild scorn.

"He'd better be counting on some really good luck," she retorted drily, ignoring the compliment, and going in a different direction. "Because he'll be needing a fairly liberal amount of it to gain approval on the home front…"

Trying to keep a lid on her ambivalence toward her husband's venture, she went on to explain the latest family developments.

Keenly aware of subtleties, and knowing both of the individuals involved, Father Riley could tell that there might've been a difference of opinion between the newlyweds.

"We all do what we have to… I'm sure Harold has the best interests of your family at heart. Men see their roles a bit differently…" he began, but faded, leaning back against the wall. Counseling people was a draining occupation.

"Have a bit more, Father," encouraged Sarah, afraid that he was failing again. "And then," she continued bossily, "you will take a real rest, in a real bed, for the remainder of the afternoon."

He started to argue. She put out a hand to stop him.

"I will see to all the patients. In fact, my friend Nettie will soon be here to help out."

She smiled, teasing.

"I'm fairly certain that the two of us can do almost as much as you can."

Relenting, Father Riley answered with a weak smile, and nodded. He took a few more bites and gulped down some more milk.

"Perhaps you're right," he agreed. Then putting up a shaky index finger he admonished her: "But only an hour. You must rouse me in an hour at most."

Sarah reluctantly nodded in guise of agreement but made no promises.

"And I'll lie down on my bedroll; I can't take a bed away from the men."

Sarah knew it was useless to argue on that point. She was temporarily satisfied with a half-victory.

His long body bent slightly at the waist, and occasionally placing a hand on the wall for support, Father Riley shuffled toward the hallway where his bedroll—a thin, dirty blanket—lay in an unrecognizable heap, crammed into a dark corner by a staircase. Sarah waited until she was sure he was going through with what he had promised. She stayed put patiently for a few minutes. Then, after hearing a few light snores, she made sure he was as well covered as possible with the poor excuse for a blanket and went to the sick rooms.

In the first ward, there were at least forty men with dysentery and in varying stages of scurvy lying everywhere, including the floor. In the next ward seethed dozens of typhoid and malaria patients, and in a third much smaller room, accident victims. Sarah waited to get accustomed to the nauseating smells, which experience told her usually took a half hour. But, she had to recognize, even after that amount of time, the stench never really dissipated. It seemed to adhere to your nasal passages even after you went home.

Along with a few other women, nurses, and volunteers, she started checking bandages, liquids, bedpans, and the sparse medicines that Father Riley obtained by hook or by crook. She inquired as to the state of mind of the men and comforted the most miserable of them. They moaned and cried out as they spoke of their families, certain that they would never see them again. Sarah tried to allay their fears, but most of the men just turned their heads away from her, and cried softly into their bedding.

Some had a wrinkled photograph tucked into their fists, some a small family memento of some sort.

She was changing some bandages on a miner who had lost three fingers when a windlass was released suddenly without warning. The attached gravel-filled bucket had smashed his hand as it came hurtling down the shaft he was digging in. He said he was lucky it hadn't taken his head off.

As Sarah put the finishing touches on the bandage, she became aware of a commotion at the entrance.

"The carbolic acid Father Riley treated you with should prevent infection, but let's keep that hand up in the air," she told the morose patient, as she got up from his bedside, and rolled a shirt under his arm to elevate it. "It'll throb less."

She looked up in time to see two men supporting a third who was keeping his foot from touching the ground.

"Got an injury here, nurse," said one of the men. "Mining accident. Where do we put him?"

Sarah was undecided for a moment. She would have to do some substituting. Beds were at a premium. She went back to the man who was sporting three fewer fingers on one hand. She explained that he could do just as well on a chair, while they took care of this new patient. After, they'd work something out.

There was no such thing as changing the bedding on a daily basis or, most of the time, even a weekly one—this, in spite of the modern knowledge that cleanliness was indispensable to healing. With Father Riley never turning anyone away, it just wasn't possible to stay ahead of the bedding situation. Nettie would be along soon to collect the worst of it.

So, Sarah had the man put into the recently vacated bed. The most they could do was to keep the wounded away from the ill, as the idea of contagion had lately been generally accepted among the medical community.

The new arrival's injury was dire, and his infection was advanced. Sarah knew that this was a case for Father Riley to consider, but she didn't want to disturb his well-earned rest just yet.

In the meantime, she cut off the miner's filthy and shredded pant leg, and tried to wash the affected area so that the dirt could be separated from the wound. This way, Father Riley could have a better idea of what was involved when he assessed it to decide whether to call in a doctor. The foul odor of rotting flesh seemed to permeate everything. She found she was repeatedly holding her breath, and was beginning to feel dizzy.

She had to get some fresh air or faint.

Placing a relatively clean towel over the wound, she patted the miner's arm. He had almost passed out and probably was not aware of much.

"I'll be right back," she whispered. "Try to sleep."

Then she rushed to the outer door where there was a stiff breeze and took in great gulps of fresh air. She leaned back against the doorjamb and closed her eyes.

"*Sarah? Ça ne va pas?* Are you not well?"

It was Nettie, her wagon loaded down with clean laundry, coming to help, and to collect what dirty laundry was waiting for her. Concern lined her forehead as she picked up a load of clean sheets.

Opening her eyes, Sarah noisily took in some more air and made a wry face.

"I just have to get my breath. It's…it's dreadful in there." She gestured towards the inside and reached to relieve Nettie of some of her burden.

Nettie listened carefully as Sarah explained the situation with Father Riley and the state of the wards, including the newest patient. Having been there every few days for laundry, and occasionally to help, she did not seem put off by any of it. Nodding in understanding, it seemed as though she was looking forward to helping.

Both women went through the doorway into the fetid atmosphere of the hospital to see what was to be done.

When he finally awoke, Father Riley was extremely put out that Sarah had let him sleep almost three hours.

"Sarah, my child, I asked you to wake me much earlier. I wasted precious…"

"But Father," she interrupted. "There wasn't anything critical enough to wake you. Besides," she continued, pivoting to try to put a positive light on it. "Obviously you needed it. You look so much better."

In her mind, she admitted that the latter was probably a small exaggeration—not an outright lie. Father Riley didn't look quite as feeble and unsteady as earlier, but his pallor and haggard physiognomy were still quite apparent.

The priest harrumphed, thought better of arguing with this uncompromising angel, and switched the subject to the patients.

They made rounds of several beds until they reached the newest patient.

Because of the smell, Sarah would've known she was near him even if she had been blindfolded. She felt her gorge rise and could hardly keep it in check.

Something had to be done.

Seemingly unperturbed by the atmosphere, Father Riley lifted the towel to examine the leg.

The patient's eyes were closed. He moaned and moved his other leg restlessly. After one brief look, Father Riley sent one of the women to fetch a doctor.

In truth, there was a small window of time when a doctor would be available. Most had exchanged their medical instruments for jiggers and whiskey glasses working long hours mixing drinks behind bars in the saloons. By five in the afternoon, they would be too busy getting their supplies ready for the evening onslaught to look at patients.

"Well, Son. What's your name?" asked the priest, putting his hand on the man's arm. "Can you hear me, my son?" He patted the arm to try to elicit an answer.

The patient moaned even louder and his eyelids fluttered. His head twisted left and right and his back arched so that his chest started to rise from the bed. Father Riley pressed down gently on his chest.

"It's all right, Son, "he said gently. "We're going to help you."

Looking around he caught sight of one of the male nurses tending to someone in one of the other beds.

"Sam, go to the dispensary and bring me the morphine powder. Hurry."

Sam recognized the urgency in his voice.

In two minutes he was back with a small flagon of powder.

Father Riley bent over and shook a bit of the precious powder right into the wound. Then he straightened up and waited for the effect to take hold. After a few minutes, the patient calmed down and the moaning subsided. A few more minutes went by, but instead of falling asleep, he opened his eyes and tried to focus on the crowd at the foot of his bed. Then he became aware of the priest, in his threadbare cassock, sitting by his side.

"Am I dying?" he croaked, his eyes widening in fear. His panicked glance went from face to face and came to rest on Sarah's. "Am I?"

To allay his fears, she tried to smile, knowing all the while, that at the very least, he would probably lose his foot.

"We're going to get you some help," she said. "There's a doctor coming very soon."

By his lack of expression, she couldn't tell if that was a comfort or not. Squeezing between the patient beds, she drew nearer to him and bent closer.

"Can you tell us your name? Or what happened?"

The man said nothing for a moment, smacking his dry lips.

"Can I have some water? I'm so…so thirsty."

One of the nurses got some water from a pitcher by the door and brought a half full tin cup to Sarah. She held her breath and put an arm behind the man's head, holding the cup to his lips. Spilling some of it that dribbled down his chin, he was able to take several swallows. Then he stopped, took deep breaths, and signaled for more. The cup was soon empty, so Sarah gently let his head fall back on the bed. He closed his eyes and breathed heavily from the exertion.

Sarah breathed through her mouth.

Father Riley motioned for everyone but Sarah and Nettie to tend to the other patients. Then he and the two women moved away from the bed out of earshot while the patient dozed off.

"We'll have to debride that wound," said Father Riley. "We should wait until he sleeps." He nodded to himself. "Too bad we don't have any maggots. They would make quick work of that dead flesh."

Then he sadly shook his head.

"I'm not sure we can save him, or his foot. He's already so infected. We have to get clean bedding to keep him from getting worse. Then we'll wait to see what the doctor says."

Sarah pursed her lips and nodded sadly in agreement.

Looking around at the rest of the ward he added, "While he's a bit more comfortable, let's not disturb him. We'll just continue our rounds."

Forgetting that he had sold his watch in exchange for supplies, he briefly searched his pockets. Coming up empty, he remembered and shrugged. "If I'm not mistaken, I think it'll be time for food distribution soon, so we'd better get ready for that, too.

Sarah nodded and patted Father Riley's arm. She knew she was in the presence of a saint and was humbled.

-7-

FOR OLD TIME'S SAKE

The music was loud, and, he thought, not always in tune.

With his foot on the rail, and his elbow on the bar, Gunther Jorgenson knocked back three fingers of whiskey in a shot glass. With a loud sigh, he slammed the glass down and signaled to the bartender for a refill.

Next to him on either side, men in various stages of inebriation lolled on the bar, staring blearily into their glasses. Some were silent as they drank themselves into oblivion; others argued over mining aspects that they had either just left, or were planning to go experience the next day. Still others tried to impress ladies dressed in lace and feathers hanging on their arms, as they paid them for an hour of companionship.

Behind Gunther, chips were thrown about on felt tables as various bets were wagered on the flic of a card or the roll of dice. Shouts and cries punctuated every action. In a corner, farther from the bar, on a hanging sheet, a Projectoscope flashed grainy moving photos of newsreels of stale events. Spectators watched them over and over, fascinated by the process, and feeling that they were now up to date on current events thousands of miles away, and months in the past.

Centrally located, a narrow stage took up a large part of the room. It was too early yet for any show to begin. Having occupied the same spot yesterday, Gunther knew what the performance would be and, he didn't have the patience to endure the predictable volley of bawdy jokes and songs that would later distract the folks who would pay a dollar fifty to be entertained.

Feeling restless, Gunther couldn't concentrate on the gambling, not that he had ever been above risking his money on a good game. He acknowledged that he had won and lost a bundle over the Klondike trip, and it had been a serious bone of contention with Sarah and Harold, eventually leading to the unfortunate rift between them. Yet, for some inexplicable reason, he was uncharacteristically apathetic about games and gambling for the moment.

He looked around in irritation.

It was always the same thing: men bragging about their discoveries or complaining about their lack of the same. The ones who had money wasted it on trying to impress the entourage by buying too many rounds or placing too many bets. Women flounced about half naked, eager to add to the pokes tied to their wrists, flirting with and flattering men in various stages of drunkenness, with that end in mind.

He wasn't falling for any of it.

"Hey, Doc!"

Motioning to the bartender for another refill, he justified the action by telling himself he had an honest source for his money. As opposed to a large number of these men, he earned a real living. Carpentry was never going to produce the fabulous amount a lucky strike at the mines could yield, but the fact remained that it was a steady income. He felt his pockets for the reassuring lumpy feel of coins. It comforted and validated him.

His thoughts returned to his original partners, with whom he had faced the harsh and unforgiving elements of the Klondike Trail—the two who had shared with him the depths of despair when things were sketchy, and elation when they reached their goal. He had always been convinced that their relationship would've gone on, unchanged forever. So he was completely blindsided when, out of the blue, the other two had cemented an alliance without him that he couldn't understand let alone accept: their marriage.

One of the women sitting on a gambler's lap reminded him of Sarah, sending a spike of angry heat through his veins. His drunken ire rose like a wild tide as he reviewed what he perceived to be the double betrayal he had suffered. It was choking him.

Damn them!

Going back years, when they were teenagers, Gunther had always taken for granted that Sarah would be his wife. As far as he was concerned, it had always been a forgone conclusion. He cursed himself that he hadn't tied the knot at some time before they had embarked on their trip north—certainly before Sarah had had the chance to meet Harold.

Why had he been so lackadaisical about their relationship?

What had he missed? Then he cursed himself all the more that he had been the one to invite Harold to travel with them. Admittedly, the invitation was mostly selfish: having the help of a third person immeasurably improved chances of success. You could always figure out some way to get rid of the unwanted individual when it came time to collect.

But everything had backfired. He regretted all his moves, but didn't feel it was his fault that things had not turned out as he had expected. He was the victim in this situation. He deserved compensation.

His blood boiled, fueled by the cheap whiskey that he was slinging back with abandon on an empty stomach.

Suddenly, it was stifling in the saloon.

Suppressing his instinct to toss some money on the green felt as a large wager, he slammed back the last of his liquor, and jammed his hands in his pockets on his way out the door.

Outside, as he staggered by some of the other saloons, it was tempting to enter and repeat his performance. But something in his addled brain was directing him to the end of Front Street and beyond.

"Hey. Hey you! Jorgenson!"

When he realized through his brain fog that he had heard his name called, his heart sank. Never a good sign when someone yelled his name from afar. Experience told him it usually meant that some kind of confrontation was in the offing.

Wobbling a bit, he turned around, his eyelids at half-mast.

Approaching just as unsteadily were two men he vaguely recognized. He squinted, forcing his lids wide open, battling the haze of alcohol to try to focus. Most of his social interactions involved gaming and money, and they were usually negative. If you never owed anyone, there wouldn't be any confrontation. Unfortunately, that was not his customary situation.

"Hey, Jorgenson…" slurred a hollow-eyed gambler, his hat mashed down to his ears, his face obscured by a huge unkempt beard.

"Where's my money? You owe me…" He coughed, and then spat into the street.

The alcohol inflating his sense of invulnerability, Gunther decided to bluster.

"Says who?" he yelled belligerently, weaving a bit, placing his feet apart to steady himself.

The two other men looked at each other. Then, with matching menacing glares, they took a few unsteady steps toward their target.

His self-confidence taking a sudden holiday, Gunther reached into his pocket, grabbed some of his precious stash of coins, and threw a handful into the street. Then he pivoted, stumbling a bit, and hurried to the end of the boardwalk without a backward glance. He knew that the two men could not resist scrambling to rescue the coins from the unctuous mud of Front Street.

It was his cue to disappear.

*   *   *

Sarah couldn't wait to lie down on her bed. Exhausted from a day of endless work at the hospital, she could barely negotiate the path uphill to her cabin.

Having had very little to eat, she looked forward to a bowl of leftover soup and a dense biscuit…after which she'd try for a healing night's sleep.

Still reeling from the sights and smells of the wards, she was nevertheless feeling a bit better about her personal contribution.

She and Father Riley had made good work of debriding the newest patient's leg wound, using carbolic acid to fight further infection, as per the instructions of the doctor. In order to ease the patient, the doctor had used a hypodermic needle to inject some morphine before work was done on the suppurating wound.

From the patient's delirious ramblings, and a few brief moments of lucidity, Sarah had gathered that he had been helped on his way back from the mines by two men with horses, heading in the opposite direction. She wasn't completely certain, but, from his descriptions, she realized that it very probably was Harold and Henry who had helped him. When she thought about it, the timeline fit just right.

Upon his return, she'd have to ask Harold about Jake Morton. That way, she'd know for sure.

As she approached the cabin, the sun was still spreading daylight even at the late hour. She could hear the tinkling of piano music emanating from the nightly revelry on Front Street.

It hardly ever stopped.

"Sarah."

She jumped.

What in the world? She'd never been accosted this far from town.

"Sarah, it's me. Gunther."

Out from behind a shed, among the long evening shadows, a tall recognizable form took shape.

Sarah pressed on toward her front door.

She hadn't talked to Gunther since they had dropped him off on the last leg of their trip to Dawson. Taking over an abandoned boat, he had used it alone to float into town, thus separating himself from her and Harold. Since then, apart from the men seeing each other occasionally at sawmills, they had broken all ties. Seeing him again after their break was more than awkward.

"Gunther?" Sarah's voice shook. Her heart was still beating rapidly from the shock. "What...what is it?"

She had a hand on the door latch. She willed herself to calm down.

"Can…can I come in?" Gunther had approached, and she was almost bowled over by the smell on him, mostly liquor.

She was trying to make up her mind, when Gunther took the key to the lock out of her hand, used it, and lifted the latch.

Suffering some kind of temporary paralysis, Sarah watched dumbly, as he pushed the door open and handed the key back.

"*Après vous, Mademoiselle*…" he said with a ironic half-bow, indicating that she should enter. "I mean: *Madame*."

He grinned crookedly, his eyes narrowing.

"Yeah, you're *Madame* now, aren't you?"

Sarah was silent.

There was unmistakable and frightening bitterness in his reference to her married state. Stepping inside, she didn't know whether to be hospitable, or to try to get him to go without his gaining entrance to the cabin.

 Not leaving it up to her, he forced his way into the living area, tripping on a box of Harold's tools as he did so.

"Hmmm, nice and cozy," he murmured, steadying himself against the wall, and looking around the cabin. He admired the small couch, hand hewn by Harold, and for which Sarah had fashioned some cushions.

"Well, well. You must be married to a skilled artist. That's quite some handiwork, I must say."

He pursed his lips as if judging it.

"Let's try it out."

Grabbing Sarah, he pulled her down on the couch, trapping her arms to her sides.

"Gunther! Stop this!" she complained loudly, struggling to get up. "Let me go! I'll get you some dinner." It was a desperate evasive tactic.

He stopped for a minute, considering the offer.

Reluctantly letting her go, he nodded. "Yes, I could use some grub," he admitted, as she quickly arose. "But I do have to say," he added in a sour tone, raising an eyebrow suggestively over the deep brown eyes she had always found so soulful.

"I can remember a time when you liked our little wrestling matches."

She was repulsed by his leer.

Why did Harold have to be gone? Her resentment toward his absence almost choked her. And how, after all this time, did Gunther seem to know that she would be home by herself?

Pushing the resentment to the back of her mind, she busied herself stoking the fire, reheating the soup, and getting out the leftover biscuits. She badly wanted to wash up and change her clothes, but that was definitely out of the question for the moment.

Waiting for dinner, Gunther had slouched against the back of the little couch, his eyes closed, his long legs stretched halfway across the room. He started to snore gently.

Sarah didn't know what to wish for: should she hope that he would doze, and sleep off his drunken stupor, or should she feed him, and send him on his way? Would that even be possible?

In any case, making her indecision moot after a few moments, he snorted awake, and sat up suddenly.

"Well, that smells good," he said, as the soup started to bubble. "You haven't lost your touch, I see."

Not sure how to respond safely, Sarah ignored the compliment. She laid out two bowls, spoons, and cups.

"Almost ready," she said, her voice barely above a whisper. "Do you want to wash up?"

"Oh, no," answered Gunther, shaking his head of thick, unkempt dark auburn hair.

"I wouldn't want to use up your water supply."

His eyes were narrow, his smile superior.

"I know you can't count on your husband to haul it for the time being…" His smile widened. "Maybe I should take over."

He definitely knew that Harold wouldn't be around. Sarah decided to gloss over his clumsy hint.

"Oh…he'll be back soon," Sarah lied casually, hoping she sounded quite sure. "He's just on an errand… Why don't you just come and sit down?"

Gunther gave her an all-knowing look, took some slow deliberate steps to the table, and slid into the chair opposite her. He picked up his spoon and waved it at her, slowly shaking his head and tsk-tsking sarcastically.

"Sarah, my dear, I saw him head out of town with that other fellow. He was packed for way more than a couple of days."

He gave her that unnatural smile again, his eyelids opening and closing in slow motion.

"So, you can say what you want…" He let the statement hang, and noisily dropped the spoon in his dish.

Sarah felt coldness surround her heart. She took his bowl to the stove and spooned in some soup. Then, setting it in front of him, she tucked a couple of biscuits next to it.

"Sorry, I don't have any butter right now."

She could barely sound civil. Going to fill her own bowl, and finding that she had lost her appetite, she barely put in a spoonful or two.

They ate without a word, Gunther slurping his soup as if he hadn't eaten in a week, Sarah barely choking down a few bites.

As she took stock of what had unfolded in the last few moments, and as she watched him wolf down his food, she had a hard time understanding how she had ever liked this man—how she could have felt secure enough to contemplate marrying him.

At the same time, she couldn't help feeling a bit of guilt over having broken off their relationship, when she knew he had always assumed that they'd be married to each other.

Her sensitive nature could understand his bitterness—that he felt betrayed—and she found herself on the verge of forgiving his bad manners. After all, there must've been a reason that she had been attracted to him besides his good looks.

When he scraped the bottom of his bowl, Sarah got up to get him a second helping. She felt a little less antagonistic.

As she picked up his bowl and was about to step to the stove, he suddenly scooted his chair back, and pulled her down on his lap.

The bowl went flying, and Sarah cried out in protest.

Wedging her between himself and the table, he tried to kiss her.

She fought.

Using the table for support, she managed to push against him so that the chair tipped over on its back with both of them still in it. His head smashed against the floor. While he was temporarily stunned by the impact, she was able to scramble free.

She had one thought: Harold's gun in the kitchen drawer.

Rushing to the cabinet while Gunther was clearing his head, and slowly getting up, she yanked open the drawer, felt toward the back of it, and withdrew the Colt.

"Get out!" she shouted, trembling, aiming it at his chest. "Out! Right now! You disgust me!"

For a long moment they stared at each other, not moving.

If Sarah had hoped to scare Gunther away, she had to rethink her expectations. He certainly didn't look daunted.

Incredibly, he still wore that peculiar smile, approaching her with uneven steps, completely ignoring the gun pointed at him. His eyes did not complement the smile.

"Or what? Or what, Sarah? You're going to shoot me now? Your ex-intended?"

He shook his head in scorn.

"Come on Sarah. Is this your idea of old time's sake? Back in the day, we enjoyed each other. Remember?"

Taking advantage of her obvious indecision, he reached out suddenly and grabbed the barrel, twisting the pistol out of her hand.

He held it high, out of her reach.

"You do know that these things need to be cocked, don't you? Or did your husband," he spat the word with great disdain, "forget to teach you that little detail?"

His glare not leaving her face, he reached above the tall kitchen cabinet, putting the pistol where she couldn't possibly get to it easily.

Suffused with blood, his face was dark, his eyebrows were knitted together over the bridge of his nose, and his mouth had taken on a cruel twist.

Sarah could hardly recognize him.

204

He approached her with slow, heavy, deliberate steps.

Sarah knew she had unwittingly touched a nerve, and she couldn't see any way of getting out of having to pay for it.

-8-

COLOR AND GRIT

The bench where their claim was located was one of the most productive in Eldorado.

It seemed the place to be.

Harold had slept much better on the gritty cabin floor than he had thought possible. He guessed that exhaustion had something to do with it.

After a breakfast of beans, bacon, and the last of Sarah's biscuits, all washed down by camp coffee, Henry had taken Harold to the area of the claim that they would work on for the next couple of weeks. Harold was very glad that he still had his rubber boots from the Chilkoot trip. Many men had cast theirs away as useless when they got to the upper elevations covered in ice and snow.

During the winter, whoever had owned the site had dug yards of thawed gravel several feet down a shaft and raised buckets of it above ground with the windlass, now silent. The resulting piles of gravel had to be carried by the bucket or wheelbarrow to the sluicing area, where it could be carefully washed away, leaving the heavier precious gold dust behind in every nook and cranny of the rocker and sluice boxes.

Henry showed Harold how to brush the gravel up the sluice boxes against the force of the creek water that was periodically allowed to flow downhill, controlled by dams at the top of the bench. As long as the creeks had water, the sluicing was conducted in stages.

The next few days, while Henry did most of the "sweeping," Harold had to do the heavy shoveling.

Loading the wheelbarrow and buckets was backbreaking work. It wasn't a small irony to Harold that this stage of mining was called "cleanup." This innocent-sounding and certainly misleading term hardly did it justice.

Harold had to stop. He leaned on his shovel, his chest heaving.

"Why don't we have other hands?" he panted. "This is a job for several men."

Henry shrugged.

"Do you want to split the profits?" he asked knowingly. "I'm not in a position to employ a load of help. But if you want to split your take with someone…" He shrugged again and returned to his task.

Harold saw the reasoning, and immediately stopped complaining. He had so much to learn.

Gold of pure quality is almost twenty times heavier than water, and about eight times heavier than rock and gravel. So, if it is pushed along or shaken with water so that it collects in the deepest crevices of the sluice boxes, it can be separated from the lighter material.

This was the basis for all the methods of coaxing gold from rock and gravel. "Riffles" or narrow barriers were often placed across the bottom of the sluice boxes about two inches from each other to trap the gold. These were occasionally removed and washed. Any trapped gold was collected with the wash water.

When most of the gravel in the sluice box had been washed or brushed away, black sand was left. Among the grains of sand, a few granules of dull yellow could be seen. All of this was carefully scooped into gold pans.

At the end of the day's labor, Harold, standing in a ditch, was able to look at his first gold pan with gold dust and tiny nuggets resting on the bottom.

Pay dirt!

It wasn't bright. It wasn't glittering. It was just dull yellow, sort of brassy. But it stood out from the black sand, full of its own significance.

He now understood the electric charge caused by this sight that most miners felt coursing through their bodies when they caught sight of the "color" in their pans. It eclipsed any other feelings; fatigue and soreness receded—and probably so did some measure of reason.

"What do you fellows think you're doing?"

Henry and Harold tore their gaze from the pans. Three men in miner's garb stood above them in their rubber boots, next to the sluice boxes, hands on hips, grim looks on their faces. One carried a pickaxe, another a sledgehammer. The third had some papers in his hand.

Henry hesitated in surprise, gathered his wits, and answered in a strong voice.

"Mining my claim. Any objections?"

One of the men stepped forward, his fist clenched at his side. He nodded dourly.

"Yeah…seeing as it's not your claim. I do have quite the objections, you can be sure."

Henry and Harold looked at each other.

Harold's heart sank, and his mind went wild.

This looked like the beginning of a "claim jumping" he had often heard spoken of. Could he have joined in this venture without adequate information? Was he about to get skunked over a technicality? Intruding images of an angry wife assailed him.

He knew that the staking of a claim depended on many variables. First you had to get to the area you wanted to claim before anyone else. You had to be the first to bury your four-foot stake at one end of the claim, and another one at the other end. Then you had to race back to town to the recorder's office and pay your fee before anyone could beat you to it.

There were many places along the way where your best-laid plans could be foiled. Harold could only hope that the original claim had been obtained properly, and that everything had been done for the sale and purchase to have been valid.

His wife's objections replayed in his mind. He didn't even want to think of how he'd have to explain this failure to her.

"What are you talking about?" growled Henry. "I came into this fair and square. Old man McWilliams sold it to me."

To be on even ground with the three men, he climbed out of the ditch that he and Harold were standing in.

"You can check the Gold Commissioner's Office. I paid the ten-dollar fee for my Free Miner's Certificate. Everything's all signed proper like it's supposed to be."

The man with the papers waved them at Henry.

"Well, here's a map of this bench," he said, angrily. "Our claim is right in this spot." He waved his hand to indicate the claim, and then pointed to the map. "Take a gander yourself."

He shoved the map at Henry who took a hurried step back and put up a hand.

"Hold on a minute. I was just at the Commissioner's Office two days ago. Everything was Kosher. I don't know what information you have, but it can't be correct."

He crossed his arms and looked back at Harold, as if he expected support.

"That map doesn't prove anything."

The three men exchanged glances, as though sharing some private information.

Harold felt extremely uncomfortable, fighting a bit of nausea, and feeling a prickling at the back of his neck—a neck that had just been bathed in sweat. Now, it was cold sweat.

He shivered.

Climbing up to stand next to Henry was all he could do to show support. Having absolutely no knowledge of the intricacies of managing this particular type of real estate, he had no idea how to help in any other way.

He felt strangely powerless.

The three half-full gold pans rested in a corner of the cabin. Henry had tried to diffuse the situation by suggesting that everyone sit around the campfire to discuss the problem. Harold went along with the plan, hoping that any conflict could be resolved favorably. He really did not want to have to admit to failure.

Henry had made enough food so that each man could fill a tin plate with dinner. He figured discussions would go more smoothly on full stomachs.

After food and considerable drink, Henry's guests said they would sleep outside the cabin. They had a small shelter a few yards away.

Harold prepared to go to bed, trying to rid himself of a peculiar thickness in his throat. He finally figured out that when your heart is in your mouth, there's no easy way to force it back down where it belongs.

Something woke him; he wasn't sure what. The cabin was shadowy and stuffy.

Harold listened, resisting the urge to scratch his chin.

He could hear some shuffling, and a metallic sound, but he couldn't tell where it was exactly. Then, against the flat light of the small cabin window, he saw a silhouette.

"Henry!" he shouted, simultaneously disentangling himself from his bedroll. "Stop, thief!"

He dove for the dark figure, but only connected with a boot. Another one kicked him in the head. For one or two seconds he saw the blinding light of a few stars. Then the cabin door opened, and fresh air rushed in. He sensed more than saw a fast-moving shadow melt into the misty light of midnight-sun dawn.

"What the hell was that?" asked Henry, sitting up on the cot, his voice thick with sleep. "What were you shouting about?"

Harold was fumbling around with a candle, trying to find matches.

"I woke up, and I knew someone was in here. I couldn't tell who it was, but I'll bet our gold pans that it was one of our dinner guests."

A match flared and Harold lit a candle. He poured some of the melting wax on the table and stuck the bottom of the candle in it until the wax hardened enough around its base that it stood by itself.

Sitting back down on his bedroll, he rubbed his head where a bump was starting to form. The flickering of the candle made the shadows jump. He leaned over and pushed the door shut before the breeze snuffed out the candle.

I knew we should've fixed the lock on the door," sighed Henry. "You can't be too careful around people who have gold on their minds."

Then he suddenly tensed and looked over into the dark corner of the cabin.

"Good God. Are the pans still there?"

Scrambling out of the cot, he went to where they had stashed the three half-full pans after the dinner guests had left. Harold froze, his heart in his mouth, as he waited for Henry's verdict.

"We were so stupid not figure out some kind of lock…" Harold started.

"Christ. One of them is overturned. You must've stopped the miscreant just in time." He turned the pan over. "Now we have our work cut out…everything spilled."

Harold did not look forward to trying to painstakingly separate gold dust from the filth on the cabin floor. He almost chuckled at himself. It would be like mining all over again.

"Who came in here?" asked Henry, hurriedly putting on his clothes and boots. "Do you really think it was our dinner guests? He reached under the cot and pulled out his Colt.

"I'm going to go out there and look around."

Checking the cylinder, and adjusting the hammer to half cock, he continued.

"If it had been me awake instead of you…" He let his voice fade, but Harold got the message.

"Wait, Henry. Wait a minute before you go out there. Let's think about this."

He watched apprehensively as Henry tucked the revolver inside his belt. He thought of using a pun about not going off half-cocked, but didn't think it was the time for jokes, as relevant as it might have been.

"What's there to think about?" Henry retorted, shaking his head. "Someone broke and entered here. They have to be held accountable. Besides," he went on. "We don't want them to get the idea that they can waltz in here and try again."

Harold wasn't sure of all the legal implications, but if the door hadn't been locked, maybe it wasn't exactly what his partner maintained. Maybe it was just trespassing. Whatever it was, Harold did not want this to escalate out of control.

Besides, out here, legal or not—serious or not—it was all moot; there wasn't any law to speak of. The person at the wrong end of the barrel was always in error.

"Are you coming with me?" asked Henry as he pushed stuff out of the way to get to the door. "Two sets of eyes are better than one."

Harold was in a quandary. While it angered him that someone would invade their cabin and try to make off with their hard-earned gold, he didn't want to be a casualty of lawless justice, especially as the identity of the fugitive was a mystery at this point.

Cursing himself for the second time for having left his pistol back home with his wife, and stifling a yawn, he followed Henry out the door into the dusky early morning light.

-9-

MISSED OPPORTUNITIES

"You're mighty quiet, young lady," commented Father Riley as he sorted medicine in the disconcertingly bare cabinet.

"You haven't lectured me on anything I might've done wrong. And it's almost noon. I'd say that's a record."

Sarah smiled perfunctorily at his attempt to lighten the mood. Folding newly laundered towels, she was getting them ready for afternoon rounds.

When she didn't say anything, the Father paused before continuing.

"Is that husband of yours home yet? I haven't seen you for a few days, so I thought maybe you were spending time with him."

Sarah bit her lips together and shook her head.

"No. And I don't really expect him for a while longer."

She shrugged dourly. "Who knows?"

Father Riley checked a few more bottles.

"Well, in his absence, I certainly hope you would feel free to consult with me if you needed anything. I'm not so old and feeble that I couldn't help…"

Sarah reached out and patted his arm, trying to smile in reassurance. For the hundredth time, she noted his appallingly threadbare sleeve.

"Don't worry, Father. If anything needs doing, I'll certainly enlist your help."

She shook her head.

"But this…it's nothing you can help with or be concerned about. I'm just preoccupied, that's all."

She picked up a pile of towels and loaded them on a gurney they used to carry things from room to room when it wasn't needed for wheeling bodies.

Not at all placated, Father Riley frowned and picked up another pile of towels. His counseling instincts were needling him. He knew unusual behavior when he saw it, no matter how subtle. His favorite helper was certainly exhibiting just that.

There were two newly emptied beds in the disease room. A couple of the men had died of a combination of malnutrition, scurvy, and respiratory infections.

The gravediggers had been by to make their grim collection.

Sarah busied herself stripping away the soiled sheets and placing them on the bottom shelf of the gurney. They had run out of clean sheets, so she'd have to wait until they were brought in from the laundry.

She was looking forward to seeing Nettie, the one who would probably be bringing them. She was glad to know that things were a lot easier for her young friend now that Sarah had had the conversation with Madame Renée. The latter was quite preoccupied with her order for the new bar counter she was expecting from Harold's workshop. She wasn't about to jeopardize that. So, following Sarah's forceful suggestion, she had reluctantly let up on Nettie, whose hands were healing quite well thanks to the lighter workload and changes in job description.

When she got to the injury room, Sarah had to stop a moment to collect herself.

Jake Morton's foot had been amputated.

There had been too much damage and infection for the doctors to put it back together in any serviceable way.

The nurses had told Sarah that since the operation, which he had barely survived, Jake had been completely silent. He had not even looked at his lower leg. Father Riley had tried to counsel him but hadn't been able to elicit any reaction from the patient.

"We need to get him out of his funk," said Father Riley, when Sarah arrived to help. "It's not unheard of for patients to die from the psychological trauma instead of the physical."

Sarah nodded. She had become quite aware personally of the impact the former could have on a person.

Lying with his eyes closed, Jake looked as though he was sleeping. Every once in a while, a moan escaped his lips. A sheet was stretched out over his bad leg, the fabric kept off his stump by a crudely fashioned cage.

Thanks to Father Riley's judicious use of donations, and clever methods to obtain medications, there was some ether, morphine, and carbolic acid in his cabinet to help with patient care.

They had actually only severed Jake's foot just short of the heel bone and saved a flap of skin to pull over the end of the stump. With some luck in the healing process, Jake would be able to walk on his stump without too much problem. Eventually, he might even be able to function without a crutch or cane. He'd probably learn to minimize his limp.

But right now, Sarah surmised, he was probably confused, not knowing exactly what he had lost, or how he could cope. And it was up to the staff to make sure proper healing took place. Sarah made up her mind that it would be her role to insure that cleanliness was paramount in the healing process.

She adjusted the sheet.

"I thought they were going to take my foot," came a groggy voice. "What stopped them?"

Sarah's puzzlement was obvious.

"But, they did take your foot," she blurted. "Didn't they tell you?"

Jake looked just as puzzled. He shook his head in disbelief.

"But...I can feel my toes. It hurts. I can't wiggle them though. Can you look?"

Embarrassed and mystified, Sarah picked up the cover in very gingerly fashion. Jake's foot was wrapped in thick bandages, so it was difficult to tell. But imagining what the bandage would look like if an entire foot was wrapped, she could tell that most of it was, indeed, missing.

Flipping the cover back over, Sarah looked at Jake.

"Jake, I'm so sorry, but most of your foot is...uh... gone. It was damaged beyond repair. The doctors did the best they could to save as much of it as possible."

Jake's expression clouded.

"But, damn it...it can't be. I can feel my foot. I can. Maybe you should check again."

Sarah shook her head.

"Jake, I don't need to. I'm sure. Try to rest. I'll go get Father Riley. Maybe he can help you with this...this feeling."

"It's a common sensation in these cases," said the Father in answer to Sarah's inquiry, as they stood in the hallway. "It's a phantom pain, caused by the damaged nerves. After about six months, it should disappear, or at least lessen to a great extent."

"Well, it must be convincing," answered Sarah. "Because...he's absolutely convinced his foot is still attached to his leg."

"That's why we have to get him to acknowledge what happened. He must look at it, and we must discuss it. Then his psychological healing can begin. Right now, he's still in denial."

When Nettie showed up with her laundry, Sarah quickly told her about Jake's situation. She had noticed that Nettie had taken particular care of him when she helped on the wards.

"Somehow, we have to help him face reality," said Sarah. "If he doesn't come to grips with it, he may never really recover."

"*Eh bien,* I will try to talk to him," said Nettie, putting a hand on Sarah's arm. "I am accustomed to sick people. I help my mother for a long time when she dying. *S'il te plaît...* please, let me try to comfort him."

Sarah nodded.

"*Très bien, ma chérie.* Go ahead. I trust you. *J'ai confiance en toi.* I'm sure the Father will appreciate your help."

Nettie smiled reassuringly, put down the bundle of sheets she was carrying, and hurried off to the sick bed.

"Sarah. Can you please take some water to the other room?"

Father Riley, juggling several objects instead of using the rolling stand, pointed to the sick room with his chin.

"A couple of the men in the last two beds are thirsty."

Glad that the request didn't involve bedpans, Sarah hurried to the water stand and filled two cups. She was giving them to the patients when one of the nurses called out to her from the doorway.

"Sarah. They need you in admitting." Sarah was accustomed to that request as she usually did any paperwork that was required.

"I'll be right there," she said, collecting the cups. "What is it?"

"I guess someone is wounded. Stabbing, I think."

"Anyone we know?

"Not sure. I think I heard him say his name was Bosley. Or Beasley. Yeah, that's it: Harold Beasley."

Sarah dropped one of the cups. Fortunately, as the patient she had given it to had been very thirsty, it was empty. Automatically picking it up and putting it back by the pitcher, she rushed out the door.

Later, in the surgery room, they had him on his stomach.

"The blade ricocheted off his scapula, went in just below it, and barely missed his lung," Father Riley told Sarah, as he patted her arm.

"The Doctor said he was extremely lucky. Nothing vital was damaged. Not even major blood vessels. Just tissue. And maybe a bruised rib."

Sarah was quiet as she processed the information. She had tried to question Harold, but he was too groggy from the morphine to make any kind of coordinated answer. She'd have to wait until the doctor sewed him up, and he came out of recovery.

Then she had a thought. She went to look for the volunteer who had alerted her.

"Who brought him in?" she asked. "Did anyone say what happened?"

It took talking to a few people before Sarah was able to figure out that Henry had brought Harold in. He had been wounded too, but much less seriously. One of the nurses was finishing up bandaging his arm.

After re-introducing herself in case Henry had forgotten briefly meeting her when he and Harold had first set out for the mines, she tried to be patient with her burning questions.

When they had him more comfortable in the only easy chair—soiled and threadbare as it was—in what had originally been a small lounge area, Sarah felt she could get her information without seeming pushy.

"So, Henry, what happened out there? How the hell did you guys end up like this?"

There was nowhere to sit, so she just stood in front of him, looking down at the top of his head. He leaned back to look up at her.

Sighing, he shook his head.

"This is not at all what I was planning on," he started, a bit hoarse. "How can everything go to hell so fast?"

He looked around. "Can I have some water? I'm parched. The dust is…"

He faded and closed his eyes.

Sarah had already slipped out to get him some in a pitcher. She poured and placed a cup carefully in his shaky grasp, ready to catch it if he couldn't hold it.

He drank two cups full.

He sighed again, leaned back in his chair, and let his head rest on the back. He closed his eyes and his features sagged. Sarah was afraid he'd fall asleep without answering her questions.

She cleared her throat.

"Don't worry," Henry said with his eyes still closed. "I'm awake. I'm just trying to remember things chronologically. Everything happened so fast, I think I'm losing perspective."

"It's all right, Henry. Take your time. I'm not going anywhere…"

At least, not unless some other crisis descends upon us.

Henry started his account with the visit from the three men. He described the dinner, and then the interruption during the early morning hours.

"So, we decided to go out and look for whoever had tried to take the gold pans. Harold didn't get a good look at the intruder, so we were operating blind. I mean, we had our suspicions of course. Our dinner guests had seen the gold."

Sarah nodded silently as she put the water pitcher on the floor.

She had been prepared to hear some outlandish scheme from the two men, but, so far, everything was logical. In their place, she probably would have reacted similarly.

"So, you went outside the cabin? Could you see anything?"

"Yep. I grabbed my Colt, in case things got wild. It was pretty gloomy, but we could see enough to walk around. Harold was right behind me."

Henry indicated he wanted more water. Sarah waited patiently for him to finish.

"Anyway, we hadn't gone more than a few yards when I heard Harold shout. I turned around and saw him rolling on the ground with someone on his back. Then someone clipped me in the legs and I went down."

He shook his head and put out his hands.

"They had come out of nowhere. The revolver got knocked out of my hand. I could hear Harold grunting. Then he yelled. I tried to scramble to get a hold of the gun all the while wrestling out of the grasp the guy who still had me by the legs."

He looked sheepishly at Sarah.

"Luckily, in my hurry to get out of the cabin, I hadn't buttoned my trousers completely, so during the scuffle they started coming off, and the guy lost his grip. I reached the gun and kicked the guy. I warned them both that I had the Colt."

Henry took a breath, getting riled as he recalled the event.

"Then Harold yelled he'd been stabbed, and for me to shoot. I hesitated because I didn't want to hit him accidentally. Anyway, it must've scared the guy because he immediately got off of Harold and ran. The other guy did the same."

"But," said Sarah, remembering something. "Didn't you say there were three guys in the original group?"

"Oh yes," nodded Henry. "And it took me a minute, but then I got a horrifying thought. Where was the other guy?"

"Oh, no," murmured Sarah. "They were distracting you…"

"Yep, exactly."

He held out his cup for more water.

"I left Harold moaning where he had fallen and rushed back to the cabin. I got there just in time to see a shadow come out. I tried to stop him and got a slash on the arm for my trouble."

He held out his bandaged arm as if Sarah needed proof.

"But apparently, he hadn't had time to get anything. As we saw later, the gold was still in the corner of the cabin. I'm glad we had moved it after the men had eaten with us."

He looked at Sarah, his lips in a cynical twist.

"You can never be too careful about anyone. It took him that crucial extra time because he wasn't sure where to look."

"Thank God for that," breathed Sarah. "But, what about Harold?"

Henry nodded.

"Well, by the time I got back out to him, others had heard the ruckus and had found him. He had lost quite a bit of blood. I was pretty sure he needed more medical attention than we could take care of out there."

Sarah nodded.

"Yes, that wound is quite deep. There was significant blood loss. You did the right thing getting him back here in a hurry."

"Well, there was a medical student out there, on one of the other claims. He did the best he could to stanch the blood flow with what I must regretfully say were some questionably clean rags. He said that Harold definitely needed expert care, or he might lose function of his shoulder or arm."

There was silence for a moment.

"So…that was the end of the great mining experience?" Sarah smiled grimly at Henry.

"I hope you put the contents of the gold pans somewhere safe."

"Yes, and I'll be taking it to the assay office. Harold will get his fair share."

Henry pursed his lips and raised his eyebrows. His tone turned apologetic.

"I hope it makes his bad experience a bit more acceptable. You can't know how sorry I am about how this turned out."

Dejectedly, he slowly shook his head.

"I really hope Harold didn't miss some business opportunities for the sake of going on what ended up being a kind of wild goose chase, instead of being home tending to them."

Sarah's face said, "Don't worry."

She patted Henry's good arm.

Then her mouth said, "I'm pretty sure he can pick up where he left off as soon as he gets better. I don't think he missed out on any business."

Of course, when she reviewed the negative events of past few days without her husband, her mind said that it wasn't just potential business opportunities that she was sorry he had missed.

Not by any stretch of her besieged imagination.

She picked up the pitcher and went back to work.

-10-

COMFORTS OF HOME

The next few days were atypical for Sarah.

She still worked at the clinic, but while Harold was still there under the doctor's care, her job centered around him, to the detriment of the other patients. She was particularly careful that Harold should not suffer shock and infection, two of the prime killers in hospital environments.

Every day, she carefully washed his wounds and applied carbolic acid. She put on fresh bandages, sometimes ripping up old clothing she brought from home when bandaging supplies ran low at the clinic. She made sure he was well hydrated and fed, despite his poor appetite.

Thanks to her capable ministrations, Harold was discharged after a few days, much earlier than anyone would've thought possible.

In the cabin, she set him up on the couch where he could spend the daytime hours.

While he was still too woozy and lacking energy, she read to him, or just kept up a one-sided conversation to keep his mind stimulated. She still put in a few hours per day at the clinic and rushed through any shopping she needed to do downtown, so that she could get home quickly.

Faster than Sarah had thought possible, as his wounds healed, the old Harold reappeared.

"Nurse! I need help. My leg itches. And I need another pillow... and some water."

"Really? Well, right now your cook is making dinner. Your nurse is on holiday. Your maid quit. Sorry, but you'll have to scratch your own leg."

She smirked as she heard him grumbling good-naturedly. That night he even felt good enough to make love to her. They had to be careful of his hurt arm, but he hardly let it have an impact. It had been too long.

Although she was immensely grateful that Harold was feeling more like himself, Sarah often rolled her eyes thinking that he had been easier to deal with when he was sicker. It was time to accelerate his recovery, before he became a real pain hanging around the cabin with nothing much to do. She was getting tired of chopping wood, hauling water, and checking progress at the workshop, on top of all her other duties, especially catering to her demanding patient. Even Father Riley had noted that she seemed inordinately tired one day.

"Sarah, my child. Please go home. You make me tired just watching you. You've been burning the candle at both ends, and you need a few days off."

His face was stern as he raised an index finger.

"I will forcibly remove you if you show up here tomorrow. Get that husband of yours back on his feet before he forgets he's not royalty."

He practically pushed her out the door.

Thinking that comments about her looking tired were rich coming from Father Riley, Sarah was nevertheless grateful to be released from her clinic duties for a while. Fatigue often overtook her to the point that she felt dizzy at times. In the late afternoon, when her stomach was at its emptiest, she even felt nauseated. Just having home duties for a while sounded good.

Feeling uncommonly positive, she hurried home to begin her forced holiday.

Even before she opened the front door, she could detect the aroma of dinner. She ignored the slightly sick feeling it caused. Harold was stirring a pot at the stove, his arm out of its sling. There were things on the table covered by towels. He was actually humming as he worked.

"Am I at the right house?" Sarah smiled her surprise and shook her head in wonderment. "I wasn't sure if you remembered the right end of a ladle to use."

Harold bowed awkwardly.

"Yes, milady, your servant is hard at work. You may sit and contemplate your new situation." He picked up a half-full wine glass from the table. "I have here a glass of super elixir for thee."

Amused at her husband's awkward attempt at some approximation of Shakespearean English, Sarah had to smile.

"Oh my God. You went into our special supply. And our good glassware."

Teasing with a reproachful expression, Sarah took the glass by its slender stem, and sat down among the pillows on the couch. She took a long luxurious sip of wine and sighed deeply. Holding the glass up to the light, she enjoyed the look of the jeweled liquid through the cut glass.

This seemed like the perfect moment to indulge; she thought she might melt into the couch. Leaning back, she closed her eyes and let her mind wander.

Pushing the cook pot to the edge of the stove away from the highest heat, Harold came over to her and removed her shoes. He swung her around, putting her legs up on the couch, and massaged her feet. For a fleeting moment Sarah worried about his arm, but she soon lost herself in the feeling of wellbeing he was generating.

A couple of sips later, her stockings were off, and Harold was inching up her legs with his caresses. With a short-lived thought about dinner burning, Sarah gave in to the sensuous release she felt thanks to Harold's attentions.

It had been an eternity.

She couldn't remember the last time she had enjoyed any physical feeling. The only thing that came close was the sensation of blissfully sinking into sleep after a hard day.

But this was better.

"Oh. I almost forgot."

Harold was kneeling alongside the couch, his lips against Sarah's cheek. "I have an even better surprise," he whispered mysteriously. "And you need to use it quickly before it gets...oh...never mind, you'll see. Close your eyes."

He started to pick her up, but yelped when the strain was too much for his sore shoulder and ribs.

"I guess you'll have to get there under your own steam..." he said, dejected. "It appears your servant needeth a little more recuperating time...Takest my hand, and keepest your eyes closed."

Sarah only sneaked her eyes open a few times to look through her lashes to make sure she didn't collide with anything.

"Well, you're so gallant, I guess I shall go wherever thou leadest," she answered with a laugh.

They ended up on the back deck, bathed in sunlight.

"Thou mayest open thy beautiful eyes," sang out Harold. "Feast them upon your...I mean...thy surprise."

Sarah found herself staring at their tin tub, filled with steaming water. Floating on the water were several different wildflowers, some upside down with small bits of stems and roots still attached.

She smiled at Harold and pulled him down to plant a kiss on him.

"Yes, master servant, this is definitely a surprise. I love it. Maybe you should get hurt and recuperate more often."

She was quite aware that it must've taken a huge effort on Harold's part to haul and heat all that water. And she got the distinct feeling that Father Riley had been in on the whole thing, sending her home at just the right time.

With some quick moves she undressed and slipped into the tub. Harold wadded a towel to make a comfortable spot for her neck.

"I shall leave you to your enjoyment," he said, trying a bow again. "There's some business inside that needs tending. Summon me when it is thy desire to…uh…" he shrugged and shook his head. "I don't know how to say 'get out' in a fancy way."

"No need," chuckled Sarah. "I understand, and I shall, indeed, summon you at that time…"

Then she leaned her head back on the towel and closed her eyes. She couldn't help smiling both with mirth and satisfaction.

Harold was definitely back to his old self.

As an able servant, Harold didn't quite come up to snuff, however. He became involved in his cooking efforts and forgot about his wife in her tub. Not wanting to distract him from his task, she dried herself off on the sun-drenched deck, and put on her nightgown and robe that were hanging on the inside of the back door. Still toweling her hair, she walked into the kitchen.

"Oops, I forgot," said Harold apologetically, his face a bit pink and sweaty, and his dark hair curling around his face due to the extra moisture. "I hope you can chalk it up my being involved in some genius moves on this stove..."

"Oh, I'm sure I'll think it was quite worth dressing myself. It certainly smells like I will." She went to the table to retrieve her mostly empty wineglass and took a long swallow.

"Anything I can do?"

Harold thought for a moment, a big dollop of something smeared on his chin. "I guess we'll be needing plates...and forks. I haven't quite gotten to that part..." He looked charmingly frustrated. Sarah felt like he might've been close to being overwhelmed. This was a great deal of activity for a recent invalid, not to mention someone who wasn't very familiar with the mysteries of the kitchen. She felt a bit sorry for him.

Against the odds however, dinner was quite the success. Sarah would've been delighted with anything she hadn't had to prepare herself, but she had to admit that Harold had outdone himself. Even though her stomach felt unsteady, she made a good show of enjoying everything.

"Did you really make all this?" she sighed, stabbing the last strawberry on her dessert plate. "I don't remember even having any of this in our pantry: mushrooms, real beef, asparagus...not to mention the strawberries and cream. And I'm pretty sure most of the shops don't have these items."

Harold's smile denoted some embarrassment, and his well-shaped brows disappeared behind the dark locks that had fallen forward due to his efforts.

"Besides," she went on. "You haven't had the time or the ability to do any shopping, lately. What has been going on that you're not telling me?"

"Uh…well…you're right." Harold pushed his hair from his forehead. "Most of the dishes are thanks to your friend, Nettie. She was able to get the hotel cook to donate to the cause. I just had to reheat most of it."

"Well, you really planned this, didn't you? Our good dishes and linen, having co-conspirators and everything." She frowned. "Is it a special occasion that I'm not aware of? If I remember correctly, our anniversary was a couple of weeks ago."

Harold got up, grabbed her hand and her glass, and led her to the couch.

They sat together, and Harold held her tight.

"It's actually a lot of occasions," he said, kissing her forehead. "The first one is that I just wanted to do something nice for you after all the work you've had to do, what with taking care of me in addition to all the other stuff."

He nodded in anticipation of her unspoken question.

"Yes, Nettie and Father Riley both contributed to this effort. He and one of the orderlies helped me with the water hauling, and she did the food gathering. I couldn't have done it without them."

Sarah nodded, feeling very grateful for her friends, and loving Harold for all the effort this had cost him.

"All right, that's one. And that would be enough. I really love everything you did, Harold." She took his face in her hands and kissed him.

"Well," he continued, after enthusiastically kissing her back. "It's also kind of another anniversary for us, loosely anyway. It's almost two years since we met. Remember that awful honky-tonk tent saloon in Skagway?"

"Oh yeah, the one with that scruffy guy with rotten teeth that accosted us? They threw him out because he couldn't pay, because they wanted to make room for paying customers. I can even recall the smell…" She wrinkled her nose at the memory.

"Yep, well, be that as it may—and of course, I can't remember the exact date—that was the first time I really laid eyes on you." He touched her cheek. "I was astounded by your beauty. In fact, I was speechless, and later, absolutely desolate that you were already taken. Little did I know. "

Sarah smiled and snuggled close.

They were quiet for a few moments, Harold rubbing Sarah's back with his good arm, his lips on her forehead. From the west window, the late summer sun sent a warm golden glow throughout the room.

"And the last thing," he added, slowly coming out of his reverie, "is that we did get a little extra income from my ill-fated adventure."

He leaned over, reached under the couch, and withdrew a little pouch. As he shook it, Sarah could hear the unmistakable clinking of coins.

"It's not a huge amount," he said, shaking his head almost dolefully. "But for a couple days' work, it's nothing to sneeze at."

Sarah gently took the pouch from his long fingers and put it on the floor without looking inside.

"I don't care," she whispered. "I'm just glad you're home."

Putting all contrary thoughts aside, she began to unbutton his shirt.

It was full daylight when Sarah stretched luxuriously, knowing she didn't have to report to work today. Next to her, the bed was empty. She could hear Harold fussing in the kitchen.

Last night had been the most comforting and gratifying time she'd had in months. After the turbulent and gut-wrenching episodes at the hospital, exhausting chores and personal responsibilities she had been obliged to fulfill, and her recent violent confrontation with her past, she had needed last night's interlude for her very sanity. She'd almost forgotten the power of the emotional transport of romantic pursuits. Harold had been so tender and caring. His whispered devotion and appreciation had warmed her very core. His touch and attentions had enabled her to recapture the magic and joy of their first times together.

Blushing, she hoped it wasn't asking too much to look forward to a few more days of the same, grateful that blissful oblivion had replaced dark concerns. Unfortunately, the latter still lurked near enough to the surface for her not to be completely free of them.

And the nerves must be affecting her stomach.

She shook off the thoughts, and swung her feet to the floor, sliding into her slippers, and reaching for her robe that had dropped off the bed.

A shadow fell across the floor.

"Sarah. What was this doing above the kitchen cabinet?"

Harold stood among the boxes that formed a temporary division between the bedroom and the living area, backlit by the morning sun.

In his hand was the Colt he had left with her.

On his face was a puzzled expression.

"I was putting one of the serving dishes out of the way up high, when I felt it clunk against this."

He frowned.

"I thought we had discussed where to keep it and decided to put it in the kitchen drawer. I know for a fact that that's where I left it."

Sarah's erstwhile feelings of wellbeing sank like a weighty stone in a dark pool of deep water.

She had so hoped that she could wish away the evil episode that the revolver now represented. In order to save Harold from heartache, she had just about successfully sworn herself to secrecy.

But she had been so consumed by her daily preoccupations that the need for putting the Colt back in its proper place had completely slipped her conscious thoughts.

If ever there was an illustration of the saying "Out of sight, out of mind," this had been an unfortunate, but perfect example of it.

-11-

WHITE LIES

Try as she might, Sarah found it impossible to come up with a plausible explanation that she calculated would make sense to her husband.

Cleaning out the kitchen drawer, or even cleaning the weapon itself—an unlikely pursuit for her—could not explain the gun's new location, completely out of her reach.

She decided to stick as close as possible to the truth, without revealing the outcome. She knew that Harold would come apart if he ever found out that his former partner had violated his wife. It would be bad enough to suggest there had merely been a threat involved. That alone would be quite enough to set him off. She was terrified of the consequences if she laid bare the whole story.

She told herself repeatedly that sometimes telling a lie was kinder than telling the truth, especially if it prevented a very harmful sequence of events. As sick as it made her feel to cross the line of not being forthright with her husband—her fear of his reaction to the truth, and the risk of destroying the harmony of her marriage, was pushing her over that boundary.

Shakily rising from the bed, Sarah pulled her robe around herself, and nudged Harold out into the kitchen.

"All right, Harold. Let me get some coffee, and I'll explain.

Her mind working furiously, and her stomach clenching again and again, she took some time carefully pouring coffee and adding some milk so as not to slosh anything.

"Let's sit down."

She went to the table and pulled out one of the chairs, indicating that Harold should take the other one, hoping all the while that he didn't notice her hands shaking. Looking intently at her, the electric blue of his eyes glinting in the sun's rays from the window, he sat in the other chair, and put the Colt in the middle of the tabletop.

Pushing it aside, she reached for his hand.

"I'm going to have to ask you to be patient," she started, gripping his hand and looking into his eyes. "This is not going to be easy to hear, but I really hope you can just…just take it calmly. I've come to terms with this…I hope you'll see that it's best that way."

Harold was frowning, his mouth in an anxious twist. He looked into his wife's emerald eyes, his brow deeply furrowed, his expression confused.

"What the hell, Sarah? What happened, and why the hell haven't you said anything? I've been back weeks…Jesus Christ."

He shook his head in bewilderment.

Sarah patted his hand and held it tight.

"I know…I know," she sighed. "I didn't want to add to your problems. I…was going to tell you when I figured you were completely better…and could think clearly."

He exhaled forcefully.

"Well, I'm better as I'm going to be. I am also a big boy and can take care of myself. You don't need to protect me…"

He whipped his hand away from hers and made a fist.

"And don't worry about me thinking clearly. I'm pretty sure my mind, at least, is completely intact."

Running the fingers of one hand through his glossy dark hair, he glowered at his wife in frustration.

Feeling desperate, and still trying to figure out how to shape her account of the "facts," she bit her lips together.

"Yes, yes," she nodded afraid things were spinning out of control. "Of course it is. I know that. I just wasn't sure what your emotional state was…you know… after getting hurt."

Sarah took a long sip of coffee, avoiding her husband's eyes.

When he didn't say anything, she took a breath and took the plunge. There was no avoiding it.

"So… one night, after work, I came home pretty late. I was about to open the front door when Gunther appeared…"

"Gunther? Good Lord. Haven't seen hide nor hair of him for a while… I wasn't even sure if he was still in town…"

Sarah nodded.

"Yes, that's what I thought too. Anyway, he pretty much forced his way in. He was filthy drunk. And mad about something. Everything. And, unfortunately, he had seen you head out of town, so he knew I was…on my own."

Harold hit the table with his fist.

"Damn it. Go on. What happened then?"

"Well, he wanted…um…food, and I thought maybe he would do better if he had something in his stomach to help absorb whatever he had been imbibing downtown."

Sarah took another sip of coffee, pushing an errant curl away from her face.

"So, against my better judgment, I heated up what I was planning to have for supper, and I gave him some."

She shook her head.

"Instead of being grateful, he mouthed off about us—you and me—getting married, and how it was supposed to be him instead of you."

"Yeah, I was pretty sure he was always upset about that," muttered Harold. "He thought he had first rights. I've always been of two minds about that."

"Same here," agreed Sarah. "I…I sort of felt sorry for him, actually…" She shook her head. "Anyway, he became pretty belligerent, and I started to get worried."

"So that's when you went for the Colt?"

She shook her head.

"Not right away, but he started talking about how I should celebrate old times with him…that I had betrayed him…that I owed him. On and on. It got more and more bitter. Soon he was so spitting mad, it scared me. I guess that's when I became frightened enough to go to the drawer."

"All right, so you got the revolver. But how did it end up way up there?" He pointed to above the cabinet. "*You* certainly didn't put it there…"

"I'm embarrassed to say that, even pointing the gun at him, I wasn't threatening enough. He just came over to me, and kept getting closer with an odd look on his face—I couldn't pull the trigger…"

"I was afraid that might happen," interrupted Harold shaking his head and tensing his mouth in irritation. "I was almost certain you couldn't bring yourself to shoot anyone…"

Sarah vigorously shook her head.

"No, no. I really couldn't pull the trigger…wasn't able to…physically."

She bit her lips in shame.

"I forgot to cock the thing. In the few seconds it took for both of us to realize that, and before I could think to do anything, he grabbed it away from me, and stuck it up there."

She pointed to the cabinet.

"So, I couldn't get to it."

Harold's asperity was obvious in the set of his jaw and his dark frown. She wondered how such a handsome face could look so ugly all of a sudden. She was sure he figured that after he had educated her on the workings of the pistol for just such a situation…he might as well not have wasted his time.

"Christ. Then what?"

This was the part Sarah had to engineer just right. Life as they knew it depended on the effect of her next words.

"Well, I told him that whatever he thought or did, things were not going to change by force. If he wanted to remain friends, he needed to get out and sober up. I told him I'd have a good discussion with him if he was reasonable about everything."

She pursed her lips in acknowledgement.

"I knew I shouldn't encourage him, but I just wanted so badly for him to get out of the cabin."

She shook her bowed head and her curls fell forward across her face. She pushed them back.

"In his present state, it was the only way I knew that he might accept things at that moment. I figured that if, in his drunken stupor, he thought there was the most remote chance that I'd change my mind about him, he might be more reasonable."

"So. Did he fall for it?" Harold looked a bit surprised. "That tactic seems rather thin."

Sarah shrugged.

"Who knows how the inebriated mind works, but I did…do know him pretty well. I was pretty sure he'd do anything to further his cause. Anyway, he calmed down somewhat, and I was able to persuade him to leave, and go sleep it off somewhere…before coming back to talk it over."

Harold was silent. Then, he scratched his chin, as he usually did when he pondered something. It was a good sign. Sarah dared to hope that she had reached him.

Encouraged, she pressed on.

"And, thank God, he never did come back. I guess I can give him credit for thinking the better of it once he got sober."

"Well, I guess you were very lucky it went your way," Harold said, shaking his head in amazement, that quickly changed to anger. "What an unspeakable bastard. Can't believe we ever partnered with him."

He got up to put the Colt back in the farthest reaches of the drawer, and slammed it shut.

Looking back at his wife, he raised a finger.

"And, if he does stick his nose anywhere near you, he's going to get a rude awakening. As it is, I think I'll try to find him, and give him an adjustment. At the very least he owes you an apology."

Sarah secretly prayed that Gunther had known better than to stick around. There was no apologizing for what he had done to her, and she was pretty sure he realized that. She wondered how he'd feel if he knew that thanks to her, he had dodged a bullet in its most literal sense.

Harold was staring out the window, the fingers of his good hand drumming on the counter. Sarah could see his jaw working. She was afraid of his thoughts.

"How about a little breakfast?" she asked timidly, hoping to distract him, and bring down the heat of the charged atmosphere.

Breakfast would normalize things.

"I can't come close to what you did for dinner, but I can whip something up to help calm the hunger pangs. How about hotcakes and bacon?"

Though obviously still preoccupied, Harold ate his breakfast with guarded enthusiasm. He had helped with it in a mechanical way, barely uttering a word. Sarah knew he'd have to work this out on his own, so she didn't interrupt his thoughts.

"I'm going to stack some of that firewood out back," he announced after the dishes had been put away. "I'm pretty sure I'll be able to start splitting some pretty soon. That'll be one less job for you."

Although Sarah felt that his arm and shoulder could use some more time to recuperate, she didn't say anything. She knew that not being able to function at optimum capacity was hard on the male ego.

For all concerned, better his shoulder should suffer than his psyche.

NUCHALAWOYET, ALASKA
FALL 1899

-12-

SECOND CHOICE

There was a definite snap to the air; fall was fast approaching. The leaves of the birches and aspen were turning at an alarming rate, and, perhaps as a perverse reminder of what was to come, falling like golden snowflakes in a rush to cover the ground.

In the early morning, thin sheets of ice gave a stained-glass appearance to the water puddles. As a kid, Sarah would've gleefully shattered them, and splashed her way through. Now, she preferred to keep her feet dry.

All about town, a new rush was on.

Gold in Nome!

All you had to do was bend down and sift through the beach sand where you didn't even have to have a claim! You'd be a fool not to take the plunge. It was easier than fishing.

It had taken almost a year for the news of the discovery on Anvil Creek, near Nome, in late 1898 to make its way to Dawson. But, once arrived, it took only a few weeks for the population of the latter to divert its focus, pack up, and sail down the Yukon for those "easy pickins on the beaches." Those who had not learned their lesson on the Klondike saw it as a reprieve: another opportunity to make it big if you hadn't already.

And most hadn't already.

Déjà vu in spades.

Amid the chaos of moving a significant proportion of Dawson's population—sometimes eight thousand in a day—Sarah and Harold had to adjust their business. People needed certain things for their trip down the Yukon and were already planning on what tools they'd need once they arrived on the beaches of Nome. Having adapted to the needs of customers, Harold and his assistants were busily trying to fill orders from wheelbarrows to shovels and saws instead of tables and chairs. They had expanded their woodworking shop to include some metal works as well.

 Sarah's sewing machine was constantly humming to keep up with the orders for new clothing, tents, and duffels.

At night, both of them fell into bed in total exhaustion, finding it harder and harder to rise the next day. As encouraging as it was to see their savings pile up, they felt they might have to cut down on the orders if they were to survive in good enough health to enjoy them in the future.

Harold's wounds had healed long ago, but he still felt occasional twinges in his shoulder and side.

Sarah's late day nausea had taken on a new significance.

Father Riley had sensed a change in his favorite volunteer who had had to cut down her hospital hours in favor of the sewing demands.

"Sarah, my child. It would greatly please me if you would take me into your confidence. I do not want to insert myself where I don't belong, but I'm concerned for your health. Is there something you should be telling me?"

It was no use hiding anything from him. He had years of experience trying to understand people and counseling them. Sarah often thought he had extraordinary mind-reading ability as well. But she could read him too and was going to make him earn the satisfaction of getting an answer.

"What makes you say that, Father?" she asked innocently. "Are you dissatisfied with my performance? I'm so sorry if that's the case…"

She smiled disarmingly, as she teased.

The father smirked good-naturedly.

"You know perfectly well that I'm eternally grateful for all you do. And…do so well," he answered, nodding.

"Don't try to shame me out of this. I'm referring to the fact that you seem to be taking your meals in a, shall I say…different way. And you seem to shy away from certain conditions here…and you like to take a little rest in the late afternoon."

He smiled and put a hand on her arm.

"In addition to all that, and I'm sorry not to be scientific about it—you have a different look about you…"

He stopped mid-sentence and took a breath.

"Are you…do you…" he cleared his throat. "Could it be that you are with child?"

It came out in a rush, and he looked surprised that he had said it.

Sarah had to chuckle.

"And how long have you been wondering this?" she asked, shaking her head at him and smiling broadly. "I can't believe that you were afraid to ask me. Did you think I would hit you over the head or something?"

Father Riley was definitely embarrassed. He just nodded mutely and shrugged. It was a rare occasion that he found no words.

Sarah hugged him.

"Good grief, Father. You know me better than that. And yes. You are correct. I am expecting a child." She raised her hands, palms up. "It has been known to happen to the best of us, you know."

Still at a loss for words, Father Riley beamed.

"And, no, as I know you're going to ask," continued Sarah. "I'm not sure when the big day will be, exactly. All I can say is that it'll be sometime next spring."

Still smiling like the Cheshire cat, Father Riley patted her hand, and moved on to the other room. Sarah knew he was already thinking about how he was going to change her job description to make allowances for her condition. And she was already thinking about how to counteract them.

Men were so clueless about pregnancy. She was sure some still thought of it as a weird disease. At the very least they figured it caused women to be more helpless, mentally challenged, and hysterical than ever, not to mentioned being severely handicapped in the decision-making process.

She'd have to do her best to correct all that.

"Are you sure you shouldn't lie on the couch and put your feet up?" asked Harold after work. "You've already put in a day at the hospital, made dinner, and now you want to sit there at that damned machine and sew all evening?"

Sarah rolled her eyes and shook her head.

"Well, do you want to take over? I've got two orders to fill by the day after tomorrow. How are you at seams? Darts? How about at following or adapting patterns?"

Harold looked dumbly at his wife, his eyes wide, his mouth in a helpless twist.

"That's what I thought," she said scornfully. "Just go do something you can manage and leave me be. And don't worry. I'll just work for a little while, and then I'll go right to bed."

At that moment, a thought occurred to her. She looked up at her husband with a sly smile.

"You could heat up some water so I can wash later. I feel like a good sponge bath…"

"Well, if I'm going to haul and heat water, I guess we could go all the way and have a real bath."

Sarah smiled.

"Yes, that would be even better. We could use one…"

"Do you think we could fit in it together like before? You're not quite that big yet…"

Sarah threw a large spool of thread at him. He ducked out the door, the spool bouncing harmlessly off the wall.

*　*　*

"Do you wish we were joining the exodus?" Sarah asked Harold one evening, referring to the massive clearing out of the population of Dawson. "Are we missing out?"

She was drawing the curtain across the small bedroom window in preparation for going to bed.

Harold was silent for a moment.

"Well, we joined the movement when we came here, and, like half the people, we didn't exactly participate in the actual mining aspect…my little adventure notwithstanding. So…no…I guess I really don't feel like we're missing out. It's much more important that you stay put."

Sarah knew that this was the ostensible reason for staying in Dawson instead of joining the race to Nome's beaches. And she couldn't help the guilt she had about being the biggest part of that reason.

"You know, getting to Nome would be so much easier than going up a frozen mountain. All we'd have to do is sit on a steamship…"

Harold shook his head.

"No, Sarah. It's still much too risky. You can't be assured that the trip down the Yukon will be uneventful. You never know who's on board with you. Christ!"

He shook his head vigorously.

"How many unsavory characters have we run across just in town here? We'd be a total captive-audience on a boat."

Again, he shook his head dramatically.

"No escape. It's like a prison on water."

He walked over to her as she sat on the bed. Plopping down next to her, he put a large hand on her belly.

"There's no way in the world I'm going to jeopardize our little nugget for the sake of some pie-in-the-sky potential riches."

With his other hand, he cupped Sarah's chin, and tenderly kissed her lips.

"Besides, I have to say, it's such a relief to live in a quiet town. So peaceful. I can hear myself think. If we went to Nome, it'd be chaos all over again. And what about care for you and the baby? We have no idea what would be available there amid all the craziness."

Sarah shrugged in ignorance.

"I guess, you're right. At least we have some health care here. I know of one doctor who said he's staying, at least till next spring. So is a midwife."

"And some people are building more permanent homes, so we'll have carpentry business for a while yet. Things just won't be as crazy as they have been."

He nodded and patted Sarah's knee.

"I don't know about you, but I will not mind the easier schedule at all."

Sarah sighed in agreement.

"I guess you're right. I'll have to wait for a letter from Nettie to know what we're missing. I hope to God she'll be all right. She wants to go stay with her uncle who's a minister of the church at St. Michael's, across the Norton Sound from Nome. I really miss her already."

She slid into bed next to Harold who wrapped her in his long arms.

"Well, I can't make up for her friendship," he acknowledged regretfully, kissing her forehead. "But you will have my undivided attention for the duration. I hope that will be enough for you."

Sarah snuggled up next to her husband, grateful for the assurance that his caresses and avowal of love provided.

If only she could be completely free from concerns that relentlessly clouded her brain. She was so frustratingly close to total happiness.

-13-

MA CHÈRE SARAH...

In a very long letter dated two weeks ago for the first few pages, and a few days more recently on the rest, Nettie had written in French, so it took a while for Sarah to make complete sense of everything. She had to go over many paragraphs several times to make sure she interpreted accurately what Nettie was trying to convey.

She was surprised to get a letter so quickly; a late steamboat had come east counting on open water for a few more weeks.

Propping her feet up on the couch, and resting the letter on her slightly expanding belly, she reread the whole thing, wishing that she had a dictionary.

"Ma Chère Sarah," she read. *"J'espère que tu vas bien..."*

The greeting was normal, but the account that followed caused Sarah a myriad of emotions.

From Nettie's writing skills and vocabulary, she realized that this young girl had had quite a thorough education. She was pleasantly surprised at Nettie's flowing and engaging narrative when using her first language.

The uneventful and lackadaisical float downriver that Sarah had pictured was apparently quite far from reality.

She thought back over the events of the last few weeks.

By the end of Dawson's second summer of craziness, the hotel business, like almost every other enterprise, had quieted down to almost none at all. As quickly as people had invaded the town two summers ago, they left in droves just as quickly, making their way down the Yukon in search of their next dream.

Or nightmare…

Nettie was a casualty of unemployment. Madame Renée was very quick to fire her help in view of the sudden loss of clientele. She contemplated following the crowd to Nome, but when she took careful count of her assets, she decided that going back south to civilization was to her advantage. She'd had enough of the frontier. It was too risky, and she wasn't about to jeopardize the reward for her hard work.

Time to enjoy the spoils.

So Nettie, with no income or job prospect, and very little in savings, decided to go stay with her uncle at St. Michael's. Once there, she could decide whether to stay, or to get passage on a ship back to Seattle or San Francisco.

In an uncharacteristically generous act, Madame Renée had paid for Nettie's steamboat passage. Sarah figured the woman owed her employee as much for her unflagging labor and contributions.

"*Tu vas me manquer…terriblement,*" Nettie said tearfully to Sarah as they hugged good-bye, at the river's edge.

"I'm going to miss you, too," answered Sarah, fighting her own tears. "You've been such a good friend. It's going to be terribly lonely without you."

"And, what is worse, I'm going to miss *le bébé* coming," added Nettie, gently putting her hand on Sarah's belly. "*C'est trop triste*. That makes me just so very sad. I want you to write to me and tell me all about it. *Jure-le moi.*"

"Yes, *Chérie*. I do swear it, of course. But you must be the first one to write and give me your address so I can have somewhere to send my letters."

Sometime later, Sarah watched as the *Louisa-Mae* sternwheeler made its way downriver possibly on one of its last voyages of the year—its lower deck seemed barely a foot above the water level—until it disappeared around the bend, leaving great smudges of smoke in its wake.

Harold put his arm around Sarah as they went back up the bank toward home. The hundreds of tents that had always occupied the space now numbered barely a dozen or so.

Trudging up the familiar path, Sarah wondered how her young friend would fare in this new chapter of her life.

"Ma Chère Sarah..."

According to Nettie's letter, the trip downriver began routinely. She had made friends with a few of the passengers. The pace downriver was pretty swift even though the boat was mostly floating with the seven miles per hour current in most spots. She spent much time on deck watching the scenery go by, occasionally seeing moose, foxes, and an occasional bear loping along the banks, as well as all sorts of birds, probably waiting for food scraps. She also caught glimpses of natives fishing or sitting around campfires on the riverbank. When her first attempts at waving elicited no response, she soon ceased. Perhaps they didn't know about waving.

Something quite remarkable caught her attention. It was a large contraption with baskets turning in the current next to the bank. At one point a large shiny fish, caught in one of the baskets, twisted and turned as it fell through a chute, and disappeared into the inner workings that she couldn't quite see. Before the boat had gone by, another fish danced down the chute to the collection box.

That machine catches fish with no one being there!

One of the crew told her that it was called a "fish wheel" or a "salmon wheel." During the salmon runs, now pretty much over, it could produce hundreds of fish per day. Now, there were maybe a half dozen daily stragglers.

But, Sarah, it is an ingenious contraption! To one side there is a holding tank that receives the fish scooped in by the baskets as the fish swim upstream. The owner just has to come by once or twice a day and collect the fish in the tank.

Unless, of course, he's afraid of thieves.

In that case it behooves him to check more often, especially at night.

Life on this steamer, Nettie continued, was like a vacation in a dream world. It was wonderful not having any responsibilities. She was delighted to meet people who were mostly focused on their next enterprise, but also taking advantage of being able to take life easy for a few days.

I must admit that, after two years of being at someone's beck and call, it is wonderful to be waited on!

Meals are taken in shifts in the big dining room—a good place to have conversation. Some people spend their time with cards and games—I must tell you that old saloon habits die hard—and some play musical instruments while others write letters. After Dawson, everything seems most civilized, easy, and relaxing.

Do you believe that Madame Renée splurged enough that I have my own semi-private sleeper cabin? I share with one person rather than to have to sleep on the lower deck with the much larger group of passengers who have cheaper tickets. It is a blessing. I do admit that I have kinder feelings towards her now. I know how she hated to part with her sous! Luckily, my cabin mate does not snore, even though she is a lady of some age and—forgive me—girth. She has interesting stories about her camp life at the mines that remind me of the tales of Father Riley's patients. We thought we were having troubled times…but our problems pale in comparison to what was going on out there in the hills. It's a small wonder that some of those men suffered so.

I will continue this letter tomorrow, as it's time for dinner. Thanks to a good cook of German origin, they are serving "carbonnades flamandes," a Belgian dish I haven't had since my childhood! I am most anxious to savor it!

Good night for now, my dearest friend.

The next part of the letter looked different. The pages were creased and wrinkled, and the handwriting looked rushed with many smudges and smears.

Tanana/Fort Gibbon

Chère Sarah,

It has been several days since I last wrote. That is because we had a fearful happening. My God! I am glad to be alive. And my life is about to change…You will be surprised to learn that in spite of the drama, I am deliriously happy…Where do I begin? You will have to be very patient with me. My mind is so mixed up with emotions, that I find it hard to write in any coordinated fashion. You may feel that I have descended into some demented state. And, guess what. I'm wondering that, myself!

Nettie's letter continued her detailed account.

They had just tied up to the dock at Fort Gibbon, in the village of Tanana—at the confluence of the Tanana and Yukon rivers known as Nuchalawoyet—to take on a load of wood for the boiler, when a lot of shouting and running footsteps could be heard all around.

Nettie had been writing her letter in the social room when someone came into the lounge shouting that the boat was under attack. At the same time Nettie heard several shots coming from the middle of the boat.

Stuffing her letter in a pocket, and ignoring counsel about staying below deck for safety, she rushed out on deck, only to find that the disturbance was not outside.

The hullabaloo was taking place near the storage area on the main deck.

After a great deal of shouting, and disturbance, Nettie saw a man being held prisoner by two other men, each holding an arm. One of them carried a pistol that Nettie could've sworn was still smoking.

"They were after the gold, I tell you," he was shouting, very red in the face. "I'm not the one you should be manhandling. Get those two thieving bastards!"

"Well, they're not going anywhere fast, thanks to you," growled what Nettie could now see was the master pilot, a snide expression sliding across his face. "That was like shooting fish in a barrel. No sport to it at all."

They lurched forward toward the gangplank, the disconcerted prisoner expostulating and fighting all the way.

When Nettie glanced once more at the bank, she saw a couple of horses approaching at a trot, their riders ramrod straight, reins in one hand, the other on their hip. They were dressed alike, and they reminded her of the mounted police in Canada.

Alaska must have a similar force, she reasoned.

You must excuse my foolishness: I guess I'm starving for entertainment and have lost my head. In my addled state, I stepped off the boat to get a better look at what was unfolding on shore. All the other passengers observed from the safety of the deck. As their shouts to me indicated, I know they thought I had lost all reason...and they could be right, I suppose.

That's when I saw him up close.

Oh, ma chère amie! Such a God-like creature I have never encountered! He sat up there, ramrod straight in the saddle, looking down at the scene, his hat casting a shadow...but then he took it off to wipe his brow. Perhaps I have been on the river too long already, and have been lulled into a kind of complacency, but my spirits lifted, and my heart jumped in my chest in a way I have never felt before.

My dear Sarah, I have tried to reason with myself. Could it be that I have seen too many hurt and ill men all this time...has my mind...no...my soul, been dormant? I may have viewed all men as victims of their obsessions and imprudent acts. But, my dear friend, I assure you that I am now fully awake! There are other ways of seeing things!

Sarah couldn't help smiling at Nettie's enthusiasm. The poor girl had been so sheltered from normal development that she was inordinately affected by natural yearnings and common reactions that had been suppressed for years. Sarah wholeheartedly wished that she could be with her friend to personally witness her newfound focus and bliss.

I was only half aware of the conflict unfolding vis-à-vis the prisoner. I did not pay attention to what was said, although I realized on a superficial level that the discussion centered around throwing the man in something called the "brig." I understand that means they intend to imprison him.

I could not take my eyes off what I now know to be a military officer. (There is an entire military fort in this place. It is not just a native village. A sign says: "7ᵗʰ United States Infantry. Companies E and F." There is much construction taking place, including what are called telegraph poles, although I'm not certain how they will function so far from civilization.)

Ma Chère Amie…You know me, I can be quite chatty under normal circumstances, but my tongue suffered some kind of instant and obscure paralysis; I could hardly speak when the soldier came over to me to ask for a description of what I knew. I sincerely hope that my hat managed to shade my red face; in fact, I redden now at the thought!

According to the rushed narrative of Nettie's letter, it took a bit of prompting by the handsome soldier before she could concentrate enough to recount the gunshots, and what she had heard from the pilot. At the end of her comments, he nodded gravely and saluted her.

She fought an urge to curtsey.

Then their attention was drawn to a procession of several of the boat crew bringing out two stretchers. One of the occupants lay on his stomach. Nettie could see bloodstains covering the back of his trousers. The other had blood all over one leg. A crowd had gathered on the deck, pointing and exclaiming.

At the same time, a wagon pulled by a couple of horses drew up along the dock. The men made quick work of loading the prisoner and the wounded. Two soldiers drove the wagon that disappeared behind a row of military houses.

My dear friend...

Please forgive the splotches above. These pages have been manhandled. I actually dropped this one in the river as I was stepping back aboard. I am rewriting what has been smudged.

We have been stationed here for several days. No one is allowed to leave because of the investigation. The passengers are restless—I suppose visions of gold disappearing before they even get to their destination are pushing them to complain. A few are threatening the crew—I've seen many pistols—but no one can disobey what I guess is martial law.

As for me...I couldn't be happier.

Even though the weather is turning very cold, especially at night, I feel an odd springtime of spirit.

Captain Beaufort...yes, he has a French name—is it a sign? Captain Beaufort...Charles, as he has bid me call him, has led the investigation on the shooting. (Apparently it occurred to prevent a theft. The two men who were shot were trying to open a strong box that was transporting gold that belonged to a bank. The shooter was employed to ensure its safe passage to Seattle.

You can see where everything ended up. Even though the shooting appears legitimate, it seems we have to wait for a ruling from somewhere before we can continue our trip downriver.)

Yes, the above is only a parenthetical thought for me. This fortuitous occurrence has had a very important consequence for me personally. In fact, (you are not going to be able to contain your astonishment) I may just stay here! Yes...here in this strange place, betwixt and between Dawson and the next real settlement at St. Michael. But thanks to the rivers, it is not as isolated as you would think. When the rivers freeze, and there are no more steamboats, they become highways for dogsled teams. Supplies are easily obtained, especially thanks to the military.

Why am I thinking of staying?

My dear friend, I recognize that this is a totally impulsive act. You will think me completely reckless.

Captain Beaufort...Charles and I... in the last several days we have become extremely close. How is that possible? It is a case of kindred spirits I believe. I've never felt so certain of anything...so at peace, and yet so alive.

Sarah leaned her head back against the pillow, putting down the pages of the long letter, and closing her eyes, before finishing it.

For some unexplainable reason, her heart rate was up, and she felt unsettled. She didn't know what to wish for.

She was all for Nettie finding great happiness after all of the contrary events she had gone through in her short life, but she was afraid that this romantic decision to stay in a remote native village in the wilds of Alaska was much more of a monumental decision than her young friend realized.

Sarah's own commitment to love had arrived quickly and under difficult circumstances, but Nettie's seemed even more sudden, and maybe ill advised.

Just a few days of consideration to make the biggest decision of your life... Even in this climate of chaotic life-changing decisions and impulsive acts, this could definitely top the list.

It put the saying "follow your heart" in a whole new dimension.

Sarah tried to calm down and finish reading her friend's words.

-14-

YOU CAN'T REFUSE

The next part of the letter contained an invitation. Sarah had begun a response to Nettie's original letter but had not sent it yet. She had not expected to hear so quickly.

Ma Chère Sarah...

I should not, in good conscience, ask you this, but I must. Forgive me...I should respect your condition, and not even make the request.

My dearest friend, would you consider coming to my wedding?

Yes, Charles has asked me to marry him. He cannot leave his post, so we will be married here at Fort Gibbon.

I'm not certain (and neither is he) what the rules and regulations are when it comes to military marriages. We are obtaining special permission. The commanding officer has been very helpful.

Will you and Harold come? I have sent an invitation to my uncle at St. Michael, and to my cousins in Nome, although I fear they will not leave their mining operations. But, the one I really want to be with me is you. You are more than family to me. I so wish we could have the conversations we used to. I miss your counsel and friendship. You are my older sister, you know. Adoptive or not, it is the same thing.

Sarah put down the letter, her gaze flicking to the window. She was startled to see a few snowflakes drift past the glass.

Her heart sank. A heaviness took hold of her—she recognized overwhelming dread. After having been through a couple of fierce winters in one of the coldest places on earth, she should've been unfazed by this pointed message from Mother Nature.

Was it her condition? Was she more conscious of her environment? She had heard of expectant mothers having sharpened senses of taste and smell. Did they also have a sharpened sixth sense?

At that moment, as if in answer, she felt a light sensation in her womb. Her hand flew to her belly.

A new communication was beginning.

Harold was of two minds about the invitation. Travel in the cold was unpleasant at best, and risky at worst. Going to Tanana by boat would soon be impossible, as freeze-up was fast approaching. Even of they squeaked by going downriver, that late in the year, there was almost no likelihood that there would be a steamboat going upriver to take them home even a few days later.

No. If they decided to undertake this venture—and Harold was not at all certain they had any business even contemplating it—they would have to wait for a substantial layer of snow, and travel by dogsled. Going too early meant forging the way yourself; there would be no clearly established dogsled trail formed by droves of others. It was a daunting venture.

"So, Sarah. When is this big event? Does Nettie even know?"

With a small shrug, and a barely perceptible shake of the head, Sarah could not be positive.

"Well, she said October, but gave no particular date. I think they are waiting for some kind of approval from the authorities."

Harold puffed out his frustration.

"If she expects people to attend, she's going to have to come up with something definite, don't you think? Crissakes! It's not like we can just stroll on over on a Sunday afternoon..."

He shook his head and let out an explosive breath.

"I really don't want to tell you what to do, Sarah, but this isn't a decision to be taken lightly in the best of circumstances. In your condition, it's certainly not that by a long shot." He sighed noisily. "If you want to know the truth, I'm really put off by your friend's request. Does she even realize what she's asking?"

Sarah smiled grimly and shrugged.

"Yes. You're right about all of that. But poor Nettie has spent a life of hardship with no one to counsel her about anything..."

"Except for you," interjected Harold. "You've been a great source of advice and counseling for her."

"Well, you're right again, and maybe that's precisely why she has no perspective about what she's asking. She's only thinking about how she wants me by her side. While it's true that I'm flattered that I matter so much to her, in a way, right at the moment, I guess her affection is as almost as much a curse as a blessing."

Harold's mouth was in a cynical twist.

"Yes, that affection could be a big problem for you. It's a hard choice, so you'd better give it a lot of thought."

He took one look at Sarah's morose expression, and sat down next to her, putting his arm around her shoulder, and giving her a squeeze.

"Look, Sarah. I'll do whatever you want. Just promise me that you'll take an honest look at all of it, and assess your situation."

She closed her eyes and nodded.

His mouth a thin line, he got up.

"Meanwhile, I'll try to find out if there are any more steamboats scheduled to go downriver. If we're lucky, we may be able to manage at least that half of the trip. We'll have to figure something out for the other half."

Sarah gave Harold a grateful look. He smiled, grabbed his hat and jacket, and went out the heavy door making sure it shut snugly with a strong sudden pull that shook the whole cabin.

It made Sarah jump, and her tiny resident too.

Harold made inquiries at the ticket office. Apparently, the steamboats would operate until the first ice shelves formed along the riverbank and ice floes made their appearance. Daytime temperatures were still able to erode what the nighttime wrought. It was to everyone's advantage that tickets be sold as long into the season as possible.

"So, what do you think will happen when we show up early?" asked Harold as he examined the contents of his clothing trunk. "We can't wait until the next steamboat. It's not a foregone conclusion that there will even be another one."

Looking through the standing wardrobe her husband had crafted for her, Sarah shrugged.

"Well…I'm hoping that Nettie will either change her date, or at least be appreciative of the fact that we made the effort to be with her, even if we don't stay long enough. Besides, I'm eager to meet this "God-like creature" of hers. I hope I'm not disappointed…" She smiled at Harold. "There aren't too many of those around this day and age…"

"And here I thought that that was exactly how you regarded me. What a let-down." His dejected look seemed almost genuine.

"Of course you're that to me," laughed Sarah, reaching up to pat him on the shoulder. "It goes without saying. From the moment, back on the trail, when you almost bought a pair of two left boots, I knew you were special."

Harold gave her a baleful look.

"Very funny. I was just looking at them. I was never going to actually buy them…"

Sarah hid her smile.

"Mm-hm," she uttered, looking askance at him out of the corner of her eye. "The sales lady certainly looked like she thought she'd made a sale…"

Indignant, Harold just shook his head.

"Do you know how hard it was to find a pair of perfect size twelve-and-half boots back there?"

When he saw his wife chuckling, he stopped. He had been slow to recognize his leg being pulled. He went on defending himself anyway.

"Right…I get it. Come to think of it, I seem to recall that you weren't even there…

Sarah just smiled serenely.

"Perhaps not…but things get around. Anyway, it was smart to get those things," she conceded, rendering moot the whole argument. "I wish I had bought some extras. What we didn't use, we could have easily sold."

Preoccupied with their own thoughts, they continued packing their gear for the prospective trip down the Yukon River, and into the unpredictable wilds of the Alaska Territory.

PART THREE

SNOWBOUND

INTERIOR ALASKA
FORT GIBBON
TANANA

-1-

ALL THE SIGNS

Days were getting shorter, losing about five to six minutes of daylight per twenty-four-hour period. If the skies threatened, darkness was even more apparent; the steel gray clouds seeming ready to burst, thus unleashing their first autumnal salvo.

Sarah was on deck, braving the cold for the sake of fresh air. Her stomach was still acting up, and even though the ride down the Yukon was mostly smooth, she didn't feel quite settled. Whether it was completely physical or partly psychological, she wasn't quite sure.

They had stopped for wood in several villages along the way: Eagle, the first American town with its trading posts, Circle, which had supported its own gold rush boom, and Fort Yukon, a large Indian village just below the arctic circle. It was when they passed Rampart and reached the Rampart Rapids that she felt very close to losing her breakfast. Luckily that was the only spot so far that had affected the ride to any extent. Sarah fervently hoped that the pilot knew the best channels to navigate.

She had heard that keeping your eye on the horizon would lessen the queasy feeling, but that was probably for ocean seasickness—not what really ailed her anyway. In her case, she knew, only time would make an appreciable difference. At the moment, she was supposedly past that critical six to eight weeks into her pregnancy—prime time for feeling "unwell." Apparently, according to those with experience, the middle months would be less bothersome. At this point, even though hurrying the process ran counter to her outlook—eight weeks or more would be an unfortunate mathematical reality—she couldn't help wishing for less nausea that the passing of weeks would probably ensure.

Superseding the biological discomfort, the constant fear that the child she was carrying was the result of the nightmarish encounter with Gunther, plunged her into a dark place where she found it hard to breathe. No matter how hard she tried, she couldn't climb out of it. Combined with her inability to tell Harold the fear she harbored, what she assessed to be her betrayal would have made her ill anyway.

"You have that glow," well-wishers gushed, nevertheless. "One can always tell."

Then they would pat her belly for good luck, never stopping to consider that their action was completely unsolicited or permitted.

She'd smile, but it hurt. She knew how she should feel, and she couldn't.

Either things were completely out of her control, or people simply saw what they wanted. She knew there was no way she could glow beatifically…unless it was an illusion caused by the sheen of sweat that occasionally broke out all over her face.

It tore her guts out to carry on as if she had no care in the world other than becoming a mother to a loved child.

Sometimes just seeing Harold's happy face was enough to plunge her into depression.

Why did it have to be like this?

She felt robbed of what she felt should be such a happy occasion; she should be blissful.

"Sarah? Oh…there you are. Harold came over to the rail. "Are you still feeling punky?"

Sarah swallowed and put on her best glowing face.

"Yes…a bit. I thought I'd get some air. Do you know how long before our next wood stop?"

"I don't think there are any more before Tanana. We're actually within seventy miles or so, all downstream."

He leaned over the rail slightly, panning the countryside, noting the thick growth of trees on the cut bank next to them. Up ahead was a curve, from which trees stuck out and bent over, sweeping the water that the current pushed past them. The boat was steering away from them, out into the central channel.

"If things go as planned," he continued to explain, "we should be there by this evening."

Sarah took this as very good news. It would be definite relief to get off this floating prison. She was counting on maybe feeling slightly better if she could get on solid dry land.

Just then, the boat lurched violently, throwing Sarah to the deck, and almost pitching Harold over the rail. She screamed in fright and pain.

"My knee! Harold! Watch out!"

Harold scrambled over to her.

"It's all right, Sarah. Just stay down. I think we just ran over something…or into something."

He bent over his wife and put his hand on her shoulder. Then he squatted down and wrapped her in his arms. She was shaking and tearful, one hand protectively on her belly, and the other one rubbing her knee.

They felt vibrations though the deck, and became aware that the bow was stationery, and the boat's stern, pushed by the current, was coming around in a semi-circle so that the boat was now almost facing directly upstream. The boat's great wheel was pushing in fits and starts against the current and whatever it had hit. There was the noise of grinding and splintering.

Shouts and screams and the pounding of running footsteps filled their ears.

Then the boat stopped vibrating and there was a confusing stillness. People were still scattering about, not sure where to go to find safety.

Sarah and Harold straightened up carefully and looked past rushing bodies over the rail.

"My God!" exclaimed Harold. "We're facing the wrong way! The boat has swung completely around."

Avoiding someone who was barreling past clumsily, he walked unsteadily to the edge of the deck, and looked down into the silty water.

"Looks like it's a sand bar," he shouted to Sarah. "We nosed into it."

Sarah looked up at him, trying to get up. He came over and helped her, and immediately noticed she was favoring her hurt leg.

"Can you walk? Shall I carry you?"

Sarah shook her head and leaned against him.

"No, no. I'll be all right." She looked around and pointed to a deck chair that was wedged upside down under some boxes.

"I just need to sit down for a minute."

Harold dragged the chair over to Sarah, who firmly gripped the armrests to ease her body into the chair as carefully as possible.

She was breathing hard, pressing her hand into her belly.

Harold put the back of his hand to her forehead, immediately noticing the sweatiness.

"Sarah. Are you all right? Christ! You look deathly pale."

She didn't answer at first, swallowing with effort, trying to ignore the pandemonium all around them.

"I don't know. Maybe I need water…"

Harold looked around and finally put an arm out to stop a lady that appeared to be wandering aimlessly, fearfully looking from side to side.

"Excuse me, Miss. My wife is feeling poorly. Could you possibly stay with her while I get some water?" He was greeted with an anxious stare. "It will only take a minute. I'll be back straight away."

The lady nodded slightly, her eyes wide. Harold was not at all reassured by her demeanor. Maybe she didn't speak English. He wasn't sure she was even aware of what was going on. Grabbing her gently by the shoulders he moved her up against the wall, next to Sarah, out of the traffic.

"Please just stay there for a few minutes. I'll be back shortly."

He was addressing both women, but only Sarah nodded in response. There was no choice but to trust the situation. He darted off towards the dining room.

Sarah distractedly watched him go. Her mouth was dry, she had a headache, and the nausea was coming in waves.

And there was something else—something she was trying instinctively to deny, but that was too insistent not to recognize:

272

subtle cramping deep inside. There wasn't much pain to speak of, but the worry it triggered was a monster.

It was decided to unload the passengers by ferrying them to the far bank by means of the skiffs normally stashed on deck. After having retrieved their coats, and everyone plus some of the cargo was safely on land, the crew worked on getting the boat loose.

The passengers and part of the cargo off, the load had lightened enough to make a difference. Ropes, pulleys. poles, and muscle all went into extricating the prow from the silt and mud. By reversing the paddlewheel, the pilot was able to finally free the boat and turn it around.

It was well into the night before anyone was allowed to climb back on board, and well into the morning when the cargo had been reloaded as well. The men were so exhausted that they slept where they fell from the exertion.

Harold had found water he put in a container to give to Sarah before they'd had to be ferried to the bank. And while the excitement of the events temporarily took her mind off her personal difficulties, her discomfort only increased as they stood and walked around for hours as the crew worked on the boat. Finally, she took advantage of one of the chairs that had been unloaded with the cargo.

Unable to ease his wife's distress, Harold walked compulsively back and forth near her, his face clouded with worry, and his fists clenched in frustration.

"Maybe you'll feel better if you eat something," he said hopefully, kneeling by her and taking her hand. "The crew brought some sandwiches over, and some hot tea. Shall I fetch you some?"

Sarah pulled her coat snugly around herself. The night temperatures were dipping appreciably. It felt like it could snow any minute.

"Yes," she nodded. "I'll definitely have some tea." She hesitated. "And I guess I'll try eating something." It was more for Harold's benefit than her own that she agreed to try some food, because she certainly wasn't hungry. In fact, the thought of food was closer to revolting than attractive.

When Harold returned with a chicken sandwich and a mug of lukewarm tea, Sarah made a valiant attempt to eat at least half of the sandwich. The tea she downed to the last drop.

At some point all the passengers were in need of relieving themselves. The men were able to take care of this, which they did with their characteristic ease. Then, stomping the brush as well as they could, they made a path for the women to follow to a clearing where some fallen logs could serve as support.

When Sarah took her turn, still slightly limping, it was much too dark for her to make any assessment of her condition; whether she had suffered any kind of untoward discharge, that could alert her to danger.

So, crouching next to a fallen spruce trunk, she took care of business along with the other women, and returned to the bank none the wiser as to what her body was signaling.

* * *

It wasn't until they were safely back on board that she was able to take stock of her situation.

Her drawers told the story. The cramping had been a sign: she was lightly spotting.

She couldn't help thinking that her ambivalence toward this pregnancy was exacting a price. More than anything, her guilt was taking on incalculable proportions.

-2-

REUNION

"*Ce n'est pas possible*...I cannot believe you are here, ...*tu me fais tant plaisir....chère amie.* My dear, dear friend.*"

Nettie was so excited she was mixing her languages.

"Oh, Sarah. I could not let myself hope. But you came. You came!"

She had Sarah in such a bear hug that it was difficult to breathe.

"And Harold, *toi aussi*...you too! I'm so...so thrilled..."

On tiptoes, she reached up and hugged him, giving him a kiss on the chin, as she couldn't reach his cheek. Bending down to return the hug, he looked slightly embarrassed and amused at this display.

"We couldn't miss your happy event," he said, smiling and patting her back. "Seemed like such an important social occasion that we must attend."

They were gathered on the bank below the village, their bags scattered around them. They'd had to wait for someone to alert Nettie that she had visitors. She had wasted no time running quite a distance to greet them.

Members of the boat crew were taking on more wood for the rest of the trip downriver. Some were carefully examining the stern wheel for damage they had not been able to assess before.

Sarah was so relieved that her journey was ending here. Dry land felt good. That and the joy of seeing her friend almost made her forget her concerns. They walked arm in arm up the bank and toward the little house where Nettie had taken up residence.

With its regular lines and a white picket fence, the house seemed out of place. Though small, it reminded Sarah of a mid-western farmhouse that could have easily been at home surrounded by an Iowa cornfield. Yet here it was in the middle of the Alaska Territory a few yards above the Yukon River. She was expecting logs, not regular siding, and certainly not painted.

Nettie noted her friend's surprise.

"It's the military," she explained. "They are building lots of houses, all in a row, with gardens and streets. This is the first one they made. It is just outside the compound, and they use it for travelers and guests. Come…there's plenty of room for you both to stay."

Plenty of room turned out to be taking Nettie's bedroom while she slept on a daybed in the living area. She would not hear of Sarah's objections.

"Non, non. Écoute-moi, mon amie. You are the one with the heavy belly, and I think you are very tired. You need good sleep. I am small and can fit easily on this daybed. You and Harold must have the comfort and privacy of the bedroom. I will not listen to your argument. You did not travel all this way to be uncomfortable."

She shook her head vigorously, and crossed her arms, a very determined look on her face.

"Je regrette, mais c'est comme ça!"

It was more than obvious that there was no deterring her from her decision. And she insisted that Sarah take a nap before dinner.

"I want you to be well rested to meet my Charles," she said, her eyes sparkling. "He has special permission to take his meals here, so he will be joining us later."

She spent some time helping Sarah unpack a few things before having her lie down on the bed, while she went to fuss over supper in the tiny kitchen. Meanwhile, Harold went off on his own to explore the village. Goods and trading always on his mind, he was anxious to see what the Alaska Commercial Store had on the shelves.

After doubting that she could fall asleep with so much on her mind, Sarah's mounting exhaustion took over nevertheless, and, after a quick gaze around at her surroundings, she fell asleep within a few minutes. Nettie tiptoed to the door to check on her. Seeing the regular rise and fall of Sarah's chest, she smiled, and pulled the door closed.

Sarah could see why Nettie had been smitten. When Charles walked into the little house, she immediately felt his commanding presence. Like Harold, he was tall and broad, and his carriage was authoritative, but the resemblance ended there. Both were very handsome, but where Harold was dark haired, had deep set eyes, and could be construed as brooding, Charles was blond and—there was no other way to put it—very sunny. Light bounced off his rosy skin and thick shiny hair. His eyes were arrestingly blue and his smile dazzled. Sarah could easily imagine that he commanded his entourage just by walking into a room.

He smiled in greeting, extending a neatly manicured hand.

"Nettie has told me so much about you," he said in a deep voice, nodding. "You have seen her through many challenges. She misses you and is so grateful…"

"Well," answered Sarah, putting a hand over his, as they shook. "The feeling is quite mutual." She looked at Nettie affectionately. "I have been lost without her."

Charles nodded in understanding.

"Well, *ma chérie,*" he said, addressing his betrothed. "The aroma in here is absolutely tantalizing. You're up to your old cooking tricks I assume?"

He gathered her up in his long arms and planted a kiss on her forehead. "And they wonder why I don't want to eat at the mess."

Nettie giggled and swatted his arm in teasing reproach.

"Charles! *Fais attention!* Our guests!"

He let her go reluctantly and looked around, not the least bit embarrassed.

"But I don't see Harold." He looked quizzically at Sarah. "Did he not make the trip? I was so looking forward to meeting him."

At that moment the door opened, and, as if summoned by the devil, Harold came in, along with a burst of golden aspen leaves that swirled in the cross current of air. He quickly closed the door.

Introductions were made as Charles went to a small sideboard and poured a liquid from a decanter into some cordial glasses. After passing them around, he raised his glass in a toast.

"Here's to acquaintances—old and new. May they enrich our lives."

"Hear, hear," said Harold lifting his glass, taking a sip, and looking at Sarah, who barely took a sip from her glass, and put it down next to the decanter.

She wasn't sure how alcohol would affect her and didn't want to risk anything. Rendering the whole thing moot, she really didn't have a taste for it anyway.

No one seemed to notice. They all spent the rest of the time setting the dinner table and talking about Dawson and the trip downriver.

Dinner was cheery; conversation animated and constant especially between the men. Outside, the wind picked up, whistling mournfully by the window, making things seem cozy inside.

"Well," said Charles after Harold gave details about the steamboat being stuck on the sandbar. "You're fortunate that they didn't try to blow it loose with dynamite. I know that sounds crazy, but it has been done."

He nodded and smiled grimly.

"And the result was somewhat less than satisfactory. They managed to dislodge it all right but damaged most of the boat and hurt many passengers." He shook his head and added prophetically. "I'm afraid that before this whole exodus is over, there will be hulks of boat wrecks scattered all over the territory."

"Just another example of men not thinking things through," complained Sarah, her cynicism more than apparent. "At least, in Canada, the Mounted Police defended those people against themselves. Sort of guarding them from their own stupidity."

She shook her head.

"Unfortunately, they don't cross the border."

Charles leaned over and patted her arm.

"Well, don't despair, my dear," he said smiling. "That's what we're here for. The United States government has been made aware of men's foibles in the Far North. That's why all the forts—Egbert, St. Michael's, Davis and the one and only Fort Gibbon right here, were established. Law and order par excellence, throughout the entire territory."

"And, I say *que Dieu soit loué pour ça,*" chimed in Nettie, clasping her hands in mock prayer. "I praise God because if not for the establishment of this fort, Charles and I...well...we would have never met. *Personellement*, I am grateful for the bad behavior that caused this..."

Sarah had to admit that Nettie's gratitude was a bit misplaced, but she could sympathize. It was logical in its own perverse way.

With Charles and Harold sent outside so that Charles could smoke a pipe, the women tended to the dishes, and putting order in the kitchen.

"I don't let him smoke that thing inside," grumbled Nettie, scowling. "*C'est dégoutant.* Most disgusting."

She smiled mischievously.

"It is the only thing he does that I do not approve of. If not for that, he is *complètement* perfect."

Her smile became a wide grin.

Sarah chuckled at her friend's expression.

"You look like the cat that ate the canary," she laughed. "But, yes, I agree about the pipe. The smell makes me...kind of sick." She made a face.

Nettie nodded and frowned.

"Yes. Especially in your condition. I'm sure that makes it many times worse."

Drying her hands on a towel, she looked intently at her friend.

"Sarah. Have I told you how much I appreciate and love that you are visiting? Especially considering everything. You seemed a bit quiet during dinner. Is…is everything going well *avec le bébé*?"

Sarah remained impassive, wondering how much she should tell her friend.

She sat down suddenly.

Nettie walked over to her and put a hand on her shoulder.

"Sarah? *Ça ne va pas?* What is wrong? Tell me, please."

Sarah decided not to stand on ceremony any longer. She looked down at the floor.

"Well, *ma chère amie*," she sighed, her forehead wrinkled, and her lips pressed together. "I am very much afraid that I'm going to lose this baby. I've been cramping and spotting…"

Nettie was quiet for a moment. Then her face lit up.

"But, Sarah. *Tu sais très bien*…you know very well that can happen at first. I remember some of the women in Dawson had that, and…*de toute façon*…they still had their babies. You just have to be careful…and not do too much."

Sarah nodded.

"Yes, I know. But this is rather late. Usually, things have settled by now."

She shook her head.

"Anyway, there's nothing I can do…besides take it easy. There's no medicine…"

Nettie put out a hand.

"But wait. There is a military surgeon at the fort. I am not sure how the rules are for taking care of regular people, but maybe he could help you," answered Nettie quickly.

Sarah smiled despite her concern.

"I'm sure his expertise is not exactly in the right field. I doubt he deals with pregnancy and childbirth too often. "

Nettie pursed her lips in thought.

"Well, *ma chère,* you may be right, but a consultation with a real doctor could maybe make you feel a bit better. He might be able to see how…the rest of you—maybe not the baby part—is faring."

Sarah nodded silently as Nettie put away some glasses. She was secretly amused that her friend was trying so valiantly to convince her of what to do.

There was definitely some logic in what Nettie was proposing. In the silence, and twisting her wedding ring around her finger, Sarah began hesitantly, "And, I'm afraid there is something else…"

At that moment the door opened. There was a rush of fresh air as the men came back in, stomping their feet and brushing leaves from their coats.

Sarah bit her lips in frustration.

For the time being, the conversation was over.

-3-

BEADS AND PEARLS

Sarah enjoyed watching the developing relationship between Nettie and her beau. It was very obvious that they were enthralled with each other. Even Harold noticed it.

They whispered in bed.

"They remind me of us," he said, cradling Sarah's head in his hands, and kissing her gently on the lips.

"When I think of all those months on the trail I was silent, being by your side every day, eating next to you, even hearing you breathe as you slept in our tent next to Gunther, a few feet from me, and behind that infernal blanket you insisted on putting up between us. Christ! I so badly wanted to kiss you like this."

He repeated his action.

"It was torture not to be able to say or do anything…and to have to watch that idiot mistreat you."

Sarah smiled tremulously in the dark. She put her hand to Harold's cheek.

"Well, at least it paid off in the end. And, if you must know, I was starting to feel the same way about you way before we ever declared anything. There was just never a good time…"

Harold made some kind of noise signifying agreement. Tossing back and forth until he found a comfortable position hugging her, he finally settled down with a shuddering sigh.

"I don't even want to dwell on the hard part," he said, his mouth on her ear, his breath tickling her. "Even the blizzards, ice, and smelly stampeders were easier to bear." He sighed again and squeezed her tight. "This does my heart so good."

One of his large hands cupping her belly, he fell silent, his face buried in her neck. Pretty soon his breathing slowed and became regular.

Alone with her thoughts, Sarah tried to make sense of her new normal: constant worry. But, amazingly, the spotting and cramps had lessened considerably since the chaos on the boat. Maybe there was some medical truth to the taking-it-easy prescription.

Did she dare hope for the best? Did she even deserve it?

Carefully taking Harold's hand from her body, she tucked it between them. Then she turned to her side, affording her belly a more comfortable position for sleep.

If only she could do the same for her head.

* * *

Arm in arm they set off for a log cabin hidden among a few tall spruce trees in the old village. The morning air was filled with smells of fallen leaves, smoke, and cooking.

"I do not have a decent dress for my wedding," Nettie had said. "And the Alaska Commercial store does not have anything suitable either."

She shrugged.

"I do not really care that much, but Charles is insisting I must have something appropriate. He says I will regret it later if I do not." She pursed her lips knowingly. "I feel he's not wanting to hear possible complaints from me when it is later…"

So, after having made some inquiries, Nettie had found the name of a native lady who was a seamstress. She bought several yards of fabric from the commercial company, and was now taking it with her, as well as an old dress in her favorite style. It would have to be taken apart to use as a pattern but could probably be put back together again. She handed it to Sarah to carry.

"I think it is here," she said, as they approached a log cabin, surrounded by everything necessary for life in the wilderness: outdoor tools, dogsleds, fishing gear, even faded dried-up flowers that must've been beautiful in the warm months.

As they got nearer to the door, a cacophony of barking and whining assailed their ears coming from behind the house.

Their knock was answered by a small child, who stood on the threshold in his—or her—underwear, chewing with great energy on something held in one pudgy hand.

"Is your mother home?" asked Nettie, bending down to eye level.

In answer, the child turned around and toddled off into the recesses of the cabin. The two women were left looking at the interior of the mudroom, an entryway that was a combination storage and bulwark against the cold.

There was a broom to be used to brush snow off boots before entering the main part of the house and a long row of hooks for all manner of clothing and miscellaneous items. Not an inch of wall or floor was bare except for a narrow path leading into the main rooms.

"Come in, come in," came a voice from within. "But close the door…"

After the brisk autumn air, the cabin was stifling hot thanks to a centrally located woodstove. It took a minute for Sarah's eyes to get used to the gloom of the interior.

There was not a spare spot to be had in the entire living area for any kind of seating. The two chairs were covered with sewing notions and fabric, as was the kitchen table. There were several pairs of new moccasins and slippers with beaded tops lined up at the edge.

A lady of indeterminate age sat at an old treadle sewing machine, in the spare light from a small window, biting a loose thread from a garment she was working on. She looked up smiling quizzically at the two strangers who had walked into her house, as if it was quite the normal situation.

"Mary? Mary Sam? I'm Nettie. I was given your name for someone who can maybe be able to help me. I hope you don't mind. I am very last minute."

She pulled out the package she had been carrying, revealing a thick bolt of fabric. Mary looked at it with interest.

"I am getting married in a few days, and I was hoping if you will have enough time to make a dress for me?'

Mary just looked at her and blinked.

"I bring an old dress for a pattern…" Nettie added, taking the dress from Sarah's arms. "I think that must to make it easier…"

Mary put down her project and nodded silently. Then she got up and examined the dress, holding it in the weak light from the window. She looked at the interior of the bodice, and at seams, and turned the sleeves inside out. Then she looked at the hem.

"Hmmm," she said, nodding. "Yes, it seems fine. Maybe I will not even have to take it apart. Please, let's see your fabric."

She reached for the folded material and fingered it.

"So, you're just having cotton?" She seemed surprised.

"Well, the store did not have much for me to choose from, especially because the big amount I need. But the salesperson say to me, it is a special weave. You see how it has a...uh... satiny side..."

Nettie pulled the folds apart to show the reverse side.

Sarah had half expected the fabric to be white but noticed that it was almost a pewter color. It was hard to be certain in the low light.

"I was thinking that some beading or pearls or maybe some lace will...how you say it...make it liven up." Nettie shrugged. "I do admit, I am not well advised of these things."

Mary smiled and nodded.

"Yes, I'm sure we can add some pretty decoration to it. I have a collection of beads and seed pearls you might want to choose from."

She pulled a large wooden box out from under the table and lifted the lid. She stepped back and held out her hand, indicating that they should approach.

"Why don't you take a look?"

An hour later, Nettie and Sarah were walking home. The sun had come out and the trees were dripping their moisture in response.

"I cannot believe how so many sewing notions and materials she has," remarked Nettie, as she sidestepped a muddy spot. "Did you see those beautiful pair of beaded slippers? I love so much those stylized flowers. She must make a lot of business."

Then her hand shot out to stop Sarah's progress.

"*Oh non. Je suis complètement idiote.* Speaking of business, I completely forgot I should discuss the price. I'm sure

Charles will expect me to know. I must be better at business. We must go back."

It took a few minutes, and they were back at the cabin they had left a few moments before.

The front door was wide open. Sarah was betting that Mary would not want that.

They were just about to go in and close the door, when they heard shouting and a scream. The two women looked at each other.

Then they heard the toddler crying.

The scene that greeted them as they hurried to make their way apprehensively to the sewing area stopped them short.

Mary was seated at her sewing machine, the toddler crying and struggling in her lap.

Holding her head back by the hair to bare her throat, a longhaired man held a knife a few inches from it.

Paralyzed, Sarah and Nettie stood stock-still in the doorway.

"Stop! Please stop!" shouted Sarah, coming alive, and taking a step forward.

Surprised by the voice, the man raised his face, shaking his greasy hair out of his eyes. The knife remained at Mary's throat.

"Who says…? Who the hell are you?" His bloodshot eyes and his slurred speech told Sarah he was far from sober. Before she could answer, he spat further invective.

"I don't need some white bitch to tell me what I can't do. Get the hell out!"

Straightening up to considerable height, he moved the knife away from Mary and pointed it at the other two.

The terrified toddler was twisting his way off Mary's lap. She tried to grab the child, but he slipped from her grasp. The man immediately grabbed the screaming baby around the belly in the crook of his arm."

Addressing Mary, he smiled triumphantly, showing gaps where teeth should've been.

"See, you stupid meddlin' bitch? He knows who he should be with. In future, mind yer own damned business."

Lurching against the table, and slashing the air with his knife, he did an amazing imitation of a dog growl, thrusting his face a few inches from Mary's as he did so.

Putting her hands up defensively, she pulled back in terror. Laughing at her, he batted her hands away with the back of his knife hand, still holding the toddler against his body with his other arm. Then, before Sarah could think to do anything, he was three inches from her face, leering and threatening.

"I don't know who the hell you are, or what yer doin' here, but it's none o' yer business either. I otta…" he waved his knife under her nose. She was so nauseated by the myriad of smells that he gave off, that the knife almost receded to secondary importance.

By instinct, Nettie grabbed his elbow to lower the weapon. He growled again and jerked his arm from her grasp. The action made him lose his grip on the child. Sarah saw an opportunity to grab the toddler, but the man pushed her to the ground regaining his grip on the screaming baby before she could get a hold of him. On some obscure level, she was amazed at his physical ability despite his inebriated state. This was not a man to be dismissed easily.

Brandishing the weapon again, he faced the three women, daring them to approach. Then, securing his grip on the baby, he brushed clumsily past them, and was out the door, his writhing burden still screaming.

Sarah struggled to get up quickly.

"No, Alfred, come back! Bring him back!" Mary sobbed loudly, rising from her chair, and looking like she was going after him.

Sarah put a hand out to stop her.

"Let him go," she said trying to put her arm around the panicked woman. "You can't accomplish anything while he's in that state. You'll only get hurt, and maybe make it worse for the child too."

"But the baby," she screamed, fighting to get out of Sarah's clutches. "He'll hurt the baby! I have to get him…"

It took both Sarah and Nettie to prevent her from running outside.

Sarah spent the next few minutes calming Mary down. Nettie poured some water from the kettle on the stove to make three cups of tea. They cleared some of the sewing from the table to make room for the cups.

"Now," said Sarah, after they had all taken a few calming sips. "What is this all about? Who was that, and why did he take the baby?"

Mary was still crying, but at much less volume. She took a handkerchief out of her sleeve and blew her nose. Then she dabbed her eyes and looked mournfully at her new acquaintances.

"That baby is my grandson, Toby. His mother—my daughter—died of the measles last year. That was her… husband. He is a damned no-good drunk criminal son-in-law. He just got out of jail, and already he's…"

She vigorously shook her head. "I need to take care of my grandson because that son of a bitch certainly can't." She looked at Sarah in despair. "What can I do?"

Well, her language certainly makes her case plain, thought Sarah. There was no ambivalence there.

"Have you tried to get legal custody? It shouldn't be too hard with his kind of record…"

Mary shrugged.

"Who will listen to me? The legal system is not very helpful for us. They think we should solve our problems in the community." She shook her head. "And, when we do, and it turns out bad, then they're ready to condemn someone without really looking into it. They usually lock up the wrong person."

Sarah and Nettie looked at each other.

"Well, Mary," said Sarah. "Now that Fort Gibbon is established, I think you can have better legal help. If you want us to, we can find out for you. The military is here to help with this kind of thing."

Mary did not look convinced.

"Thank you," she said. "But I think I will try the village chiefs first. I have a couple of relatives on the council. Maybe I can get them to do something."

She didn't look hopeful.

"Well, if you change your mind, we will gladly help you," said Sarah.

Mary nodded.

"Of course, I do have a couple of sons and brothers who might help. They can maybe use family influence…"

The three of them finished their tea. Sarah was a bit uncomfortable with that last statement but didn't discuss it.

It sounded vaguely like a threat.

After receiving assurance that this development would not affect her work on the wedding dress, Nettie and Sarah took their leave, promising to stay very much in touch. They walked quickly back through the village to get home.

"Oh, mon Dieu!" exclaimed Nettie, stopping suddenly and slapping her forehead. "I never talked about the price again."

"I don't think that would've been a good idea," said Sarah, nudging her along. "People cannot talk about business when they have so much else on their minds. Mary will have enough to deal with just doing the sewing.

Besides," she said smiling and putting a hand on Nettie's arm to keep urging her onward. "I'm sure Charles will proudly maintain that nothing is too expensive for his bride. He will think you are beautiful in your dress. You cannot put a price on that. "

Nettie beamed, and hugged Sarah with one arm.

"Tu as raison, chère amie," she said, resuming their walk "As usual, you are completely correct. Have I told you how much I love you being here…*avec moi?*"

She gave Sarah a sideways hug and giggled.

They made the rest of their way home arm in arm in companionable silence, each dwelling in the privacy of their respective thoughts.

-4-

TRUTH BE TOLD

Over dinner, the women described what had gone on at Mary's house.

"So, what do you think was actually transpiring there," asked Charles, spearing a slice of meat from the serving platter. "I wonder what recourse she has among her family members."

Sarah shrugged.

"She didn't seem sure of it, but it was definitely something she was considering. I don't know what way they have of policing themselves. Do you?"

Charles pursed his lips in thought.

"I know they have a kind of tribal council, but I don't know how much power it has."

"Well, isn't the military supposed to enforce the law around here? asked Sarah, taking a piece of bread. "Could you do something about it?" She gave some thought as to how Superintendent Steel would've dealt with this.

Charles shook his head slowly.

"Unless it's a definite and serious crime...like murder, we don't really meddle in village concerns. The natives pretty much take care of their own problems. The only time we might have jurisdiction is if the action involved a non-native person. Family disputes would not qualify."

Sarah was losing patience with what she perceived to be a straightforward problem.

"Why can't you just go into the village, question the people, and figure out how to make the lawbreakers toe the line. Why is it any different from…I don't know…if Harold beat me up or something?"

Charles chewed his food meditatively before answering.

"We haven't been here long enough for making determinations about policing the native population. That's really up to the U.S. Marshall's office. Most of the time we don't even know what is happening in the village. There are supposed to be federal marshals in charge, but there are way too few available to police such a large territory." He shook his head. "It's a bit like the 'damned if you do, and damned if you don't' saying."

Sarah frowned but kept silent.

"Believe me when I say that the villagers don't really like outside meddling," Charles continued, taking a sip from his glass. "They don't feel like they are rightfully under any jurisdiction we impose. Not our laws, nor our punishments. We're outsiders, and nothing's going to change that."

Sarah couldn't help thinking that, considering what was at stake, Mary might've welcomed some intervention even from outsiders to help her out. But she considered what Charles was saying. She had seen examples of the law used against the Indians before, and it hadn't been pretty. Maybe there was wisdom in the native attitude.

They finished their supper talking about the wedding ceremony, trying to decide if it would be completely military or whether they would ask the reverend from the St. James Mission to preside.

"Whatever you decide," began Sarah to Nettie, as they put away the dishes, while the men had gone somewhere outside.

"I hope it will be soon. Harold says there is one more barge heading up river. It would be very helpful if he and I were able to go back to Dawson on it."

Nettie nodded.

"Yes, *ma chérie*, I know. Charles has spoken to the commander of the fort. He is willing to preside if that's what we decide."

Nettie smiled.

"And I think all the men will like an excuse to take out their ceremony swords to celebrate. I think they are very much bored with only work to do."

"You're probably right about that," answered Sarah, brushing crumbs from the tablecloth. "I'm sure it will be the highlight of their season. I only hope..." She didn't complete her thought, shaking her head in a "never-mind" mode.

"You only hope what?" asked Nettie, looking intently at her friend, worry lines showing on her forehead. "*Qu'est-ce qu'il y a? Dis-moi,* Sarah. I think you are not telling me everything."

Sarah shook her head in vehement denial.

"No, no. It's nothing. I'm... just hoping everything turns out well. This is a big step for you." She smiled automatically. "I remember having a few doubts just before my wedding. But you seem so certain..."

Nettie smiled sweetly and nodded.

"Yes, I am very certain I want this with my Charles. Sarah, *je t'assure*, I have never been this happy. It is the best thing..."

She shrugged and raised her eyebrows as if a little surprised at the realization. "In my life. My whole life."

"I can see that," chuckled Sarah. "You'd have to be blind not to. I guess I won't be worried about you, then, *ma chère*."

"Well, *tu sais*, if everything else will be failing, I have you and Harold for my example," said Nettie. "I guess that if we can be like you two, everything will always be very fine."

At her friend's assessment, Sarah's smile faded and, before she could stop herself, her hand automatically went to her belly.

Nettie frowned at the sight. She bit her lips together, hesitating.

"You are not telling me everything, are you?"

She reached for Sarah's hand.

"Please, Sarah. It is my turn to be worried. *Pour l'amour de Dieu*. Please say everything to me. Is it *le bébé*? Are you still having those...those bad happenings?"

Sarah looked for a chair and sat down with a huge sigh.

"All right, Nettie. You win. I'll tell you everything."

Nettie silently drew up another chair and sat directly across from her friend. Their heads, tilted toward each other, were a few inches apart. Nettie reached for Sarah's hands.

Worried that they would be interrupted by the men coming back, Sarah rushed through a short but accurate version of her encounter with Gunther. Nettie looked horrified but kept silent until the end.

"So, I don't know for absolute certain if this is Harold's baby. My courses have always been very irregular, so it's very difficult to calculate."

There was silence as Nettie digested everything. Then she put a hand on Sarah's shoulder.

"Sarah. *Écoute-moi*. Listen. You sound like...I think you are feeling it is your fault. It is not. What could you do? He was... *un vrai cochon*...a veritable pig."

Her face twisted in disgust as she added, "This is worse than those filthy men on Paradise Alley were."

Sarah shrugged and shook her head in misery.

"I just feel like I should've fought him more. Maybe he thought I …wanted it, or something… or I owed him…"

"When you were holding a gun aimed at him?"

Nettie made a loud skeptical noise at the back of her throat. Sarah couldn't tell if it was English or French, but she got the gist.

"*Mon Dieu,* Sarah, *le pistolet*…that was not an uncertain message. He knew very well you were fighting him. It's completely his fault. I'm certain that when he sobered himself, he knew it very well."

Neither woman spoke for a minute.

"Even so," said Sarah, picking up the conversation again. "I feel it's wrong of me to say nothing to Harold, yet I also feel it will only hurt him deeply if he has to doubt the paternity of his child. And I think he might feel he's been violated in a way himself…and by an old associate...a former friend you could even say."

She shook her head again and closed her eyes.

"And I can't help feeling guilty…like I participated…I wish I knew what to do. He's so looking forward to having this child. I don't want to spoil that."

Nettie patted Sarah's hand.

"My uncle, the church minister, once told me that telling the truth about something only to free yourself of the weight of it, when you know it will hurt someone, is wrong. It is selfish."

She looked quizzically at her friend.

"Is this not such a case?"

Sarah raised her eyebrows as though deciding.

"It's sort of what I thought," she murmured. "But I can't be sure. If only your uncle was right."

She smiled drily and shrugged.

"So, what he's saying is that it's better in cases like this to be a liar than a selfish person. Maybe that's so...I guess you have to make a choice..."

At that moment, the door burst open.

"Well, you two look like you're plotting a dangerous insurrection," laughed Charles as he shook out his overcoat. "Can we join in?"

"*Certainement pas*," retorted Nettie jokingly, taking the men's coats to hang them up. "We are having women talk. It would not be interesting to you at all."

Harold walked over to Sarah and put his long arm around her.

"How's the little mother-to-be?" He kissed her forehead. "I'm back to tuck you into bed. We have to make sure you have plenty of rest."

"If you had your way, I'd be in bed all day," smirked Sarah, patting his hand. "Thanks for your attentive care, my sweet, but I'm fine, and I'll know good and well when I need to lie down."

Over some tea, the four discussed the wedding again, this time with the knowledge that the fort commander had given his approval for a full military ceremony.

As second in command of the fort, Captain Charles Beaufort had seniority accorded him. So, it was decided to have the commander preside rather than the reverend. Nettie made a reference *sotto voce* to Sarah that while her mother would not have been pleased, she herself didn't mind.

"I have not been to church in very many years," she admitted in very low tones to her friend. "It would be...how do you say... hypocritical of me to pretend..."

Part of the ceremony would involve the traditional saber arch. That was the part that Nettie was particularly interested in and awed by.

"It is such a wonderful thing," she gushed as she tried on her dress at Mary's, with Sarah watching. "No one in my family has ever had something like that."

It was with definite trepidation that she and Sarah had gone to Mary's house to see if progress had been made on the dress.

They didn't know what to expect, as they walked up to the little cabin in the trees. When they saw that the little boy was back in his grandmother's care, seemingly completely unharmed, they were much relieved. By way of explanation, Mary offered a short sentence only:

"My family took care of it."

Sarah figured that the less they knew, the better it would be for all concerned.

Even in the low light of the cabin, Sarah was amazed at what Mary's talents had wrought.

The fabric gave off a beautiful sheen falling in graceful folds to the ground. The bodice was decorated with the same stylized flowers as they had seen on the slippers, only monochromatic in white, silver, and black beads, and small pearls. The modified leg-of-mutton sleeves, or "gigot" if the proper French fashion term was used, had the same decorations, and there was an extra flounce near the bottom of the skirt also decorated with the beads and pearls.

The dress would normally have called for the wearer to have on a corset, but Nettie was so slight, that it didn't seem necessary, or even possible. An extra ruffle would fill out what lacked at her décolleté.

"It's very beautiful, Nettie," said Sarah in a hushed voice, as she trailed a finger along the beading. "Mary. You are a miracle-worker. This is much better than I envisioned. It should be in a catalog somewhere."

Kneeling for easier access to the hem, Mary smiled modestly as well as she could with a mouth full of pins.

"Yes, Mary," added Nettie, fingering the front of the dress avoiding some pins that held a seam together. "I am so grateful to you."

She paused before going on.

"Will you come to the celebration? We would love to have you."

Mary just looked down at the hem she was trying to adjust. She gave a slight shrug.

"Thank you," she said after having removed the pins from her lips. "I do appreciate the invitation." She hesitated. "I don't know if I could, though. But I really thank you."

"Well," said Sarah wanting to take any pressure off her. "You just think about it, and if you decide you want to, just come when you want. You can bring your grandson too."

Mary gave a shy little nod and went back to her pinning.

In a while, as the two other women watched in admiration, she finished doing all the pinning she needed to. The three women cleared a spot on the table and had some tea.

"I was wondering, Mary," said Sarah, examining the intricate beading on one of the slippers from a box on the floor.

"You speak English so well. If you don't mind my asking, how did you learn it?

Mary shrugged shyly and smiled.

"Well, I'm not from here," she explained. "I'm from downriver. My mother was a teacher...a white teacher from Minnesota. She made sure I learned to speak properly."

She chuckled.

"She was after my father to speak properly too, but he always had a hard time. I learned Athabascan from him."

"Oh, so you're completely bilingual then," exclaimed Sarah. "I'll bet that has come in useful at times."

"Yes, I've often had to act as an interpreter."

She shrugged again. "But sometimes it makes me feel like an outsider."

Sarah gestured toward Nettie.

"It's the same for Nettie here. She speaks at least two languages as well. "

"But my English is not so good as you yet," said Nettie to Mary, shaking her head. "I have still many troubles with it. But my Charles is very good with helping me learn."

She beamed at his mention.

Basking in their new friendship, the three women who came from far-flung corners of the world smiled and finished their tea.

With Mary's guarantee that the dress would be finished in a couple of days, and after a profusion of thanks, Sarah and Nettie left the cabin and made their way to main street.

"Let's take a look at what the Commercial Company has these days," suggested Nettie. "I'm not ready to go home yet. I need some decorative candles for our wedding dinner. And, as

I am in a buying mood, anything else that...*comment dit-on*...strikes my fancy, as Charles is always saying."

She smiled mischievously and shrugged in very Gallic manner.

"For some reason, I love that expression."

Sarah had noticed that Nettie was finding much more facility with the language. There was very little need for the translating that she had once had to resort to in almost every conversation.

She had to admit: Captain Beaufort must have very effective teaching methods.

-5-

THE SABER ARCH

The rest of the week, Sarah didn't really have time to dwell on her own problems. She was swept up into the aura of activity surrounding the wedding plans.

Nettie was in constant motion from morning to night, fussing over everything that she deemed important in making things just right for her big day.

While the ceremony would take care of itself because of military customs and regulations, she had a few personal touches in mind. And she went for a few more dress fittings before finally accepting the result and taking it home. Keeping it very secret, she packed it away out of sight. Even Sarah had not seen the completely finished product.

Sarah did wonder how the wedding night accommodations would pan out.

"Maybe we should find somewhere else to spend the night," she whispered to Harold as they prepared for bed.

"They have to have an appropriate place to…to…"

She faded with a silly look on her face."

Harold came over to her, grinning at her embarrassment.

"All taken care of," he smiled, hugging her, and planting a resounding kiss on her forehead.

"Charles has made a special reservation at the inn for a couple of nights. From having their meals served, and being waited on hand and foot, they'll be in the lap of luxury. We don't have to go anywhere."

Sarah was surprised.

"I didn't realize there was any kind of inn here," she said. "If I'd known, we'd have stayed there instead of casting Nettie out of her own bed."

Harold shook his head and made a derogatory noise.

"Do you think for a moment she would've allowed for that? I really doubt it. She wants you as close as possible."

Sarah made a moue of agreement and slipped into bed.

"Still, I feel we're imposing somehow."

Harold slid in after her and placed his very cold feet against her calves. Before she could register her shock with a loud yelp, he put his hand over her mouth.

"Shush. Just give it a minute. I'll warm you up." He removed his hand. "Anyway, we'll be gone by the time the happy couple is ready to move back in. The upriver boat will be here the next day. If things go as planned, everything will work out for the best."

He pursed his lips and raised his eyebrows in a "what more can you ask for" expression of satisfaction.

"Now. Where were we? Oh, yes. I'm supposed to warm you up in short order."

Sarah gave him a baleful glare as he reached for her.

"You have about one minute to get it done…" she growled in a low voice, huddling down in the covers and pushing his cold feet away. "If you can't measure up, you'll be on the floor in just as short order."

Harold made some kind of dismissive noise in the back of his throat and didn't waste any time getting on with his task.

As wedding ceremonies went, this one was simple and straightforward with overwhelming military overtones. Harold escorted Nettie up the aisle formed by rows of infantrymen lined up in the mess hall that could be used for multiple purposes.

In the front row, Sarah could quite easily see how stunned Charles was as he saw his bride approach. And she understood why.

Nettie was a vision of light among a sea of dark uniforms. Her face radiated happiness.

With the help of many candles—arranged by Nettie herself—the muted afternoon light that came in through the windows managed to pick up the silvery sheen of her dress and encouraged the sparkles of the hundreds of beads and seed pearls that Mary had incorporated in the design. Even though the fabric was technically gray, because of its sheen, it seemed to reflect more than a regular white dress would have. The graceful folds reached almost to the ground and shimmered rhythmically as she stepped toward her bridegroom and took his proffered hand.

Her glossy blond hair pinned in a chignon anchored a small lace veil decorated by a few white silk flowers that the two women had found on one of the Alaska Commercial shelves a few days before: "something new."   Around her neck, Nettie wore "something blue:" a length of gauze ribbon that Sarah had bought as a little gift. A small sapphire hung at the front of it; an heirloom wedding gift from her soon-to-be-husband: "something old."

As far as borrowed things went—as a kind of allegiance to her recent past—under the beautifully draped folds of her dress, she had on one of a collection of garters from her friends on Paradise Alley that had either been given to her or had been mixed with the laundry that she had collected for those many months in Dawson. Technically, it was not borrowed, but who was really paying attention?

Resplendent in his uniform, the commander of the Fort read the appropriate words, and waited for the appropriate responses from the couple. There was a small speech, the union was blessed, and then came the part that Nettie had been waiting for with great anticipation.

A dozen of the soldiers on the inside of each respective row pivoted to the side and raised their ceremonial sabers symbolizing protection, to form an arch the length of the aisle, under which the couple walked, hand in hand. The last two soldiers then lowered their sabers into a cross formation as though to prevent the couple from completely going through.

"Captain Beaufort. For passage, you must kiss your bride."

Sarah wasn't sure where the order came from, but it had the desired effect.

Charles paused, took Nettie's face in his hands, bent down, and kissed her passionately. Amongst cheers, the two crossed sabers were raised, and the couple walked beneath them, bright smiles tinged with slight embarrassment.

Along the side of the hall tables covered in white cloths were set up with small delicacies concocted by the mess chef, and champagne glasses. A couple of soldiers did the honors of pouring. The commander held up his glass and toasted the couple while everyone else raised his or her glass, and shouted, "Hear! Hear!"

The couple signed a large book that looked rather like a ledger, and a soldier filling the roll of photographer took a posed photograph of the happy couple.

Then they cut the cake that the cook had fashioned very well for someone who wasn't a baker by trade. They fed each other the first piece, without making too much of a mess.

Sarah sighed as she leaned back against Harold and took a small token sip from her champagne glass. She was gratified that things had gone so smoothly, and that, in spite of not having any family present, Nettie looked so radiantly happy. In truth, it seemed that she now had a new, very big, uniformed family to depend on.

Someone else who wasn't present was Mary. She had probably been too shy to attend. Sarah was sorry that the one person who was responsible for the dress wouldn't see the culmination of her beautiful work. It was to be hoped that, for posterity, the photographs would do it justice.

After a reasonable delay, it was time for the couple to go to their honeymoon suite. Saying good-bye among well-wishers and furtive suggestive leers from a few of Charles' best friends, the couple toured the room expressing their appreciation. When Nettie finally reached Sarah, her eyes glittered with happy tears as she enveloped her friend in a huge hug.

"Oh, my dear friend," she said, sniffing back tears. "How can I thank you enough for the happiest day of my life? I do not think I can…" She let a sob escape, as she buried her face in Sarah's neck. "I would have been so sad without you."

Sarah barely contained her own emotion as she patted her friend on the back.

"Nettie, *ma chérie,* I'm so happy to share in your happiness, you know. I wouldn't have missed this for anything."

She gathered her friend by the shoulders and pulled her gently from her hug.

"Now, go be happy with that handsome husband of yours. We will write every week, without fail. You will tell me everything…"

Nettie nodded, biting her lip to keep it from trembling, and trying to smile at the same time. Then, resignation mixed with happiness all over her face, she turned to Charles, who steered her toward the door, while he smiled his thanks at Sarah and Harold over her head.

In a few seconds, they were gone.

The room darkened a bit.

Sarah felt a physical letdown so intense that she put her arm out to Harold for support. Luckily, she had put her glass down to hug Nettie, or she probably would've dropped it.

"Sarah. What is it?"

Harold could see that something was happening. He wrapped his arm around her waist in support.

"I…I don't know," Sarah hesitated. "I just suddenly felt like… I don't know," she repeated. "I guess it's all the emotion and rush of the last few days." She looked around in a daze. "I just feel so…empty, I guess."

Harold took her over to one of the chairs that lined the wall. He sat down too and took her cold hands in his large warm ones.

"It's perfectly understandable," he said, nodding and rubbing the back of her hands with his thumbs. "I don't think you realize how much you've been doing and going through. And now, to add to it, you've suddenly had to say good-bye to someone you really care about. It all mounts up. It's very understandable that you feel like that."

Sarah nodded slightly, and put her head against Harold's broad shoulder, taking comfort in the solid feel of him. If nothing else, it was a constant that she sorely needed.

They sat for a moment watching as the men began putting some order back into the mess hall. In a few minutes, there was no sign that anything out of the ordinary had taken place in the room, just a few moments before.

Military efficiency thought Sarah. It was forbidding in a way, but also reassuring.

Back at the little house, they had some cheese and bread for supper, washed down with some tea. Neither was very hungry, and both were in pensive moods. The evening's task was to pack their belongings for the trip back to Dawson. Not knowing exactly when the steamboat would show up, they had to be prepared, starting early in the morning.

Sarah paused, absentmindedly holding some folded clothing she had been about to pack in their duffels.

"I do hope Nettie's happiness isn't spoiled by thoughts of our leaving, and that their little honeymoon will be everything she's been expecting and dreaming of for weeks…"

"Well, if it's up to Charles, it certainly will," said Harold placing his extra boots in a bag. "He's been planning everything from the candlelit dinner, and the wine, to the hot water bath, and the scented sheets…and who knows what else. I'm pretty sure all of Nettie's attention will be focused on those things, don't you worry."

Not wanting to disagree, Sarah gave a nod, and continued packing, knowing that no matter what, intruding thoughts could take over, if you let them.

Ferocious banging on the front door brought them both out of their initial deep sleep.

"Captain! Captain Beaufort. Please wake up! Wake up!"

Blinking wearily, Harold lit the bedside candle. Sarah's eyes were wide and questioning as he hurriedly pulled on his trousers.

The banging continued.

Not bothering to tuck in his shirt, he tripped his way to the door in the semi-dark, kicking away some of the half-packed bags that littered the floor.

Outside, a bright moon shone on two faces looking astonished at his appearance.

"Captain Beaufort is at the inn," Harold said in answer to their consternated stares. "He's on his honeymoon. Can I be of service?"

The two—which Harold perceived to be a man and a woman—looked at each other, in obvious quandary.

"There's some trouble in the village. Someone is asking for the captain…and also his wife," one of them finally volunteered haltingly. "One of the women…she say she know her."

By this time Sarah had grabbed a sweater and come to the door.

"Who is it?" asked Sarah, standing partly behind Harold, pulling the sweater around her shoulders. "Is it someone named Mary? Because if it is, I know her, too. What's happening?"

The two looked at each other again, looking uncomfortable out of their environment.

"This lady, my aunt, she say she worked for the captain's fiancée…er…wife. She say that his wife promised to help her…with a family problem."

Sarah put her hand on Harold's arm.

"I'm sure it's Mary Sam," she said quickly. "Her son-in-law is probably causing her trouble again. We did say we would come to her aid if she asked."

"Could we help?" Harold asked the couple, hating to think they would have to interrupt the honeymoon probably currently in progress. Wasn't the "Captain" on leave, anyway?

"My wife could act as a go-between. She's familiar with the situation…"

The couple's expressions indicated that they were obviously out of their decision-making depths. Harold decided to take the matter into his own hands. There was probably precious little in the way of precedent for these things. He didn't relish the thought of alerting the commander who was probably in a peaceful champagne-induced slumber.

He addressed the couple.

"Just give us a moment to dress. Wait here, please."

Before they could respond, he shut the door.

A few minutes later, they were following the moonlit path to the older part of the village. Prepared to turn into Mary's yard, Sarah was surprised when the couple kept going.

Before she could ask where they were headed, they stopped at another cabin, set way back from the path. Sarah could see a light in the window and could hear periodic shrieks from within. A few shadowy shapes moved around in front of the house. Sarah could hear them murmuring to each other.

The couple rushed to the door and pushed it farther open.

From the doorway, following them inside, it took a moment for Sarah, standing in front of Harold, to make sense of the scene before them.

Two men were having a tug of war with a long gun the stock of which was wedged vertically between the feet and knees of the man who was seated on the edge of the only bed. The other one was standing, but bent over, as they both tugged at the barrel, the end of which was inching back and forth under the chin of the seated man. Facing away from the group in the doorway so that Sarah couldn't see their faces, two women were screaming things that she couldn't understand, but could easily imagine.

Before anyone could act, an ear-splitting explosion rocked the scene, rendering Sarah momentarily deaf, and causing her to lose her balance as she instinctively stepped backwards in avoidance.

Putting a hand against the doorframe for support, Harold reached out instinctively to break her fall. In slow motion, she felt herself thump into him, and his arms encircle her, as the scene before her faded to black.

-6-

TOO LATE FOR REGRETS

"Sit him up. Up! He's drowning in his own blood!"

"I'm trying! Lean him against the wall. And someone, get a towel."

"Should we go get the doctor at the mission?"

English was interspersed with Athabascan phrases.

As Sarah came around, she was aware of circulating chaos. She shook her head to try to lessen an odd ringing in her ears, wondering how long she had been unconscious. Blinking a few times, she tried to sit up. Immediately she felt a hand keeping her from it.

"Not yet, Sarah. You need to lie flat for a minute."

Harold was crouched next to Sarah, his hand on his wife's shoulder, his face turned to observe the developments on the bed against the far wall.

From her spot on the floor, she couldn't see what was going on across the room, but she heard grunting and snuffling amid the cries and exclamations from people milling about, trying to do something for the victim on the bed. One of the voices struck her as familiar, even though she couldn't understand the words. A shotgun was propped up in the far corner.

Realizing that she had lost track of time, Sarah suddenly felt a rush of air as the front door was pushed completely open, and she caught the flash of uniforms, and heard another familiar voice. In spite of the unfolding drama, her first thought was random and seemingly frivolous: disappointment at her friends' spoiled honeymoon. The guards at the fort must've heard the gunshot and pulled Charles out of his marriage bed to investigate.

His attention riveted to the bed, he did not notice his friends on the floor in the dim corner. Except for the two people holding the victim sitting upright against the wall, a soggy bloody towel wrapped like an obscene bib around his neck, the crowd around the bed parted to let him through. He quickly assessed the situation.

"Jenkins, go immediately and bring back a stretcher, a wagon, and a few more hands. Quickly, man!"

Jenkins hurriedly saluted and darted out the door. A few seconds later, Sarah heard hoof beats retreating into the night.

Charles faced the crowd, and then noticed Harold, who had stood up in the dark corner of the cabin.

"Good Lord, Harold. What in the…?" he faded and then looked even more surprised as he spied Sarah, still on the floor.
"And Sarah?"

Harold came forward nodding, his face a reflection of the seriousness of the events.

"I guess you'd better get the story here, Charles, and later we'll explain our presence." He shrugged. "I really can't enlighten you much."

Surprise still all over his face, Charles nodded, instantly switching to his official mode.

*   *   *

It took some persistent questioning to arrive at some kind of coordinated account of the events that had led to the shooting.

The people who had been staying in the front yard out of the fray crowded around the doorway in a worried clump.

Sarah realized that two of them had toddlers, half asleep, in their arms. Inside, Sarah soon realized that the voice she had recognized was Mary's, speaking Athabascan. The other woman was apparently the victim's mother, and the victim was none other than Alfred, Mary's ex-son-in-law.

One of the men holding Alfred up so that he could breathe despite the blood pouring into his nose and mouth from head wounds, was Mary's brother. Sarah assumed that the other man was too—they looked very much alike. As brothers were usually in charge of bringing up their nieces, these two must've played a big role in Mary's daughter's life.

The first brother was covered by huge spatters of blood.

"He was so upset about his little son," said one of them haltingly, his English accented by his native tongue. "He did not want to live anymore. His family is against him. We tried to stop him. But he wanted to shoot himself. "He looked down and shook his head disconsolately as Alfred's panicked rattling breaths sounded from the bed. "I tried to stop him. But he's very strong."

And drunk, thought Sarah, as she stood next to Harold— thanks to one of the white man's dubious contributions. She suspected that, just as it had in the lower states, tragedies on the entire last frontier had gone up exponentially in the wake of the introduction into the culture of that single item.

Sarah stole an apprehensive look at the blood-spattered bed. She tried to make sense of it: the copious blood, the contorted sounds of Alfred trying to breathe, and, especially, the gore that had once been his face.

She noticed that one of his feet was bare.

Mary's brothers kept him upright or he would have most certainly drowned. They were trying to stanch the blood flow with little success, as demonstrated by the soggy towel catching the flow that had turned completely red.

The rest of room had become eerily silent; on some level, everyone was aware that there was nothing to do but keep a silent vigil.

Not really knowing what to do either, but feeling she must nevertheless do something, Sarah went over to Mary who had sunk into a lone chair. She put her arm around her in silence. Mary looked up at her and nodded almost formally.

"What happened, Mary? What made him do this?"

Mary just hung her head and shook it slowly. Then she shrugged as if to say she didn't know where to start.

"He was fighting the whole family," she finally uttered in a very low tone. "He knew he was wrong. He knew he couldn't care for the baby. He could not turn to anyone…"

Sarah patted her on the shoulder, encouraging her to go on.

"One of my brothers found Toby wandering around outside. When he went in the house to check…what was going on, he found Alfred with the shotgun to his chin. He was trying to figure out…how to pull the trigger…he was drunk…"

Sarah nodded, picturing the scenario. Mary's brother must have raced over and tried to pull the barrel away from under Alfred's chin. The noisy tug-of-war must have ensued.

The brother had almost succeeded.

But while Alfred's opponent was preoccupied with the location of the end of the barrel, Alfred had managed to surreptitiously wedge his toe inside the trigger guard. It had been enough to accomplish his goal of pulling the trigger. But the simultaneous action by Mary's brother had pulled the barrel out away from its lethal placement right under his chin. Instead, and maybe just as lethally reasoned Sarah, the explosion of buckshot erased his face.

As she had seen in many gunshot wounds before, she knew it was very probable that he would have been better off if there had been no struggle to alter the trajectory of the shot. It would've been instant death. It was most probable that this injury meant a long, drawn-out miserable episode that would in all likelihood lead inexorably to the same final result.

There was a commotion outside.

With a rush of cold air, two soldiers carrying a rolled-up stretcher, and a civilian with a bag rushed inside. Sarah deduced from the bag that this was a doctor, but, with no uniform, obviously not the one from the fort.

Carefully maneuvering the patient from the bed to a seated position on the stretcher, it did not take long to put a blanket over him and take him out to the waiting horse-drawn wagon. Two soldiers were lifting the stretcher, and the doctor held Alfred upright.

The burst of activity left an uneasy quiet in its wake.

Charles addressed the silent group, which had grown due to the people coming in from outside.

"There's nothing more to be done tonight," he announced gently. "There will have to be an inquiry…questioning…in the morning. Everyone will have to attend."

He looked around at the group.

"I know it's likely to be impossible for you, but you should try to at least get some rest."

"But…where they're going with Alfred?" spoke up one of the men, using the customary syntax.

"What we're supposed to do?"

318

Charles put out his hand and shook his head. "You do not need to do anything," he said. "They are taking him to the mission, where the doctor will take care of hm. You can go see him tomorrow."

There was some murmuring and milling about in the room.

"Do you want us to take you to your house?" Sarah asked Mary, who now held one of the toddlers, her grandson. "We're going back that way…"

Mary nodded. Slightly dazed, she looked around the room as though searching for some kind of answer.

"But…who's going to clean up?" she asked in a trembling voice. "This has to be cleaned… He has no family…"

Sarah patted her arm.

"You don't need to worry about that now," she said, trying to nudge Mary to the door. "The inquiry has to be conducted before anyone cleans, anyway. Come on. Let's get you home."

Hugging her grandchild, Mary hesitantly followed Sarah and Harold out into the frosty night.

The moon played hide and seek among the spikey spruce branches as a night breeze blew, leaving odd shaped shadows jumping back and forth along the path, giving it a life of its own.

Sarah kept an arm loosely around Mary, as they made their own little fog clouds with their breath. She thought about telling her how beautiful the dress had been at the wedding but realized it would seem so trivial and terribly insensitive in light of the night's happenings.

Then Mary astonished her.

"Did…Nettie have her wedding? Did she look…beautiful? I…wanted to go…but…" She shrugged and faded.

"Yes, she did," answered Sarah, squeezing Mary's shoulder as they walked slowly behind Harold along the moonlit path.

"It was a wonderful ceremony…and the dress was incredible. It sparkled and shimmered in the candlelight, and her husband was amazed. She looked absolutely beautiful, thanks to you."

Even in the dim light, Sarah could see Mary smile a bit with satisfaction.

"I'm so glad," she said, as she stopped at her front yard. "At least this night was good for someone."

Then she turned toward the dark shape of her house, still hugging sleeping little Toby.

Sarah and Harold prepared for bed for the second time that night.

"It'll be dawn, soon," said Harold, pulling back the curtain, and looking out the window, his features outlined in silver by the moonlight. "And I'm afraid we're not going to be on that steamship…"

Sarah didn't say anything as she folded her clothes and laid them on a chair. They smelled of wood smoke that reminded her of the scene at the cabin. Her stomach was unsteady, and she had a headache.

"Just come to bed and hug me," she pleaded, once more in her nightgown, as she crawled into bed. "I can't force myself to think of anything productive right now."

Harold quickly took off his day clothes and joined her.

"You're right, my sweets," he said. "Let's try to empty our minds of everything. Tomorrow will be soon enough to deal with everything."

He wrapped his arms around his wife and put his lips on her forehead. Sarah closed her eyes, breathed in Harold's calming familiar scent, willing her mind to escape to a void somewhere ...anywhere.

As usual, it was much easier said than done.

-7-

BINDING TIES

They had to be frustratingly idle while the steamship came and went.

Unlike many of the villagers, Sarah did not even go down the bank to see it dock, take on firewood, and leave. It was too much of a disappointment—she knew it would be way too depressing to watch it leave the bank and head upriver—and she was way too tired after having been up most of the night. She felt like a useless lump, knowing it was so close, yet so far.

Harold, however, less worried by his own emotional state, went down to talk to the pilot.

"He said it's doubtful that there will be another upriver steamboat, before the end of the month and freeze-up," Harold said dejectedly, as he reentered the house, peeling off his jacket, and hanging it up.

"And Christ. It feels like that could occur at any time now."

He vigorously rubbed his hands together.

"I'm afraid we're going to need our parkas and wool trousers that we didn't bring with us. Not to mention our footwear."

"Unfortunately, we weren't clairvoyant," shrugged Sarah.

"Who knew we'd get involved in a suicide attempt, become witnesses, and possibly face the ravages of winter away from home. I don't know about you, but my naïve plan was simply to attend a wedding..." She smiled drily at her husband, who returned the look.

"No fooling. Something about 'the best-laid plans…' I seem to remember. What it has to do with 'mice and men,' I don't really get."

Sarah put some leftovers on the table, supplementing them with some newly baked muffins.

"Well, I guess you have to know the entire saying for it to make sense. Anyway, there's nothing to do but ride things out and see what happens. I'm so pleased that Charles and Nettie can at least continue their honeymoon for a day or two."

She glanced around the cabin.

It was a comfort that Harold had had the foresight to pack their fur robes and hats. In the worst case, less practical than a parka, those items would go far to provide warmth.

"But now, we will certainly have to come up with a new place to stay. They can't both sleep in that rickety day bed when it's over…"

They ate their supper in companionable silence, Harold occasionally patting Sarah's hand whenever she put her fork down. Both were processing their new circumstances and trying to put things in some kind of order that made sense.

The next day, Sarah's priority was to go back to Mary's house to see what was happening.

"Alfred…didn't make it," were Mary's first words, as Sarah sat down with her. "He just died under the doctor's care at the mission. Just…died."

She shrugged and looked questioningly at Sarah.

"They say he just gave up. Just turned his head away, and gave up…"

Most of the sewing notions and paraphernalia had been put away. There was a playpen and a crib in the corner. She could see Toby asleep for a nap.

"Can you tell me how this whole thing…how it all happened?" asked Sarah softly so as not to awaken the child.

"I know this sounds uncharitable, but it's probably for the best. He would have suffered a great deal with those injuries…"

Mary nodded, her mouth a grim line.

"As much of a menace as he was," she said, her voice low. "I kind of blame myself for this whole thing. If I had tried harder, I could probably have had some kind of agreement with him. I should have tried harder… He was my son-in-law…"

Sarah knew all too well how the self-blame game worked.

"Mary, listen to me. You did try to reason with him…as well as you can with a person who's drunk most of the time, and who has a bitter outlook on everything. That man would never have listened to reason. In the end, it was him against the whole world. He saw a fight everywhere."

Mary put her head in her hands.

"I would've let him have his son at least part-time," she said, about to cry. "If he just would've listened…"

Sarah patted Mary's arm.

"Well, that's just it," she said, trying to comfort her increasingly distraught friend. "He would not have listened to you. There could never have been the agreement you're talking about. What kind of life would that've been for little Toby? He would've grown up very insecure, never knowing what the next day held for him."

There was quiet as Mary seemed to be processing what Sarah was saying.

"For where you come from, it sounds right," she finally sighed, as if she was resigned to not making herself understood.

"But it's different for us. After all this…now, I'm…I'm just…His family…they're mad at me."

"What?" exclaimed Sarah. "Mad at you? Why in the world...?"

Mary nodded with an anxious look on her face that deeply gripped Sarah and made her extremely uneasy.

"Yes...they are. Even though they didn't like what he did, and often chastised him—even fought—he was a relative...they stick with him. They say it's my fault. And...I told you...I'm an outsider to some of them. Some didn't even want Alfred and my daughter to get married because of that. Now...I'm afraid...I'm afraid..."

Sarah couldn't believe what she was hearing and didn't know where to start.

"Have they threatened you? Alfred hasn't even been buried yet. Can't they just let things be? "

Mary shook her head.

"I'm not so afraid for myself," she said tearfully, looking over at the crib.

"It's Toby. It's that...I'm afraid they'll try to take Toby."

Sarah was almost speechless.

"Don't they want what's best for him? Can't you find some kind of solution together?"

Mary's eyes shifted to Sarah with a look bordering on mockery and derision, while trying to remain friendly.

"You're talking about people up and down the river in years past—families—who sealed other families alive in their underground homes and set them on fire... all over some inherited dispute."

She shook her head ominously.

"I've been fighting one son-in-law. Now it's many people I'm up against. Sometimes the new generation doesn't even know how the dispute started, or what it was about exactly. They just know they should be fighting about something."

She gave Sarah a very troubled look.

"Family disputes never end, not even in death."

Sarah's visit to Mary had left a very bad taste in her mouth. If Mary had been totally accepted by the community, she wouldn't have been alone at a time like this, laying bare her personal struggles to a stranger of a few days ago.

Sarah understood quite profoundly that there were many conflicts and undercurrents in village life of which the white population was totally ignorant. It was as though there were a couple of parallel universes existing only yards away from each other.

There would be a potlatch for Alfred; everyone would donate a dish of food. If sparks were going to fly, it would probably be at some point during that ceremonial get together. If alcohol was added to the mixture, drama was bound to follow as sure as the evening would end with a procession to the cemetery.

As Sarah was coming to understand, the grave was not the end of life's entanglements of the departed. Legacies lived on with all the intensities and complications that life had held.

Good or bad, heritage was an inescapable fact of life.

* * *

Her clothes were beginning to bind. Allowances for growth of her belly while living in a strange place, was another thing that they could not have foreseen at the outset of the trip.

Sarah so missed her sewing machine.

"Don't worry, *ma chère*, I have pins, needles, scissors, and I also have some thread," said Nettie her voice muffled as she rummaged around in her trunk. "We will be able to make something more comfortable for you."

She nodded and smiled.

"And I'm sure we can get help from Mary for anything too difficult for us."

Harold and Sarah had moved to a vacant cabin in the old part of the village. Everyone knew it was a temporary situation, including the owner of the furnished cabin, an old Swede, who charged them a nominal fee. Having been widowed, and having found a second wife who came with her own cabin, he hadn't used this one in years.

"Yust keep the fire goin' and don' break nothing," he said, his mouth twisted into a grin, as they discussed the rental possibility before laying eyes on it. "An' if ye can, a little cleaning wouldn't be amiss. My first wife used to manage that, but she's been gone ten years now…"

Sarah nodded knowingly, picturing ten years' worth of grime, and trying to figure out where the cleaning supplies and equipment were going to come from to deal with it. For a moment, she also wondered why cleaning had stopped with the wife's passing. Then the dictum "woman's work" flashed into her brain.

Oh…of course. A disconcerting reoccurring theme if ever there was one.

Eyeing the cabin with trepidation as she and Harold pushed open the door for the first time, Sarah was relieved to find that whether dust and dirt were young or old, it could still be swept away with the same broom or cloth. It just took a bit more elbow grease.

The ceiling logs were black from smoke, and the window was but a tiny square of grainy glass—things that were to be expected. But it looked as though the first wife had tidied up and cleaned before her passing, and the remaining years that it had stood empty hadn't caused too much additional wear.

"We get a fire going, and clean up a bit, and we'll have a decent home here," said Harold, his breath in great clouds, as he looked around. "It's only for a little while anyway, until this, uh…matter gets settled."

"And the first thing," he said, pointing to the far wall, "will be to fix that bed."

Sarah figured he was already picturing more improvements to be made. The bed, indeed, was barely standing even though it was partly built into the wall.

She nodded, her mouth twisted in thought, her mind flashing back to their cabin in Dawson. She realized she was homesick for the comforts she had left behind and had taken for granted up to now.

She shivered. Even though her brain told her that it was no colder inside than out, the darkness of the closed-in space gave the illusion of much colder temperature. Maybe it was the dampness…or the gloom. She couldn't wait to step back outside into the sun's rays, weak as they might be.

"*Ne t'en fais pas…*" comforted Nettie, after having listened to Sarah's vivid and somewhat depressing description of the new living situation. "Don't worry. I will help you with cleaning." She smiled ruefully. "After all those years I was working for Madame Renée, I am a very good expert."

She was true to her word.

Not only was the cabin whipped into habitable shape in a few days, but they figured out a way for Sarah to be more comfortable in clothes.

Back during the gold rush days, when living and traveling conditions had often dictated it, some women had gladly eschewed their impractical skirts and dresses for men's clothing. To fit in the hips, most trousers were too wide at the waist. Consequently, they had to be cinched with belts, causing much uncomfortable bunching.

Bearing this in mind, the two women found several pairs of the shortest trousers they could at the Alaska Commercial store. Because they were still a bit long, they had to hem the pant legs a few inches. Then they altered the waist for a closer but adjustable fit, tailor made for Sarah's expanding anatomy.

"C'est tout à fait la nouvelle mode!" exclaimed Nettie. "I think we have invented a new style. I am going to make the same for me."

It took a while for the menfolk to appreciate the sudden change; it was hard to envision women without volumes of skirts and petticoats covering their lower half. That they had legs was now front and center. But when the men saw how much more easily the women could approach and accomplish their tasks, without yards of material getting in the way, they became firm believers.

But the unfamiliarity still made them a bit uncomfortable.

"I can't get used to constantly seeing the outline of your…you know…buttocks," grinned Harold self-consciously. "I mean…I've always known all that was there…"

He waved his hand to vaguely illustrate the point.

"But now I don't have to use my imagination…"

"I suppose you weren't aware of my legs either," quipped Sarah, nudging his shoulder, and smirking. "What did you think held me up? My petticoats?"

Harold gave her a dry look, and threw a log on the stove fire, creating a shower of sparks.

"You just get used to things being the way they have always been," he said shrugging and quickly shutting the stove door. "I suppose that, in the long run, it's possible that I may not even notice the difference...maybe."

He frowned and looked doubtful.

"But you don't really think this will catch on, do you? I mean...women in trousers instead of skirts...?"

The look on his face was incredulity personified.

"Who knows?" answered Sarah, shrugging and then holding up a forefinger. "But, for your information, I'll venture even further. I'll bet that, before long, corsets will go out of style as well. Imagine that."

She was very smug and superior in voicing her prediction.

Harold looked at her, pursed his lips in disbelief, and shook his head derisively, as if she had grown another head.

"Um-hunh." he uttered, non-committedly, so that his response could not to be construed as aimed in any direction.

Clothing styles were not his area of expertise. At great risk of losing the argument, he wasn't about to wage a dispute on the subject.

Sarah couldn't very well disagree with a non-opinion.

-8-

SNOWFALL

It was to be expected, and when it finally snowed, it was as if some tension was released. Once a good layer formed on the ground, things could be planned for in earnest. Sleds were turned right side up and repaired, and appropriate footwear, mitts, and parkas came out of storage. Even the dogs seemed to know that their contribution was soon to be exacted from them.

Charles was able to collect all sorts of outerwear for Harold and Sarah from the quartermaster's office at the fort. By the time he had delivered everything, they had more complete outfits than if they had relied on their own belongings.

Their wardrobe thus supplemented, they were much better prepared for a stay of indeterminate length.

"We're going to need an extra room to store all this," exclaimed Sarah as she started to go through the mound of clothing in the living area of the cabin. "Look, Harold. There are even towels, sheets and…good grief…a tablecloth!"

"Well, the military knows how to outfit people, and organize, that's for sure." He shrugged and raised his eyebrows knowingly. "I guess that's why we win wars."

Sarah had to agree. She was beginning to feel as secure with the U.S. Army as she had with the Canadian Mounted Police, though she missed her charismatic idol, Superintendent Steele.

But, in the U.S., the entity that was supposed to deal with any sort of policing was the office of the U.S. Marshall. The military was a separate body.

At the beginning of the Gold Rush, only one Marshall and ten deputies had been assigned duty in the entire territory of Alaska. That meant that the application of the law was sketchy rather than timely. Crimes were slow to be solved, if at all. But, often, due to the dedication and tenacity of the Marshalls, even the crimes covered up by snow at the time they were committed—usually involving a body or stolen items—often yielded clues by the Spring thaw, that the Marshall's office was surprisingly successful in pursuing to a satisfactory conclusion.

Although the office of U.S. Marshall was not really an investigative body—usually just carrying out arrests under the directive of a district judge—circumstances in Alaska dictated that they perform all the duties normally carried out be detectives and police officers. So all the outlying Alaskan villages, lacking any local or state police, counted on them to both investigate crimes and to carry out the arrests of the perpetrators.

"So, when do you think the Marshall will arrive?" Sarah asked Charles, as they ate dinner together a few evenings later. "I guess we'll have to stay here until that happens, right?"

"The fact that you two actually saw the shooting, makes you rather indispensable to the investigation," said Charles, tearing off a piece of pastry from a sausage roll.

"But I'm sure they'll release you from your obligation once you've testified."

"But it was an accident, *n'est-ce pas*?" asked Nettie, serving Charles the last of the roasted potatoes. "It is not a murder investigation…"

"Whenever there's a death, there are always many possibilities, especially when a weapon is involved," answered her husband, patting her hand. "So, there has to be an investigation to rule things out. But, to answer your question about when the Marshall will arrive, Sarah, I'm afraid your guess is as good as mine."

* * *

There's a crime been committed in Rampart," said Harold, coming in from the cold and dark a few days later, wincing as the ice formed by his breath on his mustache pulled whiskers when he opened his mouth.

It had snowed almost every day, leaving a substantial layer. Pretty soon it would be too cold for precipitation. Most well-beaten paths would harden to a concrete-like layer.

The river was a mass of slow-moving ice.

"I don't know much about the circumstances, but according to the telegraph, the Marshall is going to be there in a few days. We should go to talk to him. That way we won't have to wait so long to give our testimony."

Sarah looked up from her sewing, a blank look on her face.

"Yes, but when you say we should go to talk to him, what does that mean? That's quite a distance, right?"

Harold peeled off layers of clothing and hung them up on the large hooks by the door. Then he grunted as he removed his felt boots.

"Yes, of course. It would be a long day's dogsled ride. I'm sure the trip would be exhausting. We can't count on river travel any more, until things have been frozen for a while. I'm not sure how were going to get home now."

Sarah was silent. The idea of any kind of trip was beginning to seem onerous to her. She had begun to feel settled where they were, and reluctant to move.

"So, what do you think? You up for a sled ride?"

"You mean with your big team of three dogs?" She made a derogatory noise. "That ought to be a rather slow proposition. Would we make it by Christmas, do you think?"

Harold gave her a dry look as he poured a cup of stale coffee from the pot on the stove.

"Oh, ye of little faith," he retorted, taking a swallow and grimacing at the taste. "Charles said he could put a few teams together, with a driver or two. We would just be along for the ride."

Sarah knew that Harold had been practicing his newly acquired dogsled driving skills for a while. The fort had a few teams from which Harold had borrowed a trio of dogs, and he had bought a light sled from someone in the village. He was slowly becoming obsessed with the enterprise.

Sarah wasn't at all sure that she liked the idea of those dogs tied up behind the cabin, just feet from the back door. Apart from nightly howling, they were eerily silent most of the time, and looked brutish. When she went outside to get firewood from the stockpile along the wall, they snapped their jaws at her, with not one welcoming wagging tail to be seen.

And, to add insult to injury, there was now a perpetual caldron of fish boiling for the dogs' dinner right outside the back door as well. She could've quite easily done without it.

It seemed like Harold was becoming quite comfortable with village living. She liked the fact that he had developed an interest in something, so she kept her reservations to herself. Truth be known, both of them were adapting quite well to their new environment.

As far as her new life was concerned, Sarah saw Nettie almost every day, and they both visited Mary quite often.

Learning how to bead and make slippers, Sarah enjoyed the quiet hours sewing with her friends, learning new skills and having conversation that enlightened her to many revelations, and often made a good story.

"You know," said Mary one day, chuckling "In the not so old days, we were really ignorant about some things. Because we expected every sack brought to the store to contain sugar, we had no idea about flour. When the guys slit open the bags to taste it, they threw it all away because it wasn't sweet. When we realized what it actually was, we really got after them. After that, they always let the women check the goods."

As far as her personal relations went, it seemed that Mary's son-in-law's family had calmed down about her supposed culpability in his death. No one had overtly threatened her, and they hadn't made any attempt to take Toby away from her.

"But I'm not completely relaxing," she cautioned, nodding knowingly. "It doesn't take much to set them off. People carry grudges for a really long time. It doesn't take much to reignite the fires of revenge."

Sarah felt sorry that her friend had to remain on the defensive for life apparently. By the time someone had reached her age, it seemed like things should go more easily; she should be able to enjoy her grandson in complete freedom.

It was one of those cultural things that was difficult to understand. Mary was so obviously caught between two ethnic and cultural systems; it made her see some things more clearly, but, at the same time, the understanding of both cultures made it all the more poignant for her, and a great deal more frustrating.

After a break for tea, the three women discussed Sarah's impending trip by dogsled.

"It should be fine," counseled Mary, as she speared some beads on her long very fine needle. "You will have two or possibly three guys who are experts driving the sleds. All you have to do is make sure you stay warm. People have been travelling that way for centuries."

She laughed.

"It's probably safer than the steamboat trip. At least you'll be on solid ground most of the time…"

"Most of the time?" Sarah immediately picked up on that qualification. "When wouldn't we be?

"Well," said Mary, trying to sound reassuring to allay any fears. "At some points you might have to cross a river or something, that might have open spots. There are some short cuts sometimes…but the dogs usually know if it's safe."

Sarah thought back to Harold's grim-faced, toothy four-legged friends tied up in her back yard. Depending on their judgment seemed a stretch.

Freeze-up was upon them.

The river, thick with ice floes just a few days ago, and thickening bank ice forming treacherous layers, was now motionless. They had awakened to a completely stationary and silent waterway.

Some of the hardiest and craziest villagers had pushed their luck, trying to be the last souls get across in a skiff, dodging the crushing blocks of ice, before the river completely froze over. Some made it over, and some turned back in fear. They would try to do the same in the spring, walking across the rotting ice, trying to see who could beat break-up by the narrowest of margins.

At its zenith, the sun now barely skimmed the treetops on the far side of the river, its rays so low as to make everyone squint. In a few weeks, they would not see it at all. For a few hours, there would just be a brighter section of sky backlighting the trees to the south, before darkness returned.

This was a place where the sun rising in the east and setting in the west was only true for half the year. In the summer it rose and set in the north; in the winter it did the same in the south. Sarah hoped that schoolchildren weren't penalized for disagreeing with the general rule.

When Sarah got home, she found Harold very busy, packing clothes and survival gear.

He looked up at her, as she shook off her coat and removed her felt shoes.

"From what I hear," he said excitedly. "There are a dozen stores in Rampart. I'm sure you can probably find anything you want there."

"Good grief," said Sarah surprised. "That must mean there's quite a population. I had no idea."

"Charles said that there are over four hundred and fifty cabins—mostly for miners, of course. There are six gold-producing creeks…" he added with a sparkle in his eye. For an alarming moment Sarah thought he was going to express a direct interest in that.

"Don't worry, my sweet," he said, smiling at her expression. "I'm not planning another danger-fraught foray into the gold-mining world. I just mean everything seems to be a going concern over there. In addition, they're building a winter trail to be used for mail etc. So there's quite a bit of business from construction."

"Hmm," ruminated Sarah, her mind always open to enterprise, and relieved that Harold was resisting the lure of gold nuggets. "Sounds like, with the right business, a person could make some money. Maybe we should inquire…"

Harold pursed his lips.

"As though we don't have enough on our plates right now," he scolded, indicating Sarah's burgeoning anatomy. "That's all we need to do: start a new business from scratch in a place completely unfamiliar…"

"Oh, Harold. Take it easy. I'm just thinking out loud. It doesn't mean I'm serious."

She was silent for a moment.

"But, you know, come to think of it, no one says we have to settle in Dawson. It is in a foreign country after all. I don't know if it's important, or relevant, but maybe we should make sure our progeny is born on American land."

Holding a boot, Harold stood still, a funny frown on his face. He obviously hadn't thought about any such complications.

"I guess you could be right," he said. "It's possible that we should know all the rules of citizenship. I don't want to get ahead of myself here, but I'm quite sure I don't want Canada to press our child into its military service…if their laws permit that. Yep. We really should find those things out. Ignorance of the law is no excuse. Maybe Charles knows."

He continued his packing, a thoughtful look on his face.

-9-

OUT OF YOUR DEPTH

The new snow glittered in the slanted sunrays, reminding Sarah of a blanket of diamonds. Such a trite expression, she told herself, but apt nevertheless.

Hovering around zero, the temperature had stabilized for a few days. Sarah was trying to re-acclimatize herself to that type of severe cold that seemed to place an iron grip on you as soon as you stepped outside. After a few seconds, the inside of your nose tickled as the hairs froze and pulled when you wiggled it. Instant frost on your lashes from your condensing breath weighed down your lids: you made sure to breathe through your nose so as to warm the air a bit before breathing it into your lungs. And you were very careful to protect any exposed flesh to avoid frostbite.

Ahead of Sarah's sled moved a self-generating small factory of fog; six dogs breathing hard as they negotiated the particular ups and downs and abrupt curves of the narrow path through the spruce and birch trees, branches laden with snow.

Contrarily to what Harold had remarked in preparing Sarah for the journey, you couldn't really "just sit there." He had assured her that her role would be fairly passive.

Passive? Right, husband, master of the understatement, indeed! After hours of this, she'd be lucky to escape with light bruising and mild dislocations.

Getting knocked left to right, bounced up and down, accelerating and the braking in quick succession forced you to actively brace yourself and hang on.

And then there was her belly.

But she remembered Mary telling her that many women in her condition had travelled like this for centuries. There was comfort in that solidarity.

Firmly ensconced in her new ride, several blankets wedged around her like a cocoon, her hooded head solid against the back of the sled, Sarah couldn't easily turn her head to look back at the third sled carrying Harold. So she kept her eyes on the leading sled, and on the dogs pulling her along. The sled runners made a shushing sound as they cut through the top layer of icy snow.

Harold had wanted to ride the runners and drive the sled himself, but the designated military drivers had dissuaded him, saying that they might let him drive on the parts of the path that were fairly straightforward. He had accepted his novice status without too much dissent, and sat in silence, observing the method.

The first sled was carrying survival gear, including several sets of snowshoes. It was driven by one of the villagers who wanted to use the occasion to visit family in Rampart.

Trying to wade through the softer snow away from the trail without snowshoes would be an exercise in futility, especially for people who weren't in the best of shape or out of practice. Snowshoes were a definite necessity for life on the trail; forgetting them could be costly. Even the horses could be fitted for them; the tack shed at the fort had rows of the specialized round snowshoes ready for deployment.

Once they reached an expanse of countryside that was fairly open, the ride did become less bumpy, and Sarah found herself dozing for a few minutes at a time. Then the landscape changed back to a narrow path through tightly packed spruce trees.

More uncomfortable bumps and lumps.

At one point, the trail widened. The lead driver put up a hand. Sarah took this to mean that it was time for a break.

It was a good thing, because her bladder was about to burst, very sore from the bumps she'd had to absorb. She hated to think how many times she'd be in this predicament on this trip.

Her sled drew up even with the first sled and went slightly forward before the team slowed to a stop. As she extricated herself from all the blankets wrapping her up, she could only think of relieving herself. She hurriedly got out of the sled and quickly went for the side of the trail, fully intent on hiding behind a few bare branched bushes.

"Sarah! Wait. Don't. It's too…"

But the warning came too late. The minute she stepped off the path, she sank into the snow past her knees. It might as well have been wet concrete. She couldn't move.

The men rushed over and pulled her back up and on to the harder packed trail.

Able to walk unimpeded once more, and rather than take time to strap on snowshoes, Sarah chose to conduct business a bit farther down the trail out of sight. It was more than a breezy experience; she felt great relief to get back into the sled and wrap herself in covers, all the while cursing her challenged bladder.

The drivers and Harold seemed to be involved in some kind of discussion, their breath surrounding them in great clouds. Sarah gave up trying to make out what they were saying and was about to lean her head back against the sled to try to doze. She was slowly warming up beneath the blankets.

There was a sudden small crack as the runners of her sled jarred loose.

Her eyes flew open.

Out of the corner of one of them she was aware of a large shape up ahead before her head was slammed back against the sled as the lead line abruptly took up the slack.

Before she could gather her wits and completely focus, she got the rear view of the dogs charging down the trail and felt the sled gather speed, as they hauled her along with them.

The trees whipped by in dizzying succession.

Looking ahead she saw what she now realized was a moose loping along the trail taking advantage of the hard packed snow. Free of any commands, the dogs wasted no time in pursuit.

Gripping the sides of the sled in panic, Sarah hung on, at complete loss for what to do.

Had the brake not been set?

She heard an odd sound before she realized that she was hearing her own panicked screams. She tried to turn her head to see if anyone was following but was battered to and fro so violently that it was impossible.

Paralyzed, she could only focus on the dog team and the moose that seemed to be losing ground ahead. She didn't know whether to wish for it to get away, or for the dogs to catch up and—she hoped—stop when they reached their quarry. In either case, she couldn't begin to imagine what would happen.

Rendering the whole dilemma moot, the moose disappeared around a sudden bend in the trail, the dogs frantically tearing after it, dragging the sled around the curve. With no driver, and at such speed, the sled swung wide, with nothing to stop its wild trajectory. At the widest arc, the lead line straining, the sled flipped over a small snow berm along the edge of the trail and slammed into a tree stump.

Sarah was thrown out of the sled, landing in the snow, but not before having taken a violent blow to the body. She was vaguely aware of the empty sled getting stuck between two trees at some distance away, and the dogs barking and howling in frustration as their chase was suddenly arrested.

Then she lost consciousness.

"Sarah! Sarah! Speak to me!"

She opened her eyes. She must have gone blind, at least partially. It was dark. She felt pain and nausea. Suddenly, she sat up, put her head to the side and projectile vomited.

"Forget Rampart. We have to get her to the MacKenzie cabin. We can get her warm there."

Sarah was aware of someone's frightened voice. Nothing made sense, and her pain was overwhelming.

"My God. She's shaking so badly. How far to the cabin?"

Sarah recognized Harold's voice. She tried to utter something but wasn't able.

The next moments blended together. She felt as though she was moving, and then was aware that someone had picked her up and carried her. Fading in and out of consciousness, she couldn't keep track of time.

She had no idea where she was, nor how much time had elapsed since she had first passed out. She was in some kind of a bed, with darkness all around except for a small source of light off to the side.

"Harold?"

It was barely more than a croak. She cleared her throat, tasting something sour.

"Harold? Where am I? What happened?"

In less than a few seconds she felt her hand being squeezed.

"I'm right here, Sweetness. Take it easy. We're in a hunting cabin. You're safe now."

She was dimly aware of Harold kneeling by her side. "How do you feel? Are you warm enough? I've got a fire going. Do you want some water?"

It was a lot of questions to process, but she nodded at the last one. She desperately wanted to rid herself of the horrible taste in her mouth.

Feeling a bit better after taking a few sips from the cup of water that Harold held for her, she made a mental assessment of her condition.

Everything hurt: her back, her head, her ribs. She was close to being nauseated again, and she felt pains low down in her belly. A bandage was slipping down over her forehead. And there was something odd, something unexplainable between her legs… thickness, and moisture.

She started to pull up her skirts to pull down her custom-made pants to figure it out.

"Sarah…wait. I need to …wait. Something happened."

She felt Harold grab her hands.

Confused, she looked at him from under the slipping bandage, seeing only an outline of his features in the weak light of a lamp.

"Why? What? What happened?"

Harold dropped his chin down to his chest and closed his eyes. He was silent, as if searching for words. Sarah realized she was holding her breath waiting for him to speak.

Then, he rearranged her head bandage and, in a very low voice, spoke slowly.

"Sarah…I have to tell you…you…you've had an accident. Your driver didn't set the brake properly on your sled when we took a break. The team took off after a moose and the sled flew out of control around the curve. The sled flipped you out right by a large stump." He grabbed both her hands. "You took a big hit. It knocked you out."

Sarah nodded slowly, breathing with difficulty. Then she gestured toward her skirt under the covers.

"I don't remember hitting, but I know I saw the sled after. It was stopped. What…" She slowly shook her head in puzzlement, not really knowing what to ask.

Harold smoothed the blanket and offered more water.

She took a few experimental sips.

Putting the cup down on a little shelf behind the headboard, Harold took a deep breath. Sarah was clear-headed enough to realize he was troubled, but without the energy to figure out what might be causing it.

Overwhelmed with fatigue, she could only lie back and close her eyes.

"When we reached you, the blankets and cover were tossed around, all over the ground," continued Harold. "In a way, they actually saved you from getting too many scrapes because you had been so wrapped up. But you were bleeding from your head…and… we could see blood seeping through your skirt…and into the snow. "

Harold stopped and took hold of his wife's hands again and took a long shuddering sigh.

"Sarah, I'm so sorry. So sorry. It's bad news…" He bit his lips together, trying to find the strength to continue. "I'm afraid you…we…lost the baby."

The words came out in a rush, and he couldn't help a loud sob. In the weak light of the lamp, Sarah could see tears glistening on his cheeks.

For a moment, she felt nothing. It was as though Harold was telling a story about someone else—someone she didn't even know. But the sight of her husband's obvious distress cut right through the fog. Her eyes suddenly filled with tears.

Harold struggled to control his voice and went on.

"Peter, the native driver, recognized what was wrong when you started to moan in intervals. His wife went through the same thing. He said we needed to pack you…bind you. There was a lot of blood…lots of clots."

He shook his head as if trying to rid himself of the recollection. "The shock was just too much for you to absorb."

The vacant stare Sarah was fixing on him made him wince. He wasn't sure she completely understood the implications of what was happening to her. But her next statement made him realize that she certainly didn't.

"How…how long have I been here?" Her hand went to her lower belly, missing the former little bulge. "I don't remember…having the baby…I did have it, right?" She looked around the bed. "Where is he?"

Harold was shocked into silence; his wife had obviously not grasped the most salient part of what he had told her.

Sarah shook his arm.

"Please, Harold. I need to see him."

She looked around the cabin as if noticing that they were alone for the first time.

"Where is Peter? And the other fellows?" Her gaze came back to Harold and fear crossed her face.

"Did they take him, Harold? Did they? Where did they go?"

She became agitated, waving the arm that hurt less and thrashing her legs, undoing the bedding and the pieces of cloth that were absorbing her residual blood loss.

Gathering himself, Harold stood up and tried to hold her arm steady. He noted her feverish condition: a dangerous sign. It probably explained why she wasn't able to grasp the reality of the situation.

"Hold on, Sarah, please. I'll explain everything. You've been in and out of consciousness overnight and half the day. Christ! I tried to keep you awake but..."

He knelt back down by her side.

"The others went on to Rampart to try to get some help for you. There's supposedly a doctor and a hospital there. I thought it was better not to move you very much. To avoid more blood loss. Luckily, we were only a mile and half away from this cabin."

He patted her arm and gestured outside. "Someone should be back very shortly."

Sarah shook her head in bewilderment.

"But why did they go on? Why did they leave us behind?"

Harold got up and went to the woodstove. He poured some hot water from an antique kettle over some tea leaves in an old, cracked cup. He came back to Sarah and held it to her lips.

"Drink this. It'll make you feel better and warm you up. I promise. I'll try to explain everything to you."

Sarah took some hesitant sips. Then she gave a small cough and shuddered. A most plaintive expression painted itself across her features, and her hands gripped the covers.

"But Harold…please. Where's my baby? Why won't you let me have him? Why are you being cruel? I'm sure he needs me…"

Her face and words cut Harold to the quick. He was powerless.

The last thing he ever wanted to do was harm his wife. But he knew he couldn't protect her from the harm that had already irretrievably befallen them both. She didn't seem to understand that everyone had been on her side. It was just that there was unfortunately no help for it.

-10-

SMALL WORLD

It took three basins' worth of heated snow water to wash Sarah in any satisfactory way.

An old, waxed tablecloth served to shield the bedding as Harold painstakingly sponged bloody stains from the inside of Sarah's upper thighs with parts of one of the shirts from his duffel. After a quick search, he had found that his shirt was definitely cleaner than anything he could find lying around in the cabin.

Sarah did not respond in any great measure to his careful ministrations. Her eyes seemed to be focused on some distant point on the smoky logs of the ceiling. She didn't seem to notice that Harold tried to work as quickly as he could in order that she not get cold without blankets over her. She didn't seem to realize that he tried to ascertain that there was no more active bleeding. In fact, she didn't seem to be aware of much at all that was happening to her.

Harold tore some strips from the much-abused shirt to fasten the pad he had fashioned to absorb the seeping fluids to hold it firmly to her body. Then after having checked that his "bandages" were held well in place and serving their purpose as effectively as possible, he quickly put her skirt and the covers back over her to trap any heat that was left.

While she rested fitfully, he rinsed the remaining pieces of his shirt, and hung them over the back of a chair in front of the woodstove. They were cleaner, but still very stained. Then he quickly threw the murky water from the basin, out the door. He had also rinsed her custom trousers. They were steaming on the chair as well.

Disregarding a few dried bloodstains, he had left her wool stockings on, hoping to at least keep her feet warm. Having experienced the great cold, he had learned long ago that the temperature of your feet could affect how your whole body felt.

Terrified of his wife's apparent fragile emotional state, Harold tried to think of some way he could bring her back to reality in the most gentle of ways. He fought to but couldn't repress the memory of Peter burying formless matter in a shallow frozen grave—no more than an indentation into hard packed snow—in the waning daylight of the worst day of his life.

After reloading and stoking the fire in the stove, he decided that some food might help. Pulling out what they had packed in the way of food stores, he decided on some dehydrated potatoes and jerked meat. He supplemented that with a package of dried fruit.

It took half an hour to prepare the food. He cut the meat into very small pieces and mixed it in with the reconstituted potatoes. Then he brought a bowl of it to Sarah's bedside.

Her eyelids were fluttering, but she wasn't muttering unintelligibly, as she had before. Putting down the bowl, he tried to have her sit up, plumping the lumpy pillow behind her back and shoulders for support.

"Here you go, my sweets," he said, obviously forcing himself to sound very matter of fact—even jovial. "Let's try some of my expert 'hunter's cabin cuisine.' It's bound to make you feel better."

At first, her eyes closed, Sarah refused the food. Then, at his insistence, she half opened her mouth, and Harold quickly put a small spoonful of the potatoes on her tongue. To his great delight, she chewed quickly and swallowed. He continued and managed to get her to consume most of the contents of the bowl.

He got up and turned to fetch the fruit.

"Thank you, Harold."

He jumped at the sound of her voice. Gathering his wits, he turned around and patted her arm.

"You're so welcome," he said, somewhat formally, considering the situation. "Do you feel any better?"

Sarah nodded and tried to smile.

"Yes. That hit the spot. I...I'm sorry to be so much trouble."

Harold couldn't keep a large lump from forming in his throat. All he could do was bend over and enfold her in his arms and hug her tightly.

"Oh, Harold. Let up a bit. You're strangling me."

Feeling clumsy and not exactly sure of what to do, Harold half stood, half kneeled on the bed, his arms loosely around her.

"I think I 'm all right now. I'm thinking more clearly." She was trying to reassure him.

Harold didn't dare say anything, for fear of breaking down or saying the wrong thing. With a shudder and a sigh, he felt Sarah's forehead and cheeks.

"You feel cooler," he said finally, regaining control. "I do think your fever has broken."

It was a huge relief. An infection, even in the best of circumstances could easily mean death. It seemed that luckily all of the birth tissue had been expelled. Harold, not wanting to witness any of it, had left it to Peter to assess the situation. He had counted on Peter's personal experience for expertise in the matter and didn't really know how the man had come to his conclusion. Having no real choice, Harold decided to trust the man's judgment.

Apparently, he'd been right. If he hadn't been, Sarah's fever would undoubtedly be spiking to dangerous levels by now.

Knowing the importance of keeping hydrated, Harold made some more tea and had Sarah take as much as she could. Then she lay back down with a grateful smile and started to doze.

Harold quietly washed and dried the few dishes they had used, fed the fire, and sat in the chair by the stove, not caring that he leaned on the drying bits of cloth. There was only one other chair, and it was missing a leg.

He must've dozed off.

A huge blast of frigid air accompanied by a crashing door woke him from his much-needed slumber. By reflex, he immediately stood and faced the door in time to see a tall snow-covered figure grab the door and slam it shut against the weather.

Amid clouds of powdered snow, the figure stomped his feet, and brushed off his coat.

Harold half expected it to be one of their former companions back to help them but knew very well in the back of his mind that not enough time had passed.

He looked at the visitor's face, but the fellow's hat was still pulled low over his ears, and he had frost build up all over his whiskered face. It was his voice that rang the bell—something Harold never thought he'd hear again.

"I didn't expect to find company in this old place," growled the intruder who had obviously been counting on a solitary haven. "Much less the likes of you…"

Harold stomach clenched as did his fists. It was all he could do to restrain the impulse to step forward and smash the frost-covered face of Gunther Jorgenson, his erstwhile Gold Rush partner and former associate, and, more recently, his wife's harasser.

Throughout their journey in the Klondike, Gunther had been a thorn in his side, always trying to figure a crooked angle that could get them all in trouble. Having broken all ties, Harold and Sarah had been well rid of him as they had settled into life in Dawson City.

"What are you doing here?" spat Harold in disbelief, his lips curling down and his eyes narrowing. "What makes you think you can just barge in here like this?"

He took a menacing step forward.

"Last time I looked, you don't own this place," retorted Gunther, brushing melting frost from his beard.

"The McKenzie cabin is a well-known shelter cabin for travelers. Anyone can stay here."

He looked around.

"I do hope you're planning on replenishing what you use," he continued piously. "That's the condition for welcome use."

Harold scoffed.

"Don't lecture me on welcome use," he said, trying to keep his voice low so as not to wake Sarah. "You're a fine one to talk about welcome anything. You're nothing but a...a...."

Still a little groggy from his violently interrupted nap, he was having a hard time coming up with suitable insult.

"Just get the hell out!"

Gunther mouth turned into an insolent curl.

"Perhaps I will…perhaps I will…" he said, making a moue of consideration as he shook out his hat. "But all in good time. I need a little rest before I continue on my journey downriver."

He looked at the dishes resting on the counter.

"Maybe you'll see your way clear to share a little food with a lonesome traveler." He nodded. "Yes…and then maybe I'll consider my next moves and leave you to your own devices."

"Harold?"

Sarah had awakened to the disturbance and murmur of voices.

"Are they back?"

Harold rushed to her bedside.

"It's all right, my dear," he said, panic close to overwhelming him. "No…it's nothing. Go back to sleep."

What would happen when Sarah recognized Gunther? Would it send her back to her addled state?

"Please go back to sleep, Sarah. It's nothing," he repeated with great urgency.

But Sarah knew they were no longer alone, and the fear in her husband's voice was disturbing. She tried to sit up and get a better look into the room.

Although he knew it was futile, Harold stood in her line of sight, trying to put off the moment he was dreading.

Gunther had moved toward the stove. He held out his hands to absorb the warmth. He looked at the drying rags and frowned.

"Is someone hurt? Those are bloodstains, am I correct?"

"Oh my God," exclaimed Sarah, falling back on the bedding. "Gunther? Oh my God. Harold, is that Gunther/"

Her hand flew to her stomach.

Try as he might, Harold could not answer. Mute, he just bent down and took hold of Sarah's hand.

"Well, if this isn't just like old times," came Gunther's voice, riddled with irony. "Who'd've thought? It's the three of us all over again. Talk about a small world."

For a few frozen moments, no more words were spoken as the wind whined at the window, and the logs crackled in the firebox.

Sarah remained silent and motionless on the bed as Harold grudgingly gave Gunther some of their food: hardtack and jerked meat. There was a bit of dried fruit leftover from Sarah's meal.

It was an unwritten rule of the North that you help anyone in need, especially in winter. It was all that Harold could do to heed it. There must be some exceptions.

"All right, Gunther. Now it's time to tell me what you're doing out and alone."

By reflex, Harold looked out the window, but it was obscured by snow and frost. "You are alone, right?"

"Hmm, well," hesitated Gunther, avoiding eye contact. "You might say so... I'm sort of on the run... got involved in a booze-selling scheme to the natives. Barely escaped the jail in Rampart. My...uh...associates were not so lucky..."

Oily as ever...

A log fell in the stove, startling them. Suddenly jumpy, Gunther got up and tried to see out the window. Scraping at the glass did no good.

"Don't worry," he said turning back around. "I won't be troubling you too much longer. Got to put more distance between me and whatever son of a bitch must be trying to track me down by now. I'll be damned if I sit by and let them lock me up for such trivial offences."

He looked over at the bed, a thoughtful look on his face.

"By the way…if someone does come inquiring, I wouldn't be telling them that you've helped a fugitive. You know…aiding and abetting and all that."

His patronizing and arrogant tone made Harold sick with irritation. Seemingly unaware of his unwilling host's ire, Gunther continued.

"So. Fair's fair. You need to tell me what *you're* doing here." He looked toward the bed again and frowned. "Is Sarah all right?"

If she is, it's no thanks to you.

"Yes, she's just recovering from an incident; a sled accident. She got thrown and hit a tree stump pretty hard. Head wound and such…"

"Well, I know that head wounds bleed like the dickens," acknowledged Gunther, nodding.

He gestured towards the stained rags on the back of the chair.

"But… that looks way more significant. If that blood is all hers, she must be hurt elsewhere as well."

Damn him for noticing.

Harold was trying desperately to come up with an explanation that would be satisfactory, when Sarah spoke up suddenly.

"It's no business of yours, Gunther," she said, her voice surprisingly strong. "To be sure. But if you must know, I guess I'll have to enlighten you."

Swallowing and taking a long breath, she stopped as if still considering it for a moment.

"The fact is...that I have also suffered a miscarriage after about four months or so...as near as I could tell."

For some inexplicable reason, she realized that Gunther was secure in the knowledge that she had never divulged his transgressions. And not to protect him, of course. As obtuse as he seemed sometimes, deep down he understood people pretty well. Somehow, he knew she would have walked through fire to avoid hurting Harold with the truth. So, on some level, Sarah was sure, Gunther knew he was safe from disclosure.

In consternated silence, the men processed her statement. Harold looked mystified as to why she had said anything at all. Gunther just stared at her for several seconds. Then, something subtle and fleeting passed between them. Under her withering glare, he lowered his gaze.

"Sorry to hear that," he mumbled, picking up his coat and hat. "I'll leave you to it."

All of a sudden, he was eager to get on his way.

"Just a minute," interrupted Harold. "Not so fast. You know what you said about replenishing supplies. Well, we're low on wood. I need someone to help saw up some logs. You're not leaving until you do your bit."

Looking very uncomfortable, Gunther didn't argue. It would not help his case to alienate potential witnesses to his itinerary.

At either end of the two-man saw, exuding clouds of condensation, they made quick work of some of the dry logs that had been stacked against the side of the cabin, where they had probably lain for months or more.

As they pushed and pulled the cross-cut blade in steady rhythm, Gunther's face gradually took on an angry expression.

Finally, with an explosive breath, he let go of the saw handle and put his hands on his hips.

Harold frowned at his action.

"We're not finished yet," he said, panting a little. "Three more to go...and then there's the splitting..."

Gunther ignored the instructions. His face was red, and although he mostly panted from the exertion, it looked as though that might not be the only reason.

"I can't believe you let Sarah get hurt," he exploded angrily, with a heavy intake of breath. "What the hell? You didn't protect her. Or the baby, for that matter." He shook his head and frowned darkly, a snide expression taking shape.

"Seems like you might not be fit to be her husband...and certainly not a father."

Harold was incredulous. This was indeed rich coming from someone whose treatment of Sarah had been tantamount to slave-driving throughout the entire trip from Dyea to Dawson.

During the journey, Gunther had never listened to her opinion, never consulted her, and never put a limit on her exhausting toil. Without provocation, he was often rude to the extreme, embarrassing her, and hurting her feelings without a second thought. He had never seemed to care about her welfare. And, in the end, he had completely abandoned her to carry out his own agenda.

Wanting badly to do something, Harold had watched all this from a distance, thinking that it was not his concern, as the other two were married. It wasn't until Harold and Sarah declared their mutual love, that he discovered there was no marriage, and never had been. At that point, he had interfered in a hurry.

Still grasping his end of the motionless saw, astonishment at Gunther's temerity paralyzed him. Swallowing and taking a deep breath, he dropped his hands and came around the end of the partially severed log resting on the sawhorse, his eyes glittering with indignant fury.

Later, he couldn't remember even thinking about it, but a spasm of rage took over and he smashed Gunther's face with his fist. Too late to avoid the blow, Gunther tripped over a chunk of wood, and fell in the snow among the scattered pile of logs they had cut. Harold kicked some of them aside, and stood over him, his fists still clenched.

"You're a fine one to criticize me after how you've behaved, you sniveling bastard," he shouted down at his ex-partner. "Why the hell do you even care? You never did before, that anyone could see. What's it to you all of a sudden?"

Ignoring the interrogation, Gunther took off his mitten and felt his nose. A trickle of blood from one nostril was quickly freezing on its way down to his lip. He wiped it with a finger and looked thoughtfully at the resultant smudge. Then he looked up at Harold through slit eyes, his lips curved into a smirk. Unhurried, he gathered his legs under him and pushed himself upright until they stood nose to nose.

"Well, Mr. Righteous Indignation," he said licking his lip. "Before you start throwing your weight about, you might be a little more circumspect. Things aren't always what they seem…especially when you're not around." He shook his head and sneered. "You don't know everything."

Putting his mitt back on, he seemed to gather himself with effort to regain his temper. Then, as if nothing had happened, he shrugged and said gruffly, "Let's finish, shall we?"

Harold's jaw dropped until his teeth felt the cold, and he snapped it shut. He was so preoccupied and shocked at Gunther's behavior that he walked back to his spot by the sawhorse without uttering a word. He was also shocked by the content of what Gunther had said, trying in vain to puzzle out the meaning.

In a few minutes, without saying a word to each other, they had finished sawing the logs Harold had intended to get to. He put the saw down by the pile of wood and started to pick up an armful of logs for splitting.

"I won't be helping you split," said Gunther, walking in determined fashion over to the front porch where he had taken off his snowshoes and dropped his packs. "I've wasted too much time already."

Harold wasn't worried about having to split the logs on his own. But, as much as Gunther's imminent departure was a favorable thing, he still had many questions about the earlier discussion, and he could not put them aside. Indecisively, still holding his armful of wood, he took a few steps towards the cabin.

"Hold on, you son of a bitch. If you're referring to what you did to my wife in Dawson when I wasn't home, I'm quite aware. Consider that punch as partial payment on that account. And I've barely scratched the surface. I really ought to turn you inside out."

"Oh...so Sarah told you, did she? "

Not being able to hide his surprise, and having removed his mittens, he stepped into his snowshoes and deftly strapped them on. Then he pulled his hat lower to cover his ears, replaced his mittens, and picked up his packs. As he stepped off the porch, he quickly glanced at Harold, as though gauging the distance between them, and swiftly made his way toward the tree line. Facing away, he raised his voice to guarantee that his parting shot would be heard.

"Well, I guess that's what happens when wives get lonely. You really ought to…"

His words were lost to an angry half-growl, half-scream. It took a few seconds for Harold to process what Gunther's words were.

By the time he had reacted by dropping his armful of logs and running to catch up to Gunther on the packed snow in the small perimeter close the cabin, Gunther had reached the soft snow among the trees. Looking over his shoulder just once, he easily made his way deeper into the forest. Harold reached the tree line, but without the benefit of snowshoes, he sank in the wet snow up to his knees.

Pursuit was futile. He was at a complete disadvantage.

Shaking with frustration, and pounding the snow, he watched the distant dark figure recede among the spruce trees heavily laden with new-fallen snow.

A rifle would've served him well about now.

Giving up in disgust, he scrambled back up on the hard pack and turned toward the cabin.

The cabin door was ajar. Sarah was standing, halfway outside, grasping a threadbare quilt around her shoulders, her feet still in her bloodstained stockings, and the bandage still askew around her head.

Harold couldn't remember ever having seen his wife look so horror-struck.

-11-

GOOD FOR THE SOUL

She shivered in spite of the layers of covers Harold draped over her. Her stomach was one big hollow cavern.

Hearing Gunther on the porch, she had left the bed and had gone to the door, opening it just in time to see him trudge off to the trees.

She had heard his parting statement and seen Harold's hopeless attempt at pursuing him. Her faculties now intact, the understanding of what had transpired between the men was dawning with frightening clarity. Fear nauseated her; and with what seemed to be troubling regularity lately, she was getting tunnel vision.

She had to lie down.

Harold had hurried to the door and helped her back into bed. He rubbed her hands and her arms, trying to help her circulation. Then he put another log on the dying fire in the stove. He set some water to boil for tea and pulled the chair over to her bedside to sit down while the water heated.

He reached for her hands as she huddled under the covers.

"I don't think you should've gotten out of bed," he counseled. "I hope it didn't restart the bleeding. You need to take it easy for quite a while. Peter said…"

"It's all right, Harold," interrupted Sarah, trying to smile reassuringly. "I checked earlier when I had to use that broken down excuse for a chamber pot. Anyway, it's…well…drying up. It's just scant watery darkish fluid. Nothing bright red, and certainly not much. I'm not sure, but as there's not much pain, apparently no fever, and not much of anything draining. I honestly think I'm on the mend."

She wished she could say as much for her mental state. She knew Harold's mind was rife with questions to which there would be only awkward answers.

Harold could only pat her hand and get up to make the tea. He looked darkly thoughtful as he poured steaming water over the tealeaves.

"I hope you're right," he said, giving her the cup. "I won't feel satisfied until the doctor gives his opinion."

He looked toward the window, which was basically just a dark square. Daylight had faded some time ago.

"Someone should be back at first light with an extra sled to take us to Rampart, so we can find out for sure."

Sarah finished the tea and the leftover dried fruit. Harold had a few bites of hardtack and meat and put some order into the makeshift kitchen by the low light of the lamp. When he was finished and looking around as if trying to find something else to do, Sarah patted the bed next to her.

"Why don't you sit next to me? You're the only thing that can really warm me up, you know."

Harold gave her a disbelieving grin.

"Really? I don't feel all that warm myself…"

He scooted next to her, the bed boards groaning and squeaking under his weight. He put an arm around her, and she leaned her head against his chest. The bed was so narrow, he had to keep one foot on the floor.

It was a very tight fit that Sarah appreciated. She realized that this would preclude her having eye contact with Harold at the moment of truth she felt was rapidly approaching.

Coward! You think you can avoid confrontation by talking into his clothing?

Harold kissed the back of his wife's head, bandage and all.

"What went on out there with you two?" Sarah began, her voice muffled by his sweater, wanting to find out what Harold's understanding of the situation was. "I heard you arguing, and I saw you trying to chase him down."

"That son of a bitch was talking in riddles. He was intimating that you were on board...no...that you actually instigated that...that meeting you had with him. He totally ignored the gun part. He was acting like you actually...participated...willingly."

Sarah was silent, letting him lay out his thoughts.

"And he was so self-righteous about me treating you badly, blaming me for...for...you know...letting you get hurt, and...Christ! Even for losing the baby. Like he really cared..."

Harold stopped all of a sudden. He half-heartedly tried to get Sarah to look up at him, but realized it was an uncomfortable position for her neck.

"Any idea what his motivation is? The bastard is out of his mind, I think. After several years of a non-existent relationship, why would he suddenly even care about our...um...family? I know our marriage sticks in his craw—it's mainly his pride—and he probably still has feelings for you, but it just doesn't make sense, does it?"

Sarah took a deep breath and raised her head a bit.

"Harold. I haven't been totally honest with you. Gunther might think he has his reasons to say what he did."

"What? That you started this? That you wanted..."

"No, no. Of course not. Not at all." She shook her head vigorously, dislodging her bandage. In irritation, she quickly peeled it off.   "That's not what I mean…"

Harold was becoming agitated. He took his arm from around Sarah and tried to straighten her so that they could look at each other.

"Well, what then? Please just tell me everything, Sarah. I can't stand this wondering anymore."

He was about to get off the bed, but Sarah grasped his hand, pleading with him to make him stay.

"I will, Harold. But please hold on to me. I'll explain."
His mouth a grim line, Harold sat stiffly next to her, his hands completely inert in hers.

"What I told you about what happened in our cabin was true. It's just…it's just that I didn't tell you everything." She squeezed his hands. "I…I didn't want to hurt you, and I didn't want you to get in trouble because of what your reaction might be…"

She paused to organize her thoughts.

"Go on. I'm listening." His lips barely moved. He looked as if he was about to get a tooth pulled.

"As I told you," Sarah went on. "I intended to shoot him, but before I could go through with it, he twisted the pistol out of my hand and put it out of my reach on top of the cupboard. All that was true."

Harold was silent. Sarah looked at him out of the corner of her eye. He saw him staring straight ahead, probably preparing for the worst.

"He was irrationally angry, as well as drunk. You should've seen his face. There was nothing I could say or do to placate him. He picked me up and threw me on the bed. I couldn't successfully fight him off either physically or with any kind of reasoning. He was so crazed with anger and hate."

She shook her head.

"There was just no stopping him…"

"So, you're telling me he attacked you?" There was a sharp intake of breath. "Violated you?"

Harold ripped his hands from hers and bolted from the bed. He slammed the chair against the table. The dried rags went flying, some dangerously close to the hot stove.

"Why? Why in the hell didn't you tell me?" he shouted. "I would've skinned him alive. Beaten him to a pulp. Shooting's too good for him. He shouldn't be allowed to live. How could you not tell me, Sarah? I deserved to know. I could've done something."

He righted the chair, sat down, and put his head in his hands.

"That's why," said Sarah somberly making her point.

"That's exactly why. It would've ruined our chances for anything good. You'd have ended up in jail. Maybe it was terrible judgment, but I was trying to save our life together as we knew it."

She disentangled herself from the bedding and stood next to him. Putting a tentative hand on his shoulder, she half expected him to shrug it off. When he didn't, she went on.

"Harold. For God's sake. I hated not telling you. You have to know that. I've been unfathomably miserable because of it. My pregnancy…" She couldn't go on without sobbing. "Instead of being happy, I've been terrified. Terrified that you would find out and go crazy with anger…that you might even leave me…"

She sniffed loudly.

Harold suddenly looked up. Realization dawned on his face. He stared at Sarah.

"So…wait. You're also saying that…that the baby…"

"I don't know…for sure," Sarah said quickly, as if it made a difference. "It's possible… I just don't know…"

She stood in front of his seated form. With a loud sob, he slowly put his arms around her hips and buried his face in her belly, weighing her down.

She stayed in that position until her legs became so tired they quivered.

She dropped down into Harold's lap and he held her tightly like a drowning man would hold on to a life preserver.

The fire was down to embers when they finally stirred. Without saying anything for fear of breaking a kind of spell they were under, they both crawled under the bed covers in the narrow bed, Harold's leg once more braced on the floor.

Shivering, Sarah felt as though she'd been holding her breath for an hour. She sighed deeply as they lay wrapped in an embrace, grateful that Harold's wild anger seemed to have subsided. But she was not naïve enough to think it was all over. She didn't even want to think of what the lasting implications of her confession would be.

Yet, she felt welcome release at having unburdened her soul, glad that she had no longer had to hide anything from her husband. It was like escaping the gates of hell, because that was where she had been residing of late. Now, she was slowly regaining faith that they loved and respected each other enough to work through whatever complications might arise in their relationship.

For the moment, it was quite enough. She relaxed for the first time in months.

In spite of being cramped for space, they had both fallen asleep from all manner of exhaustion.

It was still dark when Harold carefully extricated himself from the bed trying not to awaken Sarah. He went outside to relieve himself and couldn't help reviewing the drama of the previous evening as he saw the dim pile of logs and looked in the direction of Gunther's escape.

The pale light of the three-quarter moon reflected by the snow between the trees revealed the slight indentations he had left in his wake. It was the only sign he had been here. If more snow fell—and the skies did threaten; it was warming up—it would hardly be more than a figment of the imagination.

Where is that bastard now, I wonder?

Harold tried to analyze his own feelings, imagining what would happen if they ever crossed paths again. What would his conscience allow in the way of revenge? What would his character demand?

He hadn't bothered to put on his heavy coat for his brief excursion outside, so the cold began to penetrate. He hurried back inside the cabin.

The late dawn was barely breaking when Harold put two bowls of oatmeal porridge on the table for their breakfast.

He put a few pieces of dried fruit and a bit of sugar on top to enhance the flavor.

Sarah looked a lot better after several consecutive hours of sleep. Harold felt very gratified that she attacked her bowl of oatmeal with good appetite. She seemed to be regaining some of her customary health and vigor, not to mention a more positive outlook.

Having washed out the bowls, Harold was ready to split the wood that he and Gunther had sawed to length the day before.

"I'll pack our stuff," said Sarah, drying the breakfast bowls and putting them back in the duffel. "If they're coming to get us, we should be ready. Go ahead and split the wood. I can take care of things in here and leave everything how we found it."

Except for the chair that Harold had sent crashing into the table, breaking one of the leg braces, things in the cabin were as they had found them. Fortunately, with a small measure of Harold's carpentry skills, the chair was still usable. And, in return, they were going to be leaving much more split wood than they had found.

As the logs were very dry, it didn't take Harold long to get them split; the loud cracking sound they made were like small explosions. He was making a geometrically even pile of the results of his labor against the outside cabin wall, when he heard noises from the trees that were obscured from his view by the cabin.

In the broadening daylight three dog-teams made their sudden appearance around the corner of the cabin, stopping in front. The previous silence was torn apart by whines, barks and shouts. Alerted by the sudden cacophony outside, Sarah came out of the cabin. Harold could see that she was fully dressed and seemingly ready to face another sled ride.

The drivers set the brakes and the dogs began to calm down, their tongues hanging out as they sat watching their drivers, wondering if this was a real rest stop. Harold only recognized Peter. The other two were strangers.

Moments later, everyone was inside the cabin, waiting for the water to boil for tea. It was then that Harold and Sarah discovered that the two unknowns were deputies from the Marshall's office. Peter expressed his relief that Sarah was recovering, and she thanked him profusely for his role in it.

After some discussion, discovering Harold's and Sarah's original mission in Rampart, one of the deputies explained that he could take their deposition, and that they wouldn't even have to go all the way to Rampart.

"That's a relief," said Sarah sighing. "Although, I was kind of interested to see what Rampart is like. We heard it was busy…"

"Yes. It is that," said Peter. "Much more than Tanana."

Everyone sipped tea.

"We had some trouble," said deputy Clarkson, getting down to business. "Illegal liquor sales. We got two of 'em, but the main guy escaped."

Harold and Sarah looked at each other. Their expressions did not go unnoticed. Deputy Clarkson's eyes were piercing as he looked from one to the other.

"You…uh…get wind of anything? We know he came in this direction. Lost the trail at the creek. I think the guy is pretty wily. Has survived in the wild all by himself on several occasions. Scuttlebutt is that he built a bad reputation in Dawson before he showed up out here. There's a sheet out on him. Not to mention an outstanding warrant.

Harold's ears had gone red. Neither he nor Sarah said anything while she poured tea. Then she spoke up.

"So…who is he? Do you…um…have a name? We had an acquaintance here for a bit…but…"

The deputies looked curiously at her.

"His name is Jorgenson. Gunther Jorgenson. Know him?"

There was no getting out of it, even if they had wanted to spare him. And they really didn't. He'd made his own bed.

Both Harold and Sarah nodded silently.

"Yes. We know him," admitted Harold finally. "He actually used to be a…an associate of ours…"

"But we didn't…we haven't…associated with him for several years," Sarah hurried to add. "He just appeared here, yesterday and wanted food. He was as surprised to see us as we him." She shrugged. "Of course, if we had known…"

Not sure of how to finish her sentence, she was glad when the deputy interrupted. He stood up from the bed where he'd been seated with his cup of lukewarm tea.

"When did he leave?" he asked abruptly, all business, plunking his cup on the table. "And in which direction did he go?"

Harold took him out to the porch and pointed to where he had last seen Gunther.

"He mentioned something about heading downriver…" started Harold.

"Well. That may or may not be true…" muttered Clarkson. "Knowing you'd probably say something, he could be just trying to throw us off. "

Harold kicked himself for being so naïve as not to think of that.

"Christ! You're probably right. He could've circled and gone in a completely different direction. I'm an idiot."

Clarkson smiled grimly.

"Well, I don't suppose you've spent your adult life trying to outguess criminals, have you? Nope? I, on the other hand, have learned to doubt everything they say. That approach has stood me in good stead so far."

Back inside, the men discussed a plan for the best way of pursuing Gunther. He had a start on them, but they had the dogsleds.

"Besides," said Clarkson. "He left yesterday afternoon, didn't you say?"

Harold and Sarah both nodded.

"Well, I'll wager he didn't go far. Probably camped for the night when it got dark. There are quite a few empty cabins scattered around. That means he's only had a few hours of daylight for travel so far today."

The men stood around the table and decided what the next move should be. Clarkson sent Deputy O'Leery to follow Gunther's tracks for a short distance to see if they veered off in a different direction.

Sarah could see that the original plan to get her to a doctor's care in Rampart had receded in importance. Surprisingly, the delay didn't frighten her—she felt pretty good. Liberated by her earlier confession, she didn't care where the chips fell as far as Harold was concerned. There was no longer a need to hide anything. It was so freeing.

As far as Gunther was concerned, she quietly joined the plans for his capture, but she couldn't quite match the men's obsessive desire to clap him in irons.

In spite of how she knew she should feel, a small corner of her heart had refused to harden against him.

-12-

DÉJÀ VU

Less than an hour later, O'Leery returned.

"Looks like he headed for the riverbank," he said, his face red from the cold and exertion. "I lost track just above the overflow. I couldn't tell if he went east or west."

"Pretty sure he knows how to foil a tracker," ruminated Clarkson. "We don't know but that he came right back in this direction and branched off to the north instead."

"Do you think he'd try to cross the river?" asked Harold, eyebrows raised. "He'd probably think that we'd guess it unlikely."

Clarkson pursed his lips, weighing the possibilities.

"Well, that would be fairly dangerous around here, so early in the season. Too many creeks dumping into the Yukon, and lots of overflows. Not to mention the hot springs. Depends on how lucky he thinks he is..."

Harold nodded, grimacing as he gave it some thought.

"He does seem to think he's pretty...I don't know...invulnerable. At this point I wouldn't put anything past him."

He looked at Sarah to see if she agreed, but she was just looking meditatively at the floor.

"He's no dummy, though," she added at last, looking back up at the group. "And he has a lot of wilderness experience by now." She shrugged and shook her head. "I guess time will tell as to which part of his character takes over: the risk-taking side or the cautious side."

"What about the desperate side?" asked Clarkson. "That's been known to cancel everything else out. Can't tell you how many criminals we've caught because of some stupid move desperation caused them to make."

O'Leery nodded in agreement.

"Or that Mother Nature caught," he added, smiling grimly. "She often beats us to it…"

Sarah put the last log from the hearth into the stove. The men kept up their discussion as to how to proceed. She tuned out, getting the feeling that she was probably going to be staying put for a while. She rummaged around in the duffel to find her needles and thread. There was plenty of mending to do. She even entertained thoughts of putting pieces of Harold's shirt back together to make larger rags, stains and all.

Harold came over to her, looking a bit embarrassed.

"Sarah. The deputies want me to accompany one of them to hunt for Gunther. Then we can have two teams out, which would cut the search time in half." He put his arm around her. "We'd be back by nightfall.

With two fingers under her chin he tipped up her face to look into her eyes. Then he slowly shook his head.

"I won't do it if you think we need to get you to Rampart. Or, if you want to go back to Tanana. We can go with Peter. The deputies can just go on their own, to find Gunther, I mean." He hugged her. "But if you're not comfortable being here alone a few hours, we won't even discuss it. I feel bad enough…"

Sarah sat down on the bed next to the duffel. Half a day didn't seem like much of a delay even though it meant another night in this cabin.

So, a whole day, when you counted that.

"I guess it's all right," she said. "I really do feel much better. I have plenty to sew, and I also packed a book somewhere. Show me how to light that lamp before you go."

Half an hour later, they were gone, one team eastbound, and the other more or less in the opposite direction. Members of the third dog team—Peter's—barked angrily and unremittingly in disapproval at having been left behind. Sarah wasn't sure if she was glad of the company or not.

They calmed down after she gave them water. Later on, she'd have to feed them as per the instructions from Peter.

Having often been told that sled dogs were not pets, she kept away from their jaws, and certainly didn't try to pet them. Soon they were lying down, curled nose to tail, dreaming of whatever sled dogs dreamed of.

Good dogs. Rest up. You'll be working before you know it.

Noting Harold's perfectly geometrically aligned log pile with a smile, Sarah collected a few newly split logs to take inside.

Between sewing jobs, Sarah dozed.

Noticing that she almost didn't need them anymore, she changed her absorbent rags, carefully rinsed everything out, and put the last few rags out to dry in front of the stove. She made herself a small lunch and decided to prop herself against the wall while sitting sideways on the bed to read the book she had extricated from the bottom of her duffel. She judged that there was about an hour and a half worth left of adequate light from the window. Then she'd have to move near the lamp.

Her book was a silly mystery borrowed from Nettie who had brought it with her from Dawson. It wasn't very clever, and barely kept her awake. She was pretty sure she knew who "done it" after but a few chapters.

Somewhere in her reading and dozing, the dogs started a frenzy of barking.

She was startled awake. Had she forgotten to feed them?

They must be registering a complaint, and not an alert, as it was too soon for the men to have returned.

Putting on her sweater and coat as well as her boots, hat, and mitts, she girded herself against the impending onslaught of cold, opened the cabin door, and went over to the bag of dried fish that the men had left for the dogs. She had to knock some of the fish on a rock to separate the frozen chunks from each other.

At her actions, their barking increased. Not knowing what their usual reaction was to seeing their dinner, she assumed that this was to be expected. She started to toss them each a section of dried salmon. Some sniffed at it, but most kept barking in her direction.

It was then that she sensed rather than felt something behind her. She almost jumped out of her skin. No wonder the dogs had been acting up.

"Sorry, Sarah," came a familiar voice. "I know you never expected to see me again. The best laid plans and so on…"

Sarah felt her heart skip.

"My God, Gunther. What the hell are you doing back here? People are after you, I'm sure you know…" Sarah tried to get over her initial shock.

She continued to throw fish to the dogs whose attention was now switching to their meal. Pretty soon there was nothing but growls and grunts to be heard.

"So…Harold is gone too? I assume he'd be feeding the dogs if not… He grabbed Sarah's elbow. "Did the deputies get here? Is he helping the search?"

His face was hard, his jaw clenched.

"Yes," nodded Sarah. "They're out looking for you…but I'll wager you know that…"

"Former associate helping the enemy? I knew he didn't like me…but helping them do me in? I must say I'm a bit shocked."

At first Sarah didn't say anything, but she wrenched her arm from his grasp. After a few moments, she couldn't stay silent. His idea of loyalty was so incredibly misplaced. She felt like her head was about to explode.

"Gunther. Just get out of here. I won't say anything when they get back…but just…leave. Leave!" Her face red with emotion, she started toward the cabin. The cold was starting to seep through her clothes and boots, and she was beginning to feel queasy.

Gunther bit his lips and looked pensive. Then he put his hand on her arm to stop her, and shook his head.

"Just hold on a minute." He held Sarah's gaze, clouds of his breath engulfing them both. "Sarah. Please don't tell me you're against me too. Is our previous relationship not worth anything?"

He looked so innocent and righteously indignant in the fading daylight. Some might even say entitled.

Not falling for what had to be an act, and unable to ignore visions of their Dawson encounter, Sarah's blood began to boil.

"Have you forgotten something?"

Her eyes bored into his.

"Your boorish…no…criminal behavior of a few months ago? Even if you have…I certainly haven't. How can you…"

Incensed, she couldn't finish. Tearing her arm from his grasp, she headed toward the cabin. Knowing that the unreliable old cabin door wouldn't hold Gunther at bay if he didn't want it to, she wasn't sure what she'd do to get away from him. She needed a moment to think.

The sun was very low; its slanted rays filtering their way through the heavily laden branches of the spruce trees. It wouldn't be long before the others were back. If she could just stall…

From up on the porch, Sarah looked down at Gunther.

"Look. I don't know exactly what the hell you've done that the deputies are after you for…specifically."

Gunther didn't look surprised. Sarah continued.

"According to them, there's quite a list of your offences. And frankly, I don't want to get into trouble for helping you."

She crossed her arms and shook her head. Fighting her better judgment, she continued.

"But, I'll be less than helpful to them if you get out of here and leave me…us." She stuck out her chin. "Forever."

Gunther, having shed his snowshoes before confronting her, kicked at some loose gravel in the snow, and put one foot on the porch.

"Damn it, Sarah. I can't believe you…you are so forgiving of the guy that…jeopardized your life. Yeah, that's right," he nodded indignantly as she scoffed at his statement. "It could've cost that. Not to mention…" he gestured toward Sarah's midsection. "Not to mention failing to protect your baby." He suddenly looked up at her as though the thought had just struck him. "Or, wait a minute, is it our baby? Was that why he was so careless?"

Sarah was beginning to see familiar black spots before her eyes. She leaned back against the cabin wall. This was so much déjà vu. She stared to panic as darkness closed around her consciousness.

No…no…please not now. Not now…

She leaned toward the door to open it and stumbled over the threshold. She was vaguely aware of Gunther following her and helping her onto the bed.

"Have some water, Sarah," said Gunther offering her a cup from the table. "Don't worry your pretty little head. I'm not going to abuse your hospitality."

Breathing hard, Sarah took the cup and managed to level a disdainful look at him as she drank.

"I don't remember inviting you in," she said using her sleeve to wipe her lips. "There's no hospitality to abuse. It's plain old breaking and entering…"

Well, entering, at least…

Gunther shrugged in his heavy wool coat and sniffed.

"Be that as it may, I'll thank you for a bit of food to help me on my way." He gestured toward one of the duffels. "I have a bit of my own, but I wouldn't refuse a little extra for the trip."

Sarah thought about a retort for that one but was eager for him to go on his way, so she silently removed some food from their dwindling stores, made some small packages, and tossed them on the floor by his feet.

Without so much as a twitch of an eyebrow, he quickly scooped it all up, examined it, and stuffed everything in his pockets.

"And, oh yes," he continued fastening his coat, and pulling on his hat and mitts. "I'm going to avail myself of that old sled buried out back. I don't think anyone will object. It looks like it's been there a while…"

Sarah just shrugged and pursed her lips indicating her total lack of interest in what he did, very aware that there'd be no stopping him if she even cared to.

Gunther turned toward the door and pulled it partly open, letting in a windblown powdery cloud of fine snow as he looked right and left outside. His hand still on the latch, he half turned back.

"So, Sarah. You're not going to do me the courtesy of explaining about the child..." He shook his head in mock disgust. "It's a great disappointment and not the least bit fair. I'll have to live with the knowledge that someone selfishly and carelessly took my parental rights away..."

Sarah felt like screaming at him. Instead, she just glared at him and shook her head.

"Think what you want, Gunther. That's right. You'll never know...and neither would you *ever* have known...no matter what."

His face a blank, he turned around and stepped out into the cold sunset. Sarah couldn't get to the door fast enough to push it shut behind him.

-13-

JUST DESSERTS

It was just about dark when Peter's formerly napping dogs began their frantic alert.

Sarah had been on tenterhooks for a while after Gunther had stepped outside. She could hear him on the porch fastening his snowshoes, and then scratching around the rear of the cabin probably retrieving the ancient sled. She didn't quite understand his reasoning as to the sled. She assumed that he thought it would help his progress across the snow. Perhaps it was easier to push or pull a sled than be loaded down carrying backpacks.

All the more luck to him.

There was a bit more knocking and scratching against the cabin, and then it finally stopped. Sarah held her breath. After a few moments of silence, she finally relaxed. He must have moved off by now. But she didn't have the guts to go outside and check.

Not being able to sit still, she fussed around the cabin, rearranging and repacking the duffels that didn't need it. Luckily, she didn't have long to wait for the others to return.

"Christ, Sarah," exclaimed Harold, after she had given her account of what had happened. "I can't leave you alone…" With a deep sigh of frustration, he put his arm around her and kissed her forehead. "I guess we can be glad that Gunther was somewhat intimidated…"

"Well, I don't know if that was it exactly," snorted Sarah. "But he knows on what side his bread is buttered. He wasn't about to make me mad when he was depending on my goodwill."

She looked guiltily at the deputies.

Deputy Clarkson couldn't stay silent. He came straight to the point in his very direct manner.

"So, Mistress Beasley. Which way did he go?"

Sarah shook her head and shrugged.

"I have no idea. I didn't go outside to watch him. Call me a coward, but I just stayed inside wishing him to go away as soon as possible..."

Harold gave her a squeeze. He completely understood her reluctance to be anywhere near Gunther as he left. Who knew what he might've been prompted to do if he had seen Sarah watching him.

But the Deputies had another way of looking at the situation. Now they would have to wait until daylight to circle the cabin and find tracks. It would've certainly helped them in their quest, if Sarah had been able to secretly observe his departure...even better: if she had been able to delay it...

And it was warming up enough for snow.

Preparations for spending the night in the small cabin meant pushing the sparse furniture out of the way to make room for the men's bedrolls.

After a light supper for everyone, Harold and Sarah took the bed. The men fell asleep quickly after their long day of activity, but Sarah couldn't get used to the snores, belches and other emissions from every corner of the cabin. And she wasn't able to get really comfortable with Harold unconsciously hogging more than his share of the narrow bed.

Adding to her general malaise, was the fact that she couldn't help wondering where Gunther was and what accommodations he had for the night. At least she knew he had food to sustain him for a while. She berated herself unmercifully for letting her mind wander in that direction.

Why am I even wasting precious sleep time thinking about him?

In the wee hours, about the time it started to snow, she finally fell into a fitful sleep.

She groggily woke up to early activity. Breakfast was already in evidence, and someone must have found some coffee to heat, because that unmistakable aroma was finding its way to her nostrils.

"Ah. You're awake," said Harold coming over with a steaming cup. "Try this. It ought to put you in a good frame of mind."

Sarah let the steam from the cup warm her face.

"Oh my God. Real coffee? Oh my God."

It was bliss. She was speechless.

"You have the U.S. Marshall's Office to thank," said Harold smiling at her ecstatic expression. "These guys know how to camp. And hang on to your hat. They also have some kind of cinnamon rolls…"

After a breakfast of unpredictable pleasing quality, it was time for hard decisions.

* * *

They were going back to Tanana.

Deputy Clarkson had taken their deposition about the shooting incident related to Mary's family in Tanana, so there was no need to go on to Rampart. Although Sarah was a bit disappointed at not seeing the town, she was becoming increasingly interested in a hot bath, good home-cooked food, and her own bed. As far as her condition went, the medical staff in Tanana could probably fit the bill as well as the ones in Rampart.

No matter what, it was now a moot point.

The deputies were extremely efficient at packing up their sleds and restarting their search in record time. After some heartfelt good-byes and promises that any news about Gunther would be relayed to the Tanana station, Sarah didn't pay too much attention to their departure and direction. Busy getting everything ready for her own trip downriver, she couldn't suppress excitement about going back to what she now considered her winter home and seeing Nettie again. She was looking forward to hearing all about the honeymoon. She smiled at the thought.

Peter's team of six dogs wagged their tails and gave a few sharp barks as preparations for the journey began. They always seemed to know when a trip was in the offing.

With only six dogs, the load of two people plus gear inside the sled, plus the driver on and off the runners, was considerable. So the trip back would take a little longer than the first leg had taken.

Peter acceded to Harold's request that he be allowed to drive for part of the way. Sarah wasn't sure she approved but did not voice her concerns. Now was not the time to show skepticism or lack of faith in her husband's newly acquired skills.

And he was only too enthusiastic to show off his knowledge on the subject, as they sat together in the sled for the first part of the trip home. Wrapped up together, Sarah sitting in the V of his legs, as he leaned against the back of the sled, their feet up against their gear at the front. Harold's mouth was within easy reach of her ear, so she had no choice but to get educated.

"See, the two lead dogs have to be smart," Harold stated as they skimmed through a new layer of snow through the trees, between Peter's shouted commands to the dogs of "Gee" or "Haw" or "Mush," the latter being an incorrect version of the French-Canadian expression "En marche!"

"They have to understand the driver's commands. Of course, they have to be obedient too. Most drivers are very picky when it comes to choosing those lead dogs. They can make or break the team's efficiency."

"Well, what about the others? Do they just follow? What if they don't feel like it?" Amused, Sarah was playing devil's advocate.

Ignoring her sarcasm, Harold nodded.

"Yeah, the next two are the swing dogs. You always have to make sure they get along. They have to agree with each other, but, on the other hand, they can't be too friendly with each other either."

Sarah shrugged why. Correctly interpreting her body language, Harold lectured on.

"Believe it or not, dogs can have disagreements. Sometimes their personalities clash. If they just bicker with each other, the sled will end up going nowhere. On the other hand, if they're too buddy-buddy, they play too much, and you get the same result."

"So, you're saying they have to be serious professionals at their jobs for everything to go smoothly?"

Sarah had to chuckle. She'd had no idea dog personalities were so varied, and so critical.

"And I don't know if it's just the perspective—seeing all those rear ends bouncing up and down—or I'm not observing correctly, but the last two dogs seem bigger. Are they?"

"Yep. You're right. The wheel dogs, being the closest to the sled, have to be the strongest. They do a large share of the hauling work. So they're almost always bigger."

Harold went on to discuss selection and training of puppies to make them good sled dogs, and how you had to recognize their qualities early. As the miles skimmed by, Sarah dozed, lulled by his explanations. Continuing blithely on, Harold didn't seem to notice.

After a short break for a drink warmed by a quick fire, Harold took his much-awaited turn as driver.

Feeling a bit awkward, Sarah had to sit in the sled in front of Peter, leaning against him as she had Harold.

Having been unconscious when Peter had taken care of her after her accident and miscarriage, she could only imagine how privy he had been to her most intimate parts while administering aid. He, however, seemed completely unconcerned, pointing out certain aspects of the trail and scenery, noting that they were very close to the Yukon.

Natural occurrences were probably just that to him: natural and nothing to dwell on in awkward manner. Birth, death, and everything in between were not things to be embarrassed about; they were just to be dealt with.

Suddenly he exclaimed loudly and waved his hand for Harold to slow the sled.

"Whoa! Whoa!" he shouted to the dogs who undoubtedly recognized their master's voice. All the dogs were familiar with that command. They slowed to a stop. Harold set the brake, having learned the hard way the importance of that step from Sarah's misadventure.

"I saw something odd down toward the river, when we were in that treeless area." said Peter, pointing south. "It's something that just doesn't fit. It might be someone in trouble." He shrugged. "We need to get up on the bank to get a better view."

Without waiting for the other two, he rummaged around the sled and came up with snowshoes. He threw two of them toward Harold and strapped his own on, before taking off to negotiate the slight grade up to the high bank.

Kneeling, Harold started to strap his first snowshoe on and looked helplessly at Sarah.

"I'm sorry, Sweetness. But there are only two pairs. Are you all right staying here until we come back? It shouldn't take long."

Famous last words if ever there were any, thought Sarah grimly.

"Yes. I'll be fine." She talked to the top of Harold's head as he fastened his second snowshoe. "You have any idea what he saw down there?"

Harold straightened up and shrugged, his breath a cloud.

"No idea, but we'll soon find out." He patted Sarah's arm and hurriedly headed up the rising bank behind Peter's receding figure.

Sarah decided to walk around on the trail getting her circulation going instead of sitting like a lump in the sled, getting refrigerated. A blanket wrapped around her, she went back and forth by the sled several times and slowly stretched out her walking pattern ahead of the sled.

The dogs did not know what to make of her actions. They would lie down, then sit, and then stand whenever she approached them. A couple would yip their frustration at her and jump forward, straining against their harnesses.

This was such odd behavior for a human.

With small thoughts about the possibility of running into wildlife, she peered into the woods as she walked along. The surroundings weren't very threatening. Lots of sunshine reflecting off the snow, making long shadows of the trees, gave it all a storybook quality. She doubted very much that there were packs of wolves in the vicinity, ready to attack. Any moose would stay well away from the source of growls and barks, as would any self-respecting bobcat or lynx.

As far as bears went, well, she wished them sweet dreams in their lengthy winter's nap. The only real bad guys could be wolverines—nothing much intimidated those, but even they wouldn't try to face a team of irritating noisy dogs if they had the choice.

Nope. She was safe.

She was about to turn around to head back to the sled when something out of the corner of her eye made her do a double take. Her stomach tightened as she reviewed the possibilities. It took a moment for her to realize that whatever it was wasn't moving, but its shape made it seem definitely out of place. She knew that, without snowshoes, it would take some effort to investigate.

Curiosity won out.

With a look back towards the spot where she expected Peter and Harold to reappear yielded nothing, she stepped off the trail and sank into the deep wet snow. She forced her way through, stepping as high as she could to go forward, glad for her trousers. It would've been an impossible proposition with skirts. As it was, it wouldn't have taken much to be completely exhausted with this method of propulsion. Luckily the object of her curiosity was only a few yards off the trail.

As she made furrows through the heavy snow, she concentrated on keeping her balance, carefully placing her feet in a straight line. When she finally looked up to take stock of her progress, she was shocked at the sight that greeted her.

Even though a layer of snow covered them, she recognized the navy-blue wool coat, the striped hat, and the dirty tan glove...

"Gunther! Gunther! Oh my God!"

Her last few struggling steps to his inert form didn't even register. He was seated, leaning back against the wide trunk of a spruce tree, his eyes half closed, the snow around the trunk partially trampled. What she could see of his face was the same shade as the snow. All his facial hair was covered in frost, including his brows and lashes. She was reminded of a ghost. If it hadn't been for his clothes, she might not have recognized him at all.

"Gunther! It's me. Sarah. Wake up...wake up please!"

Her heart in her mouth, she shook him until he slid sideways, his seated body forming a rigid "L" in the snow. One arm was folded against his body, his almost translucent bare hand forming a fist in front of his heart.

"Oh no...please...Gunther...wake up..."

Although denial was uppermost, her voice faded as she saw it was no use. She knew there was nothing to be done; there was no resurrecting him. But just in case, by instinct she laid her blanket around him. She tried to straighten him into his original position, but he kept falling to the side like so many building blocks.

Going back to the main trail was easier this time around, as she could go back over the little personal trail she had broken.

It was all she could do to wait by the sled for the men to return. She cried and kept brushing the tears away before they could freeze on her face. Her breathing was ragged as she paced along the trail, impatiently darting glances where she expected to see the men coming back.

Finally, she heard Harold's shout as he appeared by the bank. She hurried toward them as far as the trail allowed. He was pushing a small sled. It seemed to take forever for him to reach her.

"My God, Sarah! What's wrong? You look like you've seen a ghost."

Harold rushed to her side.

Is it…is it your belly? Are you bleeding again? Are you hurt?"

Sarah shook her head between sobs.

"No, Harold. No, I'm not hurt. It's just…just…" She started to sob. Harold held her, not knowing what to do. He looked questioningly at Peter who also looked at his wit's end.

"I…I found Gunther…" Sarah said, between sobs, her voice shaking. "He's…over there…between the trees off the trail."

She pointed a trembling finger to show them where.

"What?" Harold was immediately on the alert, his breath a great cloud. "Did he try something?" He reached under his coat where Sarah knew he kept his hunting knife. His expression left no doubt as to his intentions.

She stuck out her hand to stay his motion.

"No, Harold. Stop." She shook her head in resignation.

"He's dead. Frozen. He can't hurt us." She looked up at him, shrugging sadly. "It's over. Really over."

There was a short silence as everyone let this information sink in.

Harold and Peter looked at each other, and then, in realization, at the sled they had brought back from the river. There was no doubt as to its origin.

A few moments later, Sarah waited on the trail as the other two lifted Gunther up and brought him back to the sled. A long discussion followed as to how they would carry him to Tanana.

His body would not yield to their motions to try to straighten it out. In a macabre exercise, they strapped his seated form to the sled—which they now knew was the one he had taken from the hunting cabin the day before.

And that's not all he had taken. Before they had left the cabin, Harold had noticed the spaces in his geometrically even log pile, so he realized that Gunther had also helped himself to several split logs. Like his packs, they were probably under several feet of ice at the moment.

The three looked at their handy work. To someone who didn't know, Gunther's form simply looked like someone out for a sled ride...

Peter and Harold envisioned the scenario that must have taken place.

"He must've been trying to cross the Yukon, or at least get out into the middle for easier going," Peter explained to Sarah as they made sure the strapping was secure around the corpse.

"Unfortunately, he unknowingly, I assume, picked a spot where one of the creeks runs into the main channel. The sled was wedged on its end in the chunks of ice formed by the overflow. It took the two of us to dislodge it. All his belongings were gone…so…if he had stashed everything including matches in his packs…"

Peter just shrugged in way of further explanation.

"Judging by his clothes…and everything…" added Harold, not wanting to get too specific. "I'm pretty sure he got wet at the same time. Probably in the overflow, trying to get the sled across. After getting it stuck and losing his gear, he must've made his way up the bank to the trail on the off chance that someone might happen by."

He bit his lips and raised his eyebrows.

"And… it almost worked."

No matches, and no dry clothes to change into. The two prime elements of survival—the third being time.

Sarah remembered Deputy O'Leery's words about Mother Nature catching people and thus beating the law to their man.

Well, she had certainly won this race, with time to spare.

-14-

HANGING ON

They wended their way through the trees, knowing that there was no more time for food breaks. They would have to go until the dogs tired, even as it got dark, hoping to get near enough to Tanana for one of them to go for help.

Sarah rode in the "basket" with Harold on the runners behind her, straddling a towrope that pulled the little sled. Peter was balancing on his sled's runners, trying to keep it and Gunther's corpse on the trail without going wide at every curve. The job was almost as tiring as it was difficult. Looking back occasionally and seeing how Peter had to fight to stay on the trail, Harold wasn't sure how long his friend could be expected to withstand the assault on his body.

As the dogs had much more of a load to haul this trip, progress was slower. Harold wished they'd had an eight-dog team at least.

He kept an eye on the sun, noting with panic that it was sinking disconcertingly lower: a pale-yellow disc barely showing above the treetops to the south. Dawn and dusk in the arctic lasted much longer than in southern climes, but nightfall this late in the year still came very early. He calculated that they would be able to see where they were going for a couple more hours. After that, they'd be at the mercy of the moon and the night vision of the dogs.

Sarah had the same concerns, but her total confidence in the men provided a welcome refuge for her mind. They would get her home safely. But she couldn't help thinking about the cargo in the other sled; there was no niche offering comfort for those thoughts.

Odd how you could totally despise someone at one point in time, and then just as totally feel overwhelming sorrow at his demise just a few hours later. She didn't understand her own state of mind. It must just be a jumble of emotions, maybe prompted by a mixture of leftover hormones. Maybe it was some sort of incongruous allegiance to a former relationship. Or, it could be a normal reaction to an awful death. Whatever it was, she did not know how she was going to deal with the whole thing on a permanent basis.

One thing she was fairly certain about was that Harold's feelings about it were in all probability quite different from hers. She knew she would never be able to completely share her emotions about this with him.

It couldn't have happened to a nicer fellow.

As the miles went by, hour after hour, Harold was barely able to suppress a grimace of satisfaction. Yet, he didn't feel totally comfortable with his thoughts on the subject. In fact, a small bit of guilt at having those thoughts clouded a small corner of his mind. But, on the whole, he couldn't help feeling a certain measure of relief.

The whole thing, however awful, seemed so justified. Gunther had led the life of a reprobate, a cheat, a liar, and a rapist. Harold wasn't sure that he had any redeeming qualities that would buy him time in Heaven. And, although he wasn't comfortable with condemning anyone to eternal damnation, he rather doubted it.

"Halt! Halt!"

It was Peter calling out to Harold to stop the dogs.

A minute later, the dogs were relatively still except for their hanging tongues.

"I need a bit of a break," said Peter, panting loudly. "I was beginning to see spots."

He searched through his pack for water. He took a long swig and offered his canteen to Harold who also swallowed some.

` "I don't know how you're doing it," said Harold admiringly, handing back the canteen. "It must be one hell of a ride back there. Your legs must be aching."

Peter smiled grimly.

"Yep. I might be getting a little old for this," he chuckled. "Anyway, that's what my wife keeps telling me. I'm going to get the world's best massage after this when we get home…"

Harold smiled.

"Well, if you need a back up, I'll certainly put in a word for you," said Sarah stretching her legs. "What you're doing is above and beyond." She was studiously avoiding looking at the second sled.

Peter nodded his thanks at the compliment, and gave each dog some water, each one getting a turn lapping from a bowl he kept for that purpose.

Harold changed the subject.

"How far to Tanana now?" he asked, looking at the setting sun. "Are we going to make it before midnight?"

"Well, unless all the snow melts, or we have total darkness, I'm pretty sure that a couple of hours will do it.

Maybe three."

"Or if the dogs go on strike," said Harold. "They look pretty worn out."

The dogs had sat down; some were lying down. All of them had their tongues hanging out.

"Shouldn't we feed them?"

"If we do that, they'll think the day's work is done. No. They'll get fed when we get home. Once we get close, they'll probably pick up speed anticipating their dinner."

Encouraged by Peter's words, Sarah and Harold resumed their positions, but not before grabbing some of the last of the jerked meat to chew on the way.

Except for the moon lighting up the dogs silvery pelts as they trotted faithfully home, it was full dark when they approached the village.

Peter dropped Harold and Sarah off at their cabin and then took the whole procession of sleds and dogs to his house. Sarah was immensely glad that the contents of the other sled would not be stationed outside her bedroom for the night. As exhausted as she was, it was a foregone conclusion that the thought of the corpse a few feet away on the other side of a wall would prevent peaceful sleep.

It took a while to warm up the cabin, but Sarah was so relieved to be home that she didn't care. As the fire in the stove gained momentum, she heated water for tea and for washing.

Tomorrow she'd have a real soak in a tub with a scented bar of soap.

Harold went out to check on his own three dogs that he had left in Charles' care. The food cauldron was empty and the dogs seemed perfectly comfortable, so he assumed they had already been fed.

Sarah turned back the covers on the bed in anticipation of placing some heated rocks on the sheets to warm them. She was bound and determined that this night would be spent in comfort. Toward that end, when Harold came back in, they completely avoided discussing the main event of their trip.

"How does it feel to be able to put both legs inside the covers?" she asked Harold as they huddled together in fresh clothes and sheets, with plenty of room to spare in the bed that Harold had custom made.

He chuckled.

"Yep…in that godforsaken cabin…I wasn't sure if some rat or something would sneak out during the night from underneath and bite a toe off!" He shuddered and hugged Sarah.

"But I guess those things make you appreciate being better off all the more… and I do really appreciate this…"

He sighed, kissed Sarah on the forehead and closed his eyes. It wasn't long before they were both breathing deeply.

* * *

"Oh, *ma chère amie*," squealed Nettie, as she opened her door and saw her friend standing outside in the dim morning light. "You are back! *Grâce à Dieu!*"

She reached out and hauled Sarah inside as if she was a sack of potatoes.

They hugged for a full minute. Sarah felt tears prickling the inside of her lids.

"You must tell me everything," Nettie chattered on as she poured coffee. "I was very crazy not knowing anything. And

Charles—when he went out the door early this morning—said something about you came back last night. I was hardly awake to ask him about it. So I know nothing." She gave her best Gallic shrug.

Putting a steaming cup in front of Sarah, she sat down opposite her at the table. "You must tell me…"

She looked Sarah up and down and frowned.

"Sarah…*qu'est-ce qu'il y a?*

There was silence from across the table.

"You look…so…so…Something seems…did something happen to you?"

Sarah was having a hard time finding a starting point and keeping a handle on her emotions. Finally, she decided that a chronological approach would make the most sense. She tried not to forget any important details, but played down her own complications. By the time she had finished, the coffee pot was empty, and several muffins had been laid to waste.

Out of character, Nettie was speechless.

"So, yes, you might say something happened," Sarah chuckled wryly. "As you can see, lots of things."

"*C'est absolument incroyable,*" murmured Nettie finally, taking Sarah's hand across the table. "It is unbelievable that you should have suffered so…and me being here that whole time all comfortable and warm. *Mon Dieu!*"

She briefly closed her eyes and shook her head.

"It is awful what happened to Gunther, too. But it is his own fault." She shook her head again and waved a finger. "I hope you don't feel sad or guilty. That is what happens when you go against what is right. As my father used to say: '*Merde, alors!*'"

She drained her cup, angrily pressed the pad of her index finger on the plate to pick up the remaining muffin crumbs, and absentmindedly licked them off as she meditated.

"But Sarah. What will they do with…the body?"

"I suppose the military will store it until the Marshall sends someone to investigate, identify, and then bury it. I guess Charles will know more about that than I do. You'll have to ask him."

Nettie nodded and got up to clear the table.

"And now," said Sarah, her voice much brighter, her hands folded in front of her in a listening pose. "Let's talk about what's really important."

She grinned knowingly at Nettie's questioning look.

"Tell me all about your honeymoon, and don't skip any details."

Concerns aside, Nettie smiled broadly and hurried back to her chair.

After Nettie had filled Sarah in with great style and descriptive talent on her initial three days of newly wedded bliss, Charles came home to have a bite to eat.

"By the way, Sarah," he said, taking some effort to pull something out of his pocket while Nettie made him some lunch.

"Harold said I should ask you about this. He didn't know what it is, but he thought you might." He looked a bit uncomfortable. "I'm sorry to bring it up. It has to do with…Gunther."

Sarah's expression immediately became guarded.

"How so?" she asked in a low voice.

Nettie came around the table to where Sarah was seated and put an arm around her shoulders. She looked a bit angry that Charles should even bring up the subject.

"Well," began Charles, trying to find the best way to put it. "Do you remember how Gunther's hand was clenched to his chest...the one without the glove...I mean?

Sarah gave a quick nod, her mind immediately invaded by the memory of finding the body.

"Well," said Charles again. "It took a bit of doing, but one of the men was able to pry the fingers apart and found this."

He held out his hand. In his palm sat a small gold charm.

"It's a little four-leaf clover. It has a little loop for a chain."

He looked intently at Sarah, who instinctively stretched out her hand and then quickly snatched it back before making contact.

Her eyes downcast, she nodded.

"Yes," she whispered. "That was a birthday present I gave him for good luck before we began our...trip...up to Skagway. He had a pocket watch...from his grandfather. He looped the chains together..." She faded.

Charles was taken aback.

"We didn't find a watch, though. Just...this." He indicated his palm. "It was clenched in his frozen hand."

Sarah shook her head as if to disengage from her stupor and cleared her throat.

"We can safely assume that the watch was used for payment for whatever debts needed paying," she said with a measure of cynicism. "He probably hadn't had the watch with him for some time...Probably since the early days in Dawson..."

Charles stood with his hand still out, not knowing what to do with the little charm.

"So…maybe you should…do you want…" He held his hand even farther out.

With one look in her friend's direction, Nettie stepped forward and gently picked up the charm.

"*Ne t'en fais pas, ma chérie*," she said, going over to her nightstand and dropping it in the drawer. "Don't worry. I'll keep it for you. For later…" Behind Sarah's back, she leveled a scornful glare at her husband, who shrugged in innocence.

Nettie shook her head and rolled her eyes.

Men.

In answer to Harold's inquiry, Sarah was evasive when she acknowledged the provenance of the charm in question.

They were back in their cabin with a crackling fire and the wind whining at the window, each involved in customary evening activities.

Harold didn't press her on it. Instead, he suggested that they had another topic to discuss: the future.

"We're kind of at a crossroads here," he said, his lips pressed together in thought, as he sanded a piece of birch wood while Sarah used her wooden egg to darn a sock.

"Where do you picture us in a couple of years?"

Sarah put her work down as she mulled it over.

"I'm just happy being wherever you are, my dear," she said in a pious tone, smiling mischievously. "So far, I've followed you all over the place. Why should I change my modus operandi?"

Harold frowned.

"Are you trying to suggest that you haven't had any say in the matter? Because, if you are..."

"Oh, Harold, relax. I really don't have an opinion on the matter. I'm quite happy here. But, if you want to move on, just let me know."

She picked up her sewing.

"There's just one thing I would like to wade in on..."

"Oh, yes? And what would that be?"

Cocking an eyebrow at her, he blew some sawdust off the wood piece.

She lowered her gaze and looked down casually at her darning.

"Well, when you asked me to picture us in a couple of years, I did. And...what I saw was you, in your woodworking shop, somewhere, someday... busily making a very beautiful highchair...for our child."

Harold's expression was a study in astonishment.

Slowly putting down his project and brushing off his hands, he came to her side and knelt in front of her as she sat, his arms encircling her hips, his head against her belly.

"I'm so, so glad you said that," he whispered hoarsely into her comforting body as she patted his head, ruffled his hair, and smiled contentedly.

"I didn't dare hope."

END

Gold Mining in the Klondike

1899

Author's Note

If you enjoyed this historical novel, a favorable review from you on Amazon would be greatly appreciated. Another book you might enjoy about Alaska's rich history, *Birthplace of the Winds,* chronicles the lives of the little-known Aleut people from prehistoric times through the second world war, and on into the 1960's.

Happy reading!

Made in United States
Troutdale, OR
05/18/2024

19949216R00236